Threads Of Fate

Of Fate Series

Book 1

C.A. BLOOMING

Copyright © 2024 by Pink Office Publishing LLC

All rights reserved.

No part of this publication may be reproduced, distributed, or transmitted in any form or by any means, including photocopying, recording, or other electronic or mechanical methods, without the prior written permission of the publisher, except as permitted by U.S. copyright law. For permission requests, contact C.A. Blooming.

This story is a work of fiction. All names, characters, places, and incidents are fictitious products of the author's imagination. Any resemblance to actual persons, living or deceased, places, and events is solely coincidental.

Book Cover by @selkkiedesigns

Character Art by @avoccatt_art

Map by @studioallred

Editing by Wonder and Wander Publishing

Proofreading by @Brittany_Bookworm

Paperback ISBN 9781964087009
Hardback ISBN 9781964087016

This novel has been developed for character, pacing, plot, and emotional appeal by Hyrum M. Allred using a process based on Katherine Farmer's STORY CODE.

Content Warning

*The following novel is intended for an adult audience and contains mature content that may not be suitable for all readers. Readers should be advised that this story has **depictions of childhood trauma, mentions of suicide (in reference, not explicit scenes), explicit language, physical violence, and full sexual scenes.** This story focuses heavily on healing from your past and brings up **topics of depression, grief, drug addiction, and death.** Please use discretion and awareness of your own personal mental health prior to completing this novel, as the content may be triggering for some readers.*

To all the books that kept me safe.

COMAS

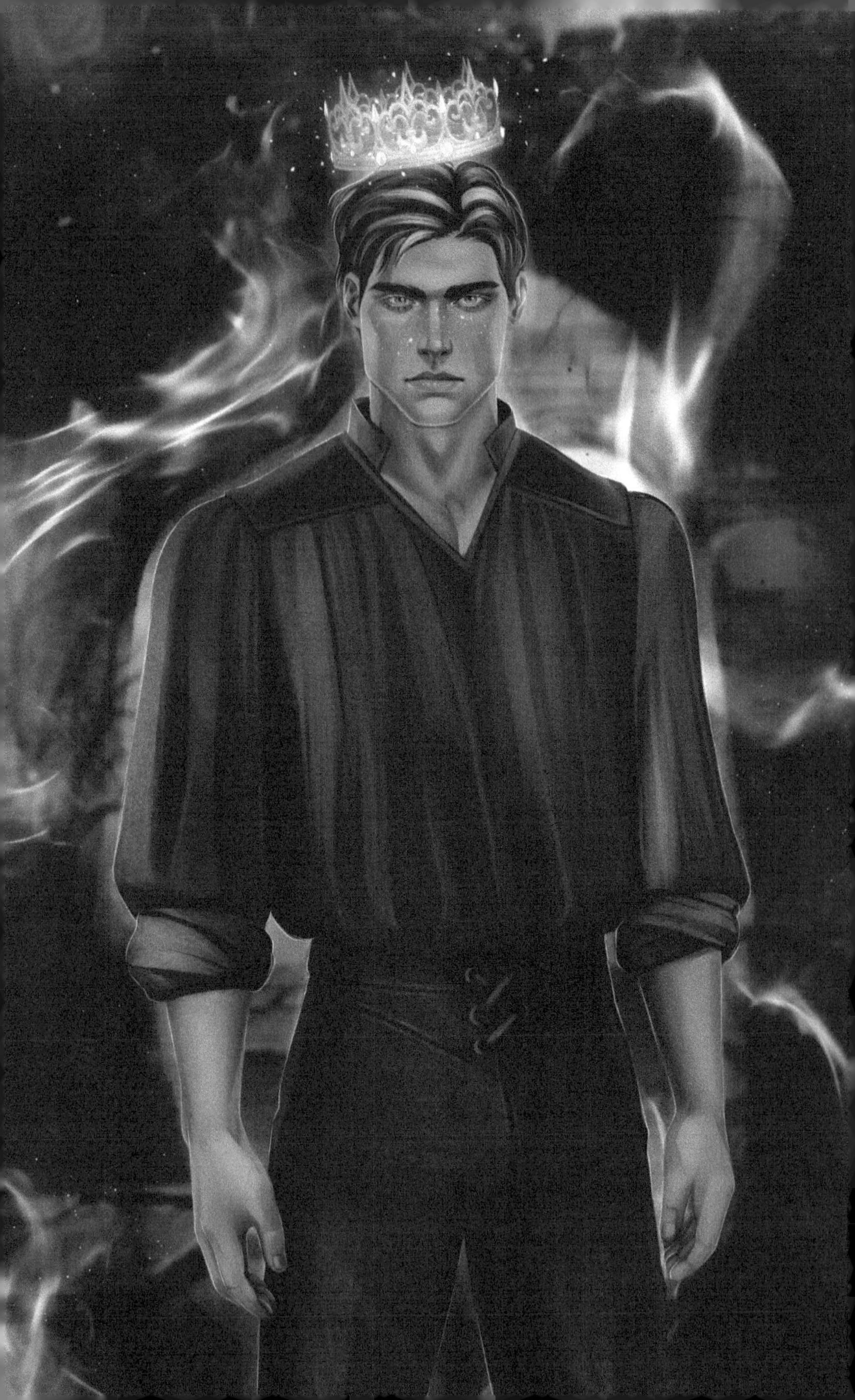

Prologue

The wind seemed to be warning Roan that day, but he wasn't able to place why. Something thick, heavy, and palpable lingered in the air as though it were taunting him. He surveyed his garden, appreciating the sounds behind the wall. Children screamed and played on the other side while their parents hushed them, reminding them to "behave in front of *his* home."

The call of the wind grew stronger, as though it were commanding him to pay attention. Roan ran his hand through his hair. Nothing had happened but yet, he couldn't shake the near-physical change lingering over him and his garden. Taking a step towards the hidden door that opened to the street, he stopped for a moment. Only he and those closest to him knew about the door. It was warded to prevent citizens of the city from seeing it—unless he'd given them permission to. He couldn't help but notice, however, that the air felt heavier near it. Letting out a breath, he grabbed the handle to ensure it was locked and found that it was.

Perhaps Lahana or Jes updated the wards.

He made a mental note to check with both of them when he went back inside. There was also the possibility he just needed sleep. The Fates knew how little sleep he'd had recently.

Rubbing the back of his neck again, he turned to walk back to the house. The air shifted once more, and he stopped in his tracks. Looking back over his shoulder, he shook his head.

Fates, I really do need sleep.

Pushing away the thought, he took a deep breath, then turned again towards the house. Suddenly, wind circled around him like an untamable cyclone determined to take the breath from his lungs.

Thud.

Something—or more so *someone*—slammed into his back, coming through the door. Anger engulfed him, and he turned around, ready to face whoever had broken through the wards. To his own surprise, he saw the intruder was shorter than him—by at least half a head.

He found himself lost in her dark brown eyes, which reminded him of safety and warmth. Flecks of gold sparkled within the brown—as if they had caught fire from her own fury. Trying to suppress his appreciation for her beauty, Roan couldn't hide his amusement when her anger hit him.

"What the hell?" she yelled while rubbing the side of her face that had collided with his back. "Why are you in my garden?"

Taking a step back, he stared at her in disbelief. "*Your* garden?"

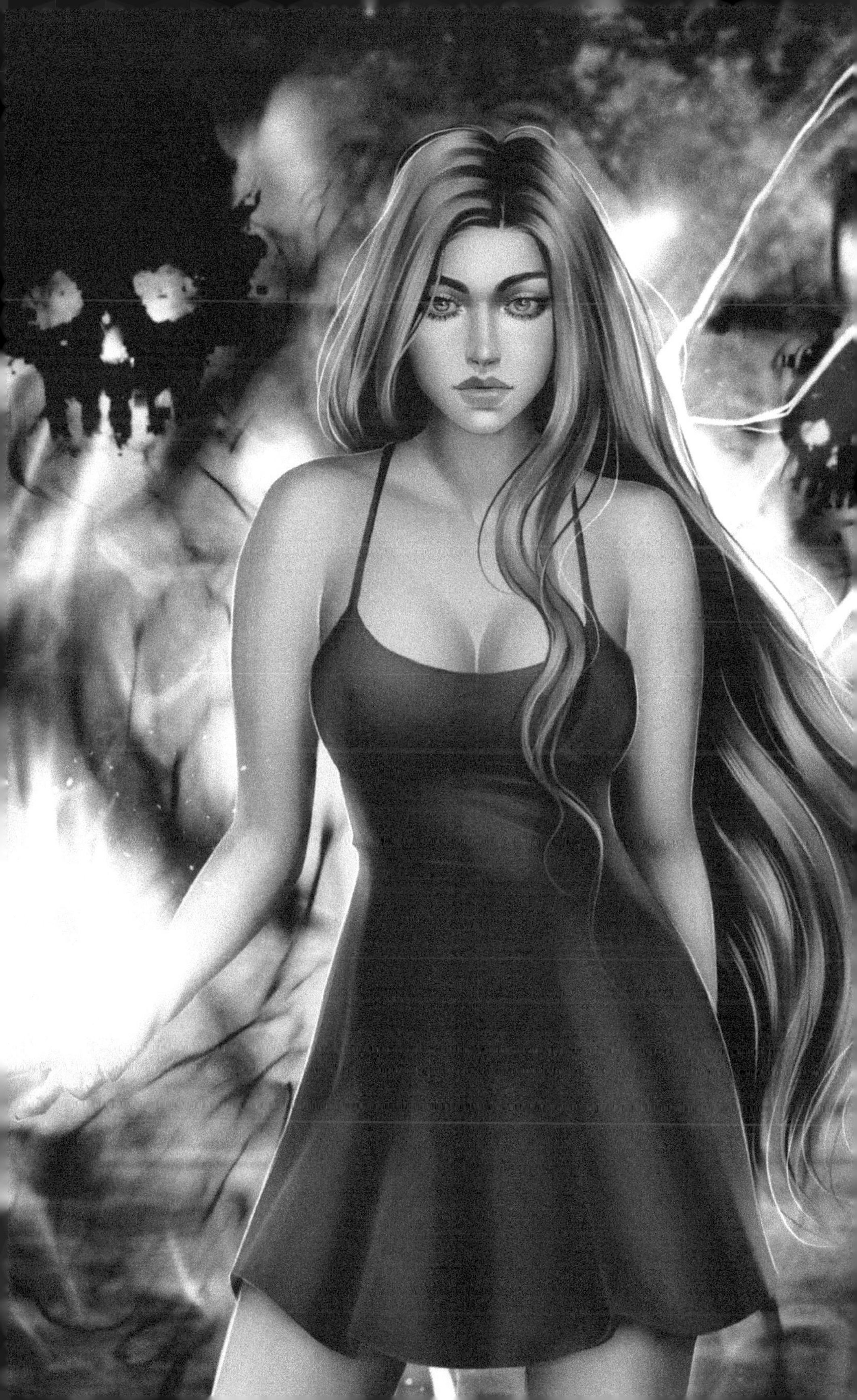

Chapter 1

Orah had always been able to sense death. It had been this consistent, invisible companion following her throughout life, alerting her to the demise of those literally and physically closest to her. She knew when her mother had passed. She also knew before she picked up her phone that her father was gone too. Just like she could sense the older gentleman sitting next to her on the plane would be gone soon. There was almost nothing she could do to distract herself from the silent thread unraveling from him and whispering to her.

Gazing out the plane window, she watched as it made its descent down into Paris. She was so close to her new life and nervous flutters flipped in her stomach with anticipation. Attempting to hold back her building anxiety, she leaned her head against the window, hoping the cool glass would ground her.

If only Dad could see you now.

A single tear landed on her cheek at the thought and she wiped it away, hoping her seat neighbor hadn't noticed. Taking a moment in her thoughts, she fondly reminisced about her father and how proud he would have been of her. If only he could have seen her taking this new step. To see she had decided to stop playing it safe and go for something she truly wanted.

The plane tires hit the tarmac and the force of it pulled her from her thoughts, shaking her back and forth in her seat. The pilot's voice sounded from the speaker, welcoming her and her fellow passengers to the Charles De Gaulle airport. Her hands shook in her lap while the voice disconnected and the small pings and loud vibrations of phones turning on filled the plane cabin. Leaning forward, she reached into her bag to pull out her own. She laughed quietly, knowing only Julian would be reaching out to see when she had landed, but she turned it on anyway.

The bright blue screen lit up and she stared at it. The lack of messages didn't upset her. If anything, it was a relief that she was able to wrap everything up so perfectly back in Boston. No relationship to cling onto, she had said her final goodbyes to her friends, her last day of work was two weeks before, and the sale of her Father's house was finalized the month prior. She had wrapped everything up like a perfect going-away present for herself.

The unbuckling of seatbelts echoed throughout the cabin, causing her to fidget nervously in her seat. The gentleman next to her cleared his throat as he stood. A pulling chill ran down her spine while something inside her screamed for her to speak. Shaking her head, she briefly considered how crazy she would sound.

As if in response, the quiet pull of death reminded her she would never see him again and what he might think didn't really matter.

Knowing it was the right thing to do, she sighed. "Sir?"

"Yes?" he replied with a smile.

"This may seem odd, but I just wanted to say that if you have any family you're close with, that you should call them and tell them you love them." His eyes widened and she forced herself to smile back. "You remind me of my late father. I would give anything to hear his voice again."

An understanding expression settled on his face. "Thank you for the reminder. I'm sure my own daughter needs to hear that from me more often." Turning away from her, he grabbed his bag from the luggage compartment, and she watched him slowly make his way up toward the plane door.

She sighed again while pulling herself up from her seat, slinging her backpack over her shoulders. After a brief walk up the aisle, she reached the door and stopped for a moment. There was no changing her mind now. A chill ran down her spine and she let out a breath.

"No going back," she whispered as her foot hit the jetway.

The walk through the airport was long and exhausting but she finally made it to baggage claim. Her chest tightened while she scanned the terminal's thick crowd for Julian. He hadn't texted or called. The only confirmation she had was a thumbs-up response when she texted him that she was boarding her flight in Boston the night before.

God, it's likely he hasn't shown up. I honestly wouldn't be upset if he wasn't actually here.

Suddenly, a high-pitched squeal echoed throughout the terminal and she turned to find its source. There was only one person in the world she knew could make a sound like that.

"Orah!" Julian's hysterical scream echoed loudly, and she grinned, running for him.

They collided into each other's arms, squealing like two children. People around the terminal turned to stare at them, but they didn't care. They held each other tightly and Orah felt as though her heart would burst from the familiar comfort of his hold.

"I've missed you." Her whisper came out choked.

His arms tightened around her and he nodded his head against her neck. "I know."

Silence settled over them again and she wondered what she could say. It had been months since they'd seen each other. Really, it had been months since Orah had reached out to him. The fact he was there in the airport, holding her, was almost a miracle. Choking back tears, Orah couldn't help but marvel at her friend. Her dependable, supportive, and loving friend who showed up for her when she likely didn't deserve it.

Pulling away from her, he grabbed her hands, dragging her to the baggage claim. They grabbed her bags, then walked silently out to the car. Trying to calm herself, her anxiety nearly overwhelmed her as she pulled open the car door and settled beside him into the passenger seat.

Looking over at him, she smiled. "Thank you for picking me up."

He turned the keys without responding and nodded his head. Her stomach dropped from his continued silence and she turned her head towards the window. She understood if he was upset with her. He had every reason to be.

They quickly made their way out of the winding roads and ramps of Charles De Gaulle, heading out past the city. Orah's anxiety battered inside of her and her fingers twitched haphazardly in her lap. But she knew she had to give him space. She couldn't push him.

Leaning her head against the window, she watched the outskirts of Paris rush by.

His long sigh startled her, and she sat up. Keeping his eyes on the road, his hands tightened on the steering wheel. "Are you okay?"

Confused by his question, she nodded her head. "Yes, of course."

He scoffed. "Orah?"

"Julian?"

Shaking his head, he laughed quietly. "Physically you may look fine. But anyone who leaves their entire life behind and buys a 16th-century chateau in another country without ever seeing it probably isn't okay." He glanced over at her and his smile dropped. "Especially not someone who cuts their best friend out of their life."

"Ju—"

Putting up his hand, he stopped her from responding. "I was there, Orah. I was there when you got that call."

Unable to acknowledge what he was referring to, she turned back to the window. "I don't want to talk about that."

"Obviously."

"Thank you for the ride." She braved glancing at him, then frowned at the sad expression on his face.

"You know I'm always here for you, Orah. The only reason I'm not calling you a selfish, entitled bitch is because of the fact that I was there the day you got that phone call."

His jab speared into her chest, but he wasn't wrong. "I am a selfish, entitled bitch."

Shrugging, he grinned. "You're the one who said it, not me."

Her eyes twinkled and she yelled with a laugh, smacking him on the shoulder. "I've missed you."

"I've missed you too." His wink made her laugh harder and she shook her head. Sighing, he grinned again. "Are you ready to put your French to the test?"

"To the test?"

"Yes, you're going to have to exclusively speak this beautiful language everyday now that you've given up your American life."

"Why do you think I picked France? What's the point in knowing the language and only using it when you're around?" Julian laughed again before using one hand to lightly shove her shoulder. Grinning at her best friend, she watched while they passed the outskirts of Paris. "Are you sure you're good to take me right to Orleans?"

"Of course, it's Saturday, I have no other plans. Are you up for another 2 hours of travel?"

"Absolutely," she replied as the city of Paris disappeared into the distance.

Tightening his arms around her, Julian let out a sigh. "I'll give you your space, Orah." Pulling away, he stared off behind her. "But, please, don't be a stranger. Take as long as you need, just know I'm always here for you."

Her heart seized and she blinked back the tears lining her eyes. "I don't deserve you."

Pretending to flip back his non-existent, long hair, he smiled. "I know."

She looked back at the car they'd driven down to pick up from Orleans. She considered inviting him to follow her back to the chateau but knew that would make their goodbye messier. Julian and his freaky intuition seemed to pick up on her thoughts and he grabbed her hand, giving her three long squeezes.

I. Love. You. Their little handshake.

Tears fell from her eyes, but he shook his head. "Don't cry. Go live in your castle. Maybe you'll find a prince hidden somewhere." Grinning, he motioned to her car and waved his hands, as if he were a mother bird sending her out of the nest for the first time.

Taking a breath to bolster her confidence, she nodded her head and walked back to the car. She knew she could do this. She could accomplish what she had set out to do. He said he would give her space and while she needed it; she knew this wouldn't be goodbye. It couldn't be.

Climbing into the car, she turned the key. The quiet hum of the engine started and she glanced back at Julian once more. Holding his hands to his mouth, his eyes twinkled. Something in his expression made her feel she didn't deserve such a good friend. Smiling, she rolled down her window as she drove off and waved goodbye. He answered with his own wide grin and squealed out a loud farewell. Grinning back, she shook her head and waved.

The country roads quickly flew past while she made her way out of Orleans. On the dashboard, her phone's navigation had her ETA at 40 minutes. Her stomach flipped back and forth again, and she let out a sigh.

She hadn't seen the chateau yet, at least not in person. She had spent the last two months on constant phone calls with the realtor, bank, and inspectors trying to finalize the sale. They definitely thought she was a crazy American—one who just so happened to speak fluent French. She believed that small factor was likely the only reason everything had gone so smoothly up to that point. If she had never been taught by her mother, they all would have likely written her off as a "rich," snobby American.

Laughing at the thought, she turned her music up and gripped the steering wheel. The minutes shown on her GPS rapidly ticked down and an oddly warm sensation settled over her the closer she got to her new home. Shaking her head, her eyes lingered back to the phone, and she gasped. Somehow, she was only 10 minutes away now. How had that happened?

Tall trees came up around the road, and she blinked, thinking she had caught a glimpse of the chateau out in the distance, but she wasn't sure. Each time she thought she saw a building a large tree quickly blocked her view.

"In four-hundred feet, turn left."

The voice of the GPS startled her. Keeping herself calm, her gaze landed on a large tree-lined driveway. That warm sensation felt almost feverish now and sweat wetted her palms against the steering wheel. Turning the wheel, she gasped as she drove down *her* driveway.

The chateau sat off in the distance like some kind of aristocratic artwork. Even in the distance, she could see how dilapidated it was, but any worry about having somewhere to sleep left her mind as quickly as it had appeared. She drove through the archway of the run-down stables, up the circled drive, and stopped right in front of the house. *Her* house, she reminded herself.

The chateau sat in front of her as if welcoming her back to somewhere she had forgotten. This feeling, this familiarity, was what she felt the moment she found it online months ago. After finally pulling herself from the dark hole of grief, the first thing she did was search for chateaus in France. She wasn't sure what she was searching for at the time—maybe something her Father would have loved, or maybe something she wanted. All she knew was that the search turned into an obsession, and she was just about to give up when she happened upon the listing *Le Château sur la Rue des Lucioles*. Right there—the Chateau on Firefly Street—as though her father himself had been sending her a message.

Stepping out of the car, she slammed the door and admired her new home. Squealing, she flung her arms up above her head and finally celebrated herself. She had gone *way* outside of her comfort zone, but she had done it. She had bought the derelict abode she now stood in front of. Spinning around and around on the lawn, she laughed while tears hit her cheeks. If everything went according to plan, she would have it up and running as an event center in about two years. She certainly had enough money from her Father's trust to more than support herself during that time and pay for any renovations needed.

The sounds of birdsong pulled her attention, and she took in her property. The tree-lined drive stretched out toward the country road. The front of the chateau had a large lawn that ended by the stables she had passed earlier. To the right of the chateau was a forested area and to the left were the gardens.

A warm breeze swirled past her while she stared at the gardens, breathing in the sweet scent. Turning, she opened the car door again and grabbed the keys she'd had the realtor mail to her the week before and pulled her bags out of the trunk. She struggled up the front steps and stopped, sticking the key into the door. A loud *click* echoed while she turned the key and pushed the door open.

A rush of cold air blew through the doors, and she shivered, stepping through the threshold. To her left was a sitting room with white cloths covering the furniture. To her right was a large library. Her eyes widened, and she dropped her bags at the front of the stairs before running for the library.

The empty bookshelves reached the ceiling, and a metal ladder sat off to the right, slightly off its track. Grinning, she spun in the room and imagined it in all its future glory. All the books and stories she would fill the shelves with. Cozy chairs that would line the walls. Soft lights that would make reading warm and comfortable. The perfect place for not only her future guests but also for herself to retreat to.

Sighing, she walked back to the main foyer and picked up her bags again. A hallway behind the sitting room caught her attention, and she remembered the inspectors telling her about the habitable living quarters located at the back of the house. Finding these quarters at the end of the hall, she set her bags down.

Now standing in a smaller sitting room, she observed her new home. There was a door that led to a small bedroom in the back and to the left of her was a very small kitchen. A dusty couch sat in the middle of the room and beside it a small dining table. Next to the kitchen was a small bathroom—it was literally everything she needed.

She considered settling in for the rest of the day, but it was still afternoon, and she had plenty of time to rest later. Setting her phone and keys on the small dining room table, she turned and headed back to the front door, ready to explore the gardens.

The warm afternoon sun hit her cheeks when she stepped onto the front steps. The summer heat tried to break its way through the trees, but the shade provided a protective layer to the property. Pausing for a moment, she surveyed the lawn. There was a stillness in the air that wasn't there when she had first arrived. Shivers ran up her arms and she let out a breath. Glancing back into the house, she considered going back inside, but the stillness shifted for a brief moment and a warm wind blew past her towards the gardens.

She had only seen one or two pictures of the gardens online and had been interested in exploring them since signing the final paperwork. Shaking off the odd feeling, she walked down the front steps and followed the wind.

She walked for about 30 minutes before happening upon a tall, ivy-covered, stone wall. For some reason it was warmer there than anywhere else she had passed so far. She cocked her head in confusion. The treetop overhead was thicker there than the rest of the property, so how was it so warm?

She absent-mindedly ran her hand over the thick, overgrown ivy cascading up the wall, when her fingers brushed against something that felt hard, almost like metal.

"What on earth?"

She stared down at the thick ivy and then back at her fingers, thinking she must have imagined the sensation. Curious, she stuck her hand through the overgrown vines and jumped back when her fingers wrapped around a warm, metal handle.

Her eyes widened with wonder. How could she have already found something hidden and secret on her first day there? She reached down to pull out her phone for pictures but scoffed when she realized her dress didn't have pockets and she had left everything inside.

Her heart beat with anticipation, and she wished there was someone there to witness her discovery. Breathing out, she pushed back the ivy and took a step back to inspect the door. It appeared to be wrought iron, but a bronze color with ivy markings molded into the metal. The overgrowth that had been concealing it before laid contently to the side where she had pushed it, as if welcoming her to inspect the hidden secret.

Smiling, she grabbed the door handle and turned it, but nothing happened. The door gave a bit of movement, as if it wanted to open but couldn't respond. She pushed her shoulder against the metal and shoved a bit while twisting the handle again.

Again, nothing.

She tried again and again with no results. Even though the door handle moved and the door shifted, she couldn't get it to open. Disappointment settled in her stomach and she kicked the door out of frustration. The metal groaned at the contact—mocking her.

She had been so hopeful that finding the door was a sign that she was meant to be there. Everything she had given up, all the risks she took to get herself to where she now stood, meant something. She groaned, kicking the door in frustration again.

Finding hidden treasures had been all that she'd imagined leading up to her leaving Boston. She'd spent hours imagining waltzing around her own personal castle, of finding hidden history deep within its walls as she began her journey to renovate it. Now, here she was, staring at a door that had been hidden with time, but she couldn't even get through it.

Her heartbeat rose, and she gently laid her forehead against the warm metal. The unavoidable spiral of thoughts hit her suddenly. She wasn't worth an adventure. She wasn't strong enough to get what she wanted. She was already a failure if she couldn't even open a door.

Tears welled in her eyes, and she laughed. Her temper built in a steady rise, and she breathed out, trying to calm herself. There was no reason to be annoyed, she could get this, she reminded herself. If she tried, she could get this.

Pulling her forehead away from the metal, she moved her hands up to her mouth and blew warm air on them. She knew it wasn't going to help with anything, but the movement gave her comfort. She threw her hand out and wrapped her fingers around the handle again. This time, it heated at her touch. Motivated by the warmth, she bore down all her weight, shoving as hard as she could. But again, nothing happened.

Cursing the stupid design and herself for not bringing her keys, she let out a scream of frustration. She believed she had found this damned door for a reason. There had to be a reason why she found her first hidden treasure there on the first day. Wondering that maybe she wasn't doing this the right way, she took a moment to think.

Those near suffocating thoughts swirled in her mind, and she let out another shaky breath. She couldn't allow herself to go down the hole she had just clawed herself out of. Her entire life now depended on her being able to gain control of herself.

Warm air circled around her feet while she thought. She took a step back. Maybe all she needed to do was take a running start at it.

"3. 2. 1." She counted down quietly and ran.

Her shoulder connected with the metal right as her hand twisted the handle. The force of her impact released whatever had sealed the door, and it finally flung open. "YES!" she yelled as she stumbled into the garden, then slammed the side of her face right into someone's back.

She was livid as both of them almost fell to the ground. Had this person been messing with her? Had they been holding the door closed that whole time? Who the hell did they think they were being on *her* property? Unable to cool her building rage, she rubbed her cheek.

"What the hell?" she shouted and looked up at who she realized was a tall man standing in front of her. "Why are you in my garden?" she demanded, wanting some kind of explanation for the obvious sick prank he'd been playing.

Taking a step back, he stared down at her with an equal level of rage that quickly turned to intrigue before he replied, "*Your* garden?"

Rolling her eyes, she scoffed. Who did this guy think he was?

Chapter 2

Roan's fury all but vanished when he registered the words coming from the woman. That language. He'd responded to her so naturally, despite not having spoken or heard it in close to sixty years.

"Yes, this is my garden," she snapped.

He didn't quite understand why she was so upset, but he took another step back, hoping to avoid any of her limbs that may have tried to connect with his face. "No. This is my garden at the back of my private residence. The most important question is, how did you get in here?"

She stared back, as if he had somehow stolen her ability to speak. Curiously, he watched her quietly take in her surroundings. Behind him, the walls of his garden seemed to blend in with the hedges that shrunk to about knee height. Beyond the hedges, his home sat across a large manicured lawn. In the garden itself, they were surrounded by flowers, finally blooming after a long cold that year. He was proud of his garden and didn't usually share the oasis he had created with many others.

"Oh my god," she whispered while her cheeks flushed with an embarrassed blush. "Did I just break into your garden? I am so sorry! I'm your new neighbor. I just moved in." She stuck her hand out as if expecting him to shake it.

Roan wasn't sure what to think of this woman. He didn't think he had ever been more confused or interested in someone in his life. Who was she? Where had she come from? He took another step back, observing the garden door that led to the street. Somehow, it had already closed itself and appeared as it had before she came tumbling out of it. He turned his attention back to her and suppressed his appreciation. She was... different.

He first noticed those brown eyes, but now he could see she also had brown hair. As the sun shone above her, hints of red glistened within it. Not a bright, stark red—no, more like highlights of auburn that appeared as though they could have caught fire at any moment. He briefly considered that maybe her fury had fueled the interesting colors.

She was also wearing a kind of outfit he had never seen before. A dark blue dress that was very short with very small straps across the shoulders. The dress clung to every curve on her body. A body he was desperately trying not to stare at. She was soft but also strong, as though she spent regular time training. Her dress stopped halfway up her thighs and despite her being shorter than him, her legs were distractingly long. Trying to control his thoughts, he admired her dress again and chuckled, knowing Lahana would have been enamored by the woman's outfit.

Her remorseful expression for trespassing turned to annoyance and she crossed her arms. "Am I amusing to you?"

"Why would you ask that?" he replied.

"You just laughed at me."

"I wasn't laughing at you. I was laughing at—" Snapping back to himself, he remembered who he was and the fact that he had no idea who she was. "It doesn't matter what I was laughing at."

Her annoyance turned back to fury as she stepped back, while her eyes slowly surveyed him up and down. He would have usually considered himself a rather confident man, but in that moment, he had never felt so aware of his skin and someone's eyes on him.

"I'm assuming you found something amusing with what I'm wearing. You're one to talk Mister, wearing clothes that are at least 300 years out of date. What are you? A cosplayer or something?"

Cosplayer? He wondered if the woman was truly mad. He had never heard of whatever it was she was referring to, and he was starting to lose his patience.

"Listen," he said while mimicking her arm crossing. "As I said, this is my garden, and you have trespassed. I suggest we get you escorted out and back into the city before I call someone to get you and I promise they will not be as understanding as I've been."

"City? The city is 40 minutes away. Let me just go back through the door, and I'll make sure I remember that I've got a grouchy neighbor behind it and that he doesn't like visitors."

"The city is behind that door," he replied bluntly.

His tone irritated her more, and she turned to walk back through the door she had just come through. She tugged on the handle, but the door didn't respond. Roan had expected this, but still found himself confused and shocked that she didn't seem to be able to go back the way she came. Sighing, he walked up behind her.

"You cannot just open this door like it's any normal door. It's heavily warded. I'm not even sure how you got through it in the first place." The handle and the wards responded to his touch as he grabbed it and turned.

Her brow furrowed when her eyes met his.

"Warded? Sir, I'm very sorry if I interrupted some kind of role-playing event, but it appears to just be you and me here. You can drop the act."

The only response he could give was a shrug, once again baffled by what she was talking about.

What an intriguing woman.

If she hadn't just broken through these wards, he would have been tempted to get to know her some more. But if Jes found out he didn't properly question her, he would be livid, and Roan didn't have the energy to deal with his moods. Pushing the door open, he gestured back toward the city street, but she appeared to be frozen in place.

"Are you okay?"

The color in her face had drained and she appeared as though she was going to be sick or possibly faint.

Pointing her finger, she managed to whisper, "That kid has fucking horns."

His head snapped back to the city street where he found one of the children he'd heard playing on the other side of the wall earlier staring at the door. He'd forgotten the children were there and briefly worried that he had likely scared them by opening the hidden door.

Turning back to the woman, he realized she'd whispered her shock, and curse, in yet another language he was familiar with. He wanted to question her knowledge of the languages, specifically the first one. He wanted to tease her choice of words. But he most certainly wanted to know why she was shocked by the child's physical appearance.

Pulling himself from his thoughts, he opened his mouth to question her, but his eyes widened when he found her knees going out from under her.

"Fates!" he yelled as he lunged forward, catching her before she hit the ground. Her body went limp in his arms and he looked down at her, perplexed by what would have caused her to faint, when Jes came running across the lawn. Roan's eyes rolled. He already knew he was about to receive an earful.

"Roan! Someone got through the garden door! What are you doing out here?" Jes projected his voice through the wind, not yet able to see the woman in Roan's arms as he sprinted toward him.

Roan glanced at him then back at the woman, letting out an annoyed breath. "Yes, Jes, I'm very aware someone got through the garden door," he muttered.

Jes arrived a moment later, and his mouth hung open in surprise. They made eye contact as he breathlessly asked, "Who is she?"

Chapter 3

I need to get up. I can't miss my plane.

Orah turned over; she didn't want to get up yet, but her new life depended on it. She couldn't leave the chateau to sit empty.

Her eyes flew open, and she sat up. "The chateau!" Her heart raced while she took in her surroundings.

She was not late for her flight, and she was most definitely not in her chateau. No, she was on a deep green, velvet couch, in what appeared to be a sitting room of some kind of stately home. Her eyes shifted to the rest of the room, and she jumped when they made contact with the strange man she ran into earlier. The man who had been in her garden, that apparently wasn't her garden.

Taking him in, she stared at the costume he wore. The flowy white shirt did little to conceal the muscled chest underneath. His pants were what she believed to be called breeches, and amusingly, he was wearing colors that coordinated with what she was wearing. A dark blue top, his breeches a complimenting brown, and long brown boots ending just below his knee cap.

Moving her eyes up his body, she was shocked she somehow hadn't noticed how attractive he was through her anger and annoyance outside. His hair was a light brown with highlights of blond. The sun from the window behind him seemed to catch the highlights as if they were a crown of light above his head. His eyes were what she could only describe as a silvery-blue. Almost ice blue surrounded with rings of silver. Reminding her of the sky when flying through the clouds. The color almost alarmingly contrasted against his darkened skin and freckles stretched across his cheeks and the bridge of his nose.

He cleared his throat and she realized she was taking an inappropriately long time admiring his features. She straightened herself. "I fainted."

His lips upturned to a slight smile. "Yes, you did. Are you alright?"

"Yes, I feel fine. I'm a bit disoriented, but I'm fine." She shifted to get herself off the couch when he jumped up to assist her. She put her hand up in response. "I can stand up by myself."

Sitting back down, he allowed her to stand. The room they were in was grand with ceilings so high she had to crane her neck to admire the golden portrait towering above them. The green couch she sat on was the simplest item in the room otherwise filled with gold framed paintings and lamps. Usually, she would have felt uncomfortable in a room filled with such displays of wealth, but this room was comfortable and, to her own surprise, cozy. She couldn't help but imagine how her own sitting room in the chateau would look someday and whether or not she could mimic the warmth and safety of this stranger's home.

Rubbing her slightly clammy hands, she decided she had to ask him about what she saw behind that garden door. "So... about why I fainted..."

He laughed and leaned back in his chair, folding his arms. "You mean that kid's *fucking* horns?"

Her face heated from embarrassment. She knew she had a mouth on her when she was alone, but she could count on one hand the number of people who had heard it for themselves. "Yes. That."

He chuckled and shrugged. "What about it?"

"What do you mean, 'what about it?'"

"I mean, what about it? I couldn't see the parents, but I would assume at least one of them has a similar pair atop their own head."

Her mouth opened in shock. "That is not normal."

His brow furrowed. "Well, that's rude."

"That's not rude!"

"Just because you mortals all look the same doesn't mean everyone else has to."

"*Mortals?*"

"You don't have to raise your voice, it's not a dirty word."

She felt herself getting dizzy again. She thought she had bought the perfect chateau in the perfect location and was quickly realizing her neighbor was insane. Standing, she glanced towards the door at the other side of the room and started walking to it. She had to get out of there and make sure to never interact with this lunatic again.

The air in the room shifted and he moved in front of her so quickly she had to take a step back to avoid running into him again. Standing between her and the door, he put up both of his hands. "Now I can't just let you leave that easily."

Her stomach dropped. Not only was this guy insane but apparently, he was also a predator and she was not in the mood to deal with an asshole after traveling all day.

"You can't tell me what to do," she responded while trying to step around him.

Again, he moved too fast for her and he blocked the door. "You really seem to think that you have any say in whether or not I let you leave right now. Honestly, if it were up to me, I probably would just let you go but remember that *someone* I mentioned calling for earlier? Well, he found you in my arms outside and I am now obligated to question you so that my Captain does not."

Her brows shot up. "Your *Captain?* You're really into this whole cosplay shit for the long haul, huh?"

He gave her an expression she couldn't quite interpret. "You keep using that word and I honestly have no idea what you are referring to."

Shaking her head, she realized that she hadn't considered that while she'd been speaking French since Julian had picked her up at the airport, she was likely using a term she wasn't sure was common in the country. "I'm sorry, it's probably the language barrier, it's been several months since I've spoken French. Your game—or what seems like a game of pretend with your clothes, and how you're speaking."

He appeared affronted by what she had said and to her own shock he responded to her in a strangely accented English. "What is French?"

Her mouth dropped open again.

Good God this man has lost grip with reality.

"The language that you were just using to speak to me. Your English is great, I can't place your accent though."

He shook his head and ran his fingers through his hair as if she had puzzled him. "I still don't know what French is and the language we were just conversing in is not my native tongue either. I haven't spoken that in years and I'm a bit relieved to know I won't be embarrassing myself by struggling to keep up with you." Sighing, he motioned for her to sit back on the couch. "I also don't know what this English is that you're referring to either, but I have a feeling it's what we're speaking now. I do, however, appreciate the compliment. My mother would probably roll over in her grave if I didn't speak either properly."

Her heart lurched at the mention of a dead parent—a situation she was too intimately familiar with. She eyed the couch his outstretched hand was pointing to and moved toward it, then stopped abruptly. "How can I trust you're not some kind of predator who's going to hurt me?"

His hand dropped to his side. "Am I a predator? Well, that will depend on who you ask." Her heart raced and she tried to figure out if she could make it past him to the door. He seemed to pick up on her building panic and continued talking. "However, I am not going to hurt you or even lay a finger on you. I just have questions, that's all."

"I don't have to listen to you," she said, folding her arms defiantly.

He mimicked the movement. "Not only are you in *my* private residence but you are also in *my* city and as the Governing God of this city and Region you do in fact have to listen to me."

She laughed now, probably harder than she should have at someone she wasn't entirely sure was stable or coherent. "*Governing God?* You think really highly of yourself don't ya?"

He stepped closer to her, taking what was obviously meant to be an intimidating stance but she held her ground as he lowered his voice. "You have no idea what I think of myself." The tone of his voice sent a shiver down her spine. He was saying so much and yet so little, but she wasn't about to let him know how she related to all he tried to hide behind his words. "As I said, I just want to ask you some questions. Please."

Maybe it was the fact he said please, or maybe it was the fact he immediately stepped back to allow her space again. She wasn't sure what changed in those brief seconds, but she found herself walking back to the couch and sitting down.

He followed behind her and sat back down on the chair he'd been in earlier. A dull ache was forming in the back of her head and she wanted to go back to the chateau but knew she could try her best to have a civil conversation. *You never have to interact with this man after today*, she told herself. It was just a few questions.

She leaned into the back of the couch, crossing her legs, and resting her hands on her knee. "Well, what do you want to know?"

He smiled at the relaxed pose she was desperately clinging to and answered simply, "Well, first I'd like to know your name. I figure if we're going to have a conversation we might as well know each other's names. It's pretty obvious that you have no idea who I am."

She didn't give a single shit who this man thought he was, but she answered him anyway. "My name is Orah."

He appeared startled by her answer and cleared his throat. "It's nice to meet you Orah. My name is Roan." *Well, that's an interesting name. Very rarely do I meet anyone whose name feels as out of the ordinary as my own.*

Shaking off her surprise, she grinned. "It's a *pleasure* to meet you, Roan." Never in her life had she felt so confident to be that sarcastic after meeting someone for the first time, but she had to assert some form of dominance when she wasn't sure she could trust that he had no ill intentions.

He smiled at her response. At least he appreciated sarcasm and wasn't taking offense at her lack of respect for his "title".

"And where are you from, *Orah*?"

It was a personal question she never knew how to answer and was unsure of whether to say where she had just left, or where she went to college. Or maybe even further back to where she was actually born and raised, the place she had tried so desperately to erase from her story. Sitting a little straighter she stared at him. "I've lived the last 4 years in Boston, I just moved to France, but I am originally from a small town in Maine."

His brows furrowed again. Holding back her laugh, she smiled. She seemed to bring that expression out of him often.

"Where are Boston, France, and Maine?" he asked.

Shocked by his response, she rolled her eyes. *Again, with the role playing.* "We're currently in the country of France, where both your home and my home next door are. Maine is a state in the United States of America. Boston is a major city there as well." She jumped, a bit taken aback at the genuine confusion that settled on his face and briefly felt shame in herself. Maybe he wasn't this dangerous lunatic after all. Maybe he was someone who had some real struggles and really didn't know where he was.

He stood up suddenly and placed his hands on his lower back as he began to slowly pace the room. "My home is not in this country you call 'France', Orah. My home is in my city Iluna which resides in the region of Nacht—the land of Nyte in the—what did you call it? Country? That might work. The Country or more so the Land of Comas. But I was born in the City of the Kings—Erde."

The room seemed to stand still for a moment when he stopped speaking. She stared at him with concern. She really didn't think he was dangerous. At least not a danger to her but she was now concerned that he was lost in his delusions and he appeared to be alone in what looked like a very large home. She glanced around for any sign of other people living there but was unable to see past the doors that looked to lead out to an open foyer.

Standing, she slowly approached him. "Roan," she said as softly and with as much empathy as she could muster. "Do you have anyone who lives here with you? Someone who maybe takes care of you?"

He stepped back briefly, and a loud laugh came from him. "You think I'm mad, don't you?"

Jumping at the accusation, she shook her head. While she did in fact think that, she wasn't going to admit it to him aloud.

"No. I just want to make sure you have friends, that's all."

He walked to the window, but she couldn't see what he was staring at. "Orah, I'm not mad. I haven't lost my mind. Honestly, between the two of us I was beginning to think you were the crazy one. In the garden you told me the city is 40 minutes away. Is that correct?"

"Yes."

"Will you come here and tell me what you see out this window?"

She froze where she stood, hesitant to get that close to him. While the window itself went to the top of the room's high ceiling, it wasn't very wide, and they would be standing shoulder to shoulder. He again seemed to sense her panic and turned to face her. "I'll step out of the way so you can see for yourself." He took a few steps to the left and leaned against the side table pushed against the wall.

Slowly, she walked up to the window. She knew what she was going to see. His estate was going to have a similar lawn to her chateau. Maybe he would also have a tree-lined drive. Maybe he would have no trees and she would see the Orleans forest swaying in the distance. She knew what to expect yet almost fell over when she made it to the window.

She was obviously looking toward the front of his house and while he did have a large lawn with trees, she didn't see the Orleans forest. She didn't see a drive that led to the main road she was on earlier. She saw a drive that led down the expansive lawn that tilted downhill, stopping at a large hedge acting in place of a fence. On the other side of the hedge was a city street; not the kind of street made for any sort of automobile, but a walking street and roads beyond it that had carriages. Actual *carriages,* all pulled a large assortment of the kinds of creatures she had grown up reading about. Beyond the carriages and people was a city. No high-rise buildings, nothing remotely modern or technological, but it was a city all the same and it was bustling with happy people who appeared to have no care in the world about how strange they looked.

She turned around quickly, not realizing Roan had moved to stand behind her. Her unexpected movement knocked him to the ground. She jumped as he yelled while he fell, and she took a step back feeling the windowsill bump against the back of her knees. Her stomach rolled as though she was going to be sick. Unsure of what to say, she glanced back at the couch feeling the need to sit down.

Standing quickly, he threw his arms out. "Please don't faint again. I barely caught you last time."

Chapter 4

Orah swayed a bit and moved her hand behind her, gripping the windowsill while steadying herself. Roan still wasn't confident she wasn't going to faint. He had almost no answer regarding who she was or where she came from, but he knew he'd shown her enough to shock her.

"I'm not going to faint," she replied, meeting his gaze.

"Are you sure?"

"Yes. I don't recall us being able to have a conversation before I fainted earlier," she snapped.

She had a point there. Despite how rattled she appeared, she seemed to be more alert. Taking a step back, he nodded his head knowing how much space was needed when processing something that didn't feel real. "Are you okay?"

Stupid question. He scolded himself for his ignorance. She was obviously not okay. Silently, she turned back to the window again.

Silence settled over the room for a few minutes before she responded quietly, "I think I've finally had that mental break I've always feared."

Oh Fates.

Roan shook his head. He didn't mean to make the poor woman question her sanity, that hadn't been his intention. They had been going around in circles, confusing each other, and he knew showing her the city would have been the proof she needed to understand she wasn't where she thought she was. "No, Orah, you're perfectly sane."

She scoffed. "Roan—if that is your name—I'm staring out your window right now watching a family of blue people with white horns on their heads being transported across the road in a carriage led by a team of Gryphons. I'm pretty sure that's a clear example of losing my sanity."

He peeked over her shoulder and saw his neighbors traveling down the road toward the center of the city. Figuring telling her their names and how harmless they are wouldn't do any good, he nodded his head. "Yes, and I can see them as well."

She turned back to him with doubt in her eyes. "I'm sorry but nothing you have said during this conversation has instilled any confidence in me that *you're* the more sane one here."

He laughed. In a way, she probably wasn't wrong. Roan opened his mouth to respond when the quiet sound of footsteps approaching the room caught his attention. As a mortal, Orah wasn't aware their conversation was about to be interrupted and Roan wasn't sure how she was going to react to another person walking into the room. The footsteps grew louder and they both turned as Jes walked through the doorway.

Jes's gaze first fell to the couch where he helped Roan lay Orah after he'd helped get her inside from the garden. He was livid with Roan and ranted about how little he cared for his own safety and, "What's the point in warding that door if any *mortal* can just waltz in whenever they please?!"

Confusion settled on Jes's face and he glanced around the room, trying to locate the woman he believed to be a direct threat to Roan. It didn't take more than a second for him to find them both by the window. He stilled in the abnormal way only he and his kin could. Roan smiled, unsure if Jes had already decided Orah was the ultimate threat to his Governing God or if he was just as intrigued by her as Roan was.

Jes glanced at Orah, then back at Roan. "My lord," he said with a bow.

Roan's lips tightened across his face while he held in his laugh. The man in front of him was essentially his brother, and the two never used formalities when addressing one another, despite their ranks.

Keeping his lips tight, Roan smirked. "Captain, please remember our guest here does not appear to speak our language."

Jes's eyes narrowed at the jest in Roan's tone. Without having to say anything, he now knew, as well as Roan did, that Roan would mock him for this formality for at least a few decades. Jes locked eyes with Orah before responding in her native tongue. "I see our *guest* is awake."

It had been a long time since Roan had seen Jes allow someone to stare at him so obviously. He was an impressive sight when you first met him, and Roan was sure Orah likely hadn't ever seen someone like Jes.

His short black hair was cut in what he claimed was the best warrior style to prevent an enemy from being able to grab hold of it. Despite its short length you could see the curls trying to force their way through the small bit of growth he allowed on top. His skin, a darker shade than Roan's, always had a warm glow that radiated from it. Another trait that only he and his kin had, as well as his golden eyes. But what Roan knew Orah was staring so intently at was not his face that many considered handsome, or the fact he was a rather large man in both height and stature. No—it was the two wings that sat slightly at attention behind him.

Roan had only seen an eagle once in his life, deep in the mountains as a boy, and when he first saw Jes's wings they were the only comparison he could think of. They were large and flecked with bits of dark brown, gold, and white. When he took flight, it was like watching a majestic creature take their first breath. After almost 200 years of friendship Roan still had an adolescent jealousy when it came to Jes's wings.

Orah's mouth hung open before Roan cleared his throat, deciding to break the awkward silence. "Orah, this is my Captain I told you about earlier. Jesiel Keita." Jes's eyebrows shot up.

Roan lifted his hand in a silent command for Jes to remain quiet. He knew Jes had thought the same thing as him after hearing Orah's name for the first time. Nodding gently, he let Jes know they would discuss the topic at a later time.

Jes nodded in acknowledgement before glancing at Orah. She fiddled with her fingers quietly, then walked toward him. Roan stared, unsure of what she was about to do when Orah stuck out her hand for a formal handshake. Suddenly, he was reminded he hadn't taken her hand earlier in the garden when she thought he was her neighbor.

"It's nice to meet you, Jesiel."

Jes took her hand hesitantly but wasn't able to hold back the large grin that spread across his face. "Fates woman, you are strong," he laughed.

Orah shrugged, "I have to be."

Jes and Roan both glanced at each other not knowing what that meant but neither pried. She was allowed to keep as much about herself private as they were.

Orah sighed and walked back over to the couch. She sat down, placing her head in her hands silently. After a few moments she sat back up and rubbed her hands over her knees. "Okay," she stated. "I don't have any idea what is going on but I'm trying really hard not to lose my shit right now. Is this real? Really real?"

Roan crossed the room and sat back down on the chair facing the couch. Jes took the chair to the right of him. Both tried to give her space. Partly because she looked as though she needed it and partly because neither of them actually knew what the woman was capable of.

Quickly Roan glanced at Jes then back at Orah. "Yes, this is real. You are in Iluna. My city."

"What do you mean *your* city?" Her eyes narrowed in defiance. He couldn't help but chuckle in appreciation at how little she cared for formality and who he was. Being pushed and questioned this way had become the highlight of his day.

"I already told you. I am the Governing God of this city as well as the region Nacht. You are in Comas, the land of the Gods and I am the God of Nyte."

She leaned back against the couch and covered her face with her hands again. "I've spent my entire life reading about lands of gods, fae, and monsters, and apparently I've somehow walked right into one of them." A low laugh came from her as she observed the room. "Do all the gods live in upscale manor houses?"

Roan smiled. It was by no means small, but it was not a grand, spacious palace that many of the others lived and ruled in. It was certainly nothing like the palace in the City of Kings where he was raised.

"Actually, my home is considered fairly modest compared to most of the Governing Gods." Jes snorted at his response. Roan knew he was thinking of his brother's home and how vastly different their lives and choices were. Orah stared at Jes as if she was unsure whether his laugh was mocking her or Roan.

"Well mister God of Night, how are you going to get me back home then?" she asked, sitting straighter on the couch.

"Back home?"

"To my chateau. My life. My *world*."

"To be able to do that I'd have to know where that was, and I can't even guarantee that I can help you. World traveling is not my expertise in power."

"What's your expertise then?"

Jes sat up abruptly in response to the question. Roan's own senses became more aware as well. At face value, Orah appeared harmless but many had been trying to discover the depth of his power for several years now and they couldn't rule out that she had been sent by those who wanted to know.

"His Lord will not be revealing what his expertise is to you," Jes responded bluntly. Orah scowled at him. The woman appeared to have lived her life so far speaking her mind and Roan wasn't sure if Jes was ready to be challenged. Putting up his hand to prevent them from ripping into one another, he spoke.

"What you don't know, Orah, is that things have been very tense here lately and my depth of power has been something of intrigue to the wrong people." Pulling her eyes from Jes, Orah's expression shifted to alarm. "However, I do not believe you have come here to harm me or to discover my hidden secrets." Roan stood, pausing for a minute in front of her. "Would you allow me to sit next to you on the other side of the couch?"

She tensed at the request and her panic flowed into Roan—a sliver of the power he'd tried to keep tucked away and hidden. Most people don't want to know that someone can physically feel what they're feeling. She glanced up at him with hesitation. "You don't have to allow me to sit next to you. I can leave you alone, but I do need to learn where you came from myself," he said softly. Biting her lip and fiddling with her fingers, she slowly nodded her head.

Letting out a relieved sigh, Roan sat down next to her. "As the God of Nyte certain parts of my powers are not a secret. Every God of Nyte who's existed before me has held the same bits of power and abilities. What do you assume those would be?"

Doubt creeped back into her eyes while she stared back at him. "Well," she puffed out her chest, as if she were trying to look and sound more confident than the emotions Roan could sense from her. "I would assume you *probably* control the darkness somehow or shadows or some shit."

Shadows or some shit. He chuckled.

While he could do some shadow magic, it was not specific to the God of Nyte, but he could control the light—or more so when the light went out. Lifting his hand, he snapped his fingers. Orah gasped as the room went pitch black. Slowly the room filled with light but not normal light. Light that can only guide you in the night—starlight.

Chapter 5

At the snap of Roan's fingers, the room went dark, and Orah's senses were alert. This man in front of her had told her he wasn't a predator, yet he had taken all the light from the room. Even the sunlight. She blinked and realized light was beginning to fill the room again, but not the same as before. Before, the afternoon sun had filled the room with a few lamps for additional light, but now, tiny lights began to flicker to life all around her. She turned to find Roan's face lit up in the dark and realized this wasn't any normal kind of light. It was mimicking starlight, and Roan looked as though he were made for it.

The light seemed to gravitate toward him. Whereas the blue in his eyes had taken center stage when they were in the sun, now the focal point was the sparkling silver the starlight revealed. The freckles she noticed earlier were lit as if they were his own personal set of constellations. A crown that appeared to be made of starlight now hovered slightly above his head. She blinked again, realizing she hadn't said a word since the lights went out.

Clearing her throat, she sat up a bit straighter. "This is..." If she was being honest, she didn't have the words to describe what it was. "...This is incredible," she managed to force out.

Roan smiled, and his constellation freckles scrunched up under his eyes. He made eye contact with Orah, lifting his hand again. She was almost sure he was about to perform a meteor shower but instead he held their eye contact and snapped his fingers once more. Gasping, she shut her eyes to avoid the blinding sunlight that filled the room. After a moment of composing herself she opened her eyes again to find he had moved closer to her than he had been before his show-and-tell of power. She noticed he was trying not to touch her, but she didn't like that he had used the dark to get closer. She moved slightly to the left and hit the arm of the couch.

Nowhere else to go.

An emotion flashed across his face that she couldn't place. She wasn't sure if it was sadness or something more dangerous, but she didn't have a chance to ponder it further before he spoke again.

"While that wasn't exactly *shadows or some shit*, I hope that was proof enough to you that what I've told you is true," he said with a sly smile.

Orah rolled her eyes. He was mocking her, but she had read enough books about *powerful*, shadow wielding men in her life that she was almost embarrassed to admit it. It was all she could assume when he said he was the God of Night.

"Yes, that was impressive, but I don't understand why you have to sit so close to me to perform a little magic trick."

A throat cleared across the room and Orah suddenly remembered his Captain, Jesiel, was still there with them. She glanced at him, still shocked by how intriguing the part-man-part-creature person was.

"His Lord has shown you but a sliver of his power and yet you question him," Jesiel said. Orah rolled her eyes again in response, unable to ignore how highly these men seemed to think of themselves. She opened her mouth to respond, but Jesiel held up his hands to stop her.

"I wasn't done." He moved closer to the couch, standing directly in front of her. "What Roan seems to be hesitant to share with you is that in order to find out where you came from, he has to be near you and yes, he does have to touch you in some way." Orah blinked, unsure how he knew the next question she was about to ask.

She turned to Roan, finding him staring at the carpet. For someone who was supposed to be this very powerful Governing God, he looked as though he was about to ask for something he had been told he couldn't have.

She let out another sigh. "Why do you need to touch me?"

Roan's eyes shot up and he breathed out long and slow. "Another portion of the power that all other Gods of Nyte have possessed is dream walking."

"Dream walking?"

"Yes."

"I don't understand."

"At night we sleep. Well, unless you're a nocturnal creature." He smirked a bit. "But I don't think you are. Either way, I can touch someone and see their dreams."

"But I'm not sleeping."

"Oh no. It doesn't work like that. Your dreams are essentially a product of your memories, including both your conscious and subconscious mind. You don't have to be asleep for me to be able to walk through them. I only need to touch you to see it all."

Orah shifted her legs uncomfortably. She didn't think she wanted this stranger in her head. Hell, most days she didn't want to be in her *own* head. "How does this help you get me back home?"

"I need to see your memories to understand where you came from," Roan replied.

"Why can't I just tell you?"

"I suppose you can, but then I'll never know if you've been lying to me."

She stood quickly, unable to hide her offense. She had quite literally been dropped into this world and he had the audacity to question her intentions. All she wanted was to go home. She didn't want to be here. Wherever *here* was.

She stared down at him, her anger slowly building. "Why would I lie to you?"

Roan's eyes softened and he motioned for her to sit down. Hesitating, she observed him for a moment. She could see that he was trying to be genuine and respectful of her space, but she didn't know if she could fully trust him.

"I don't think you've been lying to me at all, Orah, or that you would lie to me. As I explained earlier—things are tense in my Region lately, and I just have to be careful. Please understand."

Something came over her and she nodded her head, deciding to sit again. "If I'm going to be honest with you, then you have to be honest with me."

Roan nodded.

"Why did you seem nervous to tell me about this? Why did your Captain have to be the one to push you to say something?"

He jumped back, surprised by her observation. "Dream walking, or more so memory walking, can be a bit uncomfortable or even emotional for some. I can do my best to guide your mind to only show me what I'm looking for, but your mind can take control. I could accidentally pull out memories or emotions you may not want to be facing at the moment."

She gulped—that was what she feared. All those dark muddled memories she spent energy pushing down every day, that she tried to pretend were not there. She knew the truth and didn't know if she could face it all, but she also desperately wanted to go home. Orah's eyes lifted to meet his again and she nodded. "I want to go home."

His eyes flickered in understanding and he moved so close to her that their knees were now touching. He motioned for her to take his hands and she laid hers on top of his hesitantly. Closing her eyes, she braced for some kind of pain but what she didn't expect were the tears that instantly fell down her cheeks.

Chapter 6

Orah's pain was so thick that Roan could almost taste it. He stared at her now-closed eyes and the tears that were slipping through her thick lashes. Her full lips shook while her heavy emotions took over. Squeezing her hand, he tried to reassure her that she was safe and closed his own eyes.

His awareness of his own world and sitting room slipped away as Orah's memories began to fill his mind. Now standing in her memories, he could see a hidden garden door that strangely resembled his, but beyond it, weren't the city streets he was accustomed to. Instead, he could see a beautiful estate covered in trees with a large home sitting off in the distance. As he focused on the home, Orah's mind opened a bit more to allow him in. The chateau, as she called it, was in disrepair but beautiful. He smiled at the feeling of familiarity and recognition as he gazed upon her home.

She jolted slightly as her mind took them through her last few days. The first memory felt recent—perhaps just a few days earlier. She was saying goodbye to people and packing bags. She kept mentioning this chateau of hers and a new adventure. Her emotions were hopeful and excited, but under the joy was a layer of grief and fear she was trying to mask. There didn't seem to be anyone Orah was particularly close to, no real sadness in her goodbyes. There was no one it seemed she'd miss with this new life she had chosen.

Her memories shifted, and she appeared to be sitting in an elongated carriage with rows of people. To his surprise, outside of the windows were the clouds, as if the carriage itself were flying. The clouds disappeared, and Roan watched as she embraced a man in a very large room with people carrying bags around them. The man felt warm and familiar. She loved him—but not in a romantic way. More so as someone she wholeheartedly trusted. Just like before, there was a layer under the emotions she felt with him—guilt.

The guilt propelled her memories backward. Memory after memory with this man appeared. Roan took in the man's features now. His face was kind and his green eyes gazed upon Orah with nothing but love. Roan couldn't help but wonder if there had ever been anything more between the two of them. Memory after memory appeared with him. Many of them when they were younger; laughing, dancing, and drinking, but they never appeared to be anything more than friends.

His assumption was confirmed as he watched, as though he were watching through Orah's eyes, while the man danced with another man in a pub of some kind. Her emotions were light and happy as she watched her friend grab hold of his dance partner, kissing him hard on the lips.

The memory moved then to an almost bird's-eye view and Roan watched Orah join them on the dance floor. The dress she was wearing was almost scandalous and Roan worked to push down his appreciation. The dark burgundy color cut close to her curves, more so than the outfit she was wearing now. This one was shorter too and the color made the auburn in her hair stand out, even under the dark lights where she danced. Looking over at her friend, she smiled widely. Her mind felt as though it was desperately trying to cling to good memories with this friend. Almost subconsciously, Roan squeezed her hand.

Where did you come from? he thought to himself, forgetting that questions like this could guide the memories and Orah jumped as her mind raced away from her friend. She gripped Roan's hands like she was trying to steady herself and her memories went from light and airy to thick and dark. Roan's lungs constricted as though they had been filled with poisoned smoke when a blurry wall appeared in their minds.

He couldn't see past the wall very well, but he could make out who he assumed was Orah. The other person was blocked from view. He could hear raised voices. One sounded unnatural, almost monstrous, while the other sounded angry, sad, scared, and desperate all at once. Memory after memory blocked by the blurry wall rushed across his mind. He couldn't help but think how it felt as though they were barreling toward the depths of Shadus and he wasn't sure how to pull them out. The pain in the air was so thick, they could cut it with a knife, but there was a new layer of anger now—anger so real, his skin burned as though it was going to catch fire.

He squeezed Orah's hand again, trying to ground her. He wasn't sure what to do but somehow, through instinct, his one squeeze was followed by two more. As if on cue, the memories stopped abruptly. He thought her mind was done when a shimmer of light appeared, beckoning to him, calling for him to follow the light. Steadying his own breathing, he stepped through.

Observing a small lawn, Roan found a young child sitting on the grass. After a moment, he realized he was looking at a younger version of Orah. He glanced around to find a man and woman next to her, both smiling affectionately at her.

Her family.

The man sat down and Orah rushed to him. The woman laughed loudly and joined them. When the woman spoke, Roan was shocked to hear a resemblance in her voice to that monstrous one behind those blurry walls from before. Orah smiled at her and Roan's body was filled with too many emotions at once: love, hope, fear, anger, sadness, despair, and loss. He could only assume this woman was Orah's mother, and while he related, he couldn't imagine what could have happened for Orah to have all of those strong emotions attached to her.

Orah looked at the man next to her and the rush of emotions was lighter. There was still loss, sadness, and despair but the kind that came from losing someone integral to you. Roan recognized the emotions all too well. Layered within were stronger emotions of love and safety. Quickly, memories flashed with this man and Orah. Laughter, tears, fights, adventures. All the experiences you would have expected one to have with a parent. Roan felt relief that her mind seemed to be clinging to the light when a dark mist surrounded her memories. He didn't know for sure when this memory happened, but it felt recent. Recent enough that Orah's mind was working very hard not to remember.

A wail echoed through the mist, and Roan froze, suddenly being pulled back to sixty years before, when Lahana had let out the same sound.

Tears fell down Roan's face as he recognized the moment of losing someone you loved. He understood Orah a bit more now. So many of her memories were blocked and buried, but she appeared to live in a constant state of strength. She believed she put on a mask to protect herself, but he knew the truth. No one who had experienced the levels of fear, pain, and loss that she had were putting on a mask. Her strength was her own and something he admired.

He squeezed her hands once more and pulled his mind from hers. Opening his eyes, they slowly focused back on his sitting room. Jes was on the chair across from him, concern tightening his features. He jumped, realizing Roan had opened his eyes but Roan shook his head softly, letting him know he didn't need his Captain to take any action. Jes nodded his head in acknowledgement but also questioning if they would be able to trust what Orah had told them. Roan nodded slowly and looked over at Orah. Her eyes were still closed, but she had removed her hands from his. The tears were dry now but the color in her face had drained. She opened her eyes, her expression tight but desperate, as if she were silently asking if he believed her or not.

Standing, Roan walked toward the window. Her memories had shown him so much, but also so little. From what he could gather, her world was somewhere called *Earth*—he couldn't help but notice the similarity in the word to the City of Kings. He had seen the moments leading up to her going through the door, confirming why she'd assumed they were neighbors. Chuckling he shook his head at the rage she felt, believing that *he* had been the one holding the door closed so she couldn't get through. Still, he had no answers as to *how* she had gotten through.

On his side of the door the air felt thick and he had somehow known something was coming. For Orah, the door was warm—as if beckoning her to try and come through. It made no sense, but what made less sense was the thread of power Roan felt radiating through her when he held her hands. He wasn't sure how he hadn't noticed it before, but it was obvious when their hands touched.

Orah was no ordinary mortal. She somehow stepped into the Land of Gods and it had awoken a sleeping power within her. And he wasn't confident that she was aware of the power given how shocked and disoriented she was.

A warm prickling sensation sent a chill down his spine and he realized he had been silent for too long. Turning to face Orah and Jes, Roan let out a sigh. "Thank you for sharing your memories with me, Orah." She startled at the sound of his voice. She was clearly as lost in her own thoughts as Roan had been in his. "I believe what you've told me but, unfortunately, I have no idea how to get you home."

Disappointment settled across her face and she sunk against the couch. "Great. Well, what am I supposed to do now?"

He smiled. "I'm not sure but we'll figure it out. In the meantime, let's get you set up in a room upstairs."

Jes's mouth popped open at his announcement. Roan knew he wanted to say something, but the sound of the side door opening distracted them and Lahana's voice echoed throughout the house. "Roany, I'm home!"

Roan groaned, rubbing his jaw. Lahana had a terrible habit of using that damned nickname at the worst times. He glanced at Jes who nodded and walked out of the room to try and stop Roan's sister before she bombarded Orah with her own questions. Roan shut the doors behind him and turned back to Orah.

She stared at the closed doors, then back at Roan. "Who was that?" Her head cocked in curiosity. After all she had seen that day, Roan wasn't surprised to think she may have been imagining someone else who looked like Jes.

He sighed. "That was my sister." He walked back toward the couch and motioned with his hands in a silent question about whether or not she would allow him to sit next to her again. She stared at him for a moment before she nodded her head and shifted to make room for him.

He sat back down and straightened himself. He was about to speak when she interrupted him. "I'm not sure why you think I'm just going to accept your offer to stay upstairs when we've just met." He gawked at her in shock. It hadn't occurred to him that she might decline the invitation. Especially considering how rarely he opened his home to anyone.

"I don't know why you wouldn't."

She stood abruptly. "Why did you shut the doors as Jesiel left? Am I a secret you're hoping to keep from your sister?"

Again, she threw him off with another question he hadn't been expecting. "No, not at all. My sister can be a handful. I shut the doors to protect you from the onslaught of questions I'm sure she's bound to throw your way. I thought you might not want to deal with that after everything that's happened in the last couple of hours." Orah stared at him and he wasn't sure if she was upset with him or appreciative that he had thought about how she was feeling.

The answer to his question came when she spoke again. "While I can appreciate that you're concerned for my well-being, I ask that you don't make assumptions on my behalf. I can protect myself and handle any *onslaught* of questions that come my way." Orah's eyes narrowed as if she were challenging him.

He smiled; he was really enjoying conversing with her. He had thought his day was going to be mundane, but her falling into his garden made the day far more interesting than he was anticipating. "I won't make that mistake again. Don't forget, Orah, I've seen your memories and your strength. I'm aware of what you can handle."

She flinched at the mention of the emotional whirlwind they had just come out of. "I'm sorry if you saw anything that was upsetting." She glanced down at her fidgeting fingers.

Standing, he walked toward her, while making sure to keep his distance. "You don't have to apologize, there was nothing I saw that could upset me. We don't need to dwell on painful memories. Can we go back to the topic of my offer?"

Orah was unsure of what to say. She was quickly realizing that she would not be going home, at least not that day, but she didn't know if she wanted to stay with this man either. He hadn't threatened her or seemed as though he would cause her harm, but she also didn't know anything about him. She couldn't assume someone who supposedly ruled over a region and city was innately good.

Roan threw up his hands softly. She could tell he was frustrated, but she had to ensure she was protecting herself and not bowing to his Godly ego. Raising an eyebrow, he sighed, "Well?"

She crossed her arms and surveyed the room. She didn't have any idea how big the house was but by the height of the ceilings and the size of the front lawn, she believed it was much larger than her chateau. She made eye contact with him and breathed out. "I don't know why I would stay with you."

"You said that already."

"Well, it's the truth," she replied.

"If you don't stay with me then where would you go?"

"I'm not sure." Orah shrugged and looked out the window again. "Your city likely has many places for someone to stay."

His eyes followed hers and he smirked.

"Yes, that's true but you usually have to *pay* to stay in those places."

"I have money."

Stepping back, his eyes surveyed her head to toe. "Where?"

She glared at him, irritated that it was now the second time his eyes had so casually glanced over her body that day. Opening her mouth to respond to him, she glanced down at herself. "Shit," she mumbled. She was only wearing the blue dress and sandals she had put on before going to the airport. Her dress had no pockets, and she left her phone on the dining table at the chateau, although she doubted her cell would have even worked here if she had it on her. She shook her head, realizing she also left her wallet with her phone, but again, she wasn't sure if her money would have been accepted in his world.

She glared back at him and he still had that stupid smile on his face. "Okay well I *do* have money, just not here."

Roan looked back out at the city. "You are welcome to try and find a place to stay in the city if you really want to. Fates, because you came through my garden you could even tell them to put the cost on my personal tab. However, you have quite literally come from a different world and while my city is considered safe, there are many who could take advantage of your lack of knowledge regarding our customs. You may be in the Land of Gods, but that does not mean the Gods are incapable of cruelty."

Orah knew he was right, as much as she hated to admit it. Even though he was still a stranger, she had spent the majority of the afternoon with him and he did run the city. She hoped that meant she was at least safe in his home. She stared at the closed doors that led out to the house and thought she heard mumbles and the shuffling of feet on the other side. However, the sound stopped almost as soon as she heard it. She rubbed her forehead where there had been a dull ache building since she awoke on the couch.

Glancing back at him, she shrugged. "Fine. I guess it's the best option available to me."

Roan laughed and rubbed his own forehead, as if he was experiencing his own headache. "It's settled then. I'll make sure a room is set up for you." He walked toward the doors and pulled them open. Orah's eyes tried to catch the flash of green that hid behind what she could now see was a grand staircase. She had no idea who or what it was, but they were obviously eavesdropping on their conversation.

Roan chuckled. "Hello, Lahana."

A head popped out from behind the staircase and Roan's sister came into view.

What is with all the attractive people here?

Lahana was wearing a long, dark green dress that reminded Orah of depictions of Ancient Roman fashion. Her sleeves ended right at the top of her shoulder and a cape connected to her shoulders flowed back behind her. The neckline of her dress wasn't conservative, but it wasn't scandalous either. Her skin was the same dark tan color as her brother's but her long hair was at least a shade lighter than Roan's with more blonde than brown. Orah made eye contact with Lahana and couldn't help but admire her eyes. They were a brilliant green that reminded Orah of a grove of trees right after rain. Orah realized Lahana was smiling at her and took note of the lines on either side of her eyes—as though she spent most of her days smiling. She appeared younger than Roan but Orah didn't actually know how old Roan was. Any knowledge of Gods and age were from classes she had taken in school and fantasy books she'd read in her life.

The woman stood in silence before she rushed over, half yelling and squealing. "Roany!" Orah's eyes widened as the Goddess quickly spoke in the language Roan and his Captain had used in the sitting room. Roan responded, in the same unknown language before his sister's head snapped toward Orah.

"Jes told me we had a visitor." Lahana's voice was soft, but also had an intriguing air of command and confidence behind it. She, just like Roan and Jes, had an odd accent accompanying their words—an almost ethereal yet swirling hint behind everything they said, as though every word was meant to draw attention.

Roan's sister grinned wide. "I *love* your outfit." Orah blinked in shock that she was complementing such a simple dress, but she smiled anyway.

Lahana laughed nervously, then covered her face in her hands. "I'm so sorry, we haven't had a new visitor in a while, and I forget myself." She chuckled. "My name is Lahana."

"It's nice to meet you, Lahana. My name is Orah."

Lahana quickly glanced at Roan and Orah watched him shake his head out of the corner of her eye. She wasn't sure why they had all reacted to her name like this. It wasn't like any of them had what were considered common names—at least not where she was from. Deciding not to push them, she sighed. Her headache was getting worse and she hadn't felt so exhausted in a while. She surveyed the room which appeared to be a main foyer for the house. Shockingly, it reminded her of the main foyer of her chateau.

Across from the doors they had just come out of, she could see another room with a large desk in the middle and bookshelves built into each wall. At the chateau, that location had been where she had found her library too, and the only difference was the desk. Holding herself back, she refrained from rushing in to investigate what kinds of books existed in the Land of Gods and continued her survey. In the middle of the foyer was the staircase—much larger than the one at her chateau. She could see doors and a hallway at the top of the stairs but was sure there was more she couldn't see from where she stood. She wasn't sure where the kitchen or dining room were located but she assumed they were on this level of the house if it were anything like hers.

She looked back at Roan and Lahana. "So, which room will I be staying in?"

Roan stared up the stairs and rubbed his jaw. "Honestly, I haven't thought that far ahead. There are more than enough rooms to spare, but I need to speak with my housekeeper, Ms. Perri. She's more aware of which rooms are the least dusty and well maintained." He shifted his focus to the hall behind the study. "Are you hungry? I've just realized I haven't eaten anything since breakfast."

Her stomach loudly grumbled in response at the mention of food and she eagerly nodded her head. He glanced at his sister, then back at Orah. "Lahana, can you show Orah where the kitchen is? I'm going to find Ms. Perri and help her get a room ready."

"Yes, of course," Lahana said enthusiastically, motioning for Orah to follow as she began walking across the foyer toward the hallway Roan was eyeing. Orah's feet shuffled forward before remembering he'd said he was hungry as well.

"Aren't you going to need food too?" she asked him, stopping in front of the stairs.

"I want to make sure a room is ready for you when you're done. I likely won't eat with you and Lahana, but I will make sure I eat." He smiled and walked down the hallway behind the sitting room.

Orah turned back to Lahana, who motioned for her to follow. From where Orah stood now, she could see more of the house. On either side of the foyer were two hallways. The one near the study led to a large dining room on the other side of the wall. She could see a few more open doors further down but couldn't make out what the rooms were. On the side near the sitting room was a slightly shorter hallway. She glanced up the stairs, noticing that what she had previously thought was a hallway was actually another stairwell.

How big is this place? she wondered, but decided she could explore later and continued following Lahana.

They passed the dining room and approached the kitchen placed directly behind it. The door she had seen beyond the kitchen sat at the end of the hallway near a door that seemed to lead outside. On the left-hand side were even more doors.

"Those are closets and those two on the right are Jes's suite and study," Lahana whispered, taking note of Orah observing her surroundings before they stepped into the kitchen.

"Why does he sleep down here?"

Lahana shrugged. "Not sure. He claims it's because he's close to all the ground floor entrances and he feels more comfortable having easy access to them. If you ask me, I think he likes being able to sneak out without anyone knowing."

Orah chuckled at the thought of someone like him sneaking around. She couldn't imagine how sneaky one could be when they towered over most people while also having a giant pair of wings attached to your back. Lahana smiled at her laugh and nodded her head. "I think it's a funny thought too."

Lahana motioned Orah toward the door to the kitchen and Orah's stomach groaned, responding to the smells that hit her when they walked in. Lahana pointed to a round table by a bay window and Orah shuffled over. She was too tired to try and offer any help with gathering food. She sat down, realizing that she hadn't noticed the two staff kneading dough at the large island when she walked past. She smiled at them and wished she had more energy to offer a helping hand. Resting her arms on the table, she laid her head on top of them and almost drifted off to sleep when Lahana suddenly set a plate of food in front of her. The food wasn't extravagant, but it smelled incredible. There were several thick slices of what Orah hoped was seasoned beef, an assortment of sliced cheeses, some fruits she had never seen before, and a couple of thick slices of bread. She was about to serve herself when Lahana set down a small bowl with some type of spread.

"I don't know what food is like where you come from," Lahana said as she picked up the bread and began spreading it with what was in the small bowl, "But here we love a good sandwich."

Orah briefly felt as though she was going to cry at the mention of a meal so simple but apparently universal. She watched as Lahana placed the meat on the bread, layered two different kinds of cheese on top, and thinly sliced one of the fruits before placing it on top to complete the layers. She placed the sandwich on a plate and passed it to Orah.

Taking a bite, Orah's eyes rolled. She couldn't tell if she was hungrier than she had originally thought or if it was because the food was from another world, but she certainly didn't think she had ever eaten something so amazing. When she finished her meal, Lahana grabbed her plate and popped up from the table.

"Let's go see if Roan was able to get a room set up for you."

Walking out of the kitchen they nearly collided with Roan as they turned down the hall. He jumped back but smiled. "I was just coming to find you. Ms. Perri has a room ready for you. She's waiting at the bottom of the stairs."

Orah's exhaustion began to set in and all she could do was nod her head in response before she followed Lahana back to the stairs. Ms. Perri appeared stern but kind and gave Orah a slight smile as she turned to walk up the stairs without saying a word. Orah expected Lahana to leave her by this point, but she stayed by her side. When they reached the top of the stairs, Ms. Perri turned right. They passed four doors before stopping at a pair of French doors. Ms. Perri paused for a moment then pulled them open.

Orah's eyes widened as she stepped into the room. Against one wall was a very large bed with a light blue blanket laid across it. On top of the blanket were pillows in white cases and she was reminded again of the sky when flying through the clouds. Her eyes felt heavy and she found the bed, barely registering Ms. Perri pointing out the bathroom. She thanked her and Lahana quietly for their help and they shuffled out of the room, leaving her alone.

She walked up to another set of French doors and opened them softly, gasping when she stepped out onto a small balcony. She was overlooking the garden she had come through and had a near perfect view of the metal door that led her to this strange world. Her heart jumped and she thought about her chateau and how quickly something of her own had slipped away from her. Turning to her right, she found another small balcony. *I bet that one has a perfect view.*

Her chest tightened before turning back into the room, closing the doors behind her. Sleep called to her, and she made her way across the room. To her surprise the bed was warm when she climbed under the covers. *Just like a cloud*, she thought as her eyes drifted shut.

Chapter 7

Orah woke with a start and her heart raced as though it were going to burst from her chest. She knew where she was, but the room was dark, and she had no idea what time it was or how long she had been sleeping. She searched for any kind of light but was unable to find one. When she stood, however, little lights along the floorboard began to twinkle as though she were walking in the night sky.

Her curiosity about the room distracted her from the wonder she felt at the magic and she went to investigate the door next to the couch first, finding a closet. To her surprise there were a few items hanging on the racks, but she didn't feel up to inspecting them. She closed the closet door behind her and walked toward the archway. What she thought was another section of the room was actually the bathroom Ms. Perri had mentioned earlier. She was shocked she hadn't noticed it when she first walked in but figured her exhaustion had distracted her.

The bathroom had a vanity on one wall, a large tub on the other, and right next to the tub was a very large shower. Her eyes widened with excitement that there appeared to be running water there. She wasn't sure what to expect but it had not been the modern comforts she would have found back home.

She turned and walked out of the bathroom, unsure of what to do with herself. Staring at the doors that led out to the hallway, she considered braving an exploration. She thought that if the floorboards lit up throughout the rest of the house like they did in her room, she would have enough light to explore. She walked toward the bedroom doors and right as she turned the handle, a loud crash echoed on the other side. Instantly, the lights in the room went out. Jumping back, startled by the sudden darkness, she wondered whether she should investigate when the floorboard lights blinked back on and she heard raised voices. Glancing back at the room, she decided she needed to know what was going on for her own safety.

She slipped out of the bedroom and walked back the way she came earlier, following the voices. The closer she walked to the stairs, the clearer they were. They were coming from downstairs and she quietly snuck down a few steps and crouched. Lights from the open study doors lit the foyer and she could see Roan gripping the desk. Jesiel stood behind him with a hand on his back. It appeared to be a comforting touch and she wondered what exactly their relationship was.

Quietly, she watched Roan take a deep breath and walk to the other side of the room, now out of her line of sight. He returned a moment later holding a broken lamp and set it down on the desk. He glanced back at Jesiel, who was holding what she thought was a piece of paper. She jumped at the sound of Roan's voice, becoming aware she was eavesdropping on a private conversation.

"I'm not sure if I can do this Jes. What am I supposed to do?" Roan leaned against the desk and covered his face with his hands.

Jesiel set the paper on the desk and put his hand on Roan's shoulder. "I'm not sure. We both know we have no control over the Fates decision, and He's enough of a bastard that we shouldn't underestimate Him, but we also can't do anything about it right now." He removed his hand from Roan and stood a bit straighter. "We have the advantage. He's not fully aware of where your depth of power currently sits."

Roan glanced up.

"You and I both know our secrets cannot be kept forever." He stood suddenly and Orah shrunk back a bit, trying to hide from his eyes that had drifted toward the stair she was crouched on. "Not only do I have this to worry about, but I now have a strange mortal woman staying in my home. What if I can't protect her from it all?"

She covered her mouth to quiet her gasp, unsure if she should have felt fear in the moment. She didn't know who the *he* was they were referring to, but he didn't sound good. She took a breath and held it for a moment, reminding herself that she was a strong woman, and she knew how to hold her own. She believed that would even apply, at least to an extent, against a possible God or Gods.

Jesiel cleared his throat. "Roan, she's not your responsibility. I don't know why you didn't just hand her a purse of coins and let her go on her way. You said she's not a threat."

Roan's expression turned hard, startling Orah.

"Jes, you and I both know I cannot send a woman from another world out into the streets with no protection. You and I also both know there is something more to her that we need to figure out." Turning away from the stairs, Roan stared down at the paper on his desk. "I'm not sure when you became so incapable of caring for another's well-being, but she is my responsibility."

Jes's jaw tensed before he replied. "You know I am not incapable of caring for others. This is a tense time and as your Captain and bonded Beskermer, I am obligated to think of you first."

Roan's voice shifted to a teasing tone. "Yes, *Captain,* I'm very aware of your duties."

Jesiel's hands flew up in defense. "I am never going to hear the end of that. I was trying to ensure she knew your station and importance!"

"Yes, obviously." Roan laughed. "*My Lord.*" Orah stifled her laugh at the punch Roan landed on Jes's shoulder.

Any fear she had before lessened, and she felt a bit better knowing that Jes wasn't some hardass who would push to have her thrown out. He was obviously a concerned friend and seemed to have a duty to protect Roan from whatever threat he was facing.

She stood from her crouched position and held back her groan from how stiff her body was. She hadn't worked her muscles in the weeks leading up to the move and was beginning to feel it. She quietly walked back up the stairs but paused before turning back toward the bedroom. Staring up at the second staircase a few feet away, she decided she wanted a few more minutes of exploration. She tiptoed up the staircase that led to a single door at the top. Walking up as quietly as she could, she paused when arriving in front of the door. She felt a rush of fear at the possibility of falling through it to another unknown world but also knew that wouldn't happen—at least, that's what she told herself. The door handle turned with no resistance and she was surprised by the rush of fresh air as she pushed it open and stepped out onto a rooftop terrace.

The view in front of her took her breath away. She now understood why this part of the world was dedicated to the night. She had never seen the sky like this before. Stars twinkled above her, and she could see constellations she didn't recognize. All around was a blend of the aurora borealis and the way her sky at home looked when she admired the milky way high in the mountains, away from the city lights. She gasped, watching several shooting stars streak across the sky, one after another. The warm air prickled her skin and she decided she wanted to stay out there for a while before climbing back to bed.

She had forgotten she left the door open behind her until a voice spoke.

"Careful with leaving doors open around here. Apparently, mortals from another world can come through them now."

Roan held back his laugh as Orah jumped, then turned to face him.

"I didn't mean to leave it open," she glanced at the now closed door behind him.

"I know. I just thought I'd lighten the mood a bit." He walked toward where she was standing and looked up at the sky, admiring the beauty of what was his. He breathed in the smell of the night and listened to the quiet sounds of his sleeping city. From the corner of his eye, he could see her stare at him for a moment before her gaze drifted upward.

"So," she said quietly. "Did you craft this beautiful sky yourself?"

He was shocked at how close she was to the truth with her question, and he glanced at her. "Partially. It's a culmination of myself and the previous Gods of Nyte before me."

Orah met his eyes, and his chest seized while he took in how the gold flecks in her eyes lit up in the dark.

Her eyes shifted back toward the sky. "How many Gods of Night have been before you?"

Roan smiled, unable to ignore her beauty. "Too many to name, but enough to create the beauty we're staring at."

Her eyes were still on the sky and he took a step back to take her in again, thinking how exquisite she was. Her dark disheveled hair fell between her shoulders and her lower back. He could barely see any of the auburn that was so prominent in the sun. Now, it was so dark one could have mistaken it for black. She was still in the little blue dress from earlier. The tiny straps at her shoulders exposed her skin and he smiled at the freckles that dotted across her shoulders. He wasn't sure why she didn't change into one of the spare items Ms. Perri had placed in the closet, but he wasn't complaining.

Shaking his head, he scolded himself for staring at her and letting his mind drift toward inappropriate thoughts.

He cleared his throat and her head snapped toward him. "I don't know how things work in your world," Roan said, trying to hide the amusement in his tone, "But here, it's considered rude to eavesdrop on private conversations."

She stared at him for a moment before struggling out her response. "I—I don't think I heard anything important."

He knew she hadn't. He had felt her curiosity the moment she stopped at the top of the stairs. Jes had been too preoccupied in his annoyance to notice her presence so Roan tried to steer the conversation away from what they had been discussing moments before. For a moment, he worried whether or not she had seen him lose control of himself, but she wasn't reacting as if she had.

He chuckled. "No, you didn't hear anything that would be considered important."

"I don't know who you were talking about but I'm sorry to hear that he sounds like a real pain in the ass," she said casually.

His mouth hung open and he couldn't stop himself from laughing. *Fates, this woman.* She was lucky she said that comment to him and not anyone else in the land.

A smile formed on her lips and she chuckled. "Sorry, sometimes my mouth speaks before my brain can catch up to stop me."

"You have nothing to apologize for. You're not wrong in your observation."

"It seems that your Captain, Jesiel, is a great comfort to you though."

She wasn't wrong in that observation either. He wasn't sure who or where he would be without Jes in his life. He kept Roan grounded but wasn't afraid to push him. Some assumed his loyalty was because of his bonded duty, but Roan knew it was much more than that. Looking back into her eyes, he nodded. "I'm very grateful for him."

She shifted as if she were uncomfortable. "So how long have you two been partners?"

His mouth hung open once again and he laughed harder than before. *She thinks I'm with Jes.* He wasn't sure if anyone had shocked him with so many outrageous questions in one day before. He couldn't seem to stop laughing and she stared up at him with annoyance spreading across her face. To his surprise she stomped her foot, which made him laugh all the harder. He couldn't believe he'd just watched a grown woman do that. She crossed her arms in front of her. "What is so damn funny?"

He held his chest and took a deep breath in trying to stop his hysteria. "You are."

"Excuse me?"

"First your question about Jes. Fates, I wish he could have heard you ask that. I would have loved to have seen his response. Second, that little foot stomp you just did. Has no one ever told you how much it makes you look like a child?"

The heat in her fury climbed higher as she stared at him. "I didn't mean to ask a funny question. I was just trying to understand your relationship with Jesiel. Men being partners is not something uncommon where I'm from. As to the foot stomping, well, yes, I have been told it's childish." Her fury cooled to a low simmer of embarrassment with her admission.

"Men being partners isn't uncommon here either. Maybe more uncommon or unfortunately discouraged with Jes's kin but I wasn't laughing at the idea. I was laughing at how our relationship is very much not that. We're close, but not *that* close."

Roan walked over to the chairs on the other side of the roof and sat down. "If I'm being honest, I think Jes would be way less tense if he had at least one lover in his life."

Taking a seat in the chair next to him, her gaze went back to the sky. "I really didn't mean to cause offense. Whomever you're with really isn't my business."

He glanced back at her. "No offense was taken. Trust me when I tell you I'm not at all secretive about who I'm attracted to." His eyes lingered on her thick lashes, her full lips, and the way she scrunched her nose as she gasped at what he knew was the shooting star flying across the sky.

Chapter 8

They sat in silence, watching the stars shoot across the sky. She could feel Roan's eyes on her, but she was too embarrassed for how much of a fool she had made herself to look at him just yet. She couldn't believe her own ignorance in even bringing up the nature of his relationship with Jesiel. She could only imagine Julian's horror if he had heard her. Her chest immediately tightened at the thought of Julian. She wondered if he had even noticed she had disappeared with how they'd left things.

Gathering her courage, she glanced back at Roan. He jumped a bit, and his eyes shot up toward the sky. *How long has he been staring at me?* Holding back her amusement, she took a moment to take him in.

His freckles were lit up like they had been in the sitting room. She wondered if he knew they reacted to the night like that. The starlight crown that was on his head wasn't there now. Making her realize he likely made it appear with his show of power earlier. He seemed to be admiring the sky with pride, like an artist admiring their own work in a gallery. She understood his pride though, she could sit out there every night for the rest of her life and never tire of the beauty he was responsible for creating.

Yawning, she braced her hands against her chair and stood. He jumped up and she was startled by how close he was. While she wasn't a short person, he was very tall in comparison and she had to look up to meet his eyes.

"I think I'm going to go back to bed," she whispered.

He nodded. "I need sleep as well. Would you allow me to escort you back to your room?"

She knew it wasn't any kind of intimate offer, but she felt slightly uncomfortable all the same. She thought for a moment and decided there was no harm in letting him walk her down the hall. "Yes, that would be alright."

She motioned for him to walk ahead of her and followed him back to the door but took one last peek up at the stars before following him down the stairs. He turned down the hall toward her bedroom and stopped at the doors.

"Thank you for the conversation," she said quietly.

"It was a pleasure."

She turned to open her door when he spoke again. "I'm not sure if Ms. Perri said anything but the clothes in your closet are there for your use."

"How did you get items in my size? Lahana and I weren't in the kitchen for that long."

Roan grinned. "I'm the Governing God of this city. I can snap my fingers and clothing will appear."

She raised her eyebrow. "I don't believe that."

"Okay, you're right, I'm not that impressive." He laughed. "Ms. Perri's daughter is of similar height and build to you. She was married last year and left a few pieces in her closet in the keeper's cottage on the property. Ms. Perri retrieved them and placed them in the closet for you."

"Oh, wow. That's very kind of her. I'll make sure I give her my thanks."

"She was happy to help out." He smiled and gestured to the door handle she was holding.

Smiling, she slipped through the door but paused before closing it fully. She could hear him walking away and decided to see what direction his room was. To her shock, she watched him stop just one door down, opening another pair of double doors. She was unsure if she should have been alarmed that he had conveniently put her in the room next to him, but decided she needed to sleep more than stressing herself out with the thought.

Not understanding how she was tired again, she climbed back into the bed and snuggled into the blanket, laughing at herself. She wasn't sure how she had so easily accepted what was happening to her. She thought perhaps she had read too many fantastical stories in her life—that could be the only explanation of how she had justified and accepted the last day as reality. Her eyes began to feel heavy again, and she fell back to sleep, thinking of the night sky.

Orah woke to sunlight warming her cheek. She turned toward the balcony doors. She wasn't sure what time it was, and her eyes shifted to glance around the room. She jumped and pushed herself up to the top of the bed as she made eye contact with Lahana, who was sitting casually on the couch across from her.

Lahana slid off the couch and flitted to the edge of the bed. "Good morning!"

Orah glared at her. "How long have you been sitting there?"

"Maybe 2 or 3 minutes," Lahana replied with a shrug.

"Does this world have no customs regarding boundaries and not watching people while they sleep?"

"Yes, we do, but I spent a good 2 minutes knocking on your door and you didn't answer, so I had to make sure you were still here, and alive." Standing, she walked to the closet doors. "Ms. Perri left these clothes here for you. There isn't much so you and I will be going shopping today to make sure you have a proper wardrobe. Roan has let me know he's not sure how long you'll be here, so I've made it my responsibility to ensure you're taken care of."

Orah pulled the blankets off herself and hopped out of bed. "Roan told me about the clothes last night." Following Lahana into the closet, she observed what Ms. Perri had left her. "I don't need to go shopping. I can deal with repeating outfits for however long I need."

Lahana laughed behind her. "It's perfectly fine to just *deal* with things, but Roan's gone for the day and there's really not much you could do here to fill your time, so you are going to accompany me."

Orah turned to her, feeling a little annoyed. "Why is Roan gone for the day?"

Lahana twirled her hair between her fingers and shrugged. "I dunno. He's kind of a big deal here. Something about being a Governing God."

Orah snorted at her sarcasm. Despite Lahana's obvious lack of boundaries, Orah knew she was going to like her. "And you've taken it as your *personal* responsibility to take care of my clothing needs? Or have you been instructed to keep me busy, so the strange mortal woman doesn't snoop around the Governing God's house all day?"

Letting her hair fall from her fingers, Lahana's eyes gleamed. "You're very observant, you know. I'm impressed. I'll just say my answer is yes."

Walking past Orah, Lahana grabbed a simple lilac colored dress. It was a similar fashion to what Lahana had on yesterday, but without the flowing cape at the back. Holding it up to Orah she frowned slightly. "I think this might actually be a little big on you, but it should work."

Turning back toward the other clothes in the closet, Lahana's eyes moved toward the small dresser against the back wall. "Oh!" she exclaimed before turning back to Orah. Holding up a small note and then her now closed hand, Lahana smiled. "Looks like Ms. Perri left this for you too."

Lahana's hand opened and Orah laid eyes upon a dainty ring in her palm. From the size, it looked as though it would only fit her pinky finger. It wasn't extravagant, or anything special, but Orah's heart immediately jumped with excitement. The delicate band of silver leaves connected in the middle where a small and round white gem fused the two ends together.

"What is that?" Orah asked quietly, unable to pull her eyes from the piece of jewelry.

The corners of Lahana's eyes crinkled with her smile. "It will help you understand things here. Let me help you put it on."

Hesitantly, Orah held out her hand while Lahana gripped her wrist. At the touch of their skin, Lahana jumped and snapped her head up toward Orah. For a moment, the Goddess stared at Orah with her eyes wide and an emotion swirling behind them that Orah couldn't place.

Lahana slipped the ring onto Orah's pinky and shivered briefly. "I'll be in the sitting room waiting while you get ready. I'll have breakfast brought to you in about 20 minutes." Handing the dress to Orah, she walked out of the closet. Orah rushed after her, needing more of an explanation of the ring and why it was important.

Catching her at the doors, Orah watched as Lahana swung them open before quickly turning back to Orah. "I'm looking forward to getting to know you, Orah."

Orah forgot her question from the kindness Lahana seemed to emit while she watched the Goddess gracefully stride out of the room, but Orah closed the doors behind her and turned the lock. Lahana's responding yell projected from the hall. "I guess I'll have breakfast left outside your door then!"

Orah sighed while her opposite hand fiddled with the ring now on her pinky. Trying to shake off the odd warm feeling now encircling her, she walked to the bathroom. She couldn't see any lights on the wall or switches to control them, but the room appeared to be lit. The large shower called out to her and reminded her she hadn't bathed since before leaving for the airport. Shaking off her own disgust at the realization, she rushed to the shower. After fiddling with the knobs for a moment, she was relieved to find that the hot water was immediate.

Quickly stripping off her dress, she walked into the shower, closing the door behind her. Steam filled the room, and she found an assortment of soaps on a built-in ledge in front of her. None of them were labeled, but it only took her a few minutes of testing to figure out what was for her hair and her body. The body wash and the hair wash were two different scents, but they complimented each other as though they had been picked intentionally. She scrubbed herself, trying hard not to get distracted by the sweet fragrances of the soap.

She let out a sigh while she shut off the water and stepped out of the shower. Surprisingly the floor felt warmer than before she had gotten in. She stared at the floor in wonder at the magic there that was as common as electricity in her own world. After patting herself dry with a towel, she grabbed the dress off the vanity and slipped it over her head. She blushed when she realized there likely weren't any under garments available for her and cursed that Lahana had been right about needing to shop. She pulled open a couple of drawers in the vanity in front of her, finding a brush and a comb. After brushing out her hair, she searched around for anything she could use to pull it back and found a small dark tie at the back of one of the drawers. A knock at the door pulled her attention while she tied off the braid she plaited into her hair and her stomach grumbled in response, remembering Lahana's comment about sending food to her.

Pulling open the door she found a tray outside with porridge—she assumed, based on the consistency—a bowl of fruit, an empty mug, and a small pot. Turning back into the room, she held back her excitement at the familiar smell of coffee now coming from the pot. She ate quickly, deciding that the food was most definitely better in the land of Gods.

Sighing, she poured the dark fragrant liquid from the pot into her mug, then walked to the balcony doors. The smell of the fresh, near decadent air swirled with the tantalizing wisps of her drink as she pulled the doors open. Taking a deep breath in, she stared down at her mug before bringing it to her lips. "Oh my god," she gasped, as her eyes widened, and the sweet yet slightly spiced taste hit her tongue. She wasn't sure if it was coffee, but she couldn't seem to stop drinking the beverage after that first taste. She savored the rich taste with each sip and couldn't help but wonder if she could bring herself to go home after experiencing the food in this new world.

She looked to her right at the little balcony a few feet from hers. *That must be his room.* She didn't know how she felt with the knowledge that he'd put her so close to him. She wasn't sure if her room just so happened to be the most prepared for a visitor, or if it had been a strategic choice to keep her close. Deciding not to dwell on it, she turned back into her room—nearly colliding with Lahana. Orah screamed, her mug slipping from her fingers and crashing to the ground.

Stepping back, Lahana threw up her hands. "I'm sorry! You were taking a while, so I thought I'd check on you."

Orah stared down at the drink spreading across the carpet, feeling both embarrassed and angry that Lahana was in the room again without an invitation. Cursing the now ruined carpet, she bent down to pick up the mug and looked around for something to clean up the mess. Lahana bent down next to her and put her hand on Orah's. "It's okay, you don't need to clean that up."

Unable to hide her annoyed tone, Orah glared at Lahana. "What are you talking about? It's going to stain the floor."

"No, it won't. Look." Lahana pointed down casually to where the mug had dropped.

Orah's mouth popped open while she watched the carpet soak up the mess. By the time the liquid was gone, there was no trace of the dark stain that should have been there.

Fascinated, she gaped back at Lahana. "How?"

Lahana's eyes twinkled and she grinned. "Magic."

"I find it hard to believe that this is a magic house," Orah replied while standing and placing the mug back on the tray.

Lahana shrugged. "It's not a magic house per se. More like a house that's been warded in a way that keeps it running by itself."

Orah shook her head. "Warded?"

Lahana cocked her head before smiling. "Yes, warded. Think like a magical mechanism that needs to be set up for the magic to work. They have to be maintained and adjusted as needed too, depending on what you're warding." She flung her hand out and pointed around the room. "Take this room for example, when Roan checked with Ms. Perri on what room could be opened the soonest for you, she picked here. The wards are set to maintain Roan's room next door and it was easier for her to adjust the wards to this room compared to an unused one on the other side of the house."

"So, it had been a choice of convenience," Orah whispered.

"Yes, it's likely part convenience but also partly makes it easy to keep an eye on you," Lahana replied with a wink.

Orah chuckled. Her assumption hadn't been wrong in the end. Somehow, though, knowing that Ms. Perri was as much a part of the decision as Roan brought her comfort.

Orah stared down at the small ring now on her pinky. "You mentioned the ring is warded?"

Lahana's gaze moved to Orah's pinky. "Yes, Ms. Perri left a note that it would help you understand things here."

"Like the language Roan was speaking to you yesterday?"

Lahana's grin shifted to something mischievous. "You mean the language I'm currently speaking in?"

Orah's eyes widened. "What?"

"Take off the ring and ask me a question."

Hands shaking, Orah slowly slipped the ring off her finger. "What are our plans today?" she asked, somehow not fully believing the small ring held so much power.

Lahana's mouth opened and out came the same language Orah had heard Roan using the day before. Orah laughed and shook her head.

"Fuck."

Orah slipped the ring back on and Lahana laughed. "Keep it on. There are many languages in our world, but most don't speak what seems to be your common tongue."

Orah nodded her head. "But, what about me? I can't speak your language."

Lahana shrugged. "According to the note, you don't have to. I wouldn't even know you weren't using it right now. No one else will either."

"Wow," Orah whispered, while her left hand absent-mindedly twisted the ring on her pinky.

"Now about shopping," Lahana said mischievously.

Orah let out a groan. "I guess if you've been put in charge of keeping me busy then I can tolerate a bit of shopping."

Lahana squealed in response. "This is going to be so much fun!"

Orah reluctantly followed her out of the room and found herself shocked at how quickly the caffeine was hitting her. Her entire body felt as if there were a slight buzz of electricity right below her skin. Usually, coffee just made her mind feel more alert, but she also wasn't entirely sure that she had been drinking coffee.

Following Lahana down the stairs and toward the side door, she stopped while Lahana stuck her head through the open kitchen door. "Good morning, Yohan. Good morning, Xade. Good morning, Clarah."

Trying to be polite, Orah stuck her head in after Lahana and waved. She recognized the young man and woman who had been kneading dough the day before but didn't recognize the older man now standing between them. All three waved back at her hesitantly and she reminded herself to make sure they were all properly introduced soon. The sound of Lahana opening the side door pulled Orah from the kitchen, and she followed Lahana outside.

"Those were our kitchen staff. Yohan is our cook, the other two are his children, Xade and Clarah."

Orah nodded, appreciating the information. "Do they live in the house?"

Lahana chuckled. "Oh Fates no. I don't think Roan would allow any staff to live *in* the house. They have a home a few blocks away closer to the center of the city."

"Why wouldn't he want staff to live in the house? What about Ms. Perri? He mentioned a keeper's cottage on the property."

"Oh, that did come out wrong." Lahana smacked her forehead with her palm. "Roan's not this awful employer. He doesn't want the staff living in the home because he wants them to have separation between their personal lives and their work. He's also a hermit and wouldn't enjoy lots of people around all day. The only ones who live on the property are Ms. Perri and her husband—he's our groundskeeper. He maintains the grounds and stables."

Orah followed her while she walked toward a large building she assumed were the stables she'd just mentioned. "But you and Jesiel both live in the house?"

Lahana let out a soft laugh. "Oh yeah, but he can't really get rid of us. He knows there would be all-out war if he tried to kick us out."

Orah chuckled. At least Roan had a family that loved him. The thoughts of family made her pause for a moment while pain filled her chest. She pushed it down. She had decided months before that she could be her own family and it was not the time for her to wallow in self-pity.

Lahana noticed her pause and turned back to her. "Are you alright?"

Orah's lips shifted to a tight smile. "Yes, I'm fine."

Lahana stared at her for a moment before shrugging and continuing her walk to the stables. "Alright here we are," she said, as she stopped in front of open stable doors.

Orah noticed all the stalls were closed and she couldn't hear any animal noises. As she made her survey of the building an older man came out from the door next to Lahana, smiling brightly.

"Are you hoping to head out, my Lady?"

Lahana grinned back in response. "Yes, Kai. I'm taking our guest to the city for some shopping and to show her around."

The man, whom Orah assumed was Ms. Perri's husband, nodded his head with a smile and bowed lightly. Orah stepped back and threw up her hands. "Oh no, please don't bow to me. I'm just a regular old mortal. No one important."

Kai smiled at her again. "Anyone who is a guest of his Lord receives my bow. It's nice to meet you. My name is Kai Perri. I believe you've already met my wife Etta?"

Orah smiled back at him. "Yes, we met briefly yesterday. I will be sure to give her my thanks for her hospitality in person but if you see her can you tell her I'm appreciative of the clothes and especially the ring?"

"Yes of course," he said before looking back at Lahana. "The carriage is ready for your use, Lady. His Lord mentioned you may be going out today before he left." He clapped his hands and Orah had to keep herself from falling over as a carriage pulled by two Pegasi came out of the stable doors.

Lahana's hand shot out to steady Orah. "Are you going to faint?"

Orah shook her head. "Despite what your brother may have told you, that's not something that usually happens to me." She looked back at the carriage, a combination of both a carriage and a chariot. At the back was a small roof that extended over two seats. She tilted her head to the side, noticing there was no seat for a driver.

"We don't have any animals like this where I'm from. They don't have wings," Orah said, unable to hide her amazement.

Her eyes traveled back to the Pegasi and she felt as though her breath had been taken from her. The animals were beautiful and as black as the night. It felt fitting for Roan to have two pure black animals to pull his personal carriages. Both of them stared at Orah and huffed. They appeared to behave like the horses she was used to. Slowly, she stuck out her hand and approached the animals.

The one to the left sniffed her hand first, then pulled its snout away and hesitated for a moment. Orah prepared herself to step back as quickly as she could when the Pegasus knocked its head against the one on the right. The other one looked at its partner then leaned forward to sniff Orah's hand. Pulling its head away it stared at her for a moment. She held her breath, hoping she had made them feel comfortable when it finally pulled its head up and huffed out what appeared to be a form of approval. Smiling widely, Orah turned back to face Lahana and Kai and found them both gawking at her with their mouths hanging open.

She raised her eyebrow in response. "What?" She wasn't sure what she had done wrong. While she hadn't grown up around horses, she knew the basics of how to introduce herself to one and figured a Pegasus was no different.

Kai snapped his mouth closed and cleared his throat. "You are most definitely not from this world."

Unable to hide her offense, she stepped back. "What is that supposed to mean?"

Lahana responded, confusing Orah with her emphatic tone. "What Kai means is that these animals can be vicious. It's one of the reasons why Governing Gods and Royalty use them for our personal carriages. You *usually* don't just walk up to them as if they are any normal animal."

Orah turned back to the Pegasi and they nodded their heads in acknowledgement of what Lahana had said. Shrugging, Orah turned back to face her. "I didn't know. If introducing myself to them to make them more comfortable around me was a stupid choice, then the consequences would have been my own."

Lahana and Kai glanced at each other again, then Kai shrugged in agreement. "At least you're someone who accepts responsibility for their actions."

Lahana shook her head and her laugh echoed through the trees. "I guess Kai is right. No harm was done, and you appear to have been accepted by them." Walking over to the back of the carriage, she opened the door on the side and motioned for Orah to step inside. Following close behind, Orah stopped to thank Kai for his help and climbed up the small step.

The carriage was made for only two people and Orah still wasn't sure what or who controlled the animals. Lahana climbed in next to her and shut the door. Placing herself next to Orah, she tapped the side of the carriage and the Pegasus jolted forward. Waving her hand to Kai, she yelled out. "We'll be back later!"

Orah looked over at her, trying to hide her concern that Lahana had trusted these animals to just know where they were going, when Lahana suddenly stood and walked to the front of the carriage. "Nacht, Tume, we need to head into the center of the city. Preferably near the shopping district." The Pegasi both huffed in acknowledgement and the carriage jolted forward, heading down the manor's drive, toward the city. Lahana returned to her seat next to Orah and smiled.

"They understand you?" Orah asked, enamored by the animals.

Lahana nodded her head. "Oh yes, not only are they vicious when they need to be, but they are very intelligent, and we don't need any drivers. The carriages are also technically warded to travel to the correct location on the rare chance they get distracted or take a wrong turn."

"And I'm assuming Kai is the one who maintains the wards?"

Lahana responded with one of her wide smiles. "Exactly! You're a fast learner!"

The trip to the city didn't take long. They sat mostly in silence, except when Lahana occasionally pointed out significant landmarks. Orah took in the city as they went down the streets. No building was taller than 4 stories and every one of them was made from the same light gray speckled stone. She would have usually thought a gray city to be dreary, but this city appeared to naturally shine. There were few carriages on the road, but walking seemed to be the preferred method of travel. Smiling, she appreciated that instead of the sounds of honking cars she was used to back in Boston, she could hear hoofs against the cobbled roads. Beside the Pegasi pulling their carriage and the occasional gryphon, Orah didn't recognize any of the other breeds of animals pulling the other carriages around them.

Lost a bit in her thoughts, Orah was jolted forward when the carriage stopped suddenly. She watched Lahana jump to her feet and open the door, gesturing for Orah to climb down. Nervously, Orah stepped onto the street and tried her best to avoid staring at the wide range of people and people-like -creatures. Some had the same blue-hued skin she had seen on that child outside the garden door, some had wings like Jes, some had human bodies but animal-like faces, and some looked just like her and Lahana.

Lahana closed the door and brushed her hand across the neck of the Pegasus next to her. "Nacht, Tume, please return in about four hours, we should be ready for you by then."

Turning to Orah, Lahana's eyes glistened. "This is when the fun begins."

Orah smiled back at her, then looked down the street. The sound of Lahana's dress shuffling caught her attention and she glanced up to find that she'd started walking the opposite direction, motioning for Orah to follow. "We have about four hours to get you an acceptable wardrobe. I hope you're prepared for a busy afternoon."

Observing her surroundings, Orah noticed the street they were on went on for several blocks and every building was some kind of shop. Her heart fluttered with excitement while she considered all the possible things she could buy, then quickly realized she had no money. "Lahana, I don't have any money."

Lahana turned to face her. "Well, I know that. Roan said we should use his tab."

"I don't know if I'm comfortable with that."

"Orah, we either go back to the house and do nothing all day, or we accept his generosity and make sure you have what you need. I can guarantee if we return and he finds out we bought nothing, he'll drag you down here himself tomorrow and he will *not* be as fun of a shopping companion as I am."

Orah figured she was probably right and that she might as well get what she needed. Blushing, she pushed down the embarrassing thought of having Roan hovering over her while she purchased under garments.

Smiling up at Lahana, she nodded her head. "Let's shop then."

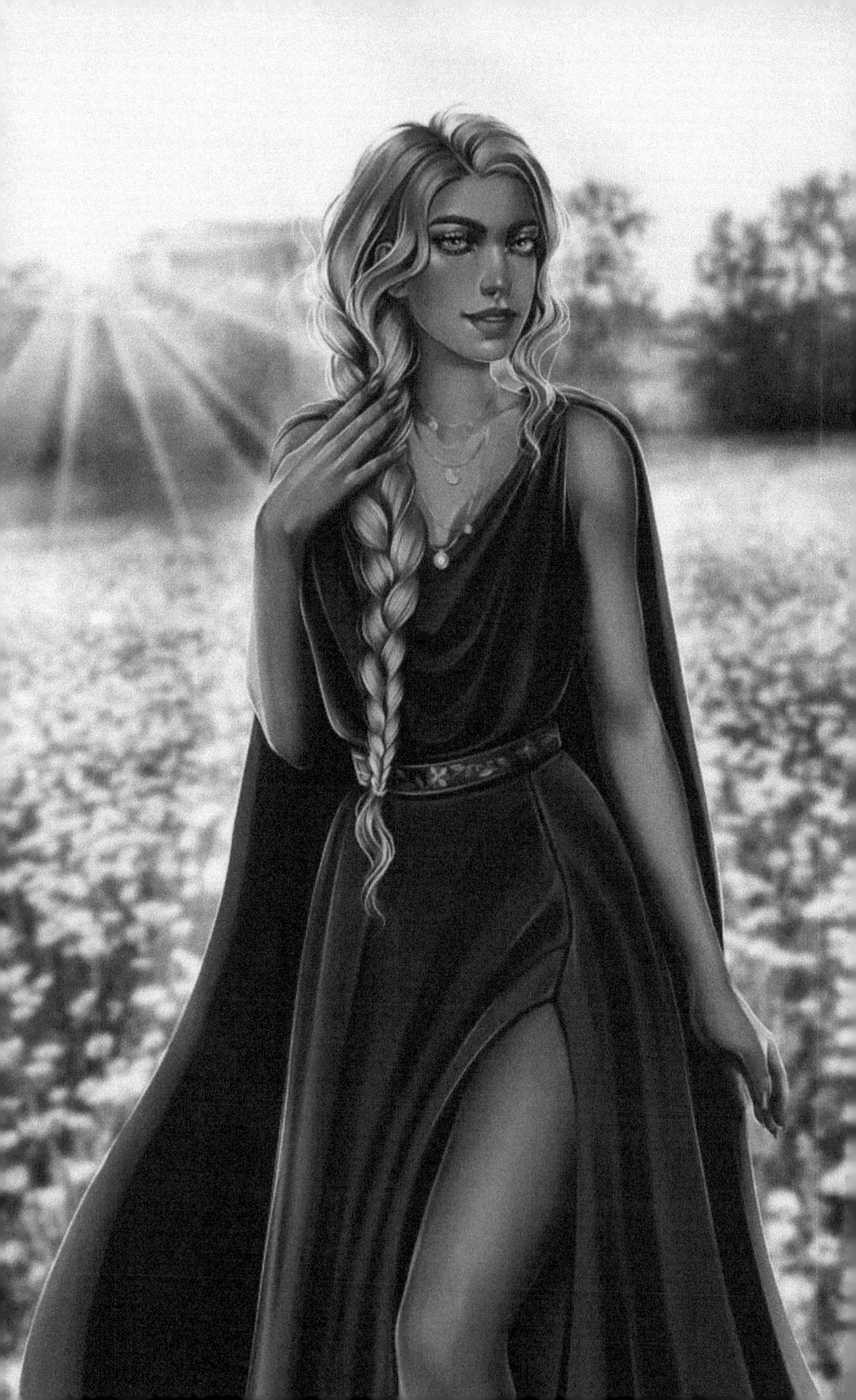

Chapter 9

Orah's arms barely held the bags in her arms as they walked through the side door of the house. She and Lahana had spent over 4 hours talking and traipsing across the city's shopping district. Most of what she was holding was actually Lahana's. She had run out of arm space when they were outside unloading the carriage, and Orah had offered a helping hand. Now they both stood laughing at how ridiculous they looked when they passed the study doors but stopped when a voice came from within the room.

"It seems you both had fun."

Orah turned to find Roan sitting at his desk with papers scattered around him. Lahana skipped into the room. "We definitely did thanks to you!" Roan's eyes went to the bags in her arms and his eyebrows shot up.

Lahana shrugged. "Okay fine. I bought all *my* things on my own personal tab. Half of what Orah is holding is also mine. She was very conservative in what she purchased."

"I hope you weren't too conservative and at least got something you wanted, not just needed," he said with a smile.

Orah cleared her throat but before she could respond, Lahana spoke. "Oh, she definitely got herself a few things she wanted. I made sure of that!"

Orah nodded. "Yes, she made sure I thought beyond just needs."

Roan nodded his head in approval. "Good, I'm glad to hear that. I've let Yohan know already but we'll be having a dinner guest this evening." Lahana's head snapped to her brother, but he put up his hand. "This is a more formal dinner so please let's be sure to dress for the occasion." Something in the way they were both looking at each other told Orah there had been a silent conversation between them.

Lahana turned to Orah. "Well, let's get these bags upstairs and get ourselves ready for dinner. I don't know about you, but I need a bit of a rest after that long day."

Orah followed Lahana up the stairs. She turned right at the top of the stairs and stopped at the first door. "This is me!" She popped the door open so Orah could partially see inside her room. It was similar to the one Orah was staying in but didn't appear quite as large. She motioned for Orah to follow her inside, but Orah shook her head. She was tired from the busy day and preferred not to be kept from resting.

"Oh alright, I guess I'll give you back some privacy. Let me drop these bags and I'll come back for my other ones." Turning and disappearing into her room for a moment, Lahana returned with empty arms. They took a few minutes in the hall sorting their bags to make sure they both had their own items before she stood to walk back into her room. Grabbing Orah's hand, she smiled brightly. "I really had fun today Orah. I know Roan has briefly mentioned how tense things have been here lately. This was just the sort of day I've needed."

Orah watched while Lahana shut her door before walking further down the hall to her own room. Closing her door behind her, Orah walked into the closet and placed her bags on the floor. She hadn't been too extravagant with what she had bought.

She was relieved to find that there was women's fashion in the Land of Gods for pants and shirts. She had grabbed a few pairs of legging-type pants and loose shirts to go with them. She also made sure to purchase a few pairs of outfits that worked well for working out. When she mentioned her intentions for physical activity, Lahana excitedly told her about a training room in the house. She'd made sure to grab the under garments she needed and two more simple dresses similar to what she was already wearing. Lahana had also insisted that Orah purchase a few formal gowns, despite her protests. Overall, she now had a sufficient wardrobe and had a remarkable afternoon.

While talking with Lahana, Orah learned that she and Roan had an older brother but Lahana wasn't too eager to share much else about their family. Orah's assumptions about age had been correct and they were both much older than they appeared. She would have placed Roan in his late twenties or early thirties, but Lahana mentioned that was about the time that aging for Gods slowed down to almost nothing. "We're *not* immortal but we're also *not* going to die of old age at the same rate as a mortal," she had said. Lahana was about 50 years younger than Roan, which shocked Orah. Lahana laughed at Orah's reaction but explained that Gods tended to space their children out over several decades. "Similar to mortals choosing to have longer age gaps for their children. Just maybe times that by 10," she explained.

Orah walked out of her closet, closing the door behind her. She was unable to wrap her head around the fact that she was in a house with people who were several hundred years old. She hadn't felt so young in a while. At 26 years old, she knew she was still young, but she had felt rather grown up for several years.

She stared at the bed and considered resting like she planned, but she wasn't sure if she actually could. She was tired but she could still feel the effects of the coffee from earlier that morning. Her entire body felt energized and had been buzzing all day and she reconsidered her thoughts on how much she loved the beverage earlier. She crossed her arms against her chest and rubbed them as if to warm herself, unsure of what to do until dinner.

She decided to go downstairs to see if Roan had a few minutes. While she enjoyed her day with Lahana, she wanted to find out if there was anything she could do to be useful or keep herself busy until they figured out how to get her home—if they could get her home. Making it downstairs, she peeked her head through Roan's study door. He didn't seem to notice she was there, and she took a moment to admire him, thinking back on the roof the night before. She hadn't been able to get the image of him staring up at the sky out of her head. Smiling, she knocked on the door lightly.

"Knock, knock."

His head popped up from the paper he'd been reading, and the corner of his mouth lifted to a smile. "Hello again."

"Are you busy?"

"Technically, yes. But I would love a break from this mundane business I'm working on right now." He motioned for her to come inside and she could now see the whole room for the first time.

Every single wall had a built-in bookcase filled with books. She turned her head to the right and found a large window identical to the one in the sitting room that looked out over the front lawn. The wall next to the window was an open walkway but she couldn't quite see where it led. "Did you have fun with my sister?" Roan asked.

Sitting down on the chair opposite of his desk, she took a deep breath. "Yes, I learned a lot about your world today."

"Oh? How so?"

"I learned that you're old." She glanced at him. "I also learned that there are different levels of Gods and not every God has the level of power that you or the other Governing Gods have."

With a smirk, he raised an eyebrow. "I'm *old?*"

"Oh yeah. I'm actually not sure how old you are. Lahana only mentioned that you have celebrated a couple centuries of birthdays and have one coming up soon."

His body tensed at the mention of his birthday, and he cleared his throat. "My sister tends to give out other people's personal information as if it were her own. Yes, I do have a birthday coming up soon. My three hundredth to be exact."

Unable to hide her shock she stared at him. "Three hundred?"

"Yes."

She leaned back against the chair. "Damn."

"Well now you are making me feel old." He laughed and stood from his desk to stretch. Orah focused on the desk to avoid staring at the way his muscles flexed as he moved.

He looks pretty great for almost three hundred, she thought to herself.

"Sorry I wasn't trying to make you feel old," she said.

"No, it's alright. I imagine it must be a shock for you. Here, mortals can maybe live to one hundred—if they're lucky. It's probably similar where you're from. How old are you?"

"Well, one hundred would be pushing it but yes, it's essentially the same back home." Thinking of home, she sighed. When she was going to get back? Shaking her head, she smiled back at him. "I'm twenty-six. I celebrated my birthday earlier in the year."

His eyes widened, and he cocked his head to the side. "Twenty-six—I don't think I can remember what my life was like when I was twenty-six."

Laughing, she folded her arms. "Well, that's because you're old."

His eyes twinkled at her joke and he stared at her for a moment. The longer he stared, the more flushed her cheeks grew. Turning her head, she broke their gazes. As if that pulled him from a trance, he cleared his throat and she turned back to look at him. The twinkle was dimmed a bit now. "So, you learned about us Gods?" he asked.

She nodded. "Yup. Lahana said that there are multiple levels. There's a King of Gods—she didn't really give much detail about him other than he's the King and runs the City of Kings. There's Gods like you—the Governing Gods who rule specific regions and cities. There's Gods—who have access to power slightly less than yours. Then she said there are Godlings who are essentially either the children of Gods or most of the people I've seen that are part creature. Then mortals. I think I remembered that all right."

Roan laughed. "Yes, you got that mostly right. Lahana seems to have left a bit out, but it's mostly the more convoluted and complicated bits."

Coming around the desk he leaned against it, slightly facing her. "I'm assuming you came in here to talk to me about something other than our ages and how the powers of the Gods work?"

Feeling nervous, she met his gaze. "Yes. I have a couple questions."

"Yes?"

"One—I know it hasn't even been a full day, but do you have any idea how to get me home yet?" He leaned back a bit more but waited for her to finish. "Two—if you haven't, can we discuss how I'm supposed to be spending my time while I'm here? Lahana can't babysit me every day."

"You're very observant. I know for a fact Lahana would have never admitted that I encouraged her to take you out today, but she definitely wasn't babysitting you. You don't need to be watched like a child." He straightened and walked over to the window. There was an obvious shift in his mood, and she wasn't sure she wanted to hear what he had to say next. "As for getting you home, no, I don't have any idea where to even begin." Turning to face her, he sighed. "Jes sent out word to Moudrost, to my Aunt, to see if she has heard of anything like this happening before, but he wasn't able to get that sent out until this morning. It may take a few days for her to find any answers for us."

Covering her face with her hands, she let out a breath. "Moudrost? Your Aunt?"

"Yes, she's the Goddess of Wisdom, which also means her Region—Moudrost—keeps track of our histories and stories. If there's anyone who will have some kind of answer, it'll be her."

"Oh, alright." Orah considered briefly what a Goddess of Wisdom would be like.

"As for your second question, you can spend your time here however you please." Roan walked back to the desk and leaned against it again while folding his arms. "What are your interests? Anything you like to do for fun?"

Orah hated when she was asked this question. Each time, she suddenly forgot everything she had ever been interested in and usually ended up fumbling her response. She stared at him while she thought. "Well, I love to read. It's almost embarrassing, to be honest. When I sold all my stuff to move to France, more than seventy percent of what I owned was books." She snuck a glance at his bookshelves while she spoke. "I really like to cook or bake. A few hours in the kitchen is always a great way for me to clear my head." Pausing, she thought for a moment longer. "Lahana mentioned you have a training room? I like to keep myself physically active if that's an option available to me."

Looking away from the books and back at him she jumped to find him staring at her. "You like books?" he asked. His eyes began to twinkle again, but this time they were like the stars.

"Oh, I love them," Orah replied. "I'll be honest, it's taking a lot of restraint for me to not be going over all of the ones on these shelves surrounding us right now."

His smile widened as he pushed off the desk and held his hand out to her. She stared at it, unsure of what he was asking, until she realized he was gesturing for her to take it. He watched her stare at his hand and chuckled. "It's not going to bite you. I just want to show you something."

She stood hesitantly and took his hand, letting him lead her to the walkway by the window. As they walked through, she let out a loud gasp. Behind what had seemed like a normal walkway was the most magnificent library she had ever seen.

There were multiple large armchairs scattered throughout the room and a few deep couches pushed up against the large windows that faced the front lawn. The ceilings were even higher than in the study and sitting room and there was a set of spiral stairs leading up to a mezzanine. Both floors had rows and rows of bookshelves. She snapped her head at him and couldn't seem to find the words to respond to what she was seeing.

"This is my library. It's an extension I had built when I took over the Region about 50 years ago." He surveyed the room proudly. "That's why it's attached to my study. There was nowhere else in the house that I wanted it to be." He walked them further into the room and her heart raced. So many books. So many stories and history that she couldn't wait to get her hands on. Breathing out long and slow, she tried to steady her emotions.

"This is beautiful."

"Thank you." His eyes went down at their hands and she realized how tightly she was gripping his. She stared at their clasped palms for a moment, a bit thrown by how warm they felt together and blinked at what she thought was a sliver of light shimmering between their palms.

Pulling her hand from his, she cleared her throat. "Am I okay to be in here?"

Out of the corner of her eye she noticed him flex his hand and rub it against his thigh before he replied. "Of course you are. Why do you think I showed you?"

"But this is attached to your personal study. What if you're busy in there?"

"Orah, someone in my position is always busy. Please come into this library whenever you want. Spend as much time here as you want. You can be here from sunup to sundown and I won't kick you out. I may check in to make sure you're alive and fed but other than that, please enjoy it."

Her eyes traveled around the room while her excitement thumped through her body. "Can I start now?" she asked eagerly.

He chuckled, shaking his head. "As much as I would love to say yes, there is that dinner I mentioned earlier, and we should both start getting ready for it." His face changed swiftly to a more serious expression. She wasn't sure what it meant and whether or not she should have been nervous, but she nodded her head.

"Tomorrow then." Turning to walk out of the room, she looked back at him once more. "I'll see you at dinner."

✦

Orah's heart was racing and she felt slightly dizzy by the time she closed her bedroom door. Since arriving in the land she had been hit with one unbelievable moment after another. She was in another world—a world where Gods ruled and lived. Magic existed there as well as animalistic people and creatures she'd never heard of. She rubbed her head. *If only dad could see all of this.*

He had always been supportive of her love of reading and would listen while she recounted the stories she had read for hours on end. As she grew older, he would poke fun of her continued love of fantasy worlds, but he still always encouraged her. Orah leaned against the door, placing her hand over her heart, and breathed out slowly. She knew in some obscure way, her father had a part in how she ended up here. If she hadn't bought the chateau, she would have never gone through the garden door.

She took in her room and its beauty, knowing she needed to get ready for dinner. She had stopped by Lahana's door on the way upstairs to confirm the time and Lahana had informed her to be ready within an hour. Breathing out, she rubbed her arms. Her body still felt buzzy despite it having been at least six or seven hours since she had that coffee. Pushing out a frustrated breath, she cursed herself. She should have known better than to drink something she assumed was similar to coffee at home. Throwing her hands out in front of her she shook them, as though she were trying to shake some of the jittery feeling from herself.

Walking to the closet she couldn't help but wonder if Lahana had actually known about this dinner with how insistent she had been that Orah buy some formal dresses. Lahana claimed you never knew when you would need something formal, but now it felt oddly suspicious. Pulling open the closet doors, Orah jumped back a bit, startled to find all the clothes she had left on the floor in bags were now hanging up and put away.

Making her way further into the closet, she pulled out the three formal dresses she had picked out. She had assumed that the fashion here would have all been similar to the dress she was wearing and Lahana's dress the day before but found herself pleasantly surprised. There didn't seem to be any one kind of specific style. The only commonality she could find was that the dresses all appeared to be long and the sleeves all on the thicker side, never shorter than the top of the shoulders. She certainly found nothing like the blue summer dress she had been wearing when she came through the garden.

She picked up the first dress that caught her attention at the shop. It was a dark blue fabric that sparkled when the light caught it. The neckline was rounded, and the sleeves ended at the elbows. The sleeves themselves were light and flowy, similar to gossamer. The dress was a tighter fit than the one she was currently wearing but still fell loosely at the waist. Comfortable but beautiful.

Grabbing the dress, she headed toward the bathroom. Her hair had been in a braid all day and she didn't think it would take much to fix it up for dinner. Pulling off the tie, she combed her hair and the waves cascaded loosely down her back. She pulled open the drawers searching for anything to hold some of the hair in place and was surprised to find the drawers that were almost empty in the morning were now stocked with essentials. Hair pins, ties, make up, a toothbrush and toothpaste, as well as what appeared to be hair styling tools. Shaking her head, Orah wondered if Ms. Perri had put them here or if the wards in the room had provided them.

After pulling half of her hair up with the pins she stared at herself and smiled, appreciating her own beauty.

Letting out a breath, she walked out of the bedroom and headed down the hall. It was quiet in the house and she didn't think anyone else had left their rooms yet. She walked down the stairs and turned toward the sitting room where she found Roan standing just inside the doors with his back turned away from her. His hair looked darker than it had earlier, and he was wearing a fitted jacket and dark pants. Everything in the way he stood and what he wore was formal and stiff and she smiled, deciding to poke him for his seriousness. Walking up behind him she tapped his shoulder. "Well, you sure clean up nicely," she teased.

He turned around and she stepped back. *That is not Roan.*

The man stared at her, obviously confused. He looked so much like Roan but also different. Darker hair, no freckles, and a bright crown hovered over his head. His dark blue eyes scanned Orah up and down as though he were going to take possession of her. A menacing smile formed on his lips while his eyes narrowed. "Who? Are? You?"

Orah immediately felt as though she needed to return upstairs and scrub her skin. Too confused to speak, a voice from behind startled her.

"You're early."

She recognized the voice and turned to find Roan standing at the bottom of the stairs. His eyes burned as though they had been lit on fire and he walked toward her and the stranger. She jumped when he casually placed his hand on her lower back, never breaking eye contact with the man. She tensed at his touch but the way this stranger looked at her made her reconsider telling Roan to remove his hand.

Roan's voice dipped low and he cocked his head. "Orah, allow me to introduce you to my brother."

She glanced up at Roan and then to his brother, who still had that predatory smile on his face. Her skin felt cold and she was unnerved by the way he kept his eyes on her. Slowly, his grin shifted to something almost wicked and his eyes widened.

"Oor-AH." He said her name with slow emphasis. "That's an interesting name. Am I correct to assume it means light?"

She blinked, a bit shocked. "Yes, you would be correct. Good guess." As subtly as she could, she reached behind her and removed Roan's hand from her back. Clearing his throat, he stepped to the side.

Roan's brother glanced between them, then back at Orah. "Oh, it wasn't entirely a guess. It sounds similar enough to someone else I knew whose name had the same meaning." He glanced at Roan and winked. Orah wasn't sure how to interpret their interaction, but she knew there was no brotherly love between them.

"Are you not going to give me a *proper* introduction?"

Roan rolled his eyes. "Orah, allow me to introduce you to my brother, Marek."

Marek's sly grin spread a little further. "My brother has never been one for formality, despite the necessity. To correct him—I'm Marek, the God of Daee." He stared at Orah as though he were expecting her to react somehow, but when she didn't, annoyance spread across his face. "I know my brother doesn't run his Region as is expected, but it is customary to bow to the Governing Gods."

"I'm not one for customs," she replied with a shrug.

Walking past him into the sitting room she held up her chin as best as she could. She almost cleared his space when his arm shot out and he grabbed her wrist. He was strong and she panicked, looking back at Roan. Marek's touch felt as though she had stuck her hand into a roaring fire. She bit back her yelp from the pain. Marek glared at her then back at Roan. "Tell me, brother, where did you get her from? Is she a gift? It's been a while since I've spent time with a mortal."

Ew.

Making eye contact with him, she slammed her foot on top of his and hit his chin with her free arm. "I am no one's *gift*."

Yelling, he let go of her and took a quick step back. She was sure he was going to attack her when Roan was suddenly between them. "Marek, I thought by now you'd have learned to keep your hands to yourself." Roan turned toward the door and Orah looked up to find Lahana staring at the three of them with her mouth open.

Marek followed his gaze and that discomforting grin spread across his face again. He bowed slightly. "Hello, Na-Na."

Lahana tensed and cleared her throat. "Brother." She walked past him over to Orah and looped their elbows together. Orah stared at her and hoped she could see the plea in her eyes, but a stern expression flashed across Lahana's face and she shook her head slowly. It appeared that Orah was stuck downstairs and any chance of escaping the dinner had gone out the window.

Lahana guided Orah to the couch and they sat down. An odd rush of wind surrounded them and Lahana leaned down, whispering, "I cannot believe I just watched you hit him in the face."

Orah's face flushed and she wasn't sure if it was from embarrassment or anger. "He grabbed me." Orah glanced up to Roan and Marek as they both sat in the chairs across from her.

Lahana squeezed her hand and smiled. "Oh, I didn't say he didn't deserve it."

Roan stared at Marek, resisting the urge to hit him. At least Orah had been the first one to throw a punch. Chuckling to himself, he wished he could relive that moment forever. Looking over at her, he watched as she shifted uncomfortably.

"So," Marek said making eye contact with her. "*Where* did my brother find you?"

Roan cleared his throat. "Orah is a friend visiting from the city."

"I didn't know you had mortal friends, brother." Marek didn't take his eyes off Orah.

"Well *brother*, considering how little we see one another I don't suppose you'd actually know if I do or not."

Finally, Marek turned to Roan with doubt in his eyes. "You didn't mention you would have company when you insisted that I come here tonight."

"I'm not the one who made a summons request for a meeting. I just insisted on the meeting place. Orah only arrived yesterday, *before* we both received our updates. I considered it rude to leave her for the evening."

Marek's eyes sparkled and Roan knew he was thinking something disgusting. "I can see why you wouldn't want to leave her alone for an evening."

Orah scoffed at his comment. "If only you were lucky enough to know how an evening with me would be."

Roan suppressed his laugh. *She is absolutely incredible.* Marek's nostrils flared in response from her hitting her mark. Nothing enraged his brother more than a quick insult and dangling something in front of him that she would never allow him to have.

Xade approached the sitting room door, alerting Roan their meal was ready. Roan gave a slight nod in return and stood. "It seems as though our food is ready. Should we go sit?"

Marek stood and straightened his jacket. Walking up to Roan, he placed his hand on his back. "Don't think your guest will be enough of a distraction to not have that discussion I'm here for." Smacking Roan's back, he walked to the dining room with Lahana rushing past Roan after him. Roan knew she would try and distract him while Roan spoke with Orah.

He turned to find Orah standing in the middle of the room. Her fury collided into him like a wave of heat and he expected her fist to connect with his own face.

"What the fuck was that Roan?" she demanded.

"That was my brother."

"Do not be a smartass. One—you touched me without my permission. Two—*he* touched me without my permission. Not only that, but his touch *hurt*. He *hurt* me, Roan. I have no idea what's going on, but I think I need to go back to my bedroom."

He stared at her, knowing she was right, but she didn't understand how much safer she was downstairs with him. "Orah, please. This dinner will be uncomfortable and confusing. I won't lie about that, but I need you in the same room as me. We cannot underestimate my brother and he has very obviously taken an interest in you."

She folded her arms across her chest. "I don't know why I should trust you right now."

He breathed out. "I've given you no reason to tonight, I know that. Please, just come and eat with us. I'll answer any questions you have afterward."

They stood in the sitting room staring at each other. Roan could feel the clock ticking and knew Marek would return at any moment to find them. She stared out the door and then back at him. Her fury cooled to a simmer and she nodded her head.

"I want honesty when he leaves. If I'm going to be put in these situations, I need to know what I'm up against."

Honesty, I can do that. She hadn't asked to be there, and he was asking her to stay. He could at least be honest with her. Roan gestured to the dining room, but she didn't look at him again as she walked out the doors toward what was bound to be an interesting evening.

Chapter 10

Orah walked past Roan toward the dining room and stopped at the bottom of the stairs. She could have easily gone up then and locked her bedroom door behind her. She knew he wouldn't have physically gone to get her. He had stopped at the door of the sitting room; his eyes were a bit panicked when he glanced back at her.

Please. He mouthed and pointed toward the dining room.

She turned to find Lahana and Marek standing at the doorway of the dining room. Marek was watching them and had that stupid grin on his face. Lahana grimaced behind him and gestured to the table. Sighing, Orah walked toward the room, expecting both Lahana and Roan to give her an honest explanation by the end of the night.

She considered briefly that she hadn't been in the room yet and she didn't know the customs for the seating arrangements. She moved to the opposite side of the table, pulled up one of the chairs and sat down. Marek moved as though he was floating on air while he sauntered over to her. The dread built in her chest in anticipation of him choosing the seat to her left. He smiled at her while he pulled the chair out but before she could blink, a rush of air blew past them and she found Lahana sitting next to her.

Lahana grinned at her brother. "Thank you, Marek! It appears you haven't completely forgotten your manners."

Marek glared at his sister and walked around the table, choosing the seat directly across from Orah. He rested his chin in his hands. "I believe tonight is going to be much fun." Roan pulled up the seat at the head of the table, directly to the right of Orah and sat down with a sigh.

"I think we all probably have different definitions of fun, brother." His gaze shifted toward the door that connected the dining room to the kitchen as Xade and Clarah appeared, holding platters of food.

They both stared at Marek nervously before placing the large platters on the table and shuffling out of the room. "You know I have never understood why you keep this house so lightly staffed. What's the point of our status and power if you don't use it?" Marek held up his hand to show a ball of light in his palm. He admired it for a moment before snapping his fingers and it disappeared quickly. "What *has* Roan told you of his power?"

Orah jumped at the question, remembering the conversation she had with Roan the day before and him informing her that the wrong people were looking into what he could do.

Clearing her throat, she shrugged. "He's the God of Night. What can't he do?" She knew she didn't sound as confident as she wanted to, but she didn't actually know what Roan was capable of.

Marek grinned. "Yes, that's the question lately. What *can't* my brother do?"

Roan stared at him and his face shifted to cool indifference. "I could say the very same thing about you. That's always the question between us isn't it? What are we both capable of?"

Marek leaned back in his chair and folded his arms. "The Fates must think we've both hit the depths of our power to call for the challenge so early into our Godhoods."

Lahana tensed beside Orah, and Roan's jaw tightened. "Where my power sits was not part of the agreed conversation when you requested this meeting."

"Why wouldn't it have been? The Fates have declared their will. It's only a correct assumption that they believe we're both up for the challenge," Marek replied.

Orah looked at Roan, unsure of what either of them were talking about, but the tension in the room was almost suffocatingly sick.

"I have no idea why the Fates would have called the challenge so soon. I think we should both be focused on what He's planning for us," Roan replied.

Marek waved his hand. "It's not our place to question Him. He'll decide whatever challenge he believes is right. I'll just do as He says and reap the rewards."

Lahana snorted now. "We all know just how willingly you obey Him."

Marek glared at her. "You know He's devastated to know you're still living all the way out here far away from the City of Kings? He told me to ask when you're going to stop slumming it out here and return home?"

She leaned back in her chair and lifted her chin. "I am home."

Orah's hands began to sweat and she wished desperately that she could leave the room. No one had yet touched the food and she was beginning to feel as though she were an unwelcome fly on the wall witnessing private familial conversations.

Marek chuckled, and reached for one of the large platters. "I'll have to at least compliment your cook, Roan. I know I'll never leave your home having had a bad meal." The tension loosened for a moment as they all silently dished up their plates. Orah stared down at hers, trying not to bring attention to herself, willing the time to go faster.

"So," Marek said loudly, "Orah, tell me more about yourself."

Jumping, Orah met his stare. She didn't want to tell him anything about herself. It felt like a trick question and that whatever she would say would be used against her. "There's not much to know."

He smiled. "Well now, I don't believe that. You're a mortal staying in the home of the God of Nyte. You have to know that's not a normal situation."

"Maybe not for you." She glared at him.

He lowered his chin and glared back. "Orah, I really am not sure what part of this Land you've come from, but you would do well to remember your place."

She raised her brow. "My place?"

"Yes, mortal. The God of Daee is speaking to you. In any normal circumstance that would be enough for you to show some respect, but this is not a normal circumstance. You are staying in the home of one of the Governing Gods. I am the brother of that God, while also a Governing God myself, and we both just so happen to be the sons of the King of the Gods. So, as you can imagine, your place is *well* below ours."

Her mouth dropped open at the revelation. She shot a look at Roan, who nodded his head. There was no way for her to know, but she felt irritated that neither Roan nor Lahana had thought to mention to her who they were.

She turned back to Marek, whose wicked grin had returned. "He hasn't told you? How curious. Remind me Roan, how long have you and this mortal been friends?"

"Long enough that I've welcomed her as a guest in my home and I am going to suggest that you stop questioning her," Roan snapped.

"But questioning mortals is so fun." Marek stood and walked around the table. Roan went to stand but seemed unable to move from his seat. The lights in the room flashed on and off and Roan appeared as if he were fighting whatever was holding him down. The table shook violently as Marek walked around to where Orah was seated.

"You see, Orah. I don't think you've seen much of my brother's power, so I'll show you some of mine. I've held him in his seat for a moment while we finish our little chat." He crouched down to meet her eyes and she moved to hit him, but found her hands fused to the table. "Oh no. I learned my lesson earlier. Those hands will stay put. Don't worry, I won't touch you." He stood again and fear flooded her body. The table shook harder now and every dish in front of her began to fall to the floor as Roan strained against his chair, as if he were attempting to stand. Marek returned to his seat and waved his hand.

Orah's hands jolted and she realized she had control over them again. In that moment of realization, the table flew across the room, splintering against the wall. Letting out a scream, Orah covered her face, expecting to be with hit with debris but nothing landed near her. She looked up, finding Roan standing between her and Marek. His hands shaking at his side while the lights in the room continued to flash on and off but more erratically than before.

Roan glared at Marek, pointing to the door. "I think it's time you go."

Marek stood casually then bowed. He locked eyes with Orah's. "Shame about the table. My brother can be so hot headed at times."

Walking toward the door he glanced back at her again. "One last thing." He smiled at Roan. "Your mortal's power is quite intriguing. Almost God like."

Orah stared at him. "What did you just say?" She thought she must have blacked out for a moment because she knew she had misheard him. Her eyes went to Roan, finding a tight, almost guilty expression painted across his face.

Marek grinned at her. "You know if I were you, I wouldn't trust friends who keep things from you." He walked to the doorway. "I'll be sure Father knows you've received word about the challenge. I'll see you in a few months, little brother."

Orah watched him leave, slowly realizing her breathing had become erratic. She thought she could hear Lahana saying her name, but she couldn't focus. The lights in the room stopped flashing but the walls swayed as though they were going to cave in.

I want to go home.

Before she knew it, her feet were moving and she was walking—no, running out of the dining room, down the hall toward the side door that led outside. She knew Roan was shouting her name, but she didn't care.

I want to go home.

She wasn't sure how she knew how to get back to the garden, but her feet carried her there. Her vision was blurred, and she could barely make out her surroundings when the door came into view.

Home.

Her chest tightened and she ran faster. Roan and Lahana ran behind her, but she didn't stop to look back at them. Nearing the door her hand flung out to the handle.

"I don't want to be here anymore!" she yelled as her hand gripped the handle.

The handle was warm like before, and hope filled her as she imagined her chateau. Her home. She thought of all her regrets of leaving everyone that loved her behind. Tears filled her eyes as she tugged on the handle, but the door didn't move.

Power. I have power, she thought.

Marek said it. Roan had all but confirmed it when he had looked at her. She had always known she was a powerful woman and whatever power she had was going to get her home.

"Orah!" Roan yelled.

Despite how disoriented she was, but she didn't turn. She tightened her grip on the handle and pushed. It groaned as if it were trying to follow her command. "I just want to go home! I just want to leave, Roan!" she screamed through her tears as she pushed harder and harder.

The door didn't move, and she let out a similar scream of rage as she had the day before and kicked the metal as hard as she could. The entire garden wall shook, and she blinked trying to clear her tears and looked up. There were threads of light lining the walls, like the vines of ivy themselves had been lit internally.

Orah stared at the light on the wall and pushed against the door again. The wall shook and the door groaned as if it wanted to open.

"Orah, please!" She didn't understand the fear and concern in Roan's tone and was too focused to care. She drowned out his pleas with her own screams. The heat from the door handle was almost too much but she bore down and pushed harder.

You can do this. You can do this.

Roan stared in shock, knowing instantly what was making the wall light up like that. She was breaking the wards. He had no idea how, but she was pulling the wards open as though they were nothing. Roan stared almost frozen in fear as she pushed and screamed. Her scream speared into his chest and he blinked back his own tears. Unable to prevent himself from feeling the pain coming off her.

He stumbled backwards as she let out a scream that sounded as though it were coming from somewhere deep within her.

Orah felt the resistance give as she pushed, so she didn't stop. She kept her hand on the handle and pushed with all her strength, screaming as loudly as she could. Finally, the door swung open.

For a brief moment, she saw a glimmer of her chateau off in the distance. Orah blinked, letting go of the handle and stepped through the threshold, ready to return to her own life. She expected her feet to land on her grassy lawn, but instead she stepped out onto a hard cobbled road. She sank to her knees. Unable to control the sobs that came.

"I had it," she whispered, covering her face with her hands. "I had it. I had it."

Her body began to shake, and warm hands gently touched her back, snapping her back to the city street she was kneeling on. Glancing up, she found Roan staring down at her. Lahana and Jesiel now stood behind him.

When did Jes get back? she wondered, staring at the terrified expression splayed across his face.

Roan stared at Orah while she kept her eyes on Jes. Jes who had just slammed into the ground, coming from the guard camp where he was meeting the new recruits. Jes stared at Orah as though he were going to attack, but Roan shook his head.

He wasn't sure what to do. Her sobs echoed down the street and he kept his hand on her back, trying to calm her.

Jes cleared his throat and Roan realized they couldn't remain outside the garden with her sobs echoing down the road. Someone was bound to come out to investigate. Removing his hand from her back, he stood. "Orah, can we get you back inside?"

Her head snapped up and she glared at him. Hot simmering rage rushed over him and she stood, pointing her finger at him. "You kept something from me." She turned to Lahana and Jes. "You ALL kept something from me."

"Yes. We did. I'm sorry that we did. Can you please come inside? I promise I'll tell you everything we know." She whirled around and before he could blink her fist connected with his chin. *I deserved that*, he thought as he rubbed his jaw.

"Did that make you feel better?" He tried to hide his amused tone, not entirely sure she would appreciate it and he didn't want to be punched again.

Glaring, she crossed her arms and walked back into the garden. "I expect honesty, Roan."

"Of course." He followed behind her and watched as she headed toward the house with Lahana following close behind. Turning, he faced Jes.

"Roan." His anger, fear, and confusion hit Roan like a solid wall.

Roan glanced back at Orah and sighed. "I have no idea what just happened." Jes went to close the garden door, but his gasp caught Roan's attention. He peeked over Jes's shoulder to the door handle he was gaping at. She had melted the metal. The handle was crushed as if she had collapsed it in her desperation.

Jes shook his head. "I'm not sure we have any idea how to handle what just walked into our lives." He watched as she and Lahana disappeared through the side door and couldn't help but agree with Jes.

Together, he and Jes made their way back into the house and found Orah and Lahana on the couch. Lahana smiled uncomfortably. Orah stared at Roan as he made his way to the chair opposite her and sat down.

She narrowed her eyes at him. "Start talking. Now."

Usually, Roan would have been shocked to have someone give him such an obvious command, but he knew she had the right. "You've got some kind of power dormant within you, and it appears to be waking up," he said.

"Explain."

"I can't really explain it, Orah. I felt it when I walked through your memories, but I don't have any idea where it comes from."

"I really think you must be delusional. I'm from a human world that, if you remember correctly, has no magic."

"I know that. I don't understand it, but it's there. We all just saw it. Have you felt any different since yesterday?"

Orah stared down at her hands, then back at Roan. "I've felt buzzy."

He nodded in understanding. She wouldn't have been able to tell what the feeling had meant. It was all so new to her.

Sitting a bit straighter, she held their gaze. "What just happened out there?"

Roan didn't know how to explain, because he wasn't exactly sure what had happened, but he had to try and give her something. "Honestly, I'm not sure. I've never seen anything like that. Orah, you literally broke through impenetrable wards."

"I just wanted to go home," she replied.

"No one here is upset about that," Roan said. Jes glared at him. Maybe Jes was upset that a mortal broke through his wards, but Roan certainly wasn't. He looked at Orah and his chest tightened. There was something about her that had been pulling at him since they met but he couldn't place what. She caught his stare and glared at him.

"Don't look at me like that."

Shocked, he jumped. "Like what?"

"Like I'm someone to pity. 'Oh poor, mortal, Orah. Going through *so* much.'"

"Orah, I wasn't looking at you with pity. I was looking at you with concern." Roan felt no pity for her. He felt admiration and intrigue. He saw the strong person she was and what he wanted was to know more about her. She held each of their stares in turn.

"I have more questions."

"Of course. I'll answer as best as I can."

"Well, first I really want to know why you manipulated and forced me to stay downstairs for that shit show of a meal." She crossed her arms and stared at him. He couldn't help avoiding her eyes. His chest felt tight and his guilt overwhelming. She was right, he had manipulated her. He had stupidly and wrongly assumed she would have been safe downstairs with him.

"I apologize. You're right. I did manipulate you to stay down here tonight, but it was what I believed to be for your own safety. My brother—well, my brother is a lot of things—but he's also cunning and dangerous." He glanced nervously at Lahana, unsure of how much he should say. Lahana nodded, encouraging him to continue. "One of his powers as the God of Daee is that people who first interact with him trust him immediately. It has something to do with the power of the sun and the warmth he radiates. It causes this feeling of trust and safety in others. However, because I am his brother and my power in a way voids that feeling of trust when we're in the same room, I believed it was better for you to be with me instead of alone upstairs." He paused for a moment and found Orah's eyebrows were scrunched together, as though she didn't believe him.

"Okay, but that still doesn't make sense. Why would it matter if I were upstairs when he was downstairs with you?"

Roan took a breath. "Because another power of the God of Daee is to be able to detect other people in a room or building by their body heat. Again, related to the sun. Marek knows how many people I have employed in my home. He was aware that Jes was gone for the evening and that the only other people who reside here are myself and Lahana. He would have realized there was an additional person here and would have tracked you down."

"Tracked me down? Roan, you wouldn't have been able to stop your brother from just stomping through your house looking for whoever it is he had detected?"

"Again, it has to do with his power. While it was evening, the sun was still up. If the sun is in the sky, my brother can essentially project himself through sunlight and appear as if he's actually in a room. I wouldn't have had any idea if he was doing it."

Her skin paled as though she was going to be sick. "Why was your brother even here?"

"He was here to discuss an announcement of sorts that we both received last night. I'm assuming he was sent by my Father."

"Your father who also just happens to be the King of Gods?"

He flinched at the anger and hurt in her voice. He and Lahana hadn't meant to keep that bit of information from her. It simply hadn't come up yet.

"Yes. My father is the King of Gods. Like his father before him and going back to the first King."

"You don't seem to like your father," Orah replied.

Lahana laughed loudly. "Orah, that is definitely an understatement!" Roan couldn't suppress his own responding laugh. Orah really spoke her mind and he liked it—a lot.

"Yes. I'm not my father's biggest fan. He has always shown a preference for Marek." He sighed and stood, realizing he needed to move. Sitting was beginning to feel suffocating. "Marek was here because the Fates have decided it's time for us to complete our second challenge."

"Second challenge?"

Here we go.

As much as he didn't want to talk about it, he had to be honest with her. "Yes, you see, there's this tradition in our world. At the beginning of time, the Fates, along with the first King of Gods, decided to enact challenges for two of his first-born sons to determine who would assume the throne upon his death. Since this first challenge, every King of Gods to exist has had two first born sons. Those sons are expected to prove themselves through two challenges." Roan walked over to the windows and stared out at his city, quieting for the night. "The sons are always given the position of God of Nyte or God of Daee. This appointment of Godhood happens at the end of the first challenge. The assumption is always that whoever is granted the Region of Daee is expected to be the King when the current King passes through Shadus. I was granted the Region of Nyte and Marek was granted the Region of Daee at the end of the last challenge fifty years ago. However, the successor has not been officially named because the second challenge has not taken place."

He couldn't see her, but he knew her eyes were on him.

"If your father has already granted Marek the Region of Day then what's the point of the second challenge, if the God of Day is usually the next King?"

His chest felt tight again. He didn't know why this was so hard for him to talk about. "*Usually* is the key word. The Fates decided that one challenge was not enough and both sons must have the chance to prove themselves twice before a final decision is made. Many generations ago there was one God of Nyte who was granted the crown. According to our history books it caused quite the upset for a while. Ironically this God that everyone had assumed would be evil and cruel was one of our most kind and fair Kings."

"When is this challenge supposed to take place?"

"While there's no set timeline for when the second challenge happens, as this is up to the Fates, it has become the normal for it to not take place for around one hundred years after the first. I received the unexpected announcement last night that it will be soon—after my birthday."

He thought back on last night when Jes came into his study with the announcement from the Fates. Fifty years was far too early for the challenge to be called and he still didn't understand why they had called for the challenge so soon.

He turned, finding Orah staring at him with a confused expression. "How soon is soon?"

"About three months."

Her eyebrow raised, and he could see there was a question forming that she wanted to ask. "How old is your father?"

He wasn't sure what he was expecting her to say, but it was not what came out of her mouth. "Oh, much older than me, Orah." Deciding he could sit again, he walked back to his chair. "But to actually answer your question, my Father has lived much longer than previous Kings. He's been

King for almost a thousand years. He's close to twelve hundred years old himself."

"TWELVE HUNDRED!" she yelled. His Father's age was impressive, but he had never seen anyone react like she had.

Lahana chuckled. "Our father's age is impressive but it's also becoming dangerous. What Roan hasn't gotten to yet is the paranoia that has come with old age. Roan explained to you that there are people looking into what his powers are, right?" Orah nodded in response. "Yes, well those people are our Father and brother. They want to know how many aspects of the King's power Roan has. Traditionally, while the challenges are set to prove who's ready, they are also supposed to pull out the dormant power in each son. The son whose power is more aligned with the King's is usually the victor. Roan has always been the more outspoken son, but his people in this Region and City respect him far more than Marek's people respect their Governing God."

"How does Roan being good to his people make your Father paranoid about where his power is?" Orah asked.

"Very observant, Orah. My Father's paranoid because he's aware I held back during the last challenge. I haven't shown my true abilities and it's beginning to anger him. With how loved I am by my people, he's worried that the wrong choice was made by appointing Marek as the God of Daee and he *does not* like to be wrong."

Orah stood suddenly to stare at the window. Roan couldn't make out her emotions, but they were heavy and tense. She sighed. "Roan, I just want to go home. Please. Please. You said you sent word to your aunt for information. Have you heard anything?"

Swallowing his gasp, he watched as she began pacing the room. He wasn't sure how to help whatever it was she was feeling but he could only imagine how overwhelming it must have been. He resisted the urge to go to her, because something told him she would have preferred anyone else's comfort to his own.

"My aunt may be the Goddess of Wisdom and our histories and stories reside in her Region, but she still needs time to track them down."

"And what if she can't find anything? What happens to me then? What happens to me while we wait? What happens now that your creepy ass brother knows about me?"

"I can keep you safe, Orah."

She stopped pacing and her glare pierced through him. "I do not need *you* to protect me." He blinked; a bit stunned by her response. Her chest moved up and down slowly and she held his stare. "I will make one thing clear, Roan. I have spent most of my life protecting myself. I can still do that in this shithole Land of Gods." Light caught his eye and he looked down to see that her hands had begun to glow. She stared down and then back at him. "Apparently, whatever power I have agrees with me." She let out a long breath while shaking her hands out and the light dissipated. Roan wondered if she had done that intentionally or accidentally.

He stood. "I believe you can take care of yourself. My home is still open to you if you would like to stay here. If not, my offer of the money and letting you leave is still on the table." Turning now, she stared out to the front doors, then to the stairs. He jumped back as she walked out of the room, watching her stop at the bottom of the stairs.

She glanced up, then back at him and sighed. "I haven't decided what I'm going to do."

He watched her reach the top of the stairs before turning back to Lahana and Jes. They all sat in silence for a moment before Jes stood and spoke. "Roan, what are we going to do?"

"What do you mean?" Roan replied.

"I mean what are we going to do with her? The power I felt at the camp when she tried breaking down the wards was almost painful. If you hadn't stopped me in the garden, I wouldn't have hesitated to deal with her."

The lamps on the tables began to shake and the lights in the room went out. Roan walked toward Jes, knowing that starlight was now pouring from his every pore. "You will not *deal* with her."

Lahana jumped in front of them, putting her hands out. "Roan snap out of it. You know he's just thinking of your safety." Roan glanced at his sister then back at Jes. Holding his breath for a moment he let it out and the lights quickly blinked back on.

"I'm sorry, Jes." He ran his hands through his hair. "I have no idea what's waking inside of her, but we have to keep this a secret. The fact that Marek felt something from her concerns me, but we can deal with that. My Father cannot find out about this."

Jes approached Roan, placing his hand on his shoulder. "We understand. If your wish is to keep her safe, then I will extend my duty to her."

Gripping Jes's hand, Roan nodded. "Thank you."

Tipping his chin down, Jes walked towards the door. "I will say this though." He looked up towards the stairs and back at Roan. "We need to keep an eye on her. We need to find out more about her. And we need to see if we can help her control whatever this power is." He exited the room before Roan could respond.

Turning to Lahana, he smiled. "Thank you for your help tonight."

She raised her eyebrow. "Help?"

"The table? You know when I lost my temper."

She grinned. "What's the point of being able to call to the wind if I don't use it?"

The sound of Orah's door closing upstairs caught his attention and he sighed. He didn't know how to approach it all, she wasn't a prisoner in his home and if she asked to leave, he would do everything to make sure she had what she needed. He thought about what he could do to find the answers to get her home and selfishly wondered what she would do if he couldn't find answers. Would she still stay then?

Chapter II

Orah fought the urge to slam her bedroom door as she got back to her room. She didn't know what to do. She could leave. Roan wasn't holding her prisoner, but then again, he was the only one who was searching for answers on how to get her home. She fell to the ground, pulling her knees up to her chin, her tears hitting the floor as a cold numbness settled over her.

She wasn't sure how long she sat there crying, but a knock on the door brought her back to reality. She decided not to answer but she stood, hoping whoever was on the other side hadn't heard her. Roan's voice came from behind the door, "Orah?" She stared at the door, too numb to care about the regret in his voice.

"What?"

"I just wanted to make sure you were okay."

Her jaw tightened, uncertain that he did care about her. He was still a stranger. "I'm fine, Roan."

"Are you sure?"

"Roan."

"Okay, I hear you. Just—" He went silent, and she hoped he had walked away, but he spoke again. "I just wanted to tell you that I'll let you know once I hear from my Aunt. If you decide to leave before I hear word, I will make sure it gets to you."

She whispered out her thanks, but she had nothing else she wanted to say to him. She stood in silence for a moment until she was sure he had left, and then turned to walk deeper into the room.

She found something in the closet to change into and rinsed her face off at the sink. She could feel herself spiraling into that familiar numb she had tried so hard to climb out of over and over again. She stared at her reflection in the mirror and frowned; her face looked like her, but also not.

The light that had been in her eyes while getting ready earlier had died. Now, they were puffy from the crying and the skin around them red and patchy. Deciding the despair now splayed across her face didn't matter, she walked back into the room.

She stared at the balcony doors and thought about the too brief glimpse she had gotten of her chateau. Turning back to the bed, her chest and legs felt heavy and she recognized her body's demand to sleep. It wasn't the kind of exhaustion she had felt the night before. No—this was different. This was exhaustion she couldn't control. The kind she had spent too long fighting off.

She approached the bed, pulling back the blankets while she stared at the mattress. She didn't know how long it would be before she climbed back out if she climbed in now. With a sigh, she crawled in anyway, pulling the covers over her head.

I don't think it matters if I don't come out.

She buried her head into the pillow as the tiredness claimed her, welcoming her to the darkness inside.

Groaning, Orah stretched her legs out in front of her. She didn't know how much time had passed. She had only moved from the bed to the bathroom and the days blurred together. She hadn't dared to open the curtain or the balcony doors. In a way, the bed had become her own personal prison. Every day that passed she considered getting up, but she physically couldn't get her body to do it. It was as though she was sinking to the bottom of the ocean and had lost the will to try and rise for air.

Food kept appearing in the room, so she had no real reason to try and venture out. At first, she had thought someone was unlocking her door to bring it to her. That was until she watched her uneaten meal disappear and a fresh one appear when she was walking back from the bathroom a day or two before. Turning in her bed, she looked toward the door. She needed to get up. She needed to move. Her fingers twitched and she balled her hand into a fist.

You can do this.

She pulled the covers off herself, pushing her body up and swinging her legs off the bed. Slowly, if she went slowly, she knew she could climb out of the bed. She stood and the room tipped a bit. Shaking her head, she cursed herself for being in bed for too long. She stared at the balcony doors, noticing the light coming through the curtain. Her first challenge—let in the light. The sunlight filled the room as she pulled back the curtains.

Staring down at herself, her muscles spoke to her, begging her to move. Her body had been still for too long. Even before the frozen pocket of time she'd been stuck in, she hadn't worked out in weeks and her muscles were reminding her of that.

Deciding not to allow herself to consider whether or not she could, she grabbed some of the clothes she bought with Lahana. *How long ago was that?* she wondered as she dressed.

The house was quiet as she walked into the hall. Briefly, she peeked toward Roan's door. Based on the light that she had let in, she assumed Roan likely wasn't home, but she also hoped he wasn't in his study. She didn't think she was ready to talk to him yet.

She looked down the other side of the hall toward Lahana's door, wondering if she were home. The house was so quiet, but she wasn't sure if it was normal with how few people lived there. Taking a deep breath, she made it to the bottom of the stairs when she almost ran into Ms. Perri.

"Oh my!" Ms. Perri proclaimed while Orah caught herself before falling back on the stairs. "Are you okay?"

Orah chuckled. "Oh, I'm fine. Just clumsy."

"You're out of your room."

"Yes," Orah replied nervously.

"Do you need anything?"

Orah hesitated. "Is Roan home?"

Ms. Perri blinked, as if surprised. "Uh. No. I'm sorry, he's not. I can call for him if you need me to."

"No!" Orah threw her hands out as if to physically stop the offer. "Sorry, no, I'm not ready to talk yet. That's why I asked."

Ms. Perri smiled. "I understand. You didn't answer my question though."

"Can you show me where the training room is?" Orah asked.

Ms. Perri motioned for Orah to follow as she turned down the hallway behind the sitting room. They walked past a couple doors before Ms. Perri stopped. "Here we are." She motioned, instructing Orah to open the door.

"I'm okay to be in here?"

She nodded. "Of course. Roan told me when you first arrived that you had full access to the house. Well, full access to every room but Jes's." She smirked.

Orah chuckled. Her feet moved her toward the door when she paused and turned back to Ms. Perri. "How long was I in my room?"

Ms. Perri's smile shifted to a sad expression. "Today would have been day seven." Turning, she walked back down the hallway and Orah watched her until she was out of view.

"Let's do this," Orah whispered, turning the door handle.

The training room was large and the equipment within was unfamiliar. At the back half of the room was a large mat, that she assumed was likely for sparring or something similar. In the half that she was standing in, there was equipment she didn't recognize. She couldn't see any specific weights, but she wasn't sure if she should have expected what she was used to at home. She turned in place, trying to figure out what to use, when her eyes fell on a sandbag hanging from the ceiling.

While unfamiliar with sandbags, she felt it would be a good way to release some of the emotions she had bottled inside of her. She walked over, searching around for any hand protection, but couldn't find any. Figuring she could make do without; she spent a few minutes stretching out her muscles. They groaned in protest, and she shook her head. "It's been too long," she whispered while she stretched her arms out to the top of her toes.

After stretching for a few more minutes, she stood and faced the sandbag. She didn't know what she was doing and briefly considered if she knew what the correct form was. She stood in what she thought was the correct position and stared at the sandbag. Pulling her arm back she breathed out and swung it forward toward the bag.

Thunk.

The quiet noise was almost insulting, and the bag swung lazily at the contact. She glared at her hand and frowned. *You can do better than that.* Pulling her arm back again, she flung it forward. But still the bag barely moved, and she felt nothing close to the release she was hoping for. Standing back, she lifted her hands.

I'm not even sure what I'm doing in here.

Her skin began to feel numb again and she peered back at the door, wondering if she had made a mistake. Maybe she should have stayed in her room. She let out a frustrated sigh and kicked the bag.

Walking to the wall behind the sandbag she slumped against it. She had been lost in the dark pit of her mind for seven days. She leaned her head against the wall, focusing up at the ceiling. Breathing out, she told herself she could either get up and try or get up and go back to sleep. Her hands tingled at the thought, as though telling her she didn't need more sleep. The exhaustion was still there though, lingering inside of her like a monster trying to welcome her back to its den, but she didn't want to follow. She gazed back at the bag again, thinking about why she had been in bed.

Because you're powerless against what happens to you. Because you have power you can't even use.

Tears built in her eyes and she stared down at her hands. The hands that had forced the garden door open. The hands that had hit Marek. Maybe if she hadn't provoked him before dinner, none of it would have happened. Her chest became tight when she thought about the dinner. The dinner where all feelings of being safe had vanished. The dinner where she had been manipulated to stay. Where she had been threatened and hurt by Marek. Anger filled her and she thought about all the times she had been put into a situation where she wasn't safe. Laughing in disbelief, a tear hit her cheek. She wasn't sure why she felt she should have been able to trust Roan. She didn't know anything about him.

She stood and approached the sandbag again, thinking of all she had a right to be angry about. All the tears, and the fear she had experienced in her life. All the loss and pain. Feeling powerless. Her way back home had been right at her fingertips, but she couldn't do anything to get there. She thought of how she got to this land and how isolated she had made herself before leaving. She thought of why she pulled away. Why she disconnected.

She resumed her previous stance before pulling her arm back and swinging it toward the bag.

Bang!

The bag swung from the hit and she grinned. *That's what I was looking for.*

Shaking off the sting of the ring biting into her finger, she mimicked the movement with her other arm and the bag shook violently in response. She thought of Marek's hand on her wrist and the blinding pain she had felt. She thought of all the other hands that had hurt her and violated her space. The words that had cut that unfillable hole inside of her. She thought of how strong she had felt for a brief moment when she pulled that door open and the hope she had felt when she saw her chateau. How close she had been to returning to the future she had been looking forward to. A scream ripped from her and she punched the bag over and over. Each time her right hand landed on the bag, the ring on her finger dug into the skin, but the pain only fueled her desire to keep going. Her tears began to fall, and her vision blurred. She could no longer see the bag, but she could feel the rush of air each time it swung back toward her as her rage took over.

"I am not powerless!" she yelled with each returning swing of the bag. "I am not a victim!"

She lost herself in the rage and the movement. Her muscles screamed as she pushed them to their limits. She knew her body was tiring but she wasn't ready to stop. Not yet. If she didn't let all of those emotions out, they were going to continue slowly consuming her and she didn't want to climb back into that bed. The only sounds that filled the room were her grunts and the creak of the bag swinging on its hook. Sweat ran down her back while she punched, over and over again, losing herself in the rhythm.

She wasn't sure how long she went before her muscles demanded that she stop. Her chest felt on fire and she grabbed hold of the bag as it swung back, instead of punching it again. She breathed in and out, trying to steady her heartbeat.

"You could probably work on your form." Yelping, Orah jumped at the voice behind her and turned to find Jesiel standing at the door with his arms folded.

"I hadn't realized I had an audience," she snapped.

He smirked. "You didn't at first. But Yohan heard you scream from the kitchen and knocked on my door asking me to check on you. I followed your yell and found you here."

Her cheeks flushed. "Oh."

"Besides, I wasn't mentioning the form to criticize you. More as advice so you don't hurt yourself." He looked at the bag and around the room. "Is this all you've been using?"

"I don't know what the other ones are for. This is the only one that resembled things from back home."

He glanced around the room. "The room is warded to recognize whatever equipment the user needs. This looks like it was for Lahana." Walking over to the wall by the door, he motioned for her to follow, then pointed to some kind of pad affixed to the wall with a knob on top. He twisted the knob and a small pointed pin popped out from the center of it. He pricked his thumb on the end and pressed the small bead of blood that appeared onto the pad.

Orah gasped as the room shifted. The mat at the back of the room remained but the half of the room she and Jes stood in transformed around them into some kind of obstacle course. There were bars for pull ups or chin ups, ropes for climbing up to the ceiling, and a moving platform that jutted against a rock wall. She blinked, unable to ignore her shock and amazement at the magic. She turned back to Jes and found him staring down at her.

"Want to see what it does for you?"

"How does it work?" she asked.

"It responds to magic."

She stepped back. "But I don't have—" she stopped, she was about to say she didn't have magic, but she remembered that wasn't true. She had powers, which meant she had magic. Gasping she watched Jes; as she approached, the pin on the pad disappeared.

"Also warded to provide a new pin after each use." Jes winked. "Safety reasons."

Following his instructions, Orah turned the knob until a new pin appeared. "I *hate* needles," she whispered, staring at the pin.

"It's okay, it really doesn't hurt," he said, motioning for her to continue.

Orah took a deep breath and pressed her thumb against the pointed end. She winced at the pressure, but realized he was right, no pain. She pulled her thumb away and blood began to bead. She glanced at Jes and he nodded, encouraging her to continue. She pressed her thumb into the pad and instinctively closed her eyes, afraid of what she would see. After a moment, he tapped her shoulder and she opened her eyes, gasping at the sight in front of her. The room was like something from her home. The mat at the back had been replaced by an oval track, there were free weights, weight machines, jump ropes, and even some manually powered exercise bikes. She found a puzzled expression on his face.

"This is interesting. Is this what you're used to using at home?"

She nodded. "Well, some of it. A lot of the cardio equipment we would use is plugged into the electricity, but I'm not seeing any plugs here."

His head cocked. "Just so you're aware, your own assumptions and imagination are the only things that can prevent the wards from creating what you want. Maybe next time don't think about what our world *doesn't* have, but instead consider what it *could*."

Surprised, she nodded her head. "Thank you."

"You're welcome. I understand the importance of needing an escape."

She glanced at the door then back at him. Her body was too tired to try anything else, but she was feeling more hopeful for what tomorrow would bring. "I think I'll excuse myself. Thank you, again." She made it to the door and had her hand on the handle when his voice behind her caught her attention.

"Oh—Orah?"

The tone in his voice was unfamiliar, and she turned back to face him. "Yes?"

He grinned. "I would consider taking a shower. I could smell you from outside the door." He winked and her mouth fell open. Staring at him for a moment, she let out a laugh.

"I'll be sure to do that right away." She winked back at him and walked out the door. Once in the hallway, she could smell what he was referring to, and she smacked her head. While she had showered recently, she couldn't remember how many days it had been. She turned to walk up the stairs, lost in her thoughts until she felt someone watching her. Turning, she found Roan's study doors open and him sitting at his desk with his mouth hanging open.

She smiled and waved. "Hi."

Snapping his mouth shut, he blinked and waved back. "Hi."

Her face flushed, remembering her need for a shower and she ran up the stairs. Frantically, she reached her room, closing the door behind her.

Climbing into the shower, a soft sob escaped her lips when the water hit her skin. While she remembered her shower days before, she had just been going through the motions of cleaning herself. Now, it felt glorious and cleansing in a different way, as though she were forming a new layer of skin as she scrubbed her tired body. She breathed in the sweet smell of the soaps, relishing in the feeling of her fingertips scratching against the top of her head.

After rinsing off, she climbed out with a sigh, noticing the warmth beneath her feet. She didn't remember the floor being warm after her last shower during those dark, quiet days. Wrapping up in a towel, she walked to the closet and pulled open the door, frowning a bit. She wanted to feel nice and suddenly felt she was too practical with her clothing choices. She decided wearing clean clothes was enough and she pulled out a pair of dark blue leggings and a gray loose shirt.

She dressed and returned to the bathroom and pulled the brush from the drawer. Her head was stinging, and tears lined her eyes by the time she had pulled through all the knots in her hair. She cursed herself for how long she had been in bed. *It could have been worse.* She reminded herself. Yes, it could have. It had been before.

Setting down the brush, she looked at herself in the mirror. Her color appeared to have returned. Her eyes still appeared hollow, but they were no longer puffy. She looked better, not fully herself, but closer.

She walked back out to the bedroom and glanced toward the open curtains. Still not ready to go outside, she remembered that she hadn't eaten. Taking a deep breath, she decided to brave the kitchens by herself and walked to her door. Peering back into the room once more she pulled the door open and walked right into Roan's chest.

"Fates!" he yelled, grabbing her arm so she wouldn't fall backwards.

"I seem to have a habit of slamming into you," she responded with a chuckle.

"I'm sorry. I wanted to wait downstairs, but I couldn't. I was shocked to see you," Roan replied.

Her cheeks flushed. "I was in the training room. I needed to move."

"Yes, Jes told me after you rushed up here. Did it help?" She nodded. His lips turned up with a responding smile. "Oh good. Please feel free to use it whenever you want. Jes said you were really taking it out on the sandbag." He chuckled, but Orah looked away. She didn't want him to know what had caused her to lose herself in that way. He suddenly released the arm she had forgotten he was holding and cleared his throat, taking a step back. "I'm really glad to see you out of your room, Orah."

"Me too." Her stomach rumbled loudly, and Roan looked her up and down with amusement on his face. His smile widened and he laughed loudly. She stared down at herself, unable to stop her own laugh. "Oh my god." She was sure she was going to drop dead from embarrassment.

"Are you hungry, Orah?"

"Oh, shut up!" She covered her face with her hands but laughed harder. After a moment of them laughing, she calmed herself. "I am actually very hungry. I was just about to head to the kitchen."

Roan stepped out of her way, motioning to the stairs. "Well, I'm not going to stop you."

They walked next to each other silently. She wasn't sure how to start a conversation and based on Roan's silence, it felt as though he was thinking the same thing. They got to the bottom of the stairs and he glanced over at his study. "I'm afraid this is where I leave you. I have to finish what I was working on and head back into the city."

She felt an odd sense of disappointment realizing he wouldn't accompany her to the kitchen, but she nodded. "I understand."

He gave her a sad sort of smile as he walked into his study and she turned down the hall. Before she got to the kitchen she stopped and glimpsed behind her, where she found him looking at her. She couldn't pull her eyes from him and the intense gaze he held. It was as though he were trying to find something hidden inside of her, perhaps the edges of the mask she always kept on. Finally, his eyes pulled from hers and he turned to close his study door. Her shoulders sagged with relief, and she fanned herself.

Her stomach rumbled again loudly as though questioning why she was standing outside the kitchen and not going in. Sounds of lively chatter could be heard behind the closed door. Orah hoped she wouldn't be interrupting anyone's day, but took a deep breath for confidence, and pushed open the door.

The conversation in the room stopped the moment she walked in. Yohan, Xade, and Clarah all appeared as if they had been frozen in place.

Orah smiled and raised her hand in a small wave. "Hello, I don't think we've all been properly introduced. I'm Orah."

Yohan gawked at his children and then back at her before clearing his throat. His accent was thick and heavy, reminding Orah of an autumn evening and a warm bowl of soup. "Hello Orah, how can we help you?"

Her hand fidgeted with the ring on her pinky while she nervously observed the room. It appeared that they were in the middle of preparing lunch, and suddenly felt as though she was intruding. She smiled at Xade and Clarah, whose fingers were unmoving in the dough they were kneading. She could smell whatever Yohan was cooking at the stove in front of her. Her chest tightened. Turning back to Yohan she found him staring at her with his eyebrow raised.

"I was just wondering if I could possibly scrounge around in here and feed myself quickly? I believe I may have slept through breakfast."

Xade and Clarah gaped at Yohan, who stepped forward, wiping his hands on his apron. "We're in the middle of preparing lunch. Should be done soon but if you can't wait until then I can grab a few things for you."

"I can grab it. I don't want to interrupt you. Whatever you're cooking smells fantastic."

Yohan smiled and approached her. "It's really no bother. Just a small break from work."

Orah peeked at Xade and Clarah who were kneading their dough again—but probably a bit too aggressively from her observation—when an idea struck her. She needed to feel useful, needed to feel as though there was a reason to get up every day. "Can I help you with your work?"

Yohan coughed and stepped back. "I—well—I couldn't ask you to do that Miss."

"You're not. I'm the one asking."

"But *we're* the kitchen help, not the guests." He peered out the door as if expecting someone to come through and reprimand them for having such a conversation.

"Please, Yohan. I'm not anyone special. I've been cooking for myself since I was nine years old. I know my way around a kitchen. I just want to be useful." He looked nervously at the door again and then back at her. He must have seen the desperation she knew was on her face because he nodded slightly. Breathing out a sigh of relief, she rushed to grab an apron from the wall across from her.

"Where can I start?" she asked while tying it around herself.

Yohan chuckled, and motioned to a bucket near the sink. "How about potatoes?"

Chapter 12

Roan stared at the wall in front of him. He could barely focus on the conversation happening in the room. The knowledge that Orah was back at the house right now and out of her room consumed his every thought. "I should have just stayed home," he mumbled to himself.

"My Lord?" Roan jumped and found one of his city officials looking at him a bit confused.

"Yes?"

"You said something?" Roan surveyed the room and ran his hand through his hair, realizing he had been lost in his thoughts and not paying attention to what was being said. His officials from the cities and towns in his Region had gathered in Iluna to discuss the details of his *grand* celebration. He must have interrupted someone based on the way they were all staring at him.

"Sorry, Thomas. I was a bit lost in my thoughts." He observed his officials, unsure of who had been speaking. "Please continue."

Thomas nodded. "As we have been discussing, we must decide the location of His Lord's three hundredth celebration."

Roan's eyes fell to the table; he had only been the Governing God for fifty years, and mundane party planning was not what he had expected. His upcoming party was supposed to be a celebration, but it now felt like a timer counting down to the challenge. While the Fates announced the challenge would happen after his birthday, he wasn't sure how soon after the celebration they would require it to start.

Glancing back at his officials, he found them all staring at him again. Thomas raised his eyebrow and motioned with his hand. "My Lord?" Thomas sounded irritated, but Roan didn't care. They had been the ones that forced this meeting, insisting the location of the party was significant.

"Yes, Thomas?"

"We asked if you had any preference for where the party is held."

Roan cleared his throat and thought for a moment. "Why wouldn't we just host it at my home?"

"Well, My Lord, don't you think we'd want to have it somewhere... larger?"

Roan rolled his eyes. His home was plenty large, but his officials wanted him to consider reopening his Uncle's old palace outside of Iluna. Him living and residing in the manor on the hill was considered abnormal for a Governing God. The Governing Gods usually liked to observe their main city from afar, like an omen in the distance warning the people not to misbehave.

"My home is perfectly capable of hosting a large number of people, Thomas."

Thomas sighed and surveyed the room. The other officials nodded their heads. They all knew Roan was right. They were also aware he did not want to spare the resources and time needed to prepare the palace for a party that would only last one night. It was both illogical and a waste.

Pushing his chair behind him, Roan stood. Every official jumped to their feet and bowed their heads. Roan suppressed his responding chuckle. They were all worried about upsetting him. They loved him, yes. They appreciated the attention, time, and respect he had given the Region, but they also feared who they believed he would become. That any wrongdoing would put them on his shortlist to the darkest depths of Shadus and the monsters lurking there.

That's not even how it works.

"It's decided then. The party will be held at my home in the manor. We can discuss the details of who will attend. Every Governing God is invited of course, but I believe we should consider other Gods, Godlings, and even some important mortals."

Thomas responded, unable to disguise his shock. "Mortals, My Lord?"

"Yes, Thomas—*mortals*. There are many of them that have built something of themselves amongst their kind and it would be significant to at least send them an invitation." Roan always felt this was the most frustrating thing about Gods and Godlings; they assumed mortals weren't important. Because of the differences in power, they believed they shouldn't give mortals a second thought. They seemed to forget that many of the wealthy and well-known mortals ran their trade routes, produced their wines, and fabricated the clothes on their backs.

Thomas bowed his head. "If that is what your Lordship wishes then we will be sure to gather a list for you to review."

"Thank you. You're all dismissed."

He waved his hand and his officials bowed before walking out the door, leaving him alone in his offices in the city center. He hadn't done much with them since taking over the Region, but his officials were used to holding business there. He preferred to allow his officials to run their own cities and towns themselves and act as a guiding hand, but that wasn't how his uncle had done things. He had ruled Nacht and no official made a change in their city without his approval. But Roan had no desire to rule like that. While his uncle wasn't a hard man, he made sure that image of himself was kept. Which was amusing to Roan; he knew who his uncle really was, he couldn't hide from Roan.

Roan turned at the sound of footsteps approaching the room and watched as the door opened. Jes walked casually into the room, sitting down at the table, and laying his feet on top of it. His wings slipped between the large gaps on both sides of the chair, designed specifically for the winged citizens in his Region in mind.

"How did it go?" Jes asked.

Roan sat back down. "As well as you'd expect. They want me to reopen Aeron's palace for the party."

Jes rolled his eyes. "They really are obsessed with that crusty old place."

Roan snorted. "Yes, they are. Aeron did a good job making it a place of significance for everyone here, especially those here in the city."

Leaning back a bit more into the chair, Jes sighed. "I think Aeron did a little *too* good of a job with that."

"I'd have to agree," Roan replied.

"Did she really seem okay when you found her in the training room?" Roan asked quietly.

"I mean. I think as okay as you can expect. Like I told you earlier, she was beating the sandbag so hard I thought she was going to knock it from the ceiling, but I think she'll be fine." Roan had to trust Jes. He had an odd ability to know what was going on with someone without them having to tell him.

"I feel so much guilt, Jes."

"Why?"

"She's here because of me. She had that awful interaction with Marek because I insisted she stay downstairs. I know almost nothing about this woman, but I just feel so much guilt. That, and I feel like I've prevented myself from even having a chance of getting to know her."

"One—you're not the reason she's *here*. We don't know why she's here. You may be the reason why she's staying in the manor, but you didn't pull her from her world. Two—you were only trying to protect her. You made a mistake, but you can come back from that. And three—" He stopped for a moment and grinned at Roan. "How much are you hoping to get to *know* her?"

Roan didn't respond; that was the real question. How much was he hoping to get to know her? She was this intriguing mortal woman who had literally walked right into his life. He had walked through her memories, he had felt some of her pain, but he knew nothing about her.

Despite that, he could feel this tug like a thread between the two of them, pulling on him to learn more. He was embarrassed thinking back to how he had rushed up the stairs after seeing her outside his study. He hadn't intended to run up there, but it had been as though his feet pulled him upstairs without his control.

Jes's expression shifted from amusement to concern. "Roan?"

Roan cleared his throat. "I don't know how much I want to get to know her, Jes. There's just something about her that makes me feel as if I've known her all my life."

Jes stared for a moment and leaned forward placing his arms on the table. "I don't know where she came from. I don't know why she's here. I don't know how she has the power she does. Fates, I don't even know why you feel this pull to her. But I think she's probably worth knowing."

Roan blinked. Out of anything he could have expected Jes to say, it wasn't that. "Where do I even start?"

"Fates, Roan. You would think we were young again and you were asking for advice on how to approach a girl. It's not complicated. She's literally living in your house. Just spend time with her." Jes laughed.

Roan knew he was being ridiculous. It wasn't as though he had never spent any time with a woman and didn't know how to interact with them. He was usually fairly confident in himself when it came to women, but he felt off balance around Orah. Not in a bad way, but it was unexpected.

Standing again, Roan stretched. "I'm done with business here. How are things at the camp?"

Jes waved his hands. "The new recruits are injuring themselves on the obstacle course, as expected, but they're good. They'll be a good addition for the Region."

While each Region was prohibited by the King to form any sort of army, they were allowed to have their own guards to oversee safety. Jes ran the Nacht guard like a well-oiled machine since Roan's Godhood appointment fifty years before. Jes was a hardass and pushed the guard to their limits but they all respected him. It had become a place of honor to sign up as a recruit under Captain Jesiel Keita's guard. Roan smiled with pride knowing their Region had the most volunteer recruits while Marek's guard was run entirely on forced conscription.

Jes stood, pushing the chair out behind him, and stretched out his wings. "Well, I guess now that both of our business is finished, we can return home." He motioned for Roan to walk ahead as they walked out of the room. Most everyone knew they were casual with one another, but likely not the full extent of their friendship. In public they had to walk under the presentation of Roan, the Governing God, and Jes, the Beskermer, always ready to protect Roan at a moment's notice.

✺

When Jes and Roan walked through the side door, Roan stopped abruptly. The door next to the breakfast table was open and he could hear an unfamiliar laugh. The sound filled his ears and his heart tugged, as if he was hearing a forgotten song. He glanced at Jes, who shrugged, seeming not nearly as phased by it as Roan was. Jes pointed to his bedroom door and Roan nodded as he walked away. Apprehensively, Roan popped his head through the side door and stared at the sight in front of him.

Orah had her hair pulled back into some kind of lopsided bun. She was wearing an apron, but it didn't appear to protect her from any of the flour covering every inch of her. She and Clarah were laughing as she cut triangles of dough. Roan's heart beat wildly in his chest.

"So, usually, they end up as triangles, but you can really cut them to be any shape you want. You just want them to be wide enough for a slice of cheese." Clarah nodded her head enthusiastically. Roan's heart jolted. Clarah was almost an adult, but he knew she missed her mother. Watching someone spending time with her like this was almost enough to bring tears to his eyes.

"My Lord?" Roan peered over at Xade, whom he hadn't noticed was grabbing something from the pantry by the table. He looked back over at Orah and found her staring at him now. Clearing his throat, he stepped fully into the room. To his surprise it appeared as though they hadn't stopped cooking all day. Yohan usually prepared breakfast and lunch but then left for several hours with Xade and Clarah before coming back to prepare dinner.

"It sounded busy in here and I thought I'd check in. You're all usually not here this time of day."

Clarah beamed. "Oh! Father still went out. He said he needed to go to the shops, but we decided to stay with Orah. Did you know she can actually cook, My Lord? And she's good! She's been showing us how to make things from her *world!*"

Orah stared down at the floor and a small simmer of her embarrassment settled over Roan. He smiled, wondering if she didn't know how to take a compliment. "That sounds fantastic. Orah, may I try something you've made?"

Her cheeks flushed and she glanced at Clarah, who was still beaming. "Um, I guess. We're just making some scones now. It was a bit difficult figuring out what was the same here compared to home for the ingredients, but I think they turned out alright."

"That sounds fantastic."

Clarah grinned and ran for Roan, grabbing his hand and leading him to the oven where a pan sat with some of the triangles inside. On the counter was a plate with finished scones on top. Roan felt Orah's warmth behind him before she spoke.

"We kind of went a bit overboard." She chuckled and picked up one of the scones. He watched as she sliced the scone in half and spread a bit of butter over both sides. Clarah returned with a slice of cheese and Orah placed it on top before sandwiching both pieces together. She held it out toward him. "It's something I grew up eating. A bit of a comfort food for me."

Roan took the scone. It smelled incredible, like flour, but he could pick up hints of the butter and cheese. Smiling at Orah, he took a bite and gasped as the taste hit his tongue. "I can see why this is something comforting to you." Realizing he was speaking with his mouth full, he covered his mouth.

Clarah laughed and turned to her brother. "Xade, he likes it!"

Orah maintained eye contact for a moment. "I'm glad you like it." She turned to go back to the table when the sound of the front door slamming open caused them both to jump. Roan felt her fear wash over him and she threw him a panicked look. Roan had no idea who had managed to get the door open, but he watched as Jes ran down the hall with his sword in his hands. Roan glanced back at Orah and then ran to see who had intruded.

Her intrigue and fear followed close behind him and he didn't know whether he should have been annoyed or impressed that she had run out to face the intruder.

Arriving at the door, Roan's anger shifted to annoyance at the man standing in front of his door with a wide grin staring at Jes, as if challenging him to wield his sword. Crossing his arms, Roan glared. "What do you want, Moros?"

Moros smiled that sly smile Roan hated. "My mother has some news for you."

Orah stopped behind Roan, staring at the man standing in the front doorway. He was about the same height as Roan. His dark hair went just past his shoulders. His eyes were a similar blue to Roan's, but there was no silver. She took in his sleeveless top that put his stark white tattoos that stopped at the base of his neck on display. The tattoos themselves contrasted against his dark skin. Orah's eyes widened. *Another attractive person?*

The man stared at Jes and chuckled. "Surprised to see you pulling your sword out in public now, Jesiel." Jesiel's hand quickly released its grip the sword at his side and he glanced at Roan. Orah wasn't sure who this stranger was, but he obviously got under their skin.

The man glanced at Orah and smiled. "I didn't know you had the kitchen help assigned to guard duty, Roan."

She looked down at herself, realizing she was covered in flour. She had lost track of time and stopped caring about the mess hours before. She folded arms.

"Moros, this is Orah, my guest. She's just been spending time with the kitchen staff today," Roan said. "Orah, this is my cousin, Moros."

Cousin. She wondered how big Roan's family actually was.

Moros walked forward and flung his hand out. A rush of ice-cold wind slammed the door shut and she gasped as the temperature in the room dropped. "Guest." He sounded out the word long and slow as he approached. "Interesting. Roan, why am I never invited as a guest?" He looked at Jesiel now. Orah's eyes followed to find Jesiel standing in that unnaturally still way he usually would.

Roan stepped forward and crossed his arms. "Because you do things like make my house an ice box, and I'd rather my favorite parts of me not freeze off. Please stop showing off."

Orah flushed at Roan's comment and cursed herself for where her mind went. Moros grinned, and the temperature suddenly rose. Staring down at her feet, she gasped, finding ice forming on the ground. "What on Earth?" she whispered.

"So, you sent word to my mother." Moros waved his hand indifferently.

Orah's brow rose. "Mother?" She didn't like situations where she had no idea what anyone was talking about.

Roan kept his eyes on his cousin. "Yes. Moros' mother is Amada, my Aunt, the Goddess of Wisdom. It appears that she's sent him here to provide us with her update. Not sure why. Moros can be rather annoying."

Orah's heart began to beat rapidly. His Aunt, the Goddess of Wisdom. The Aunt he had told her he'd requested information from. Hope filled her. She might get to go home. Roan grabbed her hand softly and she felt herself focusing again. Moros stared at their clasped hands and smiled wide. She removed hers from Roan's and stood a bit taller. "Well, if you have an update then please don't keep us waiting."

Roan snorted and turned to his cousin. Moros shook his head. "Well, considering your guest is just a mortal and I'm the God of Wintur, I would think I'd get to place the terms and conditions on when and where I share this information."

The lights in the room flashed on and off and Roan stepped forward. "Oh, do calm your temper, Roan," Moros said. "My mother made me duty bound to share this as soon as possible." He sauntered over to the sitting room and bumped into the side of Orah's shoulder. His eyes flared. "I will be waiting in here while your *guest* goes and cleans herself up. I won't talk to a walking sack of flour."

Orah scoffed. He had a point; she was filthy, and she could feel the flour against her skin, but she still didn't appreciate his attitude. "Fine, your Lordship," she said sarcastically, bowing low. Roan's eyes twinkled in amusement and she turned toward the stairs, determined to get answers out of Moros. She wasn't going to let him hold the possibility of her getting home in his hands.

Orah showered and dressed quickly before returning downstairs where she found Roan, Jes, Lahana, and Moros in the sitting room waiting for her.

"Finally." Moros flipped his hand out as if she had inconvenienced him.

"Oh, please shut up Moros," Lahana snapped.

"You should remember to respect me Na-Na, I do have some information you all asked for."

"Please get to the point, Moros," Roan interjected while he motioned for Orah to sit down on the chair next to him. Lahana and Moros were seated on the couch across from her and Jes stood near the window. His expression was tight, as though he were uncomfortable, and she wondered whether he had moved an inch since placing himself in that spot.

"My mother said that you had asked if it were possible for doors from other worlds to open." Moros turned toward Roan.

"Yes, that's right," Roan replied, obviously annoyed.

"This is so interesting. My mother was very confused as to why you would have sent word for information like this, but I think I understand."

Orah glanced at Roan, unable to ignore how tightly he was clenching his jaw. "What is it you understand?"

Moros flipped his hair back from his shoulder. "What?" He smirked "Oh. Never mind."

Roan and Lahana let out an exasperated sigh.

"Fine, I suppose I should get out with it." Moros's eyes fell on Jesiel for a moment before he began. "My mother assumed that you must have read some fantastical story in that big library of yours, but she did take the time to research any information the scholars have." He leaned back a bit and crossed his legs. "As you know, the scholars are aware of other worlds. We're all aware that the powers we Governing Gods hold here influence these other worlds." Orah tried and failed to hide her shock at the statement. Moros's eyes flashed to hers. "However, any knowledge on traveling to and from other worlds seems to be lost, or the Fates have prevented us from finding out more about it."

That's it? That's all the Goddess of Wisdom could tell us? Orah couldn't help but feel defeated.

"Thank you for the information, Moros. I'll be sure to send my thanks to Amada myself," Roan replied.

Orah watched Moros stand. "You know, Marek mentioned you had something surprising here, but he definitely left out just how surprising *she* is." Suddenly, the doors to the sitting room slammed shut and the lights faded. The room became dark and heavy. She expected to see the starlight that Roan made appear before, but the only thing lit in the room was him. His starlight crown burned as though it were on fire atop his head as he approached Moros. "My brother tends to leave out anything that doesn't benefit him."

The temperature dropped again. Orah shivered and watched the puffs of breath coming from Roan through his light when Moros spoke. "It appears that he does."

The lights faded back on and she blinked at the sudden brightness in the room. Moros walked to the sitting room doors and flung them open. Staring at them for a moment, he turned back to Roan. "Oh yes. One last thing. Not sure how I forgot to mention this. Mother said the knowledge to travel between worlds seems to align with how we travel between Regions." Roan tensed. "She thinks there may have once been doors or portals to other worlds, but she wasn't sure." Moros waved his hand and a flurry of snow enveloped him, but once the snow settled to the ground, he was nowhere to be seen.

"What does he mean about how you travel between Regions?" Orah asked, frustrated and disappointed by the lack of answers the Goddess had to offer. She thought they were back in the same place as before.

Roan stared at the doors when he spoke. "Our world is rather large, and we have doors—or more so portals—that we use to quickly get to and from each Region."

"Portals?" Orah echoed.

"Yes. They're essentially a rip in the world you can walk through. Say I wanted to follow Moros to his Region right now, all I'd have to do is go to the portal in the city and think of his Region and I'd appear there once I'd walked through."

"But you can't travel to other worlds in that way?" She was trying very hard to understand their world, but the more she learned, the more confused she felt.

Roan rubbed his jaw. "No, we can't. As Moros mentioned, we're very aware of other worlds, and it's believed that at one point there was a way to visit them, but that knowledge has been lost to time. It's why I sent word to Amada to see if she could find out anything more about it." He leaned back against the chair and stared at the ceiling, seemingly lost in his own thoughts.

Orah surveyed the room. Jesiel hadn't moved and Lahana was staring at Roan. "But I don't understand. If you have these portals to go to other Regions, can't the same magic be used to go to other worlds?"

"You would think that. But no. No one knows who created the portals to travel between regions. We believe it was the Fates, but we're not sure," Lahana responded.

"You all keep mentioning these Fates. Can one of you explain to me who or what they are?" Orah asked.

Jesiel moved now and turned to face Orah. Somehow, she hadn't noticed before that the feathers on his wings were ruffled, practically spiked straight up. "The Fates created time, Orah. Time and all who abide by it. It's also believed that the Fates created this world and every other world out there."

"Where are they?"

Jes turned back to the window. "They live on an island—the island of Tiid."

"Do they have a Governing God?"

"In a way," Jes replied, turning his attention to Roan.

Roan responded, "You see, the Fates created all. They can see the past, present, and future. They're honestly more powerful than any one of us, but because of that knowledge and power, they decided they would not rule. They appointed the first King of Gods and have acted as a sort of balancing hand since then. They won't interfere in things knowing that certain threads of fate will lead to one outcome, and others can lead to a different one, but they do their best to ensure balance. The one who guides their Island is called Eon."

"But they're not Gods?"

"They're beyond Gods. They're the Fates, they are what they are. There's not really any other way to describe it. Eon is also neither God nor Goddess. Eon is *the* Fate. Eon watches over time and is the one the Fates turn to when things begin to fall out of balance."

Orah pulled her knees up, resting her chin against them. "So, we still have no answers." She stared at the floor. The warmth she had felt while working in the kitchen was quickly shifting to that familiar numb cold. She took a deep breath and let it out. By the time she looked up she found Roan's eyes on her.

"We will keep searching. There's a chance my aunt missed something. She may be the Goddess of Wisdom, but our world is very old, and we have a lot of history. She or the scholars could have skipped over something important."

Silence fell over the room until a knock at the door sounded and Xade's voice filled the room. "My Lord? Dinner is ready."

Lahana and Jes walked past them and followed Xade out of the room, but Orah tensed at the thought of going into the dining room. Roan walked over to her chair and crouched down, lowering his voice to a whisper. "Let's go eat, Orah. We'll figure out how to get you home. I promise." She stared at the hand he had extended toward her. "Please." Roan's voice softened.

She looked at his hand and then back into his eyes. There was a sadness in his eyes that she couldn't place. Her chest tightened and she continued staring at him. Those eyes felt familiar, as though she'd looked at them in her dreams before. She blinked and stared back down at his hand. Hesitantly, she grabbed it and allowed him to help her off the chair. Gazing at their palms, she smiled at how perfectly they fit together. She stared as a light began to shimmer between their palms. Her heartbeat quickened and she looked up at Roan. He was staring at her with a smile and walked toward the door, pulling her with him. She couldn't seem to allow herself to let go of his hand as he walked past the dining room toward the kitchen.

Orah was pleasantly surprised to find what a normal dinner was like for them. Yohan and his children apparently stayed and ate at the Manor most nights, so Roan, Lahana, and Jes usually joined them at the table in the kitchen. The meal wasn't extravagant by any means, but it was delicious; a hearty stew and the scones she made with Clarah. Orah had blushed when everyone at the table loudly complimented her on her baking.

After they had finished their meal and cleared the table, Ms. Perri and Kai joined them. Yohan pulled out several bottles of wine and she sat in wonder watching as everyone laughed and drank together.

Like one happy family.

After what felt like hours, her head felt light and dizzy and she knew she had consumed too much wine and needed sleep. "Thank you for the wonderful evening. I think I'm going to excuse myself and head to bed," Orah announced, as she stood from the table.

Roan stood abruptly, rattling the table, and almost knocking everything upon it to the ground. "May I walk you up?" he asked.

Everyone's eyes turned on them and Orah's face flushed. She didn't know what it was between her and Roan, but she suddenly felt like a form of entertainment that everyone was watching. "No, I'm alright. Thank you though," Orah said, trying to ignore the amused expression on Lahana's face as she hurried out of the room. Rushing up the stairs, she turned to go down the hall to her room, but the second staircase caught her attention.

Climbing the stairs, she pulled open the door. The night air hit her in a rush, and she breathed out. Her skin prickled at the little bit of summer heat still lingering in the evening. Crossing the roof to the chairs on the opposite side she sat down.

She leaned back, gazing up at the stars, convinced she could stay out here all night. She searched for any signs of home, feeling a small glimmer of hope after the conversation with Moros, believing any one of the stars above her could possibly be her world. She cocked her head wondering if any of them was part of the Milky Way, watching over her as if to keep an eye on her until she could return. Orah closed her eyes, appreciating how quiet the city was at night. Nothing like her nights out in Boston or Paris with Julian. She laughed thinking of all the nights she spent out with him drinking well into the morning hours. If only he could see where she was now. She could practically hear what he would say about Roan. *Mon dieu! Orah please tell me you're appreciating that gorgeous man.* She flushed at the thought. She considered Roan to be attractive and had caught herself thinking about the look he'd given her before closing his study often throughout the day.

Shuddering, she stared down at her hand and thought about how hers had felt in his. Her mind imagined his hand running up her arm, down her back, up her thigh. Her imagination traveled as she wondered how it would feel to run hers over his body, appreciating him. Learning him. Her skin warmed and she let out a scream as a light burst from her palms, scattering across the rooftop. Turning her hands up she stared down in awe. They appeared normal and she had no clue what had happened. The door to the roof slammed open and she watched Roan fly through it, breathing heavily.

"What's wrong?" he asked, surveying the roof for danger.

"Nothing. I'm okay." She looked at her hands again, feeling embarrassment when she realized what had happened. Her power appeared to have reacted to her not-so-innocent thoughts about him. Light sparked in her palms again and she let out a yelp.

Roan rushed to her. "Are you sure?"

She couldn't meet his eyes, she was too embarrassed, but she nodded. "Yes. This power I apparently have seems to be acting up." He motioned for her hands, but she shook her head, pulling them against her chest. "Roan, I'm fine. Really. Just some sparks of light."

The concern in his voice shifted to amusement. "Are you sure you're okay, Orah?"

Irritated by the tone, she snapped her head up to him. His eyes glistened as if they were about to light on fire. She swallowed. "Yes."

He smiled a coy smile before placing his hands on each arm of the chair. "Nothing I can't help with?" Orah's skinned burned and she considered playing along with him.

"I'm fine," she replied, while lightly running a finger across one of his hands. He shivered, then leaned in closer. Their noses were almost touching, and her heartbeat grew erratic.

"Are you very sure you're okay, love?"

Trying to keep control of herself, she leaned toward him. "One—I'm not your 'love'. Two—please get your face out of my face before my knee connects with a part of yourself I'm sure you don't want injured."

"Oh Fates, Orah, I'm sorry." He backed up a step. "I hope you know I would never—I couldn't ever—I mean, I..."

She bit back her laugh at how he fumbled his words. Part of her wondered if her teasing had taken it too far considering how she hadn't entirely minded how close he'd gotten. The heat of his body had only fueled more indecent thoughts like the ones she'd been having before he came crashing through the door.

"I think it's been a long day and we should both head to bed," she replied, coolly, trying to hide the fire burning under her skin.

He nodded and walked towards the door, stopping before he pulled it open. She looked up at the stars and gasped as they appeared to fall down in a shower. One after another. Just like they had the first night there. She turned to Roan, finding his eyes on her. Something was hidden in his eyes, like some kind of intention he could barely control. Her cheeks flushed in response. Smiling, he pulled the door open. She kept her gaze on him, watching him close the door behind him.

Alone again, she turned back to the sky. It was lit up with different shades of blues and greens with a cluster of stars twinkling overhead. Admiring its beauty, she couldn't help but wonder how much control he had over the night, or how much it might have controlled him.

Chapter 13

Standing in front of the garden door, Orah's heart raced. The creaking hinges echoed around her and she stared while the door slowly swung open. Bright light surrounded the frame, but she could see it; off in the distance—her chateau—beckoning her to return home. Holding her hand to her chest she moved forward, ready to return to her own world, to her own life, but found she was unable to lift her feet.

The shimmering view of her chateau faltered for just a moment, and she let out a sob. She had to get home. She had to.

"You think you can leave, mortal?" Marek's voice filled Orah's ears and she twisted her head to find him behind her. Her stomach flipped at the vile smile spread across his lips and she shook her head in protest.

"Let me go home," she begged.

"No," Marek replied, lunging for her.

Orah sat up, covered in sweat as the chill of the morning air pricked her skin. Trying to gather her senses, she glanced around her. She was still on the roof. Rubbing her temple, she couldn't remember falling asleep after Roan had left her.

She wasn't usually one to fall asleep sitting up, let alone sitting up outside. All she could remember was watching Roan close the door behind him and returning her gaze to the cascading stars that flew overhead. Shivering, she pulled her sore body from the chair and walked toward the edge of the roof.

The dream had felt so real—so tangible. As though her home and life were just at her fingertips again and all she had to do was reach out to return to where she belonged. But Marek had felt just as real and fear coiled around her as if she had actually been trapped by him.

Shivering again, Orah's eyes scanned the brightening sky above her. The sun was cresting over the city with brilliant pinks and golds shining across Roan's lawn. Her eyes watered from unexpected emotion due to the beauty above her. The night sky in Roan's Region had taken her breath away several times already, but she hadn't expected the morning sky to be just as beautiful.

She pulled her eyes from the picturesque sunrise and glanced to her left to where she could see the garden hedges off in the distance. The door was just out of her line of sight, but she knew it was there. Hidden behind the greenery, somehow calling out to her.

She hadn't gathered the courage to go outside and try the door again. She hadn't wanted to feel disappointment when her attempts would inevitably fail once more. Keeping her eyes on the hedges, she puffed out her chest. She may have been scared, but she couldn't allow her fear to stop her. Turning away from the edge of the roof, she walked toward the roof door.

Rushing down the stairs and out the side door, Orah made her way to the garden. She could have been quieter when navigating Roan's manor, but she was focused on only one thing: the door—and getting it open.

Roan's large estate was beautiful with the garden nestled in the back. It took her longer than she remembered to get past the hedges, but finally the door was just a few feet from her. Her hands shook while she stared at the dulled bronze barrier. The barrier between herself and her world. The door she had never meant to go through.

Tears welled in her eyes while she scanned the wall behind the door. Stepping back in shock, her eyes widened. There were cracks in the wall. Cracks she was sure hadn't been there before and the door handle—it looked as though it had been melted and crushed. Pulling her hands up in front of her she shook her head.

How did she have powers? How had her hands, her simple *human* hands, caused so much damage? Her mind went back to the fire sparking from her palms the night before. Caused by her not-so-innocent thoughts about Roan. But how was it all possible?

Heat warmed her palm and she let out a yelp at the fire now blazing in her palm. She was captivated by the flames. The way they licked at her skin, warming her, yet not burning her. How foreign it felt but also familiar, as though the power had been hiding inside of her all this time.

Turning her head back to the door, she squared her shoulders. It was only a door. She could get it open. She could get herself back home.

Walking with her head high and her hand outstretched, she paused a few inches from the handle.

She focused on the crushed metal, thinking back on the desperation she'd felt when she'd fled the dining room. Closing her eyes, she allowed those dark consuming emotions to take over again, to take center stage. Her heart beat frantically and the heat in her palm intensified. She could feel it now. Her power. Boiling and building to the surface, trying to unlock the cage she hadn't known existed inside of her.

Letting out a scream, she gripped the handle, twisting it as hard as she could. Her other palm lit into flames and her eyes flew open. The wall towering above her groaned at the contact, but the door remained closed. Twisting hard, she pulled with all her might. Her thoughts swirled around her and her fire-lit palms grew hotter. The metal melted like ice beneath her touch, but she didn't care. She had to get home.

Blinded by her focus, she let out a yelp when Roan appeared beside her.

"What are you doing?" he asked.

Her head snapped to him and her eyes widened. She'd obviously woken him up by the way his hair was tousled on top of his head, but he was also shirtless. Painfully and distractingly shirtless. Releasing the door, she stumbled backwards while sparks of fire and electricity erupted from her palms.

"I'm trying to go home, Roan," she replied. He walked toward her, with his arm outstretched, but she backed up further. "I just wanted to try the door again, I wasn't trying to break anything," she said, hoping he would go back inside.

Air rushed around them and the ground shook as Jesiel landed beside Roan. His eyes flared in anger and his gaze darted between Orah and the handle she had just released.

Backing up further, Orah cursed the flames unwilling to extinguish in her palms. She had to calm down. Roan was staring at her as though she were a circus act, and Jesiel was staring at her as though he were about to attack.

"Orah!" Jesiel yelled. "What in the Fates are you doing?"

Irritated by the accusation in his tone, she glared at him. "I am just trying to get myself home!"

His eyes narrowed and she held her glare. The winged man walked around as though *she* were the danger. Rage built inside of her and she let out a scream of frustration at the fire still licking her palms.

"I just want to go home!" she screamed.

Her scream echoed in the air and the sky darkened. Responding lightning cracked high in the sky. Roan's eyes widened and Jesiel stepped back. Thrown off by the sudden change in weather, Orah didn't register the lightning barreling toward her. That was until Roan tackled her to the ground and the tree beside them burst into flames.

"Roan! I thought I told you and Jes you weren't allowed to train on the manor grounds!"

Orah pulled her eyes from Roan's to find Ms. Perri marching down the lawn, coming from the keeper's cottage. Roan laughed and released his hold on Orah. Pulling himself up, then offering his hand to Orah, he addressed Ms. Perri. "That wasn't me. That was Orah."

Orah's cheeks warmed and she glanced down at the ground. "I wasn't trying to destroy anything." Jesiel scoffed in response and Orah's head snapped back up.

Ms. Perri grinned. "Just be careful attacking the grounds of this manor. It doesn't respond lightly to threats." Orah's brow crumpled and she stared while the housekeeper turned on her heel and walked back to the cottage. Shaking her head, Orah glanced over at Roan, blushing again, when she caught sight of his shirtless torso.

"Distracted by something, Orah?" Jesiel asked with a grin.

"No," she bit back, crossing her arms.

Roan laughed before glancing at the door behind her. "Any luck?"

"Nothing," Orah replied. A heavy sense of disappointment settled around her and she sighed. "I just thought I would try again."

Jesiel cleared his throat. "As impressive as it is that you can rattle and even break my wards, can you try not to?"

"I've already said I wasn't trying to destroy anything!" Orah yelled back.

Jesiel's eyes scanned the wall before he shrugged. "If you weren't a guest of Roan's I wouldn't have hesitated to take you out."

Orah's eyes widened. Opening her mouth to protest, she was cut off by Roan. "Jes, let's not tease Orah too much."

Jesiel winked. "Don't worry, Orah, my duty to protect Roan is now extended to you as his guest."

"I don't even know what that means," Orah replied.

Jesiel shrugged and turned back to the house. "You know if you ever want to work on controlling that power of yours, just let me know," he called out over his shoulder. Orah watched while he walked away, making sure to keep her eyes focused on the house and not on Roan. Twisting her fingers around the ring on her pinky, she shuffled her feet.

"I'm sorry about your tree," she whispered.

Roan laughed. "It's just a tree. It can be replaced." Nodding her head, Orah glanced at Roan. His muscles flexed in response when her eyes landed on him. Losing herself in his beauty she stared for a moment before averting her gaze.

"Well, I'm going to see if Yohan has arrived yet," she said.

"There's no use in that," Roan replied.

"What?"

"There's no one in there today. It's a personal day for Yohan and his children."

Once again, disappointment settled over Orah. Her eyes traveled to the house while she considered her options. She had intended to start a schedule for herself. Schedules and maintaining them ran her life. Or more so kept her busy enough to distract her mind from the thoughts always swirling and waiting to attack. Setting up one for herself in Roan's home was how she planned to keep the darkness away while they tried to find a way to get her home. Her plan had been to start each morning in the kitchen but now it had been canceled without her control.

"What am I supposed to do today then?" she asked.

"Whatever you want."

Silently, Roan walked toward the house and Orah watched after him. Her palms buzzed and her head swam while she considered how to spend her day. Shaking off the building panic, she rushed to the side door.

The lights in the bedroom flickered on while Orah shut the bedroom door behind her. Pacing the room, she forced herself to avoid the bed calling out to her with invisible claws attempting to pull her back to its depths.

Twisting the ring on her finger, her pacing picked up. She was alone. Alone with her thoughts. Alone with the darkness she could never seem to fight off.

Slowing her pace, she backed up, planting herself on the couch. Weight settled in her chest while she pulled her knees up. She wasn't meant to end up in the bed—the prison she'd always run from.

Tears welled in her eyes while she focused on the wall across from her. She could sit on the couch all day. She could avoid the dark thoughts. She'd done it before. She could keep going.

A loud knock echoed across the room. "Yes?" she called out.

Roan's voice came from behind the door. "I've made some breakfast. I've got to work, but it's down in the kitchen for you."

Shakily, she pulled herself from the couch. "Oh, thank you. I'll be down in a moment."

Rushing to the closet, she changed her clothes from the night before, then forced herself out the door. Still aware she was going to be alone, but she could feel the darkness retreating back to the room while she walked down the hall.

The kitchen was oddly empty when she arrived downstairs. She picked up the small plate of food Roan had left her and sat at the table.

She ate quickly, then stood in the kitchen, staring at her palms. She didn't like not knowing how her power worked or even where it came from. Control over herself and her surroundings grounded her, making her feel steady and know where she was headed.

She laughed. Control: always controlling her environments, her friendships, her relationships—or lack of them. Yet, she'd ended up in a world she had no control over with more questions than answers every day she was there. How had her drive to control her new future led her to such an opposite situation?

Losing herself for a while, she finally pushed off from the kitchen island, deciding to do something with her day. Usually, she would have gone to work out, but the strain from trying to open the door had been enough of a workout for one day. Turning down the hall, her eyes lingered on Roan's study door.

There are those books.

She hadn't taken the time to explore the library despite Roan telling her she was welcome anytime. Her heart fluttered with excitement at the possible stories she would find in his books, or the information she could learn.

She approached the study door and stopped before pulling it open. She wasn't sure if it was a good idea, but she needed something to do. Moving her hand out in front of her she reached for the handle when the sound of Roan's voice behind the door startled her.

"Orah, I have no idea how long you've been out there staring at the door, but please just come in."

Heat flushed across her face. He'd said he had to work, and she'd assumed that meant him leaving the manor. The door creaked as she pushed it open.

"Hello," she waved nervously.

Roan was leaning back in his chair with his arms folded. His hair was tousled slightly, and his loose shirt clung to his body in all the right places. "To what do I owe this pleasure?" he asked, keeping his eyes locked on hers.

Embarrassed by her inability to not stare at him, she replied, "I didn't know you were home."

"So, you were breaking into my office while I was out?"

"What?" she yelled, stepping back.

His laugh echoed in the room and he slapped the top of his desk. "Orah, I'm joking. You should have seen your face. Were you wanting to use the library?"

She turned her head to the doorway in the corner of the study. "Yes, I was hoping to dive into those books finally."

He motioned to the library. She had almost passed him when he brushed his hand against her arm. "There isn't anything else I can help you with?" The touch was like a spark of electricity and the room instantly felt warm.

Trying to avoid his gaze, she shook her head. "Uh. No. Just books."

He slid his hand into his pocket while he stood. "Let me show you around. I don't have much organization set up in there."

She nodded in response, resisting the urge to touch where his hand had been. She walked through to the library, and every one of her senses knew just how closely he followed behind her. She paused in the middle of the room, unaware of where to go next.

The library was as magnificent as she remembered. "I sit in here and admire it all at least once a week," Roan said behind her. "There is almost no organization, but that area I've *tried* to keep more to our histories, whereas that area is probably more myth and legend, and that area has more fantastical stories." She watched as he pointed out each section, completely enamored by the choices. "Take your pick."

He sat down on one of the large armchairs and watched as she approached a bookshelf. She kept her eyes focused on the books but sensed him following every step she took.

"So many stories," she whispered while she ran her hands along the rows. The books were beautiful, but she always believed any large collection of books was beautiful. Finally, she stopped and picked up a book that caught her eye, but when she saw the cover, she frowned.

"What is it?" Roan asked.

Holding up the book, she turned to him. "I can't read this. I don't know what language it's in." She glanced at the ring on her pinky. "Shouldn't this ring help with that?"

He stood. "I'm not sure. I think it may have been warded only for hearing and speaking. One second." He crossed the room toward a desk tucked away in the back corner. The sounds of drawers opening, and their contents being shifted echoed across the room. "Ah! There we go!" He turned back to her, holding spectacles of some kind.

Raising her brow, she cocked her head. "What's that?"

Roan walked back to her and held them out in front of him. "They'll help you read any language you don't know. My aunt gave them to me when she first noticed my love of reading. There are many old languages that don't exist here anymore, but the books still do."

The spectacles were a silver color and small but had nothing to loop over the ears. "Do they just sit on my nose?" She glanced back at him, realizing he had moved closer. His legs were now pressed against hers. If she were to have stepped back, she would have bumped against his chest. She froze and turned her focus back to the book.

He leaned forward, the heat of his chest warming her back. His smile brushed against her ear and he whispered. "Would you allow me to show you?"

Words escaped her and she was sure she could have set the book in her hands aflame with how intently she stared at it. He pulled the spectacles up, placing each arm on either side of her head. Resting his elbows on her shoulders, he held the spectacles in her line of sight. She moved to glance back at him, but he shook his head while lowering his voice. "Don't look at me. Stay focused on the book please." Biting back a gasp, the hairs on her arms stood at the brush of his lips against her ear.

"Okay," she responded with a little squeak.

Chuckling, he brought the spectacles closer to her face. Two thin silvery threads appeared on either side when he placed them on the bridge of her nose. The threads dangled to the side until he pulled them up and they looped around each ear. With wonder, she watched the words on the cover of the book slowly shift until she could read the title.

Kings of Comas
Volume 1

She turned her head to Roan, the movement pushed her against him, and she gasped at the contact. "It's pretty impressive, huh?" he said with a whisper, still keeping his lips close to her ear.

She nodded. This was the kind of magic she wanted in her life. The histories she could learn; the stories she could live in; the worlds she could escape to. Clearing his throat, he stepped back. "That book, however, is not very impressive. A bunch of boring lineage talk."

Laughing, she set the book down. With the spectacles, she could spend every day in the library and never grow bored. She turned back to Roan, finding a smile on his face. "Please enjoy yourself today. I'm just on the other side of the wall if you need me." Turning, he walked back to his study. She watched until he was out of her line of sight and then turned back to the books, unsure of where to begin.

After searching for a bit, she found a book that wasn't either some sort of estate ledger, history book, or genealogy account. Holding it to her chest, she tried to decide which seat called to her. The sun shone through the window as though welcoming her like a sleepy house cat and she smiled, picking one of the couches in the window. Pulling the large blanket draped over the couch onto her lap, she nestled in then held up the book. She pulled open the cover, ready for a day of escape.

The First Queen

This is the tale of the First Queen. Tellings have come to know her by many titles over many ages: The Great Queen, The Beloved Queen, The Lone Queen, but we will call her by her true title, a title with no embellishment. It was she that birthed Death into the world and claimed its power for her own. It was she who first ruled all of Comas. Before there was a Queendom to rule, she governed over all the living, and all the dead. Before kingdoms and The First Kings, before History, she was The First Queen . . .

The hours quickly blurred together and Orah jumped when someone's hand touched her shoulder. "I said your name a few times, but you were completely lost in the book," Roan said.

Blushing, she set the book on her lap. "It's very interesting."

He leaned over. "Ah. I like that one. Imagining our world with a ruling Queen always sounded so much better than the long history of temperamental Kings we've had."

"It's always been a King?" She sat up, adjusting her position to allow him to sit next to her. Roan motioned for the book.

"Yes, unfortunately. I'm not sure why. It was a question I asked as a child and would pester my Father about. In response, he'd always ask me why I couldn't just accept things as they were and why I had to always question everything."

Intrigued, she sat up straighter. "What else did you question?"

"Oh everything. Why can't I be something other than the God of Nyte or Daee? Why do my questions annoy him? Why does he send me to stay with my uncle so often?" His voice shifted to something far away, as though the memories were ones he usually preferred to ignore. "That last one would really make him angry. I think it was probably his guilt and shame that I was calling him out on it."

Staring at him for a moment, she cleared her throat. "I know you said that you were made the God of Night after losing the last challenge, but who was the God of Night before you?"

"My uncle was the God of Nyte before me. It's a bit convoluted, but when my Father's Father died and my Father became King, my uncle became the God of Death. Every King of God's life is bound to the God of Death. It was one of the stipulations of the challenge the Fates set. This means when the King dies, the God of Death dies, and the successor takes their place."

"That doesn't answer how he was both the God of Night and God of Death. You said you only became the God of Night fifty years ago. If your Father is over one thousand years old then I assume your uncle is close in age, right?" Orah asked.

"Yes, that's right. To make a long story short, my Father became the King before either myself or my brother were born. When the King of Gods has no adult sons to assume the Godhoods of Daee and Nyte, the King of Gods and God of Death act as regent to the area until the sons take over. So essentially my uncle was both God of Death and Nyte and my Father was both King and God of Daee."

"But how does that work?"

Roan shrugged. "Honestly, only the Fates know. My Father sent me to live with my uncle most of my childhood and well into my adult years. Until I officially came into my Godhood, my uncle preferred to live in his palace just outside of Iluna and only went to Shadus when he needed to for business."

She looked down at the book. "I understand difficult parental relationships."

Roan smacked his hands on his knees while he stood. "Well, I didn't come in here to talk about difficult parents, I came in to see if you're hungry."

Her stomach rumbled in response. "Uh, yeah. What time is it?"

"About one o'clock."

She'd been in the library for hours and hadn't realized it.

"So, food or back to the book?" Roan asked, holding out his hand.

His hand seemed to call to her, and something urged her to take it. Reaching up she gasped at the small zap between them when their hands touched. They both jumped.

"Must be the blanket," Orah said nervously.

"Must be," he replied as he pulled her up and off the couch.

They walked hand in hand out of the library and through his office. The house felt empty as they walked down the hall.

"Is Lahana gone for the day?" she asked as they walked through the kitchen doors.

"Yes, she'll probably be gone until after dinner. She's taken it upon herself to help with the parts of planning my party that I don't want to deal with."

Orah sat down at the table, watching as Roan moved about the kitchen gathering food. "You two are really close." It wasn't a question, and she knew she was prying a bit.

"Yes, we are." Crossing the room, Roan set a plate of food down on the table. She tensed as he slid onto the bench.

"Why does she live with you?"

He was quiet for a few moments before he replied, "She came to live with me when I became the God of Nyte. My Father is unbearable to live with and she prefers my company."

"I don't have siblings, but from what I can see your relationship with her is what I would want if I had one." Orah glanced over at him and found an emotion on his face she couldn't decipher.

He shook his head. "Yes, that is until you've seen her annoy me. Then you'll feel thankful you don't have to deal with that."

"Yeah, you're probably right," she said with a laugh.

He handed her a sandwich, and they ate in silence. Finishing their meal, Roan stood, gathering the plates from the table. She watched him walk to the sink.

"Roan, why do Yohan, Xade, and Clarah take most of today off?"

A fleeting glint of sadness flashed in his eyes as he glanced around the kitchen then back at her. "It's the anniversary of Yohan's wife's passing."

The cold companion of death brushed against her, confirming what he said. "Oh." Breathing out, she stared down at the table, trying to push down her emotions. She hadn't realized Clarah and Xade didn't have a mother at home. Lost in her thoughts, warm hands gripped hers. Her eyes moved from the table to find Roan beside her once more.

He smiled, gently brushing his thumb across the top of her hand. "It used to be a really sad day here. Mila was loved and brought a light and joy to Yohan that's only been reappearing in recent years. I had to be the one to force him to take the day off each year and spend time with his children. He would have just worked straight through the day if I hadn't insisted."

Sighing, he let go of her hands. "Now it's a bittersweet day of remembrance for everyone."

Orah tried to imagine Yohan as anyone other than the warm, smiling man she was coming to know. For a moment she let her emotions wave over her. While death had been this quiet companion, she'd done her best to avoid giving it too much of her time, while also avoiding her own grief as long as she could. Several quiet moments passed before she decided she'd sat with her heavy emotions for long enough and she stood. Roan appeared startled by her sudden movement but followed close behind as she walked out of the kitchen and back to the library.

She spent the rest of the afternoon reading her book. The sun shining through the window was comforting and warm and she wondered if she ever really wanted to leave her pocket of safety. Eventually, Roan joined her with his own book and sat on the opposite side of the couch. They read together and his company provided her with an additional layer of warmth and comfort. When the sun finally set and the lights in the room twinkled on, she yawned and set down her book. "I think I'm going to head to bed now."

Roan's head popped up from his own book. "That's probably not a bad idea." Stretching as well, he placed his book beside him.

For a moment their eyes locked, and they stared at each other. Her chest felt warm and the pull to him tugged on her like some invisible string being pulled beyond her control. She didn't understand what it was she felt around him. Physically, he was attractive—she would have had to be blind not to see that—but what she felt was more than attraction. Like a chemical reaction inside of herself building every day. Her cheeks flushed as she remembered she was staring at him and he smiled wide.

"Everything okay, love?" His eyes twinkled.

Swinging her legs off the couch she stood. "Yes, everything is fine, Roan, and I thought I told you I'm not your 'love'." Meeting his gaze, she smiled.

Two can play that game.

She approached him, never breaking eye contact, noticing how his chest slowly rose up and down the closer she drew. Leaning over him, so close her chest brushed against his, she picked up his book and whispered, "Just gotta make sure we put this back where it belongs."

She was sure he stopped breathing as she rose and turned her back to him. Suppressing her laugh, she glanced around the library, not actually knowing where his book went. She walked away as confidently as she could when a rush of air shot past her, and she walked directly into his chest.

She certainly stopped breathing as she made eye contact with him. He had a wide grin on his face and the lights in the library dimmed. His freckles glowed in the dimness and his eyes lit so brightly she could see her own reflection in them. He brushed his hand down her arm that held his book.

Leaning so close his lips were right against her ear, he whispered, "I don't believe you know where that goes."

He was so close now that her chest bumped against his with every breath she took. "Goodnight, Orah," he whispered again, brushing the hair behind her ear. The air rushed around her again and she blinked, finding herself standing in the library, all alone.

"Holy shit," she panted. Her skin felt as though it was on fire, and the arm he touched felt ten times hotter than the rest of her. She stared up at the ceiling, unsure of what to do next.

Pulling her eyes from the ceiling, she allowed herself to look in the direction of his study. She wondered if he was still in there, or if he had retired to his room for the night. The room next to hers...

She held her hand against her chest and shook her head. Whatever attraction they felt was only biological, she didn't need to act on it. Acting on it would make things messy, and she did not want messy while she tried to figure out how to get home.

She walked out of the library, peeking her head into his study to ensure it was empty. The only light in the room was coming from the lamp on the corner of the desk and she found no one in the chair. Letting out a breath of relief she rushed out the door, not entirely sure what she would have done if Roan had been in there.

Turning the door handle to her room, she stopped for a moment and looked toward his. She thought she saw his door open a crack but shook her head before pushing hers open and closing it behind her.

Her heart pounded. She couldn't hear him on the other side of the wall, but she could *feel* him. As though he was this overpowering energy trying to break down the wall between their rooms, making hers feel warm and suffocating. She made her way to the bathroom, hoping a cool bath would help. Turning on the tap, she let it run until it was the perfect balance between warm but cool enough to bring her temperature down.

She stripped off her clothes and sunk into the tub. A loud sigh escaped her while her body was enveloped until only her face was exposed. She sank further, appreciating the depth of the tub.

She knew she had to make sure nothing happened between her and Roan. She didn't believe she could keep it casual like she normally did. She usually avoided relationships. No emotions, no closeness, no falling for someone and letting herself become blinded by love.

But she knew it would be different with Roan. Every time he looked at her, her skin felt hot. Every brush of his hand against hers made her feel as though she would explode. Something inside of her jolted as though she'd been stuck with electricity when he was near, and she had to do everything she could to avoid going further with him. Despite how desperately she wanted more.

She stared up at the ceiling, trying to convince herself of her willpower.

Cocking her head to the side, she watched the ceiling light up, but not from anything that was above her—from what she could see. The light was warm, reminding her of a candle in a dark room. She gasped and water flung over the edge while she sat up, realizing the light was coming from *her*. Her entire body was lit with a dim light. The ripples of water around her glowed as though they were playing in the light, beckoning it to shine brighter.

Grabbing both sides of her head, she sighed. This power she had didn't seem capable of controlling itself when she thought about him. Her cheek flushed as she considered how embarrassed she would be if he ever saw her light up like she was now. The water lapped around her and she shivered. The temperature had dropped well below the comfortable cool she had before. Gazing back down at herself, a cold chill ran down her spine, despite the warm glow radiating off her.

Pulling herself out of the tub, she wrapped a towel around her body. She was tired but she wasn't sure she could sleep. Walking into the closet, she went to search for something for bed.

Lahana had come home the day before with bags of clothes as a surprise. She noticed Orah hadn't purchased much to sleep in and claimed she needed more *"pretty things"*. Orah pulled a long night gown out of the drawer, slipping it over her head. The fabric reminded her of cashmere, the deep red color reminded her of Christmas.

Wrapping her wet hair in the towel, she walked back out to the room. Surveying the room, she knew she didn't want to get in bed yet, and her eyes landed on the balcony doors.

While she had opened the curtains the day before, she hadn't opened the doors themselves again. The view to the garden door felt almost insulting since she broke down the wards and she didn't have the energy to venture through the balcony doors again. But today she had gone out to the garden. She grabbed the handle, while nothing happened, she'd done it.

Sighing, she walked to the doors and pulled them open. Light from Roan's room poured out to her right. She stared for a moment then quieted her gasp at the voices just beyond the door.

"She's a *mortal*, Roan!" The frustrated voice sounded like Jesiel.

"Yes, thank you for pointing out the obvious." That voice definitely belonged to Roan. She almost turned to go back into her room then decided he was the one who agreed to put her room next to his. It was his own fault if he didn't keep his doors closed.

A sigh sounded from behind the door and she held herself back from leaning forward. "Roan, I know you feel something. It's obvious to literally *everyone*, but do you think this is a good idea?" It was definitely Jesiel on the other side of the door. She could tell by his grumpy tone.

The curtain swayed and the outline of Roan's figure appeared behind them. "No, of course I don't think this is a good idea. Why do you think I rushed out of that library?" Her eyes widened and she leaned forward, as though it helped her focus more on their conversation. "Jes. I—I can't explain it, but I think she feels something too."

Jes responded with an annoyed tone. "Again, something obvious to *everyone* in this house." Jesiel's silhouette appeared behind the curtain and Orah stepped back toward her balcony doors. She couldn't see him clearly, but she was sure he was staring right at her as he continued. "Just please be careful. We can't let anything, or *anyone*, cause any distraction with not only your birthday but the challenge approaching."

Roan's answering sigh was enough for her to walk backwards and close her doors as quietly as she could. She didn't need to hear how strongly Jesiel discouraged their attraction. She herself was discouraging their attraction. Whatever it was they felt for each other wasn't going to get in the way of her getting home. She couldn't let it. The lights in the room seemed to dim in response to her eyes growing heavy. Yawning, she walked to the bed and climbed under the comforter. She stared at the open balcony curtains as her eyes drifted shut and she fell asleep wondering what it would feel like to fall asleep next to Roan.

Chapter 14

Orah's days began to meld together the longer she was in the Land of Gods. She and Roan hadn't spoken much, but he spent at least an hour every day reading next to her. The day after their encounter in the library, he had chosen a chair on the opposite side of the room. Slowly, though, he'd been getting closer and closer. Now, he was right beside her.

She looked up from her book and stared at him for a moment. He was reading his book, but his body was fidgeting nervously. Her lips stretched to a tight line as she tried to hold in her laugh. He glanced at her and she quickly looked back down at her book.

He cleared his throat. "Orah?"

Her heart raced in response. "Yes, Roan?"

"I wanted to know if you would like to join me in the city center for dinner this evening. Lahana is gone with her lover for a few days and I told Yohan to go home after lunch today."

Her mind went blank as she stared at him. "Lahana has a lover?"

His face shifted through three separate expressions before he laughed. "Yes. Not sure why that's surprising though. They're fairly new and not many people know. She's gone to spend a few days away."

"Am I allowed to know who her lover is?" Orah asked.

"Her name is Fawn. She's from Spreng. That's the Region our Goddess of Spring governs and the Region Lahana will hopefully be granted." His tone shifted at the end of his sentence. "If our Father ever pulls his head out of his ass and actually grants her Godhood."

Her mind raced and she still wasn't sure if she should accept his offer to attend dinner with him. "What about Jesiel?" she asked.

"What about Jes? Does he have a lover?" Roan replied with a smile.

"No!" Heat flashed across her cheeks "No. That's not what I meant. I was asking what about him if you and I take off to dinner?"

Mischief sparkled in his eyes. "Jes is a big boy. He can fend for himself. So, do I have your answer then?"

Pulling her eyes from his, she glanced out the window toward the city. "Dinner sounds wonderful."

"Good. I'm going to change into something more suitable for a night out and I'll meet you at the side door in about thirty minutes?" He stood, brushing his pant legs. She watched the movement, trying hard to avoid her gaze from wandering and nodded.

"Yes, thirty minutes sounds fine."

His hand extended for her to grab onto and he pulled her off the couch. She lost her balance and fell against him, making him stumble back a bit. They stood there staring at one another as his hand rested on her lower back. Their breathing was almost in sync when she had to physically shake him from his hold to get him to let go.

Roan cleared his throat. "Right—so—thirty minutes and we'll meet down here again."

Orah couldn't respond before he rushed out the room and up the stairs. *Thirty minutes.* She set her book down and darted out of the room. Not entirely sure what she would wear or what was considered appropriate to wear on a night out but Lahana had given her more than enough the other day for her to sort through.

✴

The closet was a mess around her and Orah let out a frustrated groan. She'd pulled almost every item off its hanger or out of its drawer in desperation, trying to find something to wear. She let out a yell and sank to the floor. She didn't know how long she had been in there and for all she knew Roan was downstairs waiting for her.

She stared at the mess around her and her eyes caught the dress she was wearing when she first came through the garden door. Grabbing it she slipped it on, not confident it was something she should wear out with the Governing God of the Region. Sighing, she looked around her and spotted a pair of loose flowy pants that Lahana bought. When standing the legs appeared as though she were wearing a long skirt, but when she walked the loose fabric flowed around her legs. She pulled them on, tucking her dress in at the waist and admired at herself in the mirror. The blue of the dress worked well with the black pants and she smiled. Nervous flutters returned to her stomach at the thought of a night with only Roan.

A few minutes later she rushed down the stairs, stopping breathlessly at the bottom. She couldn't see Roan in the foyer and wondered if he was already waiting by the side door. Her heart beat rapidly as she took a moment to calm her nerves, reminding herself it was just dinner.

She turned to walk down the hall and her breath stopped short when she spotted Roan. He was leaning against the wall near the side door, dressed casually in a white loose shirt that stopped at his elbows and a pair of dark blue trousers. The hall was dark, but his freckles were alight and the light made his hair shine like starlight had caught it on fire.

Slowly he turned in her direction and smiled when they made eye contact. Even from where she stood, she could feel his eyes scan her from head to toe. She still wasn't sure if what she had on was appropriate but decided shaking things up a little in this new world wasn't a bad thing.

"Fates." His whisper sent a shiver down her spine as he pushed off the wall and walked toward her.

Blood rushed to her ears and her heartbeat drowned out any other sounds.

By the time he reached her all she could manage was a quiet, "Hi."

"Hello," he replied, keeping his eyes on hers.

They stood in the dark hall for a moment before she cleared her throat and motioned toward the door. "So. Dinner?"

Stepping back, he nodded. "Yes. Dinner."

They walked side by side as Roan walked down the side path, away from the stables. "The best way to show you my city is on foot. The way it's intended to be experienced," he said, gesturing for Orah to follow.

Orah smiled. Such a casual action for such a serious Governing God. Rushing after him, she followed him toward the city streets.

While Iluna appeared quiet compared to what she was accustomed to, she realized it was alive in the evening. To her surprise, the gray speckled buildings had their own natural glow. Roan nodded toward the building in front of them. "It's moonstone. That glow is starlight."

"Moonstone?" she asked.

He shrugged. "It's been here for a while. We've got a quarry where it's mined. Not sure how it got here but most buildings in Nacht are made from it."

Fascinated, she stared out at the city in front of her. Most shops appeared to be closed for the evening, but they were obviously walking toward the lively area. As they drew closer, she could hear laughter and the clattering of silverware against plates. Roan turned a corner and she stopped in her tracks. In front of them was a large courtyard surrounded by restaurants. Dozens upon dozens of tables scattered outside of each restaurant and there were people everywhere.

Live music danced between the tables and the people sitting at them, but she couldn't see where it was coming from. She felt as though she were back home. Like she had stepped back into her world into a joyous Parisian summer evening with Julian. Roan's hand brushed hers and she looked up at him. He had a gentle smile on his face, and he motioned for her to follow him.

She expected everyone to stop as soon as he stepped foot into the courtyard but instead, they all bowed their heads and smiled at him. Joy radiated off him as he greeted each person he passed. Some he knew by name and some he didn't, but he still made sure to greet them. She thought back on Lahana's comment about how loved and respected he was by the people in the Region.

The buildings around them twinkled with their starlight and the scattered trees in the courtyard appeared to sway with the music. Lost in the beauty of it all she felt a tug on her hand again. Moving her feet, she followed as Roan guided them through the crowd, heading toward a building in the far corner.

Expecting some kind of quiet restaurant, she stumbled when he pushed the doors open to a very lively pub. "It's loud but I promise it's the best meal you'll ever have!" Roan yelled. She nodded, barely hearing him over the laughter and songs filling the room. They barely cleared the crowd near the front of the pub when a loud cheer echoed throughout the room.

"To our Governing God!" A drunk, winged man yelled while holding up his mug. Similar cheers filled the room, and they were handed mugs of their own. Orah stared down at the drink assuming it was beer and glanced at Roan. His smile was almost overwhelming and the freckles on his face shone bright. Smiling back at him, she shrugged and chugged back a large drink. *Definitely beer.* Swallowing, she let out a gasp and wiped the foam from her lips.

Roan's answering laugh filled the room, and he copied her movement. Sound ceased and time froze as they stared at each other. His gaze made her feel as though he had found everything inside of herself that she tried to keep hidden and she jerked her head away. Suddenly, the room filled with bar songs again.

Reaching forward, he grabbed her hand. "Follow me!" he yelled, tugging her through the crowd.

Her beer sloshed as they weaved between people. Her responding laugh was almost outside of her control. Roan stopped once they reached a quieter section of the pub. "Here—we can talk now." She followed as he walked them to a table in the corner and pulled a chair out for her.

They ordered food and sipped on their drinks, observing the cheerful crowd in front of them. Orah wasn't usually a fan of beer, but the drink hit the spot for her that night. Her chest felt warm with each sip she took, and her nerves lowered until they were almost non-existent.

Her stomach grumbled loudly when their food was set down in front of them. Roan kept his eyes on her while she took her first bite. "Holy shit," she groaned with her mouth still full.

He barked out a loud laugh and the sound vibrated down to her toes. "See I told you!" Roan yelled. She couldn't hold back her responding smile. She'd ordered his recommendation, some kind of roasted meat in gravy over fried potatoes. It was heavy and a bit greasy, but the perfect meal to eat with a cold beer.

Leaning back against her chair she admired him. He was nothing like the serious God she'd seen at the house. While she knew he was comfortable and casual at home, in the pub he looked like he was just having fun. Like being there was all he needed to forget all his troubles.

Glancing around the room, she grinned. There were people singing, kissing, dancing, and laughing everywhere she observed. The room felt like it was breathing, and the energy thrummed through her as though it were waking her up.

She turned back to Roan, finding him staring at her while he sipped his second mug of beer. Suddenly he stood, throwing his hand out for her to take. There was a twinkle in his eye she couldn't ignore. Once their hands connected, they flew across the room, joining the other people dancing to the loud lively music.

"Roan!" she yelled, trying to get him to hear her. "Roan! I can't dance!"

Roan gripped both of her hands. "I've seen your memories, Orah. I know that's not true."

Blushing, she screamed when he grabbed hold of both of her wrists and whirled her around on the dance floor. People around them cheered and scattered to give their Governing God more room to move. The music swirled around them while her feet picked up on the rhythm. The room swirled around them while they moved around and around in a wild circle. But all she could focus on was his smile and his laugh. Even with the loud booming music filling the room, his laugh was the only sound she could hear.

His eyes sparkled again, and his grin shifted to something mischievous. Her eyes widened and she let out another scream when he grabbed her waist and lifted her high into the air. The crowd around them erupted with encouraging cheers of approval. Everyone had their eyes on them with large grins of their own plastered across their faces. Roan slowly lowered her to the ground, leaning down to whisper in her ear. "That was worth the look on your face." Laughing, she smacked him on the chest while they got lost together as the next song picked up and pulled in the lively crowd to join them.

They stumbled out of the pub a few hours later, holding each other and laughing. Orah's feet ached and her head was fuzzy from the alcohol, but she couldn't remember the last time she laughed so much. Her hand quickly found Roan's and they strolled out of the now quiet courtyard through his city's streets.

They passed several shops as they walked and every few minutes Roan stopped, pointing down a street or avenue, explaining who lived where and what shops they were walking in front of. She thought her eyes would burst from her head when they stopped in front of a dress shop and she admired the beautiful gown in the window.

His shoulder brushed against hers and he leaned down, whispering, "Like what you see?"

"It's beautiful." She cocked her head in admiration and stared at the gown for a moment. It was floor length with sleeves stopping at the top of the shoulders of the mannequin it was displayed on. The neckline was a little higher than she preferred, but the color was what caught her attention. A deep, beautiful, burgundy. A color she had been told complimented her. Shaking her head, she smiled at him. "Let's keep walking."

He grinned back at her then glanced down the street in front of them. His whole body tensed, and his hand pulled from hers.

Her smile shifted to concern. "Are you okay?"

He looked as though he wasn't breathing, and she followed his eyes to where he had his gaze locked. She could make out a large building with some kind of lot in front to park carriages. There were a few scattered around the lot and a small handful of people with luggage walking to the doors of the building.

"What is that?" She didn't like how quiet he'd gone. She reached for his hand again, but he jerked away, raking his hand through his hair.

"I didn't even think," he mumbled. "Why hadn't I thought of..." He seemed to finish his thought in his head, and she watched him unsure of what to do.

"Roan?" she touched his shoulder.

"Orah, do you want to try and go home tonight?" he asked.

Startled, she stepped back. "I thought you didn't know how to get me home."

Turning, he faced the building again and sighed. "Follow me."

Her feet refused to move from under her and she stared at him. He tugged on her hand. "Orah, follow me please."

Tears began to form, and she shook her head. "Roan, I don't understand."

Pulling her hand from his, she held it against her chest. She wasn't sure what was happening. Had he been hiding something from her? Was the carefree evening a cruel joke? Why would he have dragged her out only to mock her desire to go home?

"Orah, please don't cry. Please," he said with a near pleading tone. "The building behind me is what houses our portal." Her tears stopped and she looked past him to the doors people were now walking out of. Grabbing her hand, he squeezed. "The portal we use to go between Regions."

"Moros said your Aunt thinks the magic to travel between worlds was similar to the portal." Her words came out in a whisper.

His grip on her hand tightened. "Yes. I'm sorry. I didn't think about it until tonight. My mind feels clear for the first time in weeks and seeing the

Perambulate Building made me realize that we should at least try and see if the portal will react differently to you. I'm so sorry I didn't try when Moros first mentioned the magic being similar."

He motioned to the building again and somehow her feet moved. They walked in silence and she stared at the people coming and going from the building. Cool air hit her when he held the door of the building open for her. Stepping inside, she stared at the small line of people standing in front of a large shimmering circular shape in the middle of the room. A bright light flashed, and a man and woman stepped out from the portal. She noticed immediately they must have been somewhere cooler based on heavy coats they both wore. Her head snapped up to Roan, but his eyes were fixated on the light of the portal. He cleared his throat and everyone in the room turned to him.

There was a palpable shift in the room, something hot and radiating. Orah quickly realized it was coming from Roan. His starlight crown appeared again, and he smiled at his people. "Your Governing God requires official and classified use of the Perambulate."

As if they had no choice, everyone in the room bowed and scurried out of the front door. Roan waved his hand and the echo of the locks clicking in place vibrated against the walls. Taking her hand, he guided her toward the circle. "All you need to do is think of home before you step through. Think of your chateau. Think of your life there. Your friends. Your family."

Something inside of her screamed and pounded, yelling at her not to do as he said. She glanced at the portal then back at him. "Roan." A sob stuck in her throat. "I don't have anyone to go home to."

"Orah, no matter what you may tell yourself, you have people. I've seen people in your memories who love you," he replied gently.

Her unexpected tears ran down her cheeks, she couldn't bring herself to look at him. *Home.* She had been in his world for over two weeks now and she wasn't sure how to process the possibility of going home. He squeezed her hand. One. Two. Three.

Jumping, she gaped at him. "Why did you do that?"

"I'm not sure. Something I felt inclined to do in the moment," he replied.

Trying to push down the scream building inside of her, she took a deep breath and walked toward the portal. She could feel its warmth as she stared at the blurred wall in front of her. *Home. I want to go home.* Her feet moved to walk through but she stopped herself and turned to face him again.

"If this works, Orah, I will miss you," he said.

Before she realized what she was doing, she flung herself into his arms, kissing him on the cheek. "I'll never forget you, Roan," she whispered as she turned to face the portal again.

"I want to go home," she proclaimed loudly and walked through the portal.

Roan's heart jerked while he watched the light of the portal slowly dim and Orah fade into the distance. He wasn't sure it was going to work but as she disappeared from his sight something inside of him cracked. Standing for several minutes, he watched the portal. He couldn't feel her emotions or her warmth. Her familiar warmth that had called to him every day since she walked into his world. Sighing, he watched the portal one last time before turning to unlock the doors to allow his people back in. He stepped forward when suddenly someone slammed into his back.

Whirling around, he found Orah on her knees, staring at the floor. Her tears hit the marble and he rushed to her. "What happened?"

"I wanted to go home. I swear I wanted to go home. I was flying toward a bright light and caught a glimpse of my chateau again but then I was heading toward your manor. I couldn't stop how fast I was flying and could see my chateau fading into the distance. Then I was here again." A small laugh escaped her, and he stared, unable to hide his shock. Something happened, he wasn't sure what; the portal had shown her world, but something prevented her from being able to return. "Can I help you up?"

She nodded her head, and he looped his arm under hers, pulling her to her feet. She swayed a bit and gazed up at him. Her tears had stopped but he wasn't sure if they would come back or not. "Thank you for trying," she whispered as she steadied herself.

Keeping his hold on her, he guided them to the doors. They were silent while he waved his hand, unlocking them again and letting his people enter the building once more.

The walk back to the house was long and quiet and she didn't say a word. He wasn't sure what he could have said that would have helped how she was feeling. They approached the house and she paused for a moment. Her sadness washed over him before she moved her feet to walk again. The air was heavy and thick as she passed him, opening the side door. A noise in the kitchen pulled his attention and he glanced inside, finding Jes sitting at the table.

Jes gestured to Orah. Shaking his head, Roan put up his hand letting Jes know to stay where he was.

Roan remained close behind her while she walked toward the stairs. She hadn't spoken a word in over half an hour, and he was beginning to grow concerned. He didn't want her to hide herself in her room for another week. She reached the stairs and stopped, turning back to him. The sound of her voice startled him and he took a step back.

"I know it didn't work tonight, but thank you for thinking of it," she said.

"Orah, of course. I should have thought to try sooner and I'm sorry that I didn't."

She stared up to the hall leading to their rooms then back to him. "Will you stay with me tonight?"

His mouth hung open in surprise. He panicked for a moment, hoping she knew nothing he had done that evening had any attached expectations. She chuckled, shaking her head. "Not like *that*. I just—I don't want to be alone right now. I'm afraid I won't come out of my room in the morning if I'm alone."

Understanding what she was asking, he nodded, and she turned back toward the stairs. They walked in silence again, stopping at her door. He tried to control his thoughts about what it meant to be invited into her room. He had of course been in the room itself, but he hadn't gone in since it was *her* room.

She looked at the door then back at him. The emotions coming from her made it difficult for him to control his thoughts. She had no idea how much he could feel from her when she let her mind wander. Trying to hide his smile, he scolded himself for how liberal he'd been with teasing her whenever he noticed it. She let him know what she thought about his teasing in the library though. *Fates, did she let me know.* Clearing his throat, he tried to move his mind from the memory as she turned the handle.

There was something different about the room now that she was in it. Something brighter and sweeter. He smiled at the little piles of mess in almost every section of the room. He wasn't sure why the wards hadn't picked everything up but something about it felt so much like her that he hoped the wards never touched it.

She pointed to the bed. "I'm going to go get changed in the closet. You can lay down on that side. Remember, just sleep and companionship tonight. Nothing else, Roan." Nodding, he watched her walk into the closet, closing the door behind her.

His heart beat frantically while he kicked off his shoes and climbed under the covers. Even the bed was warmer than usual. He considered what effect she had on the wards when she walked out of the closet.

He was sure his heart stopped, and a gasp slipped from his lips while he took her in. She was wearing a dark red, long night gown, with straps almost as thin as what she had been wearing earlier. His breathing grew quicker and he reminded himself that she only asked him to be there to provide her companionship. Shaking his head, he recounted his conversation with Jes and how much he could *not* afford to be distracted.

He shifted in the bed, giving her more room and she smiled at him while she climbed under the covers. She slid next to him until they laid shoulder to shoulder.

"No funny business tonight, sir," she whispered.

His head snapped toward her and he let out a laugh. She *was* teasing him. He knew his eyes flared in response and she gasped, staring into them for a moment.

He sank further into the bed, making sure not to look at her when he responded. "Trust me, Orah. I won't touch you without your permission. Or unless you're begging me to."

Her responding gasp sent a shiver down his spine and she turned her back to him. Glancing out of the corner of his eye, he watched her for a moment. The way she lay made her appear frail. Nothing like the woman who walked around his home with her head held high. The image tugged on his heart and he slid a little closer to her.

"No touching," she snapped.

"I'm not. Just providing that companionship you asked for," Roan replied, holding back a laugh.

Orah's back was now inches from him, and he tried to steady his breathing. He was almost sure she had fallen asleep when her voice startled him.

"Roan?"

"Yes?"

"I know I said no touching. But—" His heartbeat quickened, unsure of what she was about to ask. "But can you just hold me? I feel like I just need to be held right now."

He nodded, but then realized she couldn't see behind her. "Yes, Orah, of course."

She shifted, turning so that she was facing him. He held back his gasp at the tears staining her cheeks. He hadn't felt any emotion from her or heard her make a sound. The fact she could make herself so numb and quiet made his chest hurt. Holding out his arm, he motioned for her. She slid until her cheek was resting on his chest and his arm was wrapped around her. He stared down, marveling at how well they fit together. Like two puzzle pieces finding their way to each other again.

"You know you don't have to hide when you cry," he whispered, stroking her hair.

She jolted, gripping his shirt in her hand. "It's a habit I picked up when I was a kid."

"What could have possibly made it so you hid your cries as a child?"

"Everything," she whispered as her tears formed a puddle on his shirt.

"Hey, it's okay." He moved his hand from her hair and rubbed her back. Trying his best to remind her she wasn't alone, that she was okay. Her body shook for a few minutes before she stilled. Suddenly her head popped off his chest and she stared at him. "Did you know your freckles glow in the dark?"

Raising his brow, he chuckled. "Of course I knew that but no one has ever said anything about it to me. I'm not sure why. I think it's pretty badass." She smiled, laying her head back on his chest.

"I agree," Orah said.

His hand continued rubbing her back while her breathing shifted to long and slow movements. The slowing sound of her breath and the feeling of her against him weighed against his eyelids. His hand stopped rubbing her back and he instinctively held her closer to him as he drifted off to sleep.

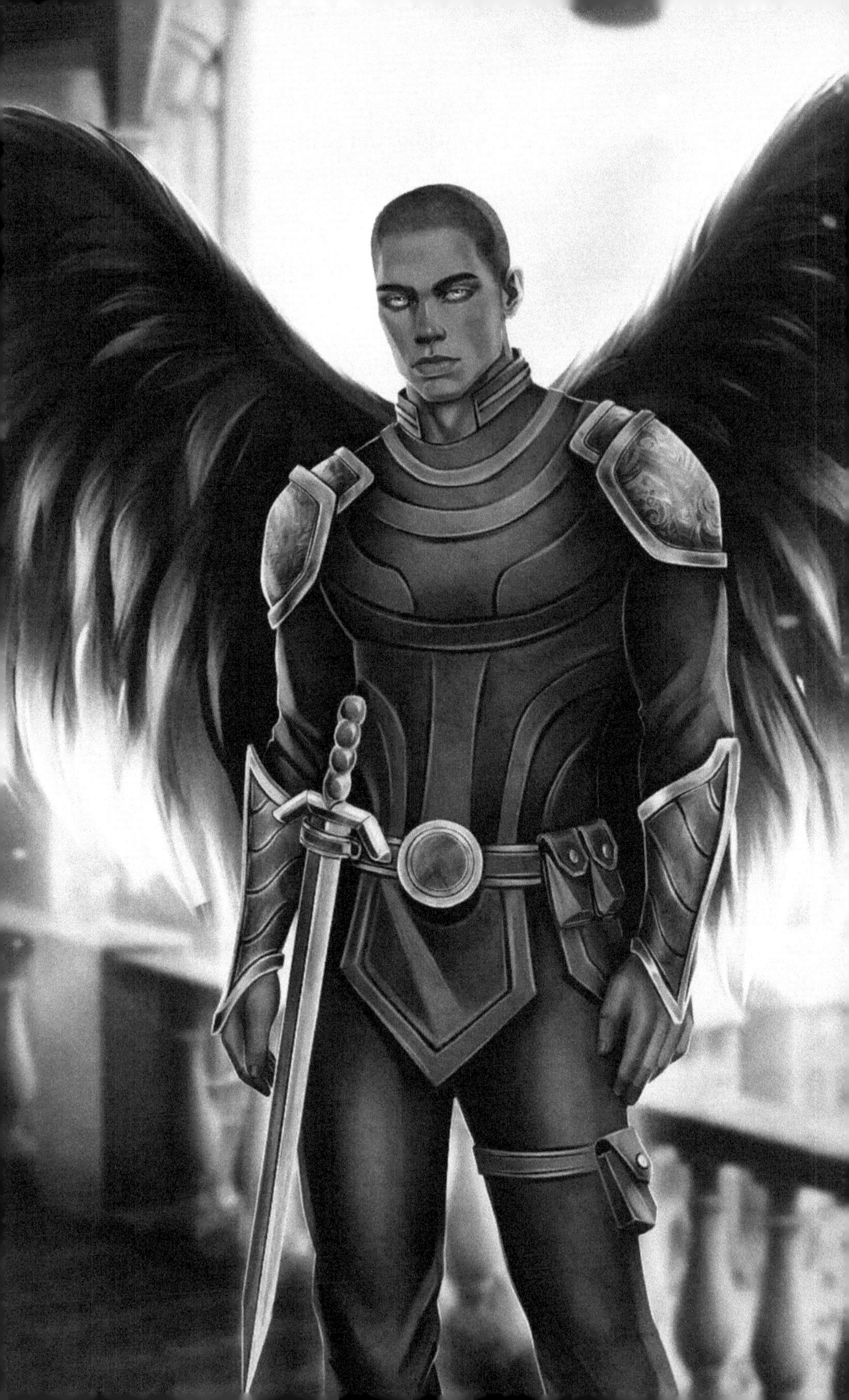

Chapter 15

Orah woke up warm. No light shone through the curtain, but she was so comfortable she didn't care what time it was. She shifted, realizing her cheek was still resting against Roan's chest. His breathing was deep and slow, telling her he was still sleeping. Carefully, she sat up, finding his freckles also glowed while he slept. She stared down at him before she looked away quickly. *I asked him to stay the night.* She wasn't sure what had come over her. All she knew last night was that she didn't want to be alone.

As quietly as she could, she climbed off the bed and slipped into the closet. Her pajama choice had been intentional. She knew she wasn't going to let anything happen between the two of them, but given how much he constantly teased her, she felt like returning the favor. She stared in the mirror for a moment and cursed herself for being so immature.

Based on how awake she felt, she assumed it was close to the time she usually got up while she slipped into her workout clothes. Quietly, she pulled the closet door open, finding Roan still asleep on the bed. "Thank God," she murmured as she slipped past him and out the bedroom door.

The house was dark and quiet when she exited her room and the floorboard lights flicked on as she walked. Last night had been a whirlwind and she needed to clear her head. While the pub had been more fun than she had had in months, the portal was heartbreaking and confusing. She hadn't expected the blinding light when she went through. She hadn't expected to see her chateau off in the distance or that the closer she'd gotten the farther away it had felt. What was most unexpected had been when she was screaming, "I want to go home," and the manor house appeared in front of her instead.

She didn't know what any of it meant and she wasn't sure she wanted to think about it all. Reaching the kitchen, she peeked inside. Yohan wasn't there and she realized she must have been up earlier than she thought. The sun was barely rising as she pulled open the side door and made her way to the garden.

She made her way across the lawn and stood in front of the garden door. Even from where she stood, she could sense the heat of the metal as she approached and glared at it. "You stupid piece of shit," she muttered.

The door mocked her every morning, beckoning her with warmth but refusing to respond to her touch again. Narrowing her eyes on the handle she knew she wasn't going to break down any wards, but she *was* going to get the door to open.

Breathing out, she gripped the handle and pushed. The metal groaned and resisted. Bracing her feet against the grass, she pushed with all her strength. Screaming while the door wiggled in defiance. Over and over again with no results.

Wind kicked up around her and she fell back as Jesiel landed on the ground, inches from her. He appeared to still be in his pajamas, and he looked pissed.

"Orah." Jes's wings flared out behind him and he stalked toward her. She wasn't sure whether to stay where she was or if she should have stood and ran. "Every day for almost a week you get up and try this door." He pointed at the door, staring into her eyes. "Every day for almost a *week* you wake me up by coming out here and messing with this door."

Rolling her eyes, she scoffed, "I can be quieter when I walk past your room." She didn't know what his problem was.

"Oh no, you're essentially as quiet as a mouse when you leave the house but those wards being messed with—those are *very* loud," he bit back, stalking closer to her.

"What are you talking about?"

Yelling, he threw up his hands. "Fates, I forget you come from somewhere with no magic. These wards are connected to *me*, Orah. I am in charge of maintaining them. Any changes in them, anyone trying to break them down alerts me. In my head, like a dozen bells going off telling me that our defenses are being attacked. Do you understand what I'm saying to you?"

Eyes widening, she glanced back at the door and then back at him. "Oh." Every day she had been going out there to test the door she'd been setting off a security alarm in his head. "Is that also why you've been up and in the training room at the same time as me every morning?"

His eyes flashed and he let out a laugh. "Yes, Orah. You wake me up with a dozen bells in my head. There's nothing else better to do with my time than train. I may be Roan's Captain, but I don't usually enjoy getting up right when the sun rises."

"Okay, well I'll make sure I don't try the door until later in the evening," she snapped.

"Oh no. I don't think so. Follow me. Right now." Turning, he walked back toward the house.

Watching him go, she contemplated whether or not she had to listen to him. She didn't have any duty or reason to do as he said, but at the same time he was terrifying, and she didn't want to face his wrath. Sighing, she ran after him, catching up right as he flung the side door open.

"You could try and not wake everyone up, you know," she whispered.

He tensed before turning to face her. "Everyone? You mean, Roan? Who, if I remember correctly, is still asleep in *your* bed."

Glaring at him, she placed her hand on her hip. "That's none of your business."

"Everything Roan does is my business. Whether you like it or not," he replied.

He stalked down the hall, heading toward the training room. When he reached the door, he threw it open, slamming it against the wall with a loud bang, then pointed for her to go inside.

"I'm not going in there with you unless you tell me why." She leaned against the wall determined to hold her ground.

"We're going to train, Orah. I'm going to show you how you can practice whatever it is you're practicing every day in a way that won't abruptly wake me up."

"Fine," she said as she pushed off the wall and sauntered into the room. She tried to hold her confident composure but jumped when he slammed the door behind him. He motioned for her to go to the ward pad.

"Prick your finger and think about that door outside. Imagine it. Think about how you can't open it and how it looks, feels, or even smells when you try."

Skeptical, she did what he said. The moment her blood touched the ward pad she stepped back in awe watching the room shift. Every last piece of equipment in the room disappeared, leaving the room empty, replaced by the exact replica of the garden door now sitting in the middle of the floor. Jesiel cleared his throat behind her and she turned back to face him.

"Now go try and open it," he said sternly.

"What?"

"I can tell you right now that the door in front of us is not warded like the one outside. You could imagine ten of these filling the room and it won't wake me up if you tried to open each one." He motioned for her to step forward.

She walked toward the door. It wasn't quite as warm as the one outside, but she still felt as though it were calling to her. Slowly, she grabbed the handle and turned the knob, but nothing happened. The handle locked at the turn of her hand. Cursing, she shoved against the door, but it didn't budge.

She fell to the ground in defeat. "This isn't doing anything."

"You need to practice. You need to know what you're practicing for, Orah. What are you trying to accomplish by getting this door open?" Jesiel asked.

Her chest tightened and she stared at the door in front of her. "I—I don't know. I don't know if I'm trying to prove a point. I don't know if I actually believe I can go home the way I came. But I just feel like I have to try to do something every day."

She jumped when his voice softened behind her. "I understand that, but you can't force something if you're not ready for it."

Her defenses became more alert and she turned to him "What do you mean if I'm not ready for it?"

"That wasn't an insult, Orah. Just an observation. There's something blocking you and you're not going to accomplish anything with your power unless you face it. I'm not even sure if you'd be able to get home once you've faced it, but you sure won't be able to do anything with it until then." His eyes moved toward the door leading out to the hall.

Her eyes followed him, finding Roan leaning against the door frame with an amused smile. "Can either of you explain to me why there's a door in the middle of the training room?"

Shaking his head, Jesiel walked up behind Roan, smacking him on the back and glancing back at her. "Ask Orah. I'm going back to bed." Orah kept her eyes on him as he left the room then looked back at Roan. There wasn't much she wanted to explain to him, so she merely shrugged.

Roan walked further into the room. The air thickened and she remembered she'd spent the night sleeping in his arms. Hoping to break the awkward tension she smiled at him. "How did you sleep?" Her cheeks flushed in response to the question that came from her.

"I slept great. What about you?" he replied, stepping closer to her.

Avoiding his gaze, she focused on the floor. "Like a baby."

Pressure brushed against her toes and she found him so close their feet were almost on top of each other. His eyes twinkled. "Great." Stepping back, he observed the room. "Were you planning on training this morning?"

"Uh, yeah."

"May I join you?"

The question startled her. She'd been coming down to the training room every day for nearly two weeks and he hadn't once joined her. She stepped back, considering whether or not she wanted to work out with him. His large frame was an obvious display of someone who worked out regularly and while she was strong, she didn't believe she could keep up with him. Her eyes traveled down the length of his body then back up to the large appreciative grin on his face.

"Well?" he asked.

Blushing, she nodded her head. "Um. Yeah. I guess that's fine."

He smiled but surprised her when he turned to walk out of the room. "Where are you going?" she asked, her curiosity now piqued.

Waving his hand behind him as a gesture for her to follow, he yelled back, "Oh, I thought we could go for a *ride*." Her eyes widened and she scoffed at his emphasis of his last word as she hurried after him.

They approached the stables the same moment Kai walked out with a wheelbarrow full of hay. Roan tilted his chin down. "Good morning, Kai. Orah and I are going to go for a ride. Could you please prepare Nacht and Tume?"

Kai's eyes darted between them and a smile spread across his face. "Of course, My Lord."

Her mouth hung open and she turned to Roan. "A Pegasus? You expect me to ride a Pegasus?"

The grin on his face seemed to be frozen in place. "What, are you not up for the challenge? We could go back to the training room and just follow your regular routine." He said the last sentence as if it were an insult and she glared at him. They stood there, keeping eye contact until Kai returned with the saddled Pegasi.

Pulling his eyes from Orah, Roan turned. "Thank you very much, Kai." Glancing at Orah again, he smiled while he approached the animals. "Tume, this is Orah. I believe you've met." He motioned with his hand for her to come forward. For a brief moment she considered going back inside, but Tume stared at her as if in greeting and she approached the both of them.

Roan kneeled down, cupping his hands together. "Step here and I'll help you up."

Orah could sense Kai staring at her and she knew it was time for her to show she was braver than she felt. Sighing, she stepped into Roan's hand. He lifted her up and she swung her leg over Tume's back. Nestling into the saddle, she couldn't help but notice how comfortable it was. Looking down, she cocked her head, observing the lap belt hanging at the sides.

"Buckle up," Roan said, patting Tume's neck. Leaning down, Orah heard his soft whisper for the Pegasus. "Good girl."

Keeping her eyes on Roan, Orah quickly secured her lap belt. Roan mounted Nacht with impressive ease and glanced at her for a moment before his grin appeared again. "Since you're new to all of this I will direct Nacht and Tume. Just hold onto the reins and don't unbuckle."

"What happens if I unbuckle?" she replied.

They were just going for a ride. While Lahana had told her the animals were dangerous, she didn't believe they would mindlessly trample her.

Roan's eyes lit up with amusement and he gazed up toward the sky. "Well, then I'd have to catch you." He leaned down, whispering something to Nacht. Before Orah could question what he meant, Tume reared back barreling up into the sky.

Orah's screams were swallowed by the wind whipping around them. The cold air pulled tears from her eyes. Blinking repeatedly, she tried to clear them, hoping her vision would adjust. The rush of air from large wing beats to the right of her caught her attention and she turned her head, finding Roan sitting confidently on top of Nacht. *Follow me*, he mouthed as Nacht dove toward the ground. Tume followed and Orah's screams were all she could hear before the Pegasus evened out and coasted a few hundred feet above the city.

Wiping the tears running down her cheeks, Orah glanced around her. The wind wasn't as harsh at that height and she turned at the sound of Roan's voice. "Beautiful, isn't it?"

She nodded, taking in the sight. The city was like a sparkling gem nestled into large mountains. She wasn't sure how she hadn't noticed them before, given their large, dark, almost purple, and imposing magnificence. Not far from the city walls, a large glittering building caught her eye. Pointing at the building, she looked over at Roan. "What's that?"

His head turned to where she pointed. "That's my uncle Aeron's palace. It's where he ruled when he was God of Nyte and where I spent a large part of my childhood." They sat, hovering above the city while Roan was seemingly lost in his thoughts as he stared at the palace in the distance. Suddenly, he shook his head and turned back to Orah. "I wanted to show you something." His heels kicked into Nacht's side and the Pegasus turned, flying toward the mountains.

Tume huffed. Smiling, Orah patted her neck softly. "Yeah, I think he's a showoff too." The Pegasus huffed again in response, heading in the direction Nacht and Roan had gone.

Orah couldn't contain the emotions that bombarded her as the mountains grew nearer. The mountains didn't just look purple, they *were* purple. Or more so a mix of purples, blues, and black. Roan and Nacht stopped ahead for Tume to catch up but Orah couldn't pull her eyes from the beauty in front of her. Catching up to Roan, they continued forward, and large trees appeared in the distance as the Pegasi began their descent.

Orah loved flying. Hoping on an airplane and going off on an adventure had always been thrilling but this—this was something else. Her hair whipped around her as the wind kissed at her neck. Her skin was cold but warm at the same time and she couldn't help but imagine how much better the experience would be at night. She stared down to where the Pegasi were descending, finding massive, black trees nestled in a meadow of lavender grass.

Her words stuck in her throat. "Roan." She couldn't get out what she wanted to say. The image below was as if she were in a painting. Nothing felt real and she wasn't confident she wasn't still in her bed sleeping. Roan smiled and hopped off Nacht. The Pegasus huffed and walked toward the other side of the meadow to graze on the grass. Orah unbuckled, deciding to hop down herself, but forgot how large Tume was and tumbled into Roan's arms.

Laughing, they fell to the ground. His arms wrapped around her waist and she landed on top of his chest. His chest slowly moved up and down against her and they stared down at each other. Time felt as though it stopped while they held their gazes. His hands were warm against her and she smiled thinking of how warm she felt when she woke up that morning. Blinking, Roan jumped, causing her to slide off his chest.

"What's wrong?"

He blinked again, staring at her. "You just glowed. Like a candle."

She peered down at herself but couldn't see what he was referring to. While she knew *what* he was referring to, she didn't look any different. "I'm not glowing."

Shaking his head, he stood. "No, you *did*. Briefly for less than a second your whole body lit like a candle." His hand extended out for her to grab onto and he pulled her up out of the grass.

"Oh."

A grin spread across his face. "What were you thinking about, Orah?"

Orah's cheeks warmed and she considered deflecting him but changed her mind. Flipping back her hair, she shrugged. "Nothing really spectacular. Just noticing how warm your hands are."

His startled gasp almost broke the stoic expression she was trying to keep on her face, and they made eye contact. Her lips tightened and she balled her fists at her side. His lips tightened in response and he broke first, laughing loudly. She couldn't hold her composure at the infectious sound and they sat in the empty meadow, laughing until their stomachs hurt.

"I like teasing you," he said while lightly bumping her shoulder with his own.

"Same," she replied while observing the meadow, taking a deep breath in. The air was just as magical as the scene in front of her. "So... are all the trees and grass in this land this color?"

"Of course not. You've seen my garden." Roan walked forward, motioning for her to follow. He walked to the middle of the meadow and to her shock, he pulled out a large blanket and basket from the bags attached to Nacht's saddle. Orah stopped in her tracks.

"Where did those come from?"

"These?" Shrugging, he sat down on the banket and set the basket out in front of him. "Oh, Kai gathered these and put them in Nacht's saddle bag before he brought the Pegasi out to us."

She wanted to question how Kai gathered what appeared to be a well thought out picnic but decided to just enjoy the moment. "So—the trees and the grass. Care to explain further?" she asked.

"The belief is they're this color to try and mimic the night sky. Considering we're in the Region of Nacht, the magic seems to make the landscape match the Region better. Here in the mountains, the trees are black and the grass different shades of purples, blues, and black. You can barely see the mountains from a distance at night. They completely blend in with the sky."

"What about the other Regions?"

"Oh, not every Region has mountains. There are many, yes, but not every one. Take Veturs for example—Moros's Region. It has large mountains with silver and white trees and grass that all have a layer of snow, however, Zomner has no mountains. At least nothing grand and large, more like hills. But what Zomner does have are lakes, rivers, and streams every few miles and it juts up against the coast. A perfect Region landscape to balance against its regular heat."

She listened intently, picking up a piece of cheese from the picnic in front of them. "This world sounds incredible."

"It is. Honestly, Nacht is just a small part of this beautiful and vast world. Maybe I'll take you to see it all one day." He shifted and looked over to her. "That is if we're not able to get you home and you want to see it all."

Her heart thumped in response. "But I'm going to go home. Right?" she asked, glancing at him.

Nodding, he stared out across the meadow. "That's the plan." Leaning back against his hands he observed the sky. "Now that I've told you about my world, I want to hear more about yours."

"What?" she asked, completely thrown off guard.

"Your world. I want to know more. You give us little bits of information when Clarah asks, but now *I'm* asking," he replied.

"Oh." Biting her lip, she thought for a moment. "We have phones."

Phones? That's all you can come up with?

"Phones?" His head turned to her and his brow lifted.

"Yeah." Orah laughed. "They're these little devices that fit in your hand and you can call anyone you want or text them. Most people prefer texting now."

Roan shook his head. "I have no idea what any of that means."

Laughing again, Orah began her tale, teaching the God of Night in the Land of Gods all about technology and phones. She explained that while his world used portals and messengers to send word to someone, in her world you can pick up the small device and connect with another person in an instant.

Roan's eyes widened with each explanation. He asked if you were required to pick up. He asked if anyone could reach you. He asked how you protected yourself from those you didn't want to reach you, a not-so-subtle nod to his relationship with his Father and brother.

And Orah explained it all, realizing she'd spent over two weeks trying her best not to think of home. Filling her days with hands-on work because she didn't have the technology to distract her. Her eyes lined with tears, realizing how desperately she wanted to curl up and watch a comfort show on the television.

Roan startled at the tears. "Are you alright?"

Orah nodded her head and wiped her eyes dry. "Yes, just missing home."

Roan grew quiet at her mention of home and motioned to the meal in front of them, encouraging her to eat. A cool breeze whirled around them and she watched as it caught his hair, tossing it playfully. Together they ate, watching Nacht and Tume graze on the lavender grass. The morning sun glistened above them, providing warm and comfortable heat. Orah sighed, stretching out on the grass and admired the sky. Roan shifted next to her, joining her.

"Did you ever try to find shapes in the clouds when you were a kid?" Her eyes scanned the sky above them. All she could see was an open blue portrait above her.

"Not so much when I was a kid, but definitely after Lahana was born. She was always admiring the sky," Roan replied.

Leaning up on her elbow, Orah turned to face him. "How does the aging thing work? Are you a child for the same amount of time as a mortal and then you just don't age anymore after a certain point?"

"Essentially, most mortals are considered adults at twenty-one. Gods aren't considered adults until about fifty, but our aging slows to almost nothing between twenty-five and thirty-five. It really just depends on the person," Roan replied.

"So, you were an adult when Lahana was born. How old was Marek when you were born?"

"Marek is only fifteen years older than me. It was quite the shock that my mother convinced my father to have us both so close together."

"So, you grew up as kids together, at least for a bit?"

Nodding, he didn't remove his gaze from the sky. Something tense and uncomfortable settled between them and she turned, deciding the topic was too sensitive to keep asking questions. They laid in silence admiring the blue sky for a while. Eventually she shifted, laying her head on his shoulder, and drifted off to sleep under the warmth of the sun.

✦

"Orah." Warm hands shook her. She didn't want to move. She was too comfortable with the sun warming her like a heavenly blanket.

"Orah, I'm sorry but we've got to go now." Opening her eyes, she found her head against Roan's chest.

She sat up. "Oh! Oh, I'm sorry!" The heat of the sun told her it was much later in the day than when they'd arrived in the meadow. She shook her head, embarrassed she had slept for so long.

Sitting up, Roan laughed. "There's nothing to apologize for. I fell asleep too, but I think I've probably missed some pretty important meetings today, so we should head out."

"I didn't mean to keep you from your day."

"Oh, it's alright. Sometimes you need to ignore your responsibilities." Throwing his hand up in a stretch, he stood then grabbed her hand and pulled her up with him. When they were ready to go, she looked out at the meadow, holding her hand against her chest, trying to soften the sad weight that settled there.

"I don't know if I'll ever get to come back here again," she whispered.

Turning back to Roan she found him smiling at her. "I'll try and bring you here again soon. Even if it's the last thing we do before you head home."

Nacht and Tume approached and Roan crouched the same way as before to help her onto the saddle. Her body ached and she chuckled, not realizing how many muscles she had used when riding to the meadow. Roan mounted Nacht and turned back to her. "Ready?"

Patting Tume's neck, she smiled back at him. "Ready." Tume reared back, launching into the air and instead of a terrified scream she let out a triumphant yell. She didn't know how much longer she would be in the Land of Gods, but she decided in that moment that she would savor every minute she had left.

The flight back to the Manor was short. Kai came running out of the stable to greet them. The smile on his face made Orah chuckle while Roan helped her off Tume. She groaned and stretched, appreciating the small ache in her legs and back. They walked beside each other toward the house when Jesiel came out of the side door.

"Look who we have here!" Jes yelled loudly. "Mr. Governing God who apparently forgot he's the Governing God today." Roan shook his head while Jesiel sprinted toward them.

"Sometimes even Governing Gods need a day off, you know." Roan smiled, shoving Jesiel lightly.

Gasping, Orah stepped back as Jesiel grabbed hold of Roan, putting him in a headlock. They spun around in circles with Jesiel holding Roan and Roan's arms flared out in a frenzy, trying to hit Jesiel. Their laughter was near contagious and Orah couldn't help but smile while watching them.

"Alright! Alright!" Roan yelled, hitting Jesiel in the stomach. "I yield!" With a laugh Jesiel released him and grinned triumphantly.

Turning to Orah he smiled. "Wanna spar, Orah?"

Stepping back, she gawked at him. "What?" Jesiel was massive, and if anything, that was an understatement.

He kept his eyes on her for a moment before he laughed. "I'm only joking. I think you might actually break if we tried."

The arrogant nature of his comment irked her, and she crossed her arms. "You don't know that."

"Is that a challenge?" he replied with a wink.

She glanced nervously at Roan, who had a very wide and almost childlike smile on his face as he looked back and forth between her and Jesiel.

"Well?" Jesiel prodded.

"Maybe another day," she replied as indifferently as she could, moving to step around him. Cool air rushed around them and he blocked her movement.

"No, I think we should try. What do you think, Roan?"

Roan's smile had somehow gotten wider and he shrugged. "I mean..."

"You mean what?" Orah yelled. She was confident there was no possibility where she could beat Jesiel. She may have known where to hit a man, but she knew he would never let her get close enough to try.

Laughing, Roan approached them. "Alright, Jes, I think we've teased Orah enough."

They both glanced at each other, then at her, grinning wide. Jesiel's eyes twinkled and he shrugged. "Yeah, I don't think she's up for the challenge." He turned to walk back toward the house and Orah's anger took over in response to his comment. Pulling back her leg, she kicked him in the back of the knee, and watched his large frame crash to the ground. Roan fell back, holding his stomach howling with laughter as Jesiel bolted upward, glaring at Orah.

"I guess you shouldn't underestimate me." She shrugged and rushed through the side door. Smiling, she walked into the kitchen to help Yohan, listening to Roan's laugh behind her. "She got you, man. Fates, you should have seen your face."

Chapter 16

Two weeks quickly turned to four. Orah wasn't sure how the time was passing right before her eyes. She had felt similar before she left Boston. The months after finding the listing for the chateau came and went in a blink of an eye, and before she knew it, she was leaving her old life behind for a new one.

She'd stopped visiting the garden in the morning now that she could have the training room wards create a door. About a week went by where she seemed to no longer be waking Jesiel up when he surprisingly met her at the training room door one morning. He grumpily mumbled something about how she may have eternally messed with his sleep schedule and they'd both shuffled into the room side by side. Together, they set the wards but after they kept to themselves.

To Orah's dismay, she had yet to get a single door open in the last two weeks. Every day she tried, and every day she ended up giving up out of frustration and resetting the wards for her usual work out. She expected more sass and opinions from Jesiel, but she had gotten neither so far. She'd felt him watching her plenty of times though.

Pulling back her hair, she headed out of her bedroom, ready for her work out. She paused at Lahana's door as she passed. Lahana had only been home for a few days during those recent weeks. She appeared to be completely enamored by her lover and spent the few days she was home talking about her non-stop. "Fawn this," and "Fawn that." Roan, to Orah's surprise, actually snapped at Lahana at dinner her first night back, asking if there was anything or anyone else in her life that she could talk about. Lahana's answering grin was enough to shut him up again and they all sat quietly listening to her continue her recount of her visit and time away.

Personally, Orah didn't find anything wrong with Lahana recounting her tales. She may or may not have been living vicariously through Lahana.

She and Roan were still spending at least an hour a day reading next to one another, but nothing had progressed. She hadn't invited him back to her bedroom again and he hadn't invited her out again.

A dull pulse of disappointment thrummed through her and she peeked back at his door. She knew he wasn't avoiding her. Things were progressing with his party planning and he spent hours every day in the city center with his officials. Jesiel had also made sure to remind everyone, on a daily basis, that the challenge was approaching, and Roan had to put as much of his focus there as he could.

She didn't know what they were doing to prepare and hadn't dared to ask. Everything surrounding Roan's magic and this challenge was an obvious secret he preferred to keep locked down.

Orah rushed down the stairs and rolled her eyes when she found Jesiel standing outside the training room door. Approaching him she tried to push the door open when he slid, blocking her.

Scoffing, she put her hand on her hip. "Excuse me." She was irritated now not knowing what his issue was.

"You're excused," he said casually leaning further into the door and completely blocking the handle.

"I'm trying to get in there."

"I know," he replied.

"So move." Orah bit back.

"No."

"What is your problem today?" The words come out louder than she intended them to and she looked around, hoping Roan wasn't awake yet.

"I have no problem. I just think it's time you and I talk about how complacent you're getting."

Her eyebrows shot up and she stared at him. "What?"

"You heard what I said. You've grown complacent," he replied with a sneer.

"Jesiel, I have no idea what your problem is today and why you woke up on the wrong side of the bed, but please move." She shoved him, but he didn't budge.

He shrugged. "I'm not moving until you at least admit I'm right."

"I have not grown complacent." Her cheeks warmed in response to the anger boiling inside of her. He had no idea what he was talking about. She was in that room trying every single day. What else did he want from her?

"Yes. You. Have." His glare burned through her and they stood as if facing off before a fight.

"Move," she demanded.

"No."

"Move your big feathery ass out of my way, now."

A smirk flashed across his face, but he still didn't budge. "I'm not going anywhere."

She let out a frustrated yell and moved to lean against the wall opposite from him. "Why do you have a problem with me?" She needed to understand what she could have done to make the man act so irritated with her constantly.

"You're a threat to Roan."

"A threat?" She had to push down her laugh. "Please explain how *I'm* a threat."

"You're impulsive but also guarded. You have all this power just brewing under the surface and there is no way to tell how it will manifest when you finally let it out. He feels something for you—which in and of itself makes him weaker than he was before you got here." She stared at him when he finished, unsure whether she should laugh or cry.

Pushing off the wall she approached him. "One—I have every single right to act however the hell I want to act. If I want to be impulsive then I can be impulsive. If I want to keep things about myself private, then I can do that too. Two—I'm not sure who made you think that whatever power I have is your responsibility but it's not. Whenever or however it manifests is my own business. And three—whatever Roan feels about me is between the two of us. But I'll have you know that *I'm* making an active effort not to act on anything. There will be nothing messier than developing feelings for someone in a world I won't be coming back to once I leave." With each point she made she walked closer to him. By the time she finished she was in front of him with her finger in his face. His eyes flared and she watched him clench his jaw while he studied her for a moment, like an eagle studying its prey.

Suddenly he moved and she jumped at the sound of the door clicking open behind him. Neither of them said a word while they walked into the room and the lights flickered on.

Gasping at the sight in front of her, she took a step back. The room was an obstacle course—larger than any she had seen him come up with over the last couple weeks. She turned toward him and found him blocking the ward pad.

"I told you that you have to admit you've been complacent. While you didn't do that, you made some valid points out there, so I let you in but I'm not letting you ward another stupid door. At least not today." He leaned against the wall and watched her, waiting for her reaction.

Her stubbornness gave into her curiosity and she sighed, smacking her hands against her thighs. "How have I been complacent? Please *enlighten* me."

"You're not trying anymore," he said.

"Yes I am."

"No, you are not, Orah. You seem to forget I'm watching you every single day. I watch you ward the door into existence, I watch you try the handle, and I've watched your determination and strength while pushing against the door loosen with each passing day." His observations hit her like a wave. He wasn't wrong when she thought about it, but she didn't know if she liked how observant he had been. It made her feel seen in a way that only Julian had made her feel.

"Well?" he asked, breaking the silence between them.

"So what if I have?" She folded her arms, shifting to a more defensive position.

"Complacency will not allow you to take control of that power. Complacency also means you stop searching for a way home. Do you not want to go home, Orah?"

She had somehow known what question he was leading up to, but she wasn't expecting the tears when the question left his lips. His feet moved, as if to come toward her, but she threw up her hands. She didn't need his comfort. She didn't need anyone's comfort. What she needed was to face the hard truth he had blatantly made her see. Breathing deeply, she wiped her tears.

"You're not wrong." She surveyed the room. The room that transformed with magic. A literal dream come true for the woman who was used to burying herself in stories of other worlds. "I don't one-hundred percent know if I want to go home. I think that's mostly because trying to find a way there feels hopeless, but I also don't know what I'm going home to."

Without realizing what she was doing, she sank to the floor and cradled her head in her hands. Movement above her caught her attention and she watched as he sat down across from her.

"Why wouldn't you know what you're going home to?" The kindness in his eyes was genuine and her defenses crumbled.

Just like Julian.

"You remind me of my friend."

"Is he also a handsome, winged man?"

Laughing, she shook her head. "No, but he has this way of knowing things about me before I do. Or even worse, knowing things I kept private and telling me he knew at the most inopportune times."

"Roan tells me it's my uncomfortable talent."

"He's not wrong," she chuckled, glancing back down at the floor. "Before I bought my chateau, I had a life. I had a job I loved and friends. Two, or actually, now three-ish months ago, I bought the chateau on a whim and decided to leave it all. You would think me randomly picking up and leaving would have shocked the people I loved, but unfortunately it didn't. The months leading up to my move, I spent isolating myself. Declining dinner invites, faking sicknesses to cancel plans, not answering calls, even going as far as pretending I wasn't home when they showed up unexpectedly." She thought back on how far she had gone to break the ties she'd formed. The relationships she had just let slip through her fingers.

She glanced at him and found Jesiel staring at her, but he wasn't looking at her with pity—no, he was looking at her as if he understood and that somehow felt worse.

"I'm not sure if there's anyone to go home to because I made sure there was almost no one left for me," she admitted.

He sighed and she watched as he leaned back against his hands. "I don't talk to my family." He laid down against the floor, resting his hands on his chest while he stared at the ceiling. "They're hard and old fashioned in some ways. I didn't even attend my own father's wake when he passed away several decades ago. Going back there, to a place I've removed myself from, scares me more than diving into the depths of Shadus." He sat up again. "What I'm trying to say, Orah, is that I understand." He stood. "But, while I haven't tried and time has strained the relationships past repair, you still have time. Several months of isolation may feel long to you, but in the grand scheme of things it's just a sliver of time."

The constant heavy weight on her chest lightened slightly. "Thank you, Jes."

A twinkle flashed across his eyes. 'Oh, don't thank me yet. Stand up."

"What?"

"I didn't ward this room with this obstacle course for nothing. You and I are going to start training together now," Jes stated.

Orah blinked, unable to come up with a response. The obstacle course was almost military and like nothing she was used to. "Jes, I don't need to train like you. I came down here to work out and move my body, not train for something big."

"What you don't seem to understand, Orah, is that just you being here is something big. Something neither Roan nor I have heard about in our lifetimes. Right now, you may be tucked away safe in his home but what happens after the challenge? What happens if you're still here after the challenge?"

They stared at each other as she stood. He had a point. A month had already come and gone, and she was still nowhere closer to getting home. While Roan spent every day buried in books trying to find answers—they still had none. This challenge was nothing insignificant and she needed to know how to take care of herself on the off-chance things got out of control.

Jes smiled when she stood, his wings flared out behind him and he settled them in a pose that reminded her of a soldier. His eyes twinkled and he glanced back at the course. "Let's begin."

✷

Orah thought she might hate Jes—no—she *knew* she hated Jes.

The cold training room floor bit against her hot body, and she couldn't seem to catch her breath. He had been barking his orders at her for a few hours now. No matter how much effort she put into trying to get through the course it didn't feel like enough.

"Get up," he demanded.

She stared up at him hovering over her. She was covered in a thick layer of sweat and he was barely winded. "I'm not moving." Folding her arms, she looked past his head up at the ceiling.

"You either get up or I'll make you get up." There was amusement in his tone that she didn't like.

Her eyes locked onto his and she glared. "You wouldn't dare."

Leaning down, he hovered above her face. "Is that a challenge?"

Fear rushed over her, realizing he would likely swing her over his shoulder. Keeping her eyes on him she stood. "Fine. Are you happy?"

"Not really, but at least you're not laying on the ground anymore," he replied as he walked back over to the wall she had been trying to climb and pointed up. "You still need to scale this wall and ring that bell on the other side. Then we're done."

"Jes, I'm tired. Can't we pick this back up tomorrow?"

"No, we can't. Tomorrow will be something different. I'm trying to push you past your comforts. You won't break this complacency if you don't push yourself."

She glanced up at the wall and then back to him. She hated that he had a point. She never moved forward in her life by staying where she was comfortable. Sighing, she walked over to the wall and took it in. She didn't understand how it fit in the room. It was several feet high with a large platform at the top. There were no ropes or anything to provide assistance to someone trying to get up to the top. The only slight advantage appeared to be that the wall itself was inclined, as though a running start was supposed to help.

Jes tapped his foot impatiently while she observed the wall. Turning back to him she crossed her arms. "If I do this then you have to answer a question."

He glanced at the wall then back at her. She didn't know if he was going to agree but he nodded his head. "Alright. I can make that deal." Smiling, she turned back to the wall and breathed in.

Her muscles protested while she considered how she would get up the wall. She didn't think she had ever pushed them this far and while she wanted to climb back into bed and have a long nap, she wanted to prove him wrong even more. Letting out her breath she backed up a few steps. A running start really appeared to be the best way to get up there.

"3. 2. 1," she muttered to herself and she sprang forward toward the wall. Her feet hit the wood and she made it about a quarter of the way up before she slammed against the smooth surface. Smacking her chin on the way down. Jes's responding grunt echoed in the room and rage filled her. She would beat this wall. She would prove him wrong.

She ran. She slipped. She hit her face. Over and over again. She could feel his eyes on her back with each attempt she made. He didn't poke fun though or say a word. As though he were waiting in anticipation to see if she could accomplish the obstacle.

Tears of frustration lined her eyes and she stepped back a few steps farther than she had with her last attempt. She screamed as she ran forward, and her feet hit the wall. Using all her remaining strength she pushed her body upwards but knew the momentum wasn't enough. Out of desperation she flung out her hand and yelped in surprise when a golden rope of light flew forward and connected to the top of the wall. "YES!" she screamed, gripping on to the rope with both hands, pulling herself up. Her feet hit the wall and she started to scale upwards. There were no sounds in the room other than the sounds of her own breathing. It took her longer than she wanted to get to the top given how tired her body was, but she made it.

Triumphantly, she smiled down at Jes and found he hadn't moved, but his mouth was dangling open. She peeked behind her, finding the wall sloped even further on the opposite side and slid down, landing ungracefully at the bottom. Ahead of her was the bell Jes mentioned and she sprinted for it. Grabbing it, she shook it as hard as she could, then gasped when the room shifted around her.

"What did you do?" Jes yelled from the other side of the wall when it suddenly vanished, and she could now see him clearly.

Scoffing, she glared at him. "I rang the bell. Like *you* told me to." She stumbled back when a set of doors slowly rose from the middle of the now empty room. Jes threw her a stern expression she couldn't translate.

"Don't touch those doors." He was obviously nervous and the hairs on her arms stood in response. Swallowing, she nodded her head.

"Come here." He pointed to the space next to him and she scurried over. She wasn't sure but she didn't believe ringing the bell had anything to do with the doors appearing in front of them.

Jes cleared his throat and turned to her. "Did you do this?"

"Do what? Conjure doors? Jes, I haven't even been able to open the fake doors in here," Orah replied.

He stared at her before turning back to the door. "I don't know what this is, but we need to get Roan." Grabbing her hand, he pulled her from the training room, slamming the door behind him.

He pointed to the ground. "Don't move. Do you understand me? Don't move from this spot. It might take me a few minutes to track him down." She nodded her head in response and watched as he sprinted down the hall.

Orah's legs groaned while she leaned against the wall, staring at the training room door. She didn't know how long Jes had been gone for, but it was certainly longer than a few minutes. A low hum called to her the longer she stared at the door. Pushing away from the wall, she glanced down the hall. She didn't know how long they were going to be and Jes technically wasn't in charge of her.

She walked toward the training room door and pushed it open. The golden doors were still in the middle of the room. The hum was stronger and the air in the room had an almost metallic taste to it. Hesitantly, she walked towards the doors and gasped at the heat coming off them.

"Like at home," she whispered, putting her hand out to feel their heat. A content sigh escaped her when her hand made contact. It was warm just like her garden door had been, but these doors weren't the same. These doors were solid gold with symbols of stars, the sun, the moon, and planets engraved around them. Taking a step back, she admired their size. They were so large they reached the top of the ceiling and each door had a handle placed right in the middle of them. Handles that hummed loudly while she stared longingly.

"There's nothing wrong with taking a peek," she whispered, grasping one of them. "Nothing wrong with it at all."

The handle turned with no resistance and the door clicked, swinging open a crack. Blood rushed to her ears and the world drowned out around her. She stared at the door in awe. *I did it. I got one of these damned things to open.* Slowly she pushed it open and stepped back. It was as though she were looking at the portal in the city center, but through the blur she could see something. She wasn't sure what it was, but she could see gold and light. Her eyes watered, not able to break her focus on the image off in the distance. Without her control her feet moved forward when suddenly hands wrapped around her waist, pulling her backward. Unsure of what was happening, she watched in horror as the door slammed shut and the doors disappeared.

"NO!" The scream tumbled out of her and she wriggled out of the arms holding her back. "What did you do?" Tears flowed down her cheeks and she fell to the ground. She glanced back up to where the doors were, finding Jesiel standing in their place. His nostrils flared and his hands fisted at his side.

"What did I do?" he demanded, walking toward her. "I told you to stay in the hall."

"You're not in charge of me!" she yelled back.

Jes stepped forward but someone's quiet groan caught her attention. She looked back, finding Roan kneeling on the ground behind her. *He's who grabbed me.* Roan glared at her, his eyes burning with obvious rage, and she stumbled. She hadn't seen that expression on his face before.

Standing and not breaking their eye contact, Roan lowered his voice. "Orah, what did you do?"

She stared at him in both shock and irritation. "What?" They both had to stop acting like she had done something. "What did I do? I finished that stupid fucking obstacle course *your* Captain forced me to do! That's what I did!"

Roan rushed toward her, grabbing both of her arms, and pinning them to her sides. The lights in the room flashed on and off and there was an almost chilling blue light surrounding him. "No, Orah! What did you do with those doors? Where did they come from? What did you *do?*" he demanded, tightening his hold on her arms.

The unexpected pressure from his hands on her shocked her. Struggling to get out of his firm grip, she stared at him. *This man better get his hands off me before I get a chance to kick his balls in.*

Her thoughts turned wild and as untamable as the fury rising within her. Her arms grew hot and Roan jumped back letting out a yelp, rubbing his hands. Staring down, she marveled at the scorch marks now on the sleeves of her shirt. He stared at his hands while the lights stopped flashing and his color returned to normal.

She glared at him. "I had nothing to do with that door appearing. I may have opened it, yes, but nothing *I* did made those doors appear." Tears of anger and frustration spilled over while she held her gaze.

How dare he touch me. How dare he grab me like that.

They all stood in silence, staring at each other. The room grew uncomfortably cold but none of them dared to move. Roan and Jes kept their eyes on Orah as if they expected her to cause some kind of destruction.

Sighing she slumped to the ground, putting her face in her hands. Jes cleared his throat and she peeked through her fingers as Roan joined her on the ground.

"Orah," Roan said.

"Don't talk to me," she replied.

"Orah."

"Roan, you do not talk to me right now. You have no right to talk to me. You grabbed me. You grabbed me as if you were going to hurt me." She looked away from him and down to the ground. She didn't know what she had seen behind the golden doors, but she wanted nothing more than to be there instead of in that room with them.

"I'm sorry," he whispered before standing. She watched him walk toward Jes, tapping him on the shoulder. Jes nodded and they both glanced at her once more before walking out the door.

Alone in the quiet room, her tears hit the floor. Her familiar numb companion wrapped her with its chill while quiet sobs came from her. *Always being grabbed. Always being hurt.* Her tears fell rapidly while she sat there in the quiet numb cocoon, unwilling to move, unwilling to allow anything to break past her protective walls enveloping her.

When her tears finally dried, she pushed herself off the floor and walked toward the door. She turned back to where the golden doors had been before walking into the hall and stumbling over a pair of legs.

"I'm sorry." Roan popped off the ground and stepped back. "I couldn't leave you alone. I need to explain."

Orah put up her hand. "I don't want an explanation. An explanation is an excuse for how you reacted."

"But Orah, those doors," Roan interjected.

She shook her head and something in her heart fractured. She didn't know what she was going to do when she left the room—until that moment. Sighing she peered down the hall toward the front door then back to him.

"I want to leave," she stated.

"I know that. I'm still trying to find out how to get you home. I just need to explain."

Putting on her bravest face, she stepped forward. "No, Roan, not home. Here. This house. I want to leave, and I want to leave as soon as I can."

Chapter 17

Stumbling backward, Roan stared at Orah unsure if he had heard her correctly. She wanted to leave him, his home. He had told her he wouldn't stop her if she ever made that decision, but he never expected her to.

"If that's what you want," he replied.

"It is." She averted her gaze.

He knew he'd made a mistake. Those doors rattled something deep inside of him and he allowed himself to lose control of his temper. He was always losing control of his temper at the worst possible times.

"Do you want to stay here in Iluna or were you hoping to go somewhere further? I could send word to Lahana and see if you could go somewhere in Spreng."

"I don't know where I want to go yet. I think right now just that purse of money you offered. If that's still an offer?"

"Yes, of course." He nodded his head, but she still refused to look at him.

Sighing she moved to walk down the hall. "Thank you."

"Orah?" He had to explain to her what had happened. He watched her body tense in response to her name, but she didn't turn around.

"Roan, whatever it is you want to say right now, please don't," she replied.

His chest tightened and he felt that thread between them strain. "Just one thing. It might take a day or two to get the money you'll need together and get you packed with whatever you want to bring, but I won't stop you from leaving." Her shoulders slumped and she nodded her head as she walked toward the stairs.

He watched her walk away but couldn't bring himself to move for a while. Jes eventually found him and motioned down the hall as a request for Roan to follow. Roan's heavy feet somehow carried him, and he followed Jes into the study. Slumping down into his chair, he covered his face with his hands and let out a sigh.

"What happened?" Jes asked.

The concern in Jes's voice irritated Roan. If Jes hadn't pushed her so hard none of it would have happened. She would have still wanted to stay. Roan would have still been able to help keep her safe.

"She's leaving," Roan responded.

"Where will she go?"

"That's up to her. She's a grown woman. I'm not her keeper."

"Roan, you can't possibly let her just go after what just happened in there."

"After what just happened? What would that be, Jes?" Roan replied, his voice rising with his anger. "Are you referring to how you pushed her like a madman or how the throne room doors to the fucking Palace of Kings somehow appeared in the middle of that room!" The room was now pitch black except for Roan. The temper he fought everyday had swallowed up the light like a ravenous monster.

"You're not wrong. I pushed her. I did. She has power, Roan. Insane power that I don't think either of us are fully aware of how deep it goes. That room was warded to that obstacle course. She didn't touch the ward pad once but somehow when she rang that bell the room shifted in response to her. I don't know if she did actually make the doors appear but we both know who they would have led to and we can't let her out there alone," Jes stated, keeping his voice calm and steady.

The light on Roan's cheeks burned his skin while he stared at Jes. His Beskermer, his brother, a man he would trust with his life. Roan breathed in and out, his head cleared, and the lights slowly faded on. His temper had already caused too many consequences and Jes couldn't be one of them.

"We don't know if He'd find her," Roan whispered, slumping against the back of his chair. He wasn't confident in his response. Power to call a portal to the City of Kings was certainly enough to catch his Father's attention.

Jes's eyebrows rose. "Roan, you know they say denial is the first sign of acceptance."

Roan chuckled. "Hopefully she just decides to stay in the city or at the very least in Nacht and we can keep an eye on her. I'm not forcing her to do anything, Jes."

Both of them were aware what had happened wasn't good. Too many possibilities existed as to what could happen next. Too many questions were left unanswered the moment she walked out of Roan's door.

Jes stood from his seat and stretched. "I'm sorry for my part in this, Roan. I made a mistake and I hope you know how sorry I am for that."

"It's not me that you owe an apology to," Roan replied.

"I know."

Roan watched Jes walk out of the office and stared at the stairs. Orah was likely up there now, packing her things. He wasn't confident how much she would end up taking, considering he provided most of it. He leaned against his chair. He'd spent a majority of his life feeling helpless against the things that occurred around him but he didn't believe he had ever felt worse than he did now.

The fear and anger he'd felt when he came through the door to the training room was blinding. Staring at those doors, he could see Erde clearly. He could see all the years he walked the halls of his Father's palace toward the throne room, through those golden doors. He wasn't positive if it even was the palace he'd seen, or if his memories from childhood had made him believe he had. He could, however, sense the portal was calling to her. Like a siren tempting a man to its cave. Shuddering, he tried to push down the thought of what would have happened if he hadn't stopped her.

He couldn't imagine the surprise she would have been for his Father. This beautiful mortal woman just waltzing into His palace without a care in the world. *He probably would have killed her on the spot.* A shiver ran down Roan's spine. It didn't matter now, they stopped her from going through. He may have broken something between them, and her anger was valid, but he stopped her. He protected her.

But you also hurt her. You grabbed her. You grabbed her as if she were one of Father's spies.

Groaning he stood and paced his study. Every instinct in him believed she was a threat. For a brief moment he'd viewed her as the enemy and treated her as such. His stomach rolled in response. *Fates, I'm a monster.* His Father's paranoia had created Roan's own where he couldn't separate real threats from his own fear.

He stopped his pacing and walked into the library. Observing the room, he found bits of Orah scattered throughout. A book left on top of a shelf, piles of blankets thrown across nearly every chair and couch, even piles of books for her to read later.

"So, I know where they are when I'm ready for them," she'd proclaimed when he'd questioned why they were left out. He'd always felt that the library was his own personal room in the house, but it never quite felt like his own. Now—now—he could only see it as Orah's.

Taking one last look, he turned and walked out of the room. He had to find Ms. Perri and let her know Orah would be leaving. He also had to gather funds for her. He wasn't sure he would be able to figure out how to get her back to her world and felt responsible to ensure she was taken care of. He had no doubt she wouldn't allow him to provide enough funds for as long as he hoped. If she decided to stay in the city, he would check with Yohan to see if he knew of anyone looking for help. Orah was a damn fine cook and Roan was confident she would be able to live comfortably working for some of the Gods in Iluna.

Leaving his office, he turned down the hall toward the kitchen but paused at the quiet cries coming down the hall. Startled by the sounds, he paused, trying not to disrupt the conversation.

"But Orah, why do you have to go?" His heart tugged from the sounds of Clarah's cries.

When did Orah come downstairs?

"I just do, Clarah. I'm sorry." The cracked sound of Orah's voice tugged on Roan's heart. Her voice was as broken up as Clarah's. He cursed himself. He did this.

"Will you at least stay in the city?" Clarah sniffed and the quiet sounds of Yohan's comforting hushing floated down the hall.

"I'm not sure. But I will promise that if I do, I'll come and visit you at home often," Orah replied.

Roan couldn't help but take note of Orah's emphasis on the word "home" and how she had made sure not to say "here." She likely had no plans to see his home again, or at the very least, never step through its doors again.

He turned back toward the foyer to find Ms. Perri. Orah probably wouldn't allow Ms. Perri to help her pack but Roan knew this housekeeper needed to be made aware the wards to Orah's room could be reset in a few days. A noise in the hall behind the sitting room ventured down toward him and Roan followed it to the training room. He was surprised when he found Ms. Perri standing in the middle of the room making little tsk noises while she surveyed the room.

"Ms. Perri?" he asked, stepping into the room.

"Roan, when are you going to start calling me Etta again?" Something in the sad almost disappointed way she smiled at Roan told him she already knew Orah was leaving.

"Etta was what I called you as a young boy running after you for entertainment when my uncle wasn't home," he responded.

Ms. Perri had been his mother away from home, but as he grew older the comfort of addressing her by her first name had somehow become uncomfortable. Roan placed himself next to her then glanced around the now empty room. There wasn't one piece of equipment out, but the air was heavy. As if all the oxygen had been sucked out and was slowly being replenished.

Quietly, his voice barely above a whisper, he spoke, "Did Orah tell you?"

"No, Jes did," Etta replied.

Roan nodded. No one would have known the relationship Jes had with Etta. If she had been Roan's mother away from home as a child, she had become Jes's mother as an adult. Roan smiled at her. On the outside Etta appeared hard and stern, but the woman had a heart practically made of gold.

His voice stayed a whisper as he glanced at the floor. "I messed up." The admission was painful for him to voice.

Etta rubbed his back in a comforting motherly way and made a small disapproving tsk. "Roan, we all mess up. Do you think that I never lose myself with Kai? I've been married to the man for over six decades now and sometimes I think I might kill him."

Appreciating her humor, Roan laughed. "Etta. This is different."

"Oh, knock it off. You and I both know that you would have never hurt that woman," she replied.

"We don't know what I'm capable of."

Roan winced at Etta's responding smack against his shoulder. The small weathered woman may have looked fragile, but she was strong. Both physically and in her opinions. "Roan Durel. We do not pity ourselves in this house. I will not allow it. I know your heart. I know your intentions, but most importantly *you* know who you are. You would have never hurt her."

His lips tightened while he held back his laugh at her sternness. She wasn't wrong. He knew who he was and he worked every day to keep his temper and anger at bay. Despite what he knew, however, he also knew Orah deserved to trust she was safe, and he had broken that trust.

"I have to let her go," he said.

Etta's small hand squeezed his arm, "I know you do. She's not your prisoner and you're not going to treat her as such, but maybe there's a chance she'll come back." A moment of silence passed between them before Etta glanced around the room. "You know, I use this room sometimes," she whispered.

Roan's eyes widened. "What?" His mind couldn't conjure any image of her in the room other than resetting the wards for cleanliness.

Etta stood a bit taller and nodded her head. "When life feels like it's out of control this room offers me a quiet you won't find anywhere else." His eyebrows rose and he stared at her, trying to understand what she was saying. He opened his mouth to speak but she held up her hand, continuing her thought. "This room has a way of providing me with the exact quiet I need when I'm desperate for it. Isn't it interesting that doors would appear?" Turning, she looked up at him with a stern expression on her face. "The wards on this home are not easily violated. I think even your Father would find that difficult. Are you certain they were His doors that you saw?" Abruptly she turned and walked out of the room.

Roan stood there, almost paralyzed from his confusion while he tried to process what she had said. Now alone in the room, he stared at the spot the doors had been. He sighed, if he hadn't seen it with his own eyes he wouldn't have believed it. He glanced back to the door Etta walked out of. Maybe she was right. Maybe if he were patient then Orah would come back and whatever it was between them wasn't actually broken beyond repair.

It took Roan half a day to get enough funds for Orah gathered. She didn't know where she wanted to go but decided an inn in the city would be her best option until she made her decision. An odd tension seemed to settle over the house the day of her planned departure. Word of Orah leaving was sent to Lahana but she was unable to arrive back to Iluna in time for goodbyes.

He leaned against his desk chair, staring up at the ceiling trying to think of anything other than her departure. The stack of papers in front of him was supposed to distract him, but he hadn't been able to focus on anything other than her. The study was suffocating, and he wasn't sure how he was going to be able to manage working there with so many fragments of Orah lying about the library on the other side of the wall. He thought he would likely make more use of his offices near the city center. Something his officials would appreciate.

His study door creaked open and he glanced over, finding Jes watching him.

Jes's eyes glimmered with guilt. "Are you going to be okay?" Cautiously, he made his way into the room, sitting down at the chair across from Roan.

Roan nodded, glancing back up at the ceiling. "Yes, I'll be fine. I'm a big boy Jes. Nothing ever really went far between us. I can get over a crush."

Jes's responding snort pulled Roan's eyes from the ceiling back at his Beskermer. "Yes, because you have acted like what you feel for her is only a crush." The blunt and honest response made Roan chuckle. There Jes was again, using that uncomfortable talent of his, always knowing more than Roan wanted him to.

Roan knew what he was about to say next wasn't completely true, he knew Jes did as well, but he sighed and forced it out anyway. "Honestly though, I will be okay." His gaze on Jes turned serious, enacting his position as Governing God, "Just make sure she's watched at least while she's staying in Iluna. Even after that, if we find out where she goes, I want someone nearby at all times."

"You know she's too observant to not pick up on someone trailing her, right?" Jes responded, holding his lips tight in an obvious attempt to push down a smile.

"Well, you'll just have to find me someone she won't notice. Alright?"

Jes nodded his head before looking back at the study doors then to Roan.

Dread settled in Roan's chest, the look on Jes's face was one he didn't like. "Is there something more we need to discuss?"

Jes stood and shut the study door. "The Fates have decided on the date of the challenge."

The world disappeared for a brief moment while Roan stared down at the papers on his desk. While he had been waiting, he didn't expect the dread and anger now coursing through him. His response was barely audible, "It took them long enough. They were faster with deciding last time. When did they decide?"

Jes approached Roan's desk, handing him the announcement. "Exactly one month after your birthday."

Roan couldn't bring himself to read the proclamation. Nodding he glanced up at Jes. "All this means is that we have more time to prepare."

"Prepare for what, Roan? To throw the competition again like last time?" The anger in Jes's voice shocked Roan.

"You know exactly why I held back last time," Roan replied.

"Yes, but you don't have to hold back now. Don't be afraid. You won't become Him if you allow yourself to fight at your full capacity."

"Enough." The temperature in the room shifted to a chilling cold with Roan's command. Standing he put out his hand, he would not be lectured. They knew the date now and that was all that mattered. "We have more important things to worry about today than this challenge."

"More impor—" Jes's eyes widened. "Are you talking about Orah leaving? That's more important than the challenge?"

"Jes, enough." Roan moved across his study, heading to the doors. Pulling open the door Roan glanced back at Jes once more. Jes's expression was hard, as though he wanted to say more but held himself from speaking. They glared at one another then a clearing throat behind Roan startled him. Turning back to the open door, he found Orah standing in the foyer.

She glanced between the two of them nervously. "Am I interrupting something?"

Jes opened his mouth to respond before Roan cut him off. "No, nothing. Can I help you with anything?"

Fidgeting with the ring on her pinky, she stared at Jes. "I just wanted to let you know that I've decided to leave after dinner this evening. Yohan and I are going to go get me a room during his afternoon break and then I want to eat with everyone one last time." Her eyes shifted to the floor.

She still hasn't looked at me.

"Not everyone. Lahana won't be able to make it back in time," Roan replied, trying not to allow himself to feel hurt by the lack of eye contact.

"I know. I've invited her to dinner in the city when she gets back. Just the two of us," Orah replied.

"She'll love that." Roan glanced back at Jes, finding him unmoving, staring at the floor. Roan told Jes he owed Orah an apology and the guilt coming from Jes told Roan that was what he was gathering courage to do.

Stepping forward, Jes breathed out, "Orah."

The air in the room shifted to a stifling heat and she glared. "I don't want to hear it, Jesiel."

Swapping an alarmed glance between themselves, Roan and Jes stepped back, allowing Orah more space. Jes's shoulders lifted in a defeated shrug. "I guess I deserve that," he muttered as he slid past Orah and through the study doors. She watched him stalk silently down the hall before turning back to Roan.

"I'll see you at dinner," she whispered, still refusing to look at him.

✦

Dinner was a melancholy experience. Yohan put forth one of his best meals, but the group ate in silence. Jes decided not to join and left the house after the interaction with Orah outside of Roan's study. He was likely out in the city center drowning his regrets alongside his new recruits. Roan wished, multiple times, throughout the evening that he had been able to join Jesiel instead of suffering through the awkward meal.

"So, Orah." Kai cleared his throat while everyone else at the table jumped from the unexpected breaking of silence. "Were you able to get a room set up for yourself?"

"Yes, I was. Thank you for the recommendation you gave to Yohan. We were able to get me a comfortable room."

Kai gave Roan a subtle glance and Roan nodded in return. The recommendation hadn't been Kai's. Roan was aware of the owner of the inn and knew it was a safe place for Orah to stay while in Iluna.

Uncomfortable silence settled over the room again while everyone finished their meal. Roan glanced at his family. The family he had spent over five decades building. He didn't view Yohan and his children or Kai and Etta as employees They took care of him. They supported his endeavors and aspirations and there was a part of him that had hoped Orah was becoming one of them.

Shaking his head, he tried to push down the guilt in his chest. He couldn't help but feel responsible for it all and despite Etta's firm scolding on not pitying himself, he found himself feeling that way anyway. There he sat at a silent table full of people. There was no drinking and laughing to enjoy. No jokes or storytelling. Not even Clarah pestering Orah to tell them all about her world and her life. None of what Roan had grown accustomed to over the previous weeks. There was no way for him to not feel responsible.

He watched Orah as she stood from the table. Despite the push inside of him to stand he remained in his seat while she hugged the others.

"I'll meet you at the gate in an hour," Yohan whispered, releasing her from his arms.

Now alone in the room, Roan and Orah stared at each other. He couldn't bring himself to pull his eyes from hers when she had done everything she could the last day and a half to avoid his. Finally, he pulled his gaze and admired her beauty, admiring her from head to toe. Doing everything he could to memorize the red in her hair, the gold in her eyes, the freckles that dotted her shoulders. When his eyes landed back on hers again, he smiled at the blush now spread across her cheeks.

He motioned toward the kitchen windows. "Look at you, going out into the big, wide Land of the Gods."

A grin cracked across her face, then she glanced at the floor. "Thank you for the money. I promise I won't mooch off you forever. If I never make it home, I will get myself employment."

Mooch? He chuckled to himself. One of those words she used that was as equally amusing as it was confusing. "Just take care of yourself, please."

She nodded and looked toward the doors. A tight cold tugged at Roan—her apprehension and nerves. He realized he was likely keeping her from gathering her bags. Stepping aside, he gestured out the kitchen doors. "I don't want to keep you or make you late to meeting Yohan outside."

Tucking her chin in, she whispered, "Thank you," before rushing out of the kitchen. She paused before walking down the hallway. Standing under the door frame, she observed the kitchen, as though she were committing every last detail to memory. Sighing, she patted the frame then turned and walked down the hall.

Staring after her, Roan sighed. *You're going to wait until she walks out the front gates.* He was unable to accept that she was leaving until he watched her walk off his property with his own two eyes. He glanced around the quiet kitchen and felt a tug of sadness from the meal they'd all experienced. He wished they could have all had better goodbyes. Really, he wished there hadn't been any goodbyes.

Walking back to the table he sat down, losing himself in his thoughts. He didn't want to sit in his study and make her feel as though he were watching her, but he also didn't want to follow her upstairs. Leaning his chin against his palms he stared at the wall.

✷

The clock in the study chimed, echoing down the hall and he jumped, the hour had come and gone faster than he'd expected. Standing with a stretch he rushed out of the room. He'd given her space, but he wanted to be there when she walked away.

He rushed down the hall, reaching the stairs right as she arrived at the bottom. Stopping, she glanced down the hall, past him, then toward the front door. As though she were trying to decide which door to go through. With a sigh she picked up her bag and turned her head to him.

"For what it's worth, Roan. I wasn't completely miserable staying here. I just," she paused. "I just think it's time I leave."

Stepping forward, Roan nodded his head. "I understand, Orah. For what it's worth, you have my most sincere apology." Her bag clattered to the ground loudly and her hand flew to her mouth, covering her gasp at Roan lowering himself to a bow. He knew she deserved his respect, and she would receive nothing else when she left his home. Slowly he stood, staring at the tears lining her eyes. Twisting her head to the side he watched her hand quickly move to her face to wipe the tears away.

His voice was barely above a whisper, he said, "Can I help you with your bag?"

Keeping her eyes from his, she shook her head. "No, I got it. I'm just going to go out the front door. It's silly, but I can't bring myself to go out the side door."

She picked up her bag and walked toward the front door. Roan crossed his arms against himself, trying to warm the cold broken feeling growing inside of him. He watched her make her way to the door when his skin prickled. Eyes widening, his senses went on alert the moment her hand reached for the handle.

His arms flew out in front of him and his voice rose in panic. "Orah! Don't touch that—" His warning was cut off, and he watched in horror as the door was flung off its hinges.

Chapter 18

Thrown back by the force of the door coming off its hinges, Orah fell back. Her body shook and her power danced under her skin. Glancing up, she tensed, finding Marek now where the door once stood. A predatory grin spread on Marek's lips while he glanced at her bag on the ground, then behind her at Roan.

"Why, Orah, leaving so soon? If you need somewhere to stay, I've got a warm bed you can climb into," Marek said.

Roan moved to stand between her and his brother. "What are you doing here?"

"Father sent me." He sauntered past Roan, knocking him with his shoulder as he walked to the sitting room.

Roan's gaze followed Marek before he turned and whispered to Orah. "If you want to leave you can walk out that door or go upstairs, but I would suggest you do it now."

Orah stared into the sitting room as Marek sat down casually and grinned at her. "I'm not going anywhere. I'm not going to let your brother scare me," she replied as she pulled herself to her feet.

Nodding, Roan lowered his voice more. "Do not engage with him. Do not let him know what happened in the training room—please."

Orah nodded in agreement, then walked toward the sitting room. Her power danced more wildly inside of her, full of anticipation for the conversation that was about to unfold.

Roan followed close behind her and closed the sitting room doors. Marek's grin remained, his eyes traveled up and down the length of Orah's body. "Orah, why don't you come sit with me." His eyes sparkled while he lightly tapped his thigh. Keeping her eyes on him, Orah sat down on the chair across from him.

She maintained her eye contact with Marek. His eyes darted to her side and she turned to find Roan sitting down in the chair next to her. Roan had an expression of cool indifference on his face, but she knew it was a mask. One she wasn't sure Roan held confidently enough to convince his brother.

Finally breaking their gaze, Marek lazily wiped his pant leg. "So Roan, what have you been up to?"

"What?" Roan replied with a scoff.

"You heard me. What have you been up to here in your sad little Region?"

"Marek, why did Father send you?" Roan asked.

"My question is related to why Father sent me." Marek stopped fiddling with his leg and looked up at Roan. Orah jumped at the expression on his face. Something almost evil and sickening was hidden behind the smile he forced. Roan shifted in his chair uncomfortably and Marek grinned wider before clearing his throat. "I'll ask again. What have you been up to?"

"Nothing terribly exciting. Party prep." Roan's answering shrug seemed to irritate Marek and he leaned forward, nostrils flaring.

"Well, that's a lie. And before you try and tell me you don't know what I'm talking about, I'll keep going." With a wink, Marek turned to Orah then glanced at Roan. "Father felt an odd, small burst of power yesterday morning. It took him all day, but he finally tracked it down to here. What did you do and please tell me how you managed to block him from tracking it immediately? I thought he was going to light the throne room in flames when he realized it came from here."

Orah held her unphased expression as desperately as she could while she took in what Marek was saying. A small burst of power yesterday. The doors. That was yesterday. That had been *her*.

Roan scoffed. "We both know Father is getting old and paranoid. Bursts of power can come from anywhere and just because it came from Nacht doesn't mean it came from here."

"Oh see, you're wrong in that assumption. He tracked it *here,* to this quaint little building you call home." Marek observed the room as if in disgust. Every muscle in Orah's body fought the urge to respond. Gripping the arms of her chair, she kept her eyes on him as his gaze settled back to Roan. "So, are you going to tell me what you've been doing or am I going to have to force it out of you?"

Marek's calm threat forced a scoff from Orah, and his eyes locked with hers. As suddenly as he'd looked at her, she felt her breath being pulled from her lungs. Panicked she glanced over to Roan, finding him straining in his chair, his eyes wide with terror. Orah looked down, watching her chair as it slid toward Marek. Struggling, she pushed, trying to force herself out of her chair but her body wouldn't respond.

It took only a few agonizing seconds before Orah found herself and her chair directly in front of Marek, only an arm's length away. His eyes traveled down the length of her and his lips tightened with his grin. "You know, I thought I told you to sit with me, *mortal*." His hand flew out to grab her chin and Orah blinked, questioning whether she had gone crazy. She watched both fascinated and terrified while his arm slowly turned to wood. As though his limb had been replaced by a tree branch. Marek let out a scream of agony and his eyes darted to the sitting room door. The pain loosened his control on Orah, and she whirled around, finding Lahana standing in the doorway with Jes standing behind her.

Lahana walked into the room with her arm outstretched and her own predatory grin wide across her face. "You know, *brother*, I thought we warned you the last time you were here that you should keep your hands to yourself." Cocking her head, she flicked her wrist and Orah watched, stunned, as Marek's own hand slapped himself across the face. Orah's eyes widened, understanding now just how powerful Lahana was. She had total control of Marek's limb and Marek appeared incapable of fighting her off.

Marek, his cheek now red from his own slap, stared at his arm in shock, then glared at Lahana. "You felt like showing off tonight I see. How does it feel to know you have so much power but Father refuses to grant your Godhood? I've heard you've been spending a lot of time with Dagny's daughter. What was it again? Oh yeah, Fawn."

Lahana let out a small breath at the mention of Fawn's name but didn't release her hold on Marek's arm. "It doesn't matter if *Father* refuses my Godhood. You and I both know Roan will do the honor for me when the time comes." Roan shifted in his chair.

Catching the movement, Marek smiled. "It appears our brother doesn't have the same belief in himself that you do. I mean, he didn't even try to defend his little mortal tonight."

As the insult left Marek's lips, the room was suddenly black. The only sound was the echo of Roan's chair clattering to the ground. Orah blinked, unable to see anything but she could hear him approaching where she still sat in front of Marek. The voice that filled the room sent a shiver down her spine. It was Roan, but it wasn't. It was deep and almost gravely. Every instinct in her told her to run but one small thread inside of her begged her to stay put.

Slowly starlight, now radiating from Roan's every pore, lit the room. Roan was now inches from Marek. He grabbed Marek's chin. "You know if I wanted to I could fill that arrogant head of yours with nightmares." Marek's eyes widened in obvious fear and Orah looked down, finding shackles of starlight holding Marek in his place on the couch. Roan's chilling, yet almost familiar, deep voice filled the space again. "What does the God of Daee fear, I wonder?" Roan stepped back. "It wouldn't be hard to find out. Just a quick walk in that cowardly mind of yours and I'd know." Turning back to Lahana, Roan grinned. "I bet he's scared of daddy." Marek jumped at the mention of his Father. Orah watched, with bated breath as Roan slowly turned back to Marek with an unrecognizable smile on his face. "Seems I hit a nerve, *brother*."

Captivated with the interaction between the two, Orah wasn't aware of the person approaching her from behind. She let out a quiet yelp when a pair of large arms wrapped around her waist and pulled her across the room. Cursing she twisted back and found Jes holding on to her. He shook his head, warning her to stay still and quiet. Nodding her own, she turned back to watch Roan, while pushing further into the comfort of Jes's protective hold around her.

Now standing next to Roan, Lahana smiled and dropped her hand. Marek's arm fell against his lap and he stared at the branch-like limb. Shrugging, Lahana stared down at her creation. "One of Father's healers should be able to help with that." Marek appeared as though he was unable to speak while Lahana slowly backed away toward Orah and Jes.

Orah jumped when Marek stood abruptly and glared at Roan. "I have no idea what you are doing here but you better stop. Father sends His warning. He expects to not have to send another." Jes's arms tightened around Orah when Marek passed, stomping out of the room through the broken front door.

"You're okay," Jes whispered. His arms were still holding her protectively and she breathed out, not ready to move from the hold. Roan sighed across the room and ran his hands through his hair. Orah took in the room and her chest tightened. When she made eye contact with Lahana tears lined her eyes and she let out a sob.

"Thank you," she managed to choke out.

Nodding, Lahana smiled. "Of course, Orah. Jes came to Tuuli to pull my head out of my ass, demanding I come home to give you a proper goodbye. It appears the Fates helped us arrive just in time."

Jes shifted behind Orah, releasing his hold around her before rubbing his hand across his jaw, whispering quietly, "I have got to figure out how to adjust these wards to keep your family out."

Roan's head snapped to Jes and he smiled, throwing his head back, his laugh echoed in the room. Lahana's responding laugh startled Orah and soon the room filled with everyone's laughs. From the outside, it likely would have appeared that they had all lost their minds. Perhaps they had but the break in tension was precisely what they all needed.

Clearing his throat, Roan calmed himself and walked out of the sitting room to the front door. Orah turned and watched in awe while he repaired the splintered wood with a few casual waves of his hand. She couldn't ignore his strength when he picked up the door as though it weighed nothing and set it back on its hinges.

"I didn't know he could do that," she whispered.

Leaning down next to her Lahana responded in her own whisper, "There are many things even I don't know that Roan can do."

Orah, Lahana, and Jes walked out of the sitting room to join Roan in the foyer. Orah's chest was heavy and she stared down at her bag. She didn't know whether or not she should leave after what had happened. Glancing up, she noticed Roan also staring at her bag intently. His head turned slowly, and they made eye contact. Jumping, Orah quickly glanced back down to the floor. She had no idea what she needed to do, but she knew she couldn't leave anymore.

Roan's quiet voice was all she could focus on as he spoke. "Orah, I know I told you that I wouldn't stop you from leaving but—" he stopped. "But I'm going to ask that you reconsider your choice."

For a moment, she wasn't sure how to respond. She knew she could technically leave but something told her Marek would come after her for his own sick entertainment. She was realizing that her power yesterday, that door, had called Marek there. It alerted the King somehow and she had no confidence she could control whatever it was, at least not in that moment.

She'd felt the growing power swimming frantically beneath her skin all day and she needed help understanding it.

"I'll stay," she replied.

Lahana jumped next to her but Orah kept her eyes on Roan while he nodded. She wasn't able to make out the emotion on his face. but she felt as though a weight had been lifted off her shoulders. Perhaps she hadn't actually wanted to leave. Perhaps all she needed was to know that he wouldn't have stopped her if she did.

Jes cleared his throat and they all turned to him. Orah let out a shocked yelp, finding him in front of her on one knee with his head bowed low. "Orah." He paused and glanced up at her. "Orah, what is your surname?"

"Excuse me?"

"What is your surname? I need it," he responded.

Lahana elbowed Orah in the side. Orah looked over to find an encouraging smile on Lahana's face before turning back to Jes. "It's Clark. My last name is Clark."

Jes nodded and they held their eye contact. "Orah Clark, I offer you a warrior's apology for my part in all of this. I offer you not only my apology, but I offer you a Beskermer's bond. From this day to either the day you leave this world or the day I take my last breath you have my protection." Lahana's gasp pulled Orah's gaze from Jes. Glancing up, she found Roan staring at Jes with tears lining his eyes. Noticing her gaze, Roan wiped the tears away and nodded toward Jes. Orah looked back shocked to find Jes still on his knee. "Not only do I offer you my protection, but I also offer you my friendship." He stood, while he finished his proclamation. The air in the room was heavy in response and the four of them stood in deafening silence.

Orah's chest tightened while she stared up at his now towering figure standing over her. She didn't know what he just offered but it felt important, like something she needed to respond to. Putting her hands out in front of her, she walked forward and grabbed hold of his. "Jesiel Keita, I accept your apology, your bond, and your friendship." They looked at each other for a moment when a warm zap between their palms startled her.

He tightened his grip. "I look forward to a very long friendship, Orah Clark."

A long sigh echoed behind them and she turned to a grinning Lahana. "I don't know about you three, but I could really use a drink right now," Lahana said.

Releasing her hands from Jes, Orah smiled and glanced at Roan. "I think I know just the place."

A grin spread across Roan's face and he turned to his sister. "Oh, I don't know if Lahana is ready for The Burning Boar."

Jes let out a choked laugh and Orah turned back to Roan. "THAT is the name of that place?"

His amused smile grew, and he glanced back at Lahana. "What do you say? Wanna have some fun?"

Eyes narrowing, Lahana grinned back. "You know I can handle anything thrown at me."

"Oh Fates," Jes sighed, shaking his head.

Orah could feel her eyes twinkle with delight while she looked at them. She knew they had to talk about what had happened, but she also knew they needed to blow off some steam as well. Excitement thrummed in her chest as Roan bowed sarcastically and the front door slowly opened in front of them. Grinning up at Orah, he winked. "Ladies, after you."

Lahana let out an excited squeal while she skipped forward, looping her and Orah's arms together. "I have no idea what you did to almost chase this woman away, so she's walking with me," she yelled back behind her. Orah stumbled next to her, laughing while they crossed the front lawn. As they crossed the hedged fence, Orah paused for a moment to admire the house. The lights twinkled in the windows and she smiled, thinking how much the house appeared to be waving them off for the night.

"So," Lahana leaned her head toward Orah. "What *did* Roan do to drive you off?"

"He—" Orah suddenly felt nervous. She didn't want Lahana to think she was trying to make Roan look bad.

Lahana gave Orah's arm a reassuring squeeze. "It's okay, we don't have to get into all of that now." Glancing behind her, Lahana announced loudly, "I mean we ALL know how much of an ass he can make of himself."

Jes barked out a laugh behind them and Orah glanced back at him. She was surprised by how casually Jes now walked. His wings were held at a relaxed stance while he sauntered down the street with his hands in the front pockets of his trousers. Meeting her eye, he nodded.

At first glance, one would have assumed the group was going out for a relaxing night out. No one would have been able to guess the experience they'd all had back at the Manor. Twinkling lights next to Jes caught Orah's attention and she glanced back to find Roan's freckles lit up under the night sky. His body was slightly turned toward Jes, as though he were actively listening to whatever Jes was saying, but his eyes were focused on Orah.

"Oh Fates, Roan! Will you stop showing off!" Lahana abruptly stopped and threw her free arm up to point at the sky.

Orah pulled her gaze from Roan's right as shooting stars flew overhead. Specifically, four stars following one after another. When the fourth disappeared off in the distance Orah's palm heated in response. Staring down at her free hand, her eyes widened. It was lit similarly to when she was in the tub, but it wasn't the soft candle-like light. It was as though her palm were a cloud and the light was starlight falling as raindrops that dissipated before hitting the ground.

Her eyes glanced back to Roan, who stared as though he were in a trance. She didn't know what to make of his obvious shock, or whether or not she should have been scared herself. Roan's eyes met hers and a grin spread across his face, she couldn't hear what he whispered but it wasn't hard to interpret.

Beautiful.

The walk to the pub didn't take long. Orah noticed how much quieter the room was compared to the night she and Roan were there alone. The bartender waved at them enthusiastically when they entered and led them to quiet corner table. Orah sat down, thinking back on the beer she and Roan enjoyed together. She wasn't sure if she was in the mood for beer but didn't have to think too hard when Lahana rushed to the bar and ordered for the four of them.

A few minutes later Lahana returned, arms full of bright pink drinks. Jes groaned next to Orah. "Lahana, if I drink anything that color, I'm going to hate myself in the morning."

Grinning, Lahana set one drink in front of each of them. "Then don't hate yourself." She winked, grabbing her glass and tilting her head back, drinking the beverage in one go.

Orah glanced between Roan and Jes. "Lahana, I knew I liked you." She grabbed her own glass and threw it back, just like Lahana. She shivered when the alcohol hit her stomach. The drink was sweet, but the flavor was unfamiliar. Her body warmed instantly as though it was exactly what she needed to rid the cold chill of uncertainty after Marek's visit.

The music in the pub soon picked up around them and the room filled with more people along with the melody. After several more brightly colored drinks, Orah found herself dancing with Lahana. With their hands entwined they spent the night cheering and laughing while they bounced, jumped, and twirled around the room.

For Orah it felt as though a puppet master were pulling on invisible threads, guiding her, and the lack of control felt glorious. Throwing her head back, she let out a laugh when Lahana grabbed her hand and spun her out toward the middle of the room. Orah flung her arms above her head, calling to that invisible puppet master to guide her where they wished. The room spun around and around her while she allowed the music to guide her, briefly she worried she may have been sick when she collided into someone's chest. Not anyone's chest, she realized—but Roan's.

"Caught you," he whispered, but somehow, he was still loud enough she could hear him over the music. His hands settled around her waist and her senses realigned. The room swayed and she teetered to the side for a moment.

Roan's grip on her tightened. "Whoa, let's not fall."

Orah admired the smile on his face. *I like that smile.* He moved his hand toward her face. Out of instinct, she flinched, and his smile disappeared. Dropping his voice, he stared at her. "Orah, I would never hurt you."

Her chest tightened and her knees buckled under her. Shaking her head, she tried to push down the panic and the memories clawing for their chance to come out and play. Turning her head away from him, she whispered, "I've heard that before."

His hold around her waist loosened and he let her step back, gathering her space. The room spun and she teetered again. "Oh God, I might be sick," she groaned, realizing just how much alcohol she'd consumed.

His arms wrapped around her again, balancing her. "I've got you."

The alcohol's grasp took full control and she looked up at him again with a drunken smile. "Has anyone told you that you're pretty?" Immediately her mouth slammed shut. Her eyes widened with realization at how loudly she had spoken, basically shouting over the music in the room. His eyes sparkled with amusement and his eyes focused on her mouth. Heat flushed to her cheeks while she watched him watch her.

"I don't know if anyone has used that word when complimenting me," he replied. His arms flexed against her waist.

I think I might die if he keeps holding me like this.

"Stop looking at me like that," she snapped.

The music in the room faded away and he lifted her chin. "Like what, Orah? Like I don't want you to drunkenly crash to the floor?" His grip tightened while he pulled her body closer. "Or like all I'm thinking about is what your lips would feel like against mine?"

Her heart beat frantically while she stared up at him, desperately avoiding staring at his own full lips. His arms tightened around her, as though he was aware of the reaction she was having to his comments.

"Roan –" She couldn't seem to get the words out. She thought about what kissing him would be like. *Hell, it would probably be fantastic.* But they couldn't. He knew they couldn't. "Roan, we can't."

"Why not, Orah?" The quiet, almost indecent way he whispered her name sent shivers down her spine. His eyes were still lingering on her lips and the very small sliver of control she had started to slip.

Taking a deep breath, she turned her chin from his grip. "It's too messy. We both can't deny that there's something here, but I can't have messy. I need to be able to get home." He pulled his arm away from around her waist. Something firm behind her startled her and she peeked back to find he had been guiding them to barstools. With his hand, he motioned for her to sit.

"Let's get you some water," he said.

He hadn't responded to what she'd said, and she wasn't sure if he was supposed to. She was the one keeping him away. She was the one who wouldn't allow whatever it was between them to happen. The bartender placed a large glass of water in front of her and her stomach rolled at the thought of drinking anything. She knew, however, that she had to sober up to be able to walk back to the manor. Movement and a rush of wind beside her pulled her away from her drink and she glanced up to find Roan staring at Jes, still sitting at the table across the room.

Turning back toward her, he smiled and leaned down. His whisper tickled her ear and the hair on her arms stood in response to the brush of his lips. "For what it's worth, Orah. If we do get you home—I will spend the rest of my life searching for a way to find you again."

The music in the room flooded back into her ears and she blinked, finding him now across the room with Jes. Her chest heaved up and down and her head swam. She wasn't sure what to make of what he said and she couldn't keep herself from staring at him. He didn't glance at her again, but she knew he was still somehow paying attention.

After a few glasses of water and an hour later they were all heading back to the manor. Lahana had joined Orah at the bar while they both sobered up. Orah listened, captivated, while Lahana told her all about her time in the Spring Region. From what Orah learned, Lahana had the power to become the next Goddess of Spring but her Father refused to name Lahana as successor of the Region. With all the time Lahana spent with the Goddess of Spring, learning about the Region and its people, she had grown close to Fawn. Who, to Orah's surprise, was the Goddess's daughter. Lahana explained that as the daughter of the King of Gods her ascension to Godhood overrode any offspring from that Region's Governing God or Goddess. Because her powers manifested as a near replica to the Goddess of Spring's it was assumed Spreng would be where Lahana would one day Govern.

"If that day ever comes," Lahana grumbled.

Fawn, however, didn't seemed bothered that Lahana was expected to become the Governing Goddess. Lahana's description made Fawn sound like a wonderfully interesting person. She was the calm to Lahana's wild storm. Where Lahana could push important matters to the side, Fawn brought her back down to face them first.

Strolling down the city streets, Lahana's eyes sparkled. "Oh, but she knows how to have fun!" She grinned at Orah. "She may be serious, but once the work is done, she is *wild*. We literally jumped off a cliff the other day. Just jumped and I had to guide the wind to help us land."

Roan stopped abruptly in front of them and whirled around. "You did what?"

"I. Jumped. Off. A. Cliff." Lahana puffed out her chest as she emphasized each word.

The expression of rage on Roan's face was almost enough to scare Orah but then he sighed, running his hand through his hair. "I might have to have a word with Dagny about this daughter of hers."

"You will do no such thing, Roan. We're both adults and can do as we please," Lahana replied, glaring at her brother. Pulling her gaze from the standoff, Orah realized they were now in front of the manor.

Jes slinked over to her and whispered, "Don't get in the way. Lahana's just trying to remind Roan she's not a helpless little girl."

Orah fidgeted uncomfortably and looked back at the house. Jes's own discomfort appeared to get to him and he cleared his throat. "I don't know how long you both want to have your little standoff but I'm going inside to bed." His comment pulled Roan and Lahana's focus to him and a wide grin spread across Jes's face. Turning to Orah he put out his hand. "Orah, care to join me?"

Taking his hand, Orah choked on a laugh and grinned back at him. "I would love to."

Roan stumbled, his eye darted frantically between Orah and Jes as though he were trying to decipher if she had just accepted an invitation to Jes's bed. Coughing he shook he head and turned to his sister. "Okay, Lahana, you've made your point. Just be careful."

Amusement flashed across Lahana's face. "I could say the same thing," she replied.

Jes gripped Orah's hand and whispered, "Roan is so much fun to tease." Nodding, Orah glanced back at Roan, who appeared as though he were going to burst his own hand from how tightly he was holding it in a fist.

They all walked toward the front door while Jes pretended to whisper sweet nothings in Orah's ear. She could feel Roan's annoyance boiling. Like his anger was a palpable heat that he had no control over. She wasn't sure if it were funny or cruel, but Jes seemed too preoccupied with annoying Roan to notice.

The front door slammed open in front of them, startling Orah. Jes sighed then turned back to Roan. "Fiiine, Orah. I guess my Governing God prefers guests to stay in their own rooms, alone." With a smirk, he winked at Orah. "That is unless the guest is inviting *him* into said rooms."

A low almost snarling sound came from Roan and Orah turned around. Her eyes widened and she could do nothing to hold back her laugh while she stared at him. "For all the books I've read, I've tried to imagine what it meant when the man snarls and you've just given me a free demonstration."

Lahana's eyes widened as she dropped to her knees. "Orah!" Holding her chest Lahana couldn't seem to get out whatever else she wanted to say through her laughs.

Orah's eyes connected with Roan's and they both laughed. He sighed, "I'm being ridiculous. We've all had too much to drink. Let's head to bed and talk tomorrow."

Nodding, Orah walked toward the stairs, expecting everyone but Jes to head up with her but was shocked when Roan motioned for Jes to follow him to his study. Lahana, shrugged. "Probably some business they need to attend to."

Lahana looked at the stairs then down the hall to the kitchen. "You head up. I need more water. I'll see you in the morning."

Orah watched Lahana walk away, she was tired but didn't think she could sleep. Sighing, she walked up the stairs and stopped at the top. She glanced down the hall then to the second stairs case in front of her. She wasn't sure where to go when her eyes traveled back to the end of the hall and door at the end—Roan's door. An electric buzz flowed through her while she imagined what it would be like to surprise him in his bed. The shock that would be on his face. Her palms warmed while she thought about the way his eyes lingered on her lips and the way his arms felt wrapped around her. Closing her eyes, she imagined what the brush of his lips would be like. The ways their hands could explore each other.

Right as the thought of his hands on her crossed her mind a burst of flames shot out from her palm, lighting the carpet in front of her into flames. "Shit!" she whispered, rushing to stomp them out. Panicked, she waited to see if anyone would rush up the stairs. After a few silent seconds she breathed out a sigh of relief. No one had seemed to notice her outburst or the smell of charred carpet. Looking back down at the carpet she gasped, watching while it mended itself back together.

An embarrassed flush heated her cheeks, and she shook her head. *Get a hold of yourself.* She stared at his door for another moment before deciding to go up to the roof.

Orah kept finding herself called up to the roof, unable to get enough of the beautiful sky. She observed what appeared to be a version of the aurora borealis that she knew from home. She had seen it before, but the colors now were bright and overwhelming. With pinks and purples mixed with the blues and yellows. Each color swaying as if they were calling to each other. Despite her searching she hadn't found any more shooting stars. She was aware that the ones she'd seen earlier had been from Roan, but she still felt disappointed that no more appeared.

Orah turned toward the sound of the roof door opening, already knowing it was joining her. She found him casually leaning against the door frame with his arms across his chest. "I keep finding you up here," he said.

"Finding me or following me?" she replied.

Smiling, Roan pushed off the door frame and made his way to the chair next to her. "Despite what you might think, it is finding. I come up here often. That's why there are chairs out here."

They sat in silence staring up at the stars and she resisted the desire to stare at him. She watched the sky, thinking about the events of the day. How ready she had been to leave the house. She didn't know what she had been thinking. What would she have done once she'd gotten to that inn? Where would she have gone? Shaking her head, she scolded herself. If she left, she would lose the resources Roan had to help figure out how to get her home. A dull ache built in her head while she thought about what happened with Marek and how close he had been to grabbing and forcing her to do whatever he intended in that moment.

"What's a Beskermer bond?" Orah asked.

Roan's head snapped away from the sky over to her. "What?"

"Jes—he offered me his Beskermer bond. What is that?"

Roan stared at her for a moment before answering. "Beskermer is the name of the race that Jes comes from. They're sort of between Godlings and Gods. Beskermer means protector. Their lives revolve around the bonds that they bind themselves to." Looking back up at the stars, he breathed out. "For Jes to offer you his Beskermer bond is a big deal, Orah. You will never have anyone for the rest of your life that will fight so hard to protect you."

"But what does it mean? How does it work?"

"Well technically Jes is only allowed to offer his Beskermer bond to God Royalty and he already did that over 200 years ago to me so I'm not quite sure how it'll work now."

"Jes is over 200 years old?"

Roan laughed. "You always seem to focus on the most miniscule bits of information. Yes, Jes is just a few years younger than me."

"Rude," she replied, glaring at him.

He laughed again. "It wasn't meant to be rude; I apologize."

"How did you meet? When did he bind himself to you?" she asked.

Roan grinned at her and shifted as though he were excited. "Well, that's a story in and of itself. When the children of the Governing Gods and the other Gods are young, many decide to send them to the region Guerra—our War Region. There's a school there. Its whole point is to learn our histories and regular school lessons but also to learn the art of war. How to use your mind logically. How to train your body. How to run a successful Region. The Beskermer also have the privilege to send their children there and it's expected by the time graduation hits that at least the children assumed to ascend to a Governing God will have a bonded Beskermer." He stopped for a moment.

Orah leaned forward and her chair tipped. She let out a gasp, not realizing she had been on the edge of her seat. She couldn't help it though. Every time one of them gave her more information about how their world worked, she couldn't seem to soak it in fast enough.

Roan glanced at her engaged position and smiled. "Anyways, most of the time the bond is decided because both the Godly child and the Beskermer child are a logical choice. Either they're psychologically compatible, physically compatible, or so on. Very few have a friendship with one another. That's where Jes and I were a sort of anomaly. We were friends almost instantly. We annoyed each other, yes, but we have always been friends. Our friendship became more important than finding someone to protect me. When graduation came there was no other choice besides Jes. I knew there was no one else in the world who would have my back like he does. The school and my Father were besides themselves. They thought our friendship would be a weakness and that it would get in the way of the hierarchy of the Gods and Beskermer, but we didn't care."

Orah's brow rose. "What do you mean, hierarchy?"

"I can command Jes to do anything I wish. If I wanted him to peel the paint of my walls slowly, I could tell him to. Technically, tonight I could have told him to take his hands off you and stop whispering in your ear." Orah stared at him in shock, unsure how to respond. He continued, "But that's never been how it works between us. He pushes me but he knows when to stop. He knows when I've made my final decision, and nothing will change that. But he also keeps me in line. Keeps my head out of my ass so to say."

"So, what does that mean for me and Jes? Would I be able to command him?" Orah asked.

Roan's eyes widened. "What? Oh Gods, no." His quick response irritated her, and her brows crumpled with annoyance. Putting up his hands he shook his head. "No, it's not like that. I mean you guys didn't have a ceremony with the Fates involved. That's how the bond is enacted. The families of each participant are there, and the Fates seal the bond with a blood oath. His bond is real and don't take that lightly but it's not sworn by blood so you can't control him."

Orah let out a breath of relief. "Oh, good. I don't want to have that power over someone."

For Orah it was cruel to command someone who was invested in protecting you. She didn't understand why Roan and Jes's close relationship wasn't normal, she would assume a pair would need trust like that to have a successful bond. A thought crossed her mind and she turned to Roan. "What about Marek? Does he have a Beskermer bond?"

"Of course he does. His is actually Jes's cousin. But they have a different relationship. Strictly business and Marek commands him to stay in his home whenever he wants. In a sense, Marek mocks the importance of the bond and having someone duty bound to protect you."

"What about Lahana?"

A sad look flashed across Roan's face. "My father loves Lahana in his own way. He never expected to have another child, as I've told you before. When she was born, he refused to send her to the school. She got private tutors and an incredible education, but never had the chance to find her Beskermer. She used to get really upset about it but once she moved in here, she said Jes is hers by proxy."

Orah's eyes traveled to the door that led inside, unable to push down the sadness she felt. She wondered how Lahana must have felt with Jes's proclamation to her earlier. It must have come as a shock and Orah told herself to check on Lahana later.

"She's not upset about what happened today." Orah whipped around to see Roan's eyes on her.

"You don't know that," she replied.

He nodded his head. "I do though. She is just as relieved as I am that Jes made that effort with you. I know he's been a hardass and he's pushed you since you arrived. I was starting to worry that you two would never get along."

Orah scoffed while leaning back against her chair. "I mean, *I'm* still not sure if we'll ever get along."

Orah didn't have to see him to know that he was staring at her. His gaze felt as though a hole was burning into her skin. Her hands shook in her lap and she tried to keep her eyes on the sky. Silence settled between them and she wasn't sure who would break it first. Her spot in the chair felt suffocating and she tried, desperately, not to look in his direction. After several agonizingly silent minutes he cleared his throat.

"Orah. About what happened at the pub."

Flexing her fists in her lap she kept her eyes upward. "It's okay, Roan. You didn't do anything wrong."

"I didn't say that I did. I just—I want you to know that I'll respect your decision." From the corner of her eye, she watched him stand from his seat. She turned toward him, finding him looking down at her with a smile. "But I also wanted you to know that you'll most definitely regret that decision as well." Her mouth popped open while she tried to gather a witty response when he winked and walked away.

"Arrogance doesn't suit you, Roan!" she yelled after him.

He let out a loud laugh and shrugged his shoulders. "You're welcome to your opinion, Orah." She watched him close the door behind him.

Too messy. Way too messy.

Chapter 19

Loud knocking on the door jolted Orah awake. She felt as though she had only been sleeping for a few hours and based on the way the light came through her curtains, she was sure she was right. Swinging her legs off the bed, she made her way to the door. "Yes?" she called out, obviously annoyed. No voice responded, and she angrily pulled her bedroom door open, finding Lahana standing there grinning.

"Good morning! Roan wants us all to talk downstairs. He said we can do it around the kitchen table." Lahana did a little whirl as she turned and walked down the hall.

Muttering to herself, Orah closed her door and walked to the closet to find something to wear. She didn't understand why Roan couldn't have waited until they'd all gotten a few more hours of sleep. It wasn't as though he hadn't also been up late.

"Maybe Gods don't need as much sleep as lowly mortals," she grumbled while she pulled a long summer dress over her head.

Turning, she looked in the mirror, taking note of the lack of sleep around her eyes. Frowning at the bags, she admired her dress; at least she was happy with that. It was one Lahana bought her. It flowed down to her feet, covering them. The neckline was a halter style with thick straps tying at the base of her neck and long tails of fabric cascaded down her back. The color reminded her of sunrise—a mix of yellows and oranges. At least the color of the dress made her feel awake.

She rushed out of the room, curious as to why she'd been woken so abruptly. But the longer she was awake, the more irritated she felt with him. She huffed, hoping whatever he had to say was important. When she arrived at the bottom of the stairs she turned and found Jes standing in front of the kitchen doorway.

"Any idea why Roan woke us all up?" she said, walking toward him. She jumped back with a yelp when Roan popped out from the other side of the door and smirked.

"I'm not the one who gathered everyone."

"What are you talking about? Lahana woke me up saying you told her you needed to talk to all of us," Orah asked.

"Same here. She almost broke down my door to pull me out of bed," Jes replied.

Roan motioned for them to follow him into the kitchen. "She told me Orah had an announcement." Orah and Jes followed Roan into the kitchen and they all gathered around the table. They passed confused glances between one another when Lahana finally entered the room.

"Oh good! You all got up." She walked toward the table and her bright grin shifted to something serious and grim. Sitting on one of the chairs opposite of Orah, she stared at the three of them. "Now, you three are going to explain to me what happened."

"What are you talking about now?" Roan asked.

Lahana's eyes narrowed and she stared at her brother. "I'm talking about what happened that made Orah want to leave? What happened that brought Marek back to this house? What haven't you three told me?"

"Something happened in the training room two days ago. Jes created an obstacle course for me and when I finished, a set of golden doors appeared in the middle of the room," Orah replied.

Lahana's face changed from serious to scared. "What do you mean golden doors?"

Orah opened her mouth to explain when Roan interrupted. "You know what golden doors mean and not just any doors." He rubbed his jaw before continuing. "The doors were identical to the ones that lead to the throne room in the Palace of Kings. Size, color, and symbols. Orah was able to get one open and I could see the city behind the wall."

Orah's head snapped toward Roan, sure she hadn't heard what he'd just said. *The Palace of Kings.*

"Like a portal," Lahana gasped, covering her mouth with her hand.

"Exactly. I lost my temper and grabbed Orah. It was inexcusable. I wasn't able to control myself initially and could have hurt her. She decided she was ready to leave here after that." He looked down at the table. "Understandably."

Still covering her mouth, Lahana shook her head in disbelief. "But what does that have to do with Marek showing up?"

"I'm not sure. He said that Father felt strange magic, but it took Him an entire day to track it here. Not just to Nacht, but He was able to track it to the house. Marek was here on behalf of Father to provide a warning to me to stop messing with whatever they assume I'm messing with. They don't seem to know it was Orah," Roan replied.

Orah jumped and glared at him. "I didn't do anything, remember? I may have gotten that door open but I sure as hell did not bring it here."

Next to her Jes sighed. "We don't actually know that Orah. You could be right, but we could also be right. It's a mystery right now. All that matters now is Marek and their Father don't suspect you."

"I wouldn't count on Marek not at least suspecting. He may be arrogant but he's observant. It's just whether or not he tells Father about Orah existing," Lahana said.

Shocked, Orah stared at Lahana. "You don't think Marek's told Him about me?"

"Trust me," Roan responded. "If He knew about you, He would have come for you personally."

Fear settled in Orah's stomach. She hadn't heard anything positive about the King of Gods and she didn't want to consider what it would mean if He came for her. She glanced at Roan and he nodded his head, silently confirming the fears running through her mind.

Roan shifted out of his seat and stood. They all watched while he walked to the kitchen island and leaned against it, crossing his arms over his chest. "We need to figure out how to get you home, Orah. Immediately. My birthday is less than 8 weeks away and something big feels like it's about to happen. I can't explain how I know but it's almost as if the Fates are trying to warn me."

"But how can we get me home if we don't know how to get access to my world?" Orah asked.

"Last night I had Jes send word to Amada again. I want to find out if something can be done with the portal magic we already have. I know she said the knowledge of traveling to other worlds has been lost but I don't feel like that's entirely true. Maybe misplaced, but I don't think it's gone forever."

"What if you can't get me home before your birthday?"

The atmosphere in the room shifted. "That's not an option."

"Doesn't matter if it's not an option it might be reality, Roan," Orah scoffed.

"Then we better pray to the Fates that the warning in my gut is wrong," Roan replied.

Dread hit her and she stared at him. She knew he was trying to help but she was also aware that he didn't know what to do. The uncomfortable realization settled between the four of them and they sat in silence.

Next to her Jes shifted. "I have a proposition," he announced.

"Yes?" Roan's eyebrows rose, unable to hide the curiosity on his face.

"I train Orah," Jes stated.

"I thought you *training* her is what got us into this mess in the first place," Roan shot back. Startled, Orah glanced at Lahana, who shrugged in response.

"I do it at the camp. Away from the house. Orah, you need to learn how to control that magic. Not only that, but you need to learn how to protect yourself. As your Beskermer, I insist," Jes replied.

Roan grinned. "I don't know if Orah is ready to have her ass kicked by Captain Jesiel Keita."

"Excuse me?" Orah's eyes darted to Roan and she scowled at the grin on his face. "Maybe *Captain Jesiel Keita* isn't ready to have his ass kicked by me."

"This is going to be fun!" Lahana said with a laugh.

Roan walked back to the table. "I haven't heard one person describe being trained by Jes as fun."

"Maybe not for Orah, but it'll be fun for me to watch," Lahana replied.

"We can train Jes. As much as Roan doesn't want to admit it, I don't know if I'll be home soon and I want to be prepared for whatever might happen," Orah said with her attention on Jes.

Jes slid off the bench and stood. "We'll start today. First things first—change out of that dress. You may look fantastic in it, but you can't train in that."

Lahana gasped and Orah's mouth hung open from the compliment. "I didn't know you were capable of complimenting a woman," Lahana responded sarcastically.

Shrugging, Jes glanced at Roan. "I dunno but each time I compliment Orah, Roan turns an interesting shade of red." Orah's head snapped to

Roan, whose jaw was clenched tight like he was about to burst from annoyance.

"Are you two sure you're not actually brothers?" Orah said while she slid out of her seat.

"Wouldn't that make all of our lives so much easier," Lahana replied as she leaned back in her chair.

Orah turned to Jes. "I'll be back down in about 10 minutes, Jes."

"I'll be waiting by the stables," he nodded, then walked out the room.

Orah rushed out of the kitchen, making it to the bottom of the stairs before she sensed someone behind her. Turning, she found Roan standing in the hall, staring at her.

She cocked her head. "Yes?"

Roan shrugged. "He wasn't wrong."

"Who wasn't?" She did not have time for him to be obscure.

"Jes. You do look fantastic in that dress." He smiled and turned to his study door. Forcing herself upstairs she refused to peek back at him. She couldn't give him the satisfaction.

※

After dressing into something more functional, Orah met Jes at the stables. Kai greeted her with a grin. "Etta and I were very pleased to hear that you aren't leaving us."

"I guess you all are stuck with me for a bit longer," she replied.

She found Jes standing off to the side, observing her with Kai. Kai glanced at Jes then dipped his chin down. "Let me go grab Tume for you."

"What's the camp?" Orah asked Jes while she walked toward him.

"It's where the Region's guards train. I'm in charge of the guard and the camp. It's my duty as Roan's Beskermer and Captain," Jes replied.

"Why can't we use the training room?"

"Because last time something happened that caught the attention of the King. I would prefer to keep Roan's home protected from him. So we'll train out in the open."

Orah couldn't argue with him there. She caught Kai out of the corner of her eye while he led Tume out of the stable. Tume was just as beautiful as always. Her majestic black mane sparkled underneath the sun and her powerful wings were tucked in tight against her. Kai stopped a few feet in front of Orah and Tume dropped her head low as if in a bow. Instinct took control of Orah and she mimicked the movement.

Jes's startled gasp pulled her attention away from the Pegasus. "How did you know to do that?" His eyes were wide while he gaped at her.

"I dunno. It just felt like the appropriate thing to do in the moment," Orah said.

Approaching Tume, he nodded his head and slowly extended his hand. She sniffed it briefly then nodded in approval. Orah stood and watched while he crouched down, like Roan, and cupped his hand as a step for her. It only took a few seconds for him to lift her into the saddle and for her to get herself settled.

Buckling her strap, she glanced at him. "What about you?"

His eyes twinkled and a giddy grin spread across his face. Tume let out a startled neigh, stepping back when his wings snapped out to his sides. "I have my own means of transportation," he said. Wind rushed around them but he kept his eye contact while shooting straight up into the sky. Orah's head snapped upward while she tried to keep her eyes on him. He became a speck in the blue sky so quickly she had to blink to believe it. She watched in wonder while his wings straightened out and he soared high above her.

Just as rapidly as he'd flown upward, he descended down toward her and she panicked, thinking he was headed straight for the ground. She let out a scream when he stopped inches from the ground, hovering impressively.

"Well, what are you waiting for?" he said, motioning to the sky.

Orah stared down at Tume. She had no idea how to get the Pegasus to move. Leaning down, she ran her hand up and down Tume's mane. Dropping her voice to a whisper she spoke to the Pegasus, "Tume, let's show him not to mess with us ladies." Tume's hooves kicked excitedly at the grass and Orah gripped onto the reins right before they both shot into the sky.

Orah didn't scream this time. This time her chest felt as though it were going to explode from the onslaught of emotions that flooded over her. She surveyed the world below her, taking in the beauty. The city below her sparkled under the sun but she felt like it was waving at her. As though the city and land themselves were friends welcoming her back home. Shaking her head, she looked over to Jes.

He flew at her side with a wide grin on his face. "Good job, Orah."

Orah smiled then patted Tume's neck. "I didn't do anything. I just trusted Tume had me." Jes veered to the right and Tume followed close behind. Keeping her eyes ahead, Orah watched them grow closer to a small mountain range.

"Where is this camp?" she shouted over the wind.

Jes responded, somehow as clear as if he were sitting next to her "Just down there. Only about a fifteen-minute flight from the city." He pointed to a large valley surrounded by the mountains. The closer they flew the more she could make out a wall surrounding most of the camp with several buildings grouped together. Little dots of people moved about the camp below. At the back was a large archway and a smaller mountain behind it.

Jes pointed to the archway. "Behind there is the obstacle course. That's where we're going to train."

"Not in the camp?" Orah asked.

"No, the recruits would get too distracted if I showed up with a pretty woman," he replied.

"Are there no women guards?"

"Of course there are women guards. They're usually the best of us. What I mean is my guards have never seen me with a woman and if I show up with you it'll start unnecessary gossip and distraction."

She smiled at him. "Won't they want to use the obstacle course?"

"Nope. They can't see that it's you on this Pegasus right now. They'll recognize me and assume you're Roan. Once they see us heading to the training course, they'll avoid it. They respect Roan but he scares the shit out of them."

"Why?" Orah asked, shocked by how casually Jes had made the statement.

"Because they believe that he's the next God of Death. These Pegasi are used in different ways. One being Aeron riding his almost identical black Pegasus to collect souls every now and then. As much as they respect Roan and how he governs the Region, the future his Father has publicly assigned him to means many fear him and try to avoid getting on his bad side."

"The God of Death can just collect souls whenever he wants?"

Jes chuckled and shook his head. "Oh of course not. There's a natural cycle of things. As scary as Aeron likes to make himself seem, he can't cross that line. But most Godlings and mortals don't know that, so myth and legend run rampant."

Orah nodded her head but her quiet companion Death shook its head in response as if in disagreement. Shaking off the bitter cold running down her spine she looked back at Jes. "Are there no Gods in your guard?"

"There are but it's mainly made up of Godlings and mortals. Gods have this air of entitlement I don't like. While my guard is made entirely of volunteers, I still have the final say. I prefer the Godlings and mortals. They want to make something of themselves and they protect the cities and towns here with purpose," he replied, while he admired his camp from above.

Jes shot out ahead of Orah and Tume, flying over the lower mountains behind the camp. Tume let out an almost irritated huff and hurried after him. Jes landed with a loud thud and Tume followed close behind. Twisting back and forth in the saddle, Orah took in the course surrounding her. Parts of it were built into the mountain but there were many obstacles scattering the flat earth below them. To the right were large platforms jutting out from the mountain. There appeared to be some sort of zipline at the top of where the platforms stopped. The end of the zipline sat several hundred feet away on the ground. A few feet from the end of the zipline were military-like, low barbed wires that she assumed were for guards to crawl under. All around the ground were vertical pillars of different sizes and platforms floating in midair.

"Let me help you down," Jes said, approaching her. He stretched his arms out for her to use for support. She unbuckled herself and grasped each of Jes's large arms. Slowly, he lowered her and clicked his tongue at Tume. Huffing, the Pegasus stared at him then glanced at Orah.

"I'm fine. Go get some shade," Orah whispered, stroking Tume's mane. Tume let out a huff of approval then turned to make her way toward the archway to a shaded area with a few trees scattered near the entrance back to the camp.

Turning back to Jes, Orah crossed her arms. "Well, where do we start?"

Walking toward her Jes grinned. Orah's eyes widened with panic. Suddenly she wasn't sure whether or not she was in danger. Glancing backward she calculated how quickly she could get back to Tume when Jes's arm extended toward her. Screaming she ducked and covered her head with her arms.

Jes stared at her before letting out a laugh. "Orah, relax, look behind you."

Snapping her head back, she blushed when her eyes found the wardpad on the wall behind her. Turning back to him she gave him an apologetic smile. "This course can be warded?" she asked.

"Yes, it's how we keep the guards and recruits continually improving themselves. If the course never adjusted, they would never be challenged," he replied.

"Do you ward it or do the recruits?"

"I ward it for the recruits when they're in here as a group. Same with the existing guards stationed here to assist with training. But when someone wants to come here alone, they can ward the course to benefit their skills or powers. The wards are set up to provide courses that will push the users' powers. It's how I train any Gods or Godlings who come through here to utilize their powers and have better control over them."

"And the mortals?" she asked.

"It works for the mortals but someone with access to magic has to do it for them. That's usually me or their training officer. If we have a mortal who, for example, is really quick on their feet, the training officer or myself will think about that skill set when setting the wards and the course will provide the necessary challenge to keep them fast on their feet," Jes replied.

"Interesting. And you're planning on using this course to train me? I understand trying to get my powers to come out and control them but what about other ways you can prepare me?" she asked, glancing out at the course behind him.

"Other ways?"

"I want to learn how to fight. I'm strong, I know that, but I don't know how to fight and would never be able to protect myself from someone faster than me," Orah stated.

She glanced back to Jes, finding him grinning at her. "So you're asking me to spar with you?" he asked.

Trying to hide her own grin, she shrugged. "Spar, train. Tomayto, tomahto."

"What?" His laugh echoed around the course.

She blushed. "It's a saying where I'm from. Meaning different words or different ways to say things can have the same meaning."

"I need to hear more phrases from where you're from then." He smiled. His eyes sparkled and Orah wasn't sure if it were from amusement or anticipation that she asked him to train her. Or anticipation that she'd just given him permission to kick her ass repeatedly.

His eyes fell to the wardpad next to her and he motioned to it with his hand. Taking a breath for confidence she turned the knob, watching the pin appearing in the middle. Shutting her eyes, she pricked her thumb and placed it on the pad. She waited while the ground shook beneath them and the shifting sounds of the course changing echoed around her.

"Whoa," Jes whispered behind her.

"What?" Turning back to the course her mouth hung open. It was similar but different from before. There were still platforms that jutted out of the mountain, but these ones were spaced further apart. Between each platform was a kind of cylindrical arm that appeared to be made from the mountain itself. Each arm popped in and out of the mountain repeatedly, reminding Orah of video games from when she was a child. The last platform ended at the top of the mountain and below were spires shooting out from the ground. Each spire was a different size but they each had some kind of large ring attached to it at different angles. Across from where the spires ended was a large hole in the ground with a roaring fire in the middle. Beyond the firepit lay a wall identical to the one that appeared in the training room but at the top of this wall was a single bronze door.

Chapter 20

Sweat ran down Orah's back while she took it all in. She had no idea how any of the obstacles were supposed to entice her powers to come out.

"Okay, so, I think this course intends to kill me," she said, glancing back over to Jes.

"Then don't die," Jes replied with a smirk.

She turned back to the course. Warmth hummed in her chest. Something was calling to that power—all she had to do was let it answer. She moved to head toward the platforms jutting from the mountain when Jes pulled her back.

"Wait," he said.

"What?"

"The other day in the training room. You had said you had a question for me that you would get to ask if you got over that wall."

"Oh, yeah. I was curious what it was between you and Roan that made you so protective, but he and I talked last night. I think I understand now," Orah replied.

"You do?" Jes asked.

"You're his Beskermer but more importantly you're his friend."

"Well, Orah Clark." Jes waved his arm out in front of him. "Go get your ass kicked."

The warm hum inside of her grew stronger while she approached the first platform. Taking her first step up, she watched in fascination but also horror as the cylinder arm jolted in and out of the mountain as though it were a battering ram designed to take her out. Her hands buzzed in response and she looked down.

Maybe if I just jump when it goes into the mountain, I can make it.

She stared at the arm while it disappeared into the rock briefly. She observed it for a few seconds trying to grasp any kind of pattern. Finally, she leapt forward right when the arm disappeared. She landed on the next platform with a loud grunt and the cylinder behind her flew forward, barely missing the edge of her shoes. Bolting upward she stood, then repeated the process to get to platform two, then three, then four. Standing on platform four, she jumped to five, sure she had the pattern of the cylinders down but that surety cost her. Platform five was further from four than the others had been. Her eyes widened and her hand flew out in front of her grasping at the air when the arm between four and five jolted out from the mountain and slammed into her side.

Time stood still and she was hurled to the ground. Hitting the dirt, pain erupted through her side. She bit back her scream while her vision blurred and her chest tightened. Her breath left her lungs and she laid staring at the blue sky, sure she had possibly taken her last breath.

Relax! Relax!

Her vision cleared and her chest loosened while air filled her lungs again. After a few moments laying on the warm dirt, she sat up and surveyed the platforms. Her eyes narrowed and her curses flew out of her mouth outside of her control.

"Orah?" Jes's voice sounded far away. "Orah, are you okay?"

Turning to find him, she winced from the bolt of pain that shot up her side. Biting her lip, she let out a deep breath and grabbed her side. "I'm good!" she yelled.

I'm very much not good.

"You will not let this beat you," she whispered.

Blinding pain almost knocked the air back out of her when she stood and tried to steady herself. Making sure to breathe, her feet moved toward the platforms. Same as before, she got through platforms one to four. Standing on the fourth platform she stared at the fifth. The cylinder jolted out from the side of the mountain repetitively and her hands tingled in anticipation.

"Orah! The course is trying to challenge you. Feel your power. Let it help you!" Jes yelled.

So much easier said than done.

She turned back to the platform in front of her. The jump was definitely farther than the others had been from each other. Glancing back at the three behind her, she considered retracing her steps and calling it a day.

"Orah, don't you dare give up." The tone in Jes's voice startled her. She glanced down to find him now standing near the first platform. "This is challenging your power. Let it help you. You don't have to figure it all out by yourself. Your power is there to guide and support you."

Orah scoffed at how easy he must have thought it was to just accept help. The power thrumming inside of her might have been hers but she didn't know how she got it. It didn't feel like it was hers exactly. It hadn't ever been there to help or guide her through her life. Never showing up to protect her. Never stopping her pain. Her thoughts ran rampant inside while she stared down at Jes.

That growing power called to the hidden anger she kept buried deep inside. The bitterness she rarely allowed to come to the surface jumped, ready to be let out to play. She wasn't sure what she was even doing there; trusting had never been easy for her, yet there she was trusting Jes when she wasn't sure she could even trust herself.

"Orah, we don't have all day," Jes said from the ground below.

Shaking her head, she turned away and stared at the platform.

Trust.

The word felt bitter on her tongue. She thought back on all the times she trusted and her trust had been broken. She thought of trusting one of the few people who she should have been able to count on in her life and the black hole of despair that trust allowed in. She thought of her father and how thoroughly she trusted him but even he eventually left her as well. Tears welled in her eyes and her gaze locked on the platform ahead.

How could she trust this power if she couldn't trust those closest to her?

How could she trust the power wasn't there to hurt her in some way?

How could she trust herself when she didn't even know what she was doing most days?

Her chest tightened and her anger begged to be let out. She stared at the obstacle course designed to supposedly help her learn how to protect herself. To protect herself from people like Marek.

I wouldn't even be here if I hadn't forced that damned door open.

Her vision blurred and she cursed herself and her stubbornness. How unwilling she was to just leave the door alone and come back another day. That had always been her thing – she could never leave things alone.

She poked.

She prodded.

She demanded the right things to be done. She wanted her way when it felt unfair.

Her breathing became low while the anger consumed her. Her body hummed and that darkness seemed to smile, clawing itself out of its hidden depths.

If only she could have left things alone she could have avoided so much pain in her life. If she didn't insist on pushing, perhaps certain things wouldn't have happened. If her anger hadn't driven her to lash out, perhaps certain people would have still been there.

She could no longer see the platform. Her vision was blurred by the tears falling down her cheeks. Her hands felt warm and tingling and a strange buzz hummed from the tips of her toes to the top of her head. She laughed a low guttural laugh, as though she'd lost complete control of herself.

How convenient this power would have been years ago.

Why hadn't it shown up when she needed it most?

When she was most vulnerable?

Darkness clawed up her throat and she threw her head back, letting out a scream. Sounds around her went out but the last thing she heard was Jes's curse below her.

It's warmer. She blinked away her tears.

Large hands on her arms startled her and her feet lifted off the ground. "What the hell?" she screamed, thrashing at the hands gripping her. They rose into the air and she stared down in horror. The obstacle course was on fire.

"Orah you need to calm down right now." Reality came back and she realized Jes was who had her – Jes's hands held her arms.

A large gust of wind next to her pulled her gaze from the hypnotizing flames and she looked to her right. Tume was now hovering next to her watching the flames. Relief washed over Orah, she would have never forgiven herself if her fury had injured the Pegasus.

Taking a deep breath in then out she watched mesmerized while the flames shrank further and further with each breath she let out. They hovered over the course while she breathed until finally the flames reduced to smoldering embers. Nothing appeared to have been destroyed, but a heavy layer of smoke surrounded them when they landed back on the ground.

Jes set her down and she rubbed her arms. "I'm definitely going to bruise," she whispered, while her fingers brushed tender spots.

"Bruise?" Jes snapped his head to her. His eyes were wide with either anger or surprise. Maybe both. "You're worried that I *may* have bruised you after pulling your ass from a fire you set? What were you doing up there to cause a fire to erupt?"

They stared at each other while she considered his question. "I was thinking," she said.

"Thinking? About what? The firepits of Shadus?" his hands fell, smacking against his thighs.

"Well, since I don't actually know what that is or looks like, no. I was–" Stopping herself, she stared at him. He didn't need to know what she was thinking about. "I was just thinking. That's all."

His eyes narrowed. "Orah, no one that was thinking about anything good sets an entire obstacle course on fire."

"It doesn't matter what I was thinking about," she snapped.

"If you want me to train you, then you need to be honest with me," he bit back.

"I will be honest as best as I can, Jes."

Stepping back, his eyes scanned her up and down. "You can't control whatever magic you have if you can't accept yourself or what lives inside you."

Irritated, she crossed her arms "You've said this before. I don't need advice on how to deal with my traumas."

Shock flashed across his face. "Traumas?"

"We're not getting into that. Let's make a deal. You will train me and I will figure out my own shit inside my head." He opened his mouth to respond but she threw up her hand, stopping him. "I will figure out my own shit *myself*," she said, firmly.

For a moment he looked as though he was going to argue but instead he nodded, stepping back. "I'm not sure what you've lived through Orah but I won't pry. I'll accept your deal."

"Thank you," she grimaced. "Did I break your course?"

"No. This isn't the first time someone's power has caused a little destruction," he said with a laugh.

She watched him walk toward the wardpad, motioning for her to follow. He pricked his thumb, pressed it against the pad. In an instant the destroyed obstacles were replaced by the course she'd observed when they first arrived. As though her flare of anger hadn't happened.

Amazed and slightly amused she turned back to him with a grin. "Well. Now that that's fixed, how about the other half of our training?"

He shook his head sternly. "We're not sparring today, Orah."

"What? Why not?" she asked.

With a smile he approached her then poked her side. She jumped back screaming from the jolt of pain and glared at him. "What did you do that for?"

"You're injured. I'm not teaching you how to fight when you were knocked through the air and onto your ass," Jes replied.

"I could get injured every single day we're out here. Does that mean you'll perpetually put off teaching me to defend myself?" she asked, sure she was making a valid point.

"No. What it means is that we need to be better prepared tomorrow. There are tonics you can take to help protect yourself from injuries. We'll want to grab some from the city before we come back."

Trying to hide her grimace as she shifted, she placed her hand on him and scowled. "And once we have those, you'll teach me how to fight?"

He gave her a sly smile "Yes."

The anticipation of what was to come was almost painful while she imagined all she could accomplish there. What she could possibly discover about herself. What she could possibly accept about herself...

She turned back to walk toward Tume and tilted slightly from the pain in her side reminding her it was still there. Jes rushed to her, steadying her. "We better get you back to the house," he whispered. His hands wrapped around her shoulders and he slowly guided her to Tume. "May I?" he asked, pointing to her waist then toward the saddle.

"Oh – yeah but be careful, please." He wrapped his hands around her and lifted. Her side spasmed in protest and she let out several pants trying to ignore the pain.

Jes grimaced. "Are you going to be good to fly?"

"I think so. You said it's only fifteen minutes, right?" She tried to tell herself fifteen minutes was nothing, but just sitting in the saddle was already agonizing.

Concern flashed over his face and he buckled the straps around her. "Yes, but I think you're more injured than you realize. Fifteen minutes may feel like fifteen hours."

"There's no other way to get back, right?"

"Correct," he replied.

"Then I guess we better go then."

Nodding he patted Tume, whispering something she couldn't hear. Tume looked back at Orah cautiously then back at Jes. With a nod and a huff she reared back and shot into the sky. Tears sprung from Orah's eyes at the jolt of pain that cascaded through her. Tume flew as though she were trying to take it easy but Orah's side screamed in protest. She tried her best to sit as still throughout the ride, keeping her eyes on the city as it grew closer.

Jes hadn't been kidding that the time it took to get back would feel longer. When they finally descended, Orah let out a breath of relief that she would be out of the saddle soon. She gasped when they landed and found Roan standing by the stables talking to Kai. Slowly he turned and she knew somehow he was aware she'd been injured.

"What happened?" His question was more of a command and she stared at him in shock.

Landing next to her, Jes bowed his head. "The course warded itself to try and invoke her powers. She was thrown to the ground on her first try."

"How?" Roan's voice echoed through the trees surrounding the stables.

Orah and Jes glanced at each other nervously. Taking a deep and very painful breath Orah replied, "There were platforms coming out of the mountains and these cylinders shooting in and out of the mountain. I jumped from one platform to the other and the cylinder thought it needed to stop me." She lifted her shirt to show him and winced. Roan and Kai's responding gasps surprised her and she looked down. *Shit.* She hadn't taken a moment yet to check herself out and found a large bruise running right above her hip to the top of her ribs.

The ground shook and Roan turned to Jes. "Did you seem to forget that she's a mortal?"

"She's a mortal with powers, Roan." Jes stood taller with his arms folded.

Orah rolled her eyes. She was getting tired of them acting as though they knew more about her well-being than she did. She patted Tume's neck and the Pegasus lowered her front legs, understanding Orah's request. Unbuckling Orah hopped out of the saddle, landing on the ground with a soft "Umph." Standing as steadily as she could she straightened herself hoping neither Roan nor Jes could see the pain now rattling her bones.

They both turned their attention from each other and rushed to her side. Throwing up her hands, she stopped them and held onto the saddle for support. "Despite what either of you think, I know what's best for myself." Looking at Roan she stood a little straighter. "I know you feel that my wellbeing is your responsibility, but it's not. I know what I'm getting into by training at a magically controlled course. Jes told me today we were both unprepared and that won't happen next time."

Roan was silent, seeming to contemplate his response before he nodded. "I understand. Jes can you please run to the healer and grab as many tonics as you can?" Orah kept her eyes on Roan while Jes launched himself into the air.

Roan walked toward her with his arms out. "I know you said you've got yourself but you look like you might fall down at any moment. Can I help you inside?"

As if on cue, her legs shook under her and she nodded her head. "I think that's probably wise," she replied. Expecting him to wrap his arms around her shoulders like Jes had at the camp, but instead he scooped her up into his arms. "Shit!" The curse flew out of her mouth from the pain that spasmed in her side.

"I've never heard anyone curse as often as you do." Roan laughed.

She blushed. "That's not even the worst thing I've said."

He did nothing to hide the amusement in his response. "Oh I know."

She clutched the back of his shirt while he made his way inside. Ms. Perri met them at the bottom of the stairs and stared at Orah. "What did you do to yourself?" Ms. Perri asked, covering her mouth with her hand.

Orah smiled. "Just a bit of training. I'm fine."

Ms. Perri's eyes shot to Roan and he nodded. "She'll be okay. Jes ran to the healer for tonics. But I need help getting her door open upstairs." With a nod Ms. Perri rushed beside them while Roan tried to walk up the stairs as slowly as he could. Each step he took was more agonizing than the last and Orah was covered in a thin layer of sweat by the time they made it to the top.

Roan leaned down whispering in her ear, "I know you can't really control it but could you try not sweating so much? You might slip out of my arms." His joke shocked her and she let out a laugh followed immediately by groans of pain.

"Oh. Please don't make me laugh," she said.

"Why would I ever not try and make you laugh?" he replied.

Too shocked to know how to respond she looked up when he stopped at her bedroom doors. Ms. Perri ushered them into the room while she pulled back the covers to Orah's bed.

"There are more pillows there than when I woke up this morning," Orah observed, staring at the plush mountain on the bed.

Ms. Perri nodded. "The room seems to know you need them."

Catching the odd glance Roan gave Ms. Perri, Orah wasn't sure what it meant but she didn't care. Her body spasmed from the pain and all she wanted was to be put down somewhere comfortable. Roan leaned down and set her on the bed gently.

Wincing at the movement, Orah whispered, "Ow."

"Did I hurt you?" he asked, pausing himself to prevent moving her further. Orah couldn't help but notice his arms were still under her, pinned between her backside and the bed.

Blushing at the heat of his touch, she shook her head. "No." Her response was barely above a whisper. With a nod, he continued and slowly pulled his arms out from under her. They kept their eyes locked on each other for a moment before a voice clearing behind them forced them to break their trance.

"My Lord, I think I'll help our guest out of her training clothes," Ms. Perri said sternly.

Giving Orah a nod and a quick wink, Roan walked towards the bedroom doors. "I'll return once Jes comes back with the tonics. Take care of her, please." Roan addressed the last sentence to Ms. Perri before he turned to the bedroom door.

Orah watched while he closed the door behind him. She couldn't pull her mind away from how his hands felt on her. Ms. Perri cleared her throat again and Orah shifted her gaze from the bedroom door.

"Is there anything in particular that I can grab from the closet?" Ms. Perri asked.

"I think there might be some night gowns that Lahana brought that would be easy to slip on over my head," Orah replied.

Nodding, Ms. Perri walked into the closet. Orah listened to her rummage around and decided to try and shimmy her leggings off while alone for a moment. Orah's body felt stiffer with each movement and she was covered in sweat again by the time she kicked the leggings onto the floor when Ms. Perri returned. Orah's eyes widened, alarmed by what was in the housekeeper's arms.

"I can't wear that!" she yelled. Her cheeks went hot and she stared at the very sheer and very short black nightgown. Shaking her head, she cursed Lahana, sure she must have snuck in the outfit with the bags of clothes she'd bought Orah.

With a shrug Ms. Perri walked toward the bed. "This is short and easy to get on over your head. The light fabric also won't put pressure on the bruise I'm sure you have. Everything else is heavy, or too long for you to be able to move comfortably in."

Orah shook her head, unsure if she could allow Ms. Perri to help her into something so risqué. "Okay, well what about some of the night shirts and bottoms I know are in there?"

"I just watched you almost pass out from Roan bending down to put you on this bed. Do you think you'll be able to pull your own pants down to attend to your needs in the bathroom?" Ms. Perri replied with a scowl.

"Fine."

"Arms up please," Ms. Perri instructed.

Reluctantly she lifted her arms and yelped in pain. Shaking her head, she stifled a sob. "I don't know if I can."

"Let me help."

Ms. Perri's callused hands brushed against Orah's skin while she gently helped pull the shirt off Orah. Sweat ran down Orah's spine while they worked together, in slow movements. Orah was sure she would pass out from the pain when her top finally came up over her head.

Ms. Perri shook her head in disapproval once Orah's bruise was fully on display. Orah's stomach flipped while she stared down at herself, finding a bruise encircling her bust and traveling down her side.

Orah's arms crossed over her chest in a painful and near pathetic attempt to cover herself and her bra. Ms. Perri laughed. "We need to get that off you. It's putting pressure on your injury."

Orah watched while the housekeeper fished something out of her apron. A few seconds later, she pulled out a pair of silver scissors. Orah's cheeks flushed. Shaking her head, she tried to sound stern through her pain. "You are not cutting this off me and baring my tits out to the open air."

Ms. Perri let out a loud and slightly rough laugh. "Orah you seem to have forgotten I'm also a woman and I see *tits* every day I live. If you lean forward, I'll cut down the back and cut the straps off so it slips off once we get the nightgown over you. You can also hold it against your chest until the last second."

"Oh," Orah replied. "Yes, that sounds alright."

Ms. Perri offered her hand and helped Orah lean forward. "Can you bring your arms up to your chest?" Ms. Perri asked.

"Yes," Orah replied.

Breathing in and out, Orah pulled her arms up and braced them against her chest holding the bra in place. The cold shock of the scissors sent a shiver down her back while Ms. Perri cut the back and then snipped the straps so they were no longer connected. Orah kept her eyes on the comforter in front of her lap while Ms. Perri grabbed the night gown and slipped it over Orah's head. Slowly she pulled it down so it rested right at Orah's shoulders.

"Now, can you lift your arms just a bit to get them through?"

Orah's vision blurred from pain but she nodded her head. The night gown was now lowered enough and with her still leaning forward she knew she could slip her arms through the straps without issue. Ms. Perri held the first strap open while Orah pulled her arm through. Then they repeated their movement for the other side. The cut fragments of the bra fell to Orah's lap. Gently, Ms. Perri placed her hand on Orah's back and helped lower her back onto the pillows.

Orah had forgotten how sheer the nightgown was until the comforter brushed against her while Ms. Perri pulled it up. "Oh!" Orah shifted, trying to find somewhere more comfortable in all the pillows.

"I'm not sure how long it'll take Jes to come back from the healers. She's usually very busy this time of year," Ms. Perri said.

"This time of year?" Orah asked confused. It was warm enough she assumed it was summer and in her world one was less likely to get sick during the summer.

Ms. Perri smiled. "Yes, the children are all out of their tutoring and schools so lots of injuries for her to heal."

"Ah. That makes sense," Orah replied with a smile. Summer break appeared to be yet another universal experience then.

"Do you think you can sleep with how much pain you're in right now?" There was concern in Ms. Perris' eyes.

"Actually, yes I do." Orah's body hummed in response as though celebrating that she finally paid attention to what it had silently been asking for.

Ms. Perri nodded. "Good. Either myself or Roan will be back with the tonics once they arrive. I'll also make sure he doesn't forget your drink." She said the last part with a wink.

Orah watched while she gathered the sweat-stained and smoke-filled clothes while she made her way to the bedroom doors. "Thank you, Ms. Perri."

With a smile, Ms. Perri looked back. "Orah, please call me Etta."

She turned to walk out the doors again but Orah called out to her.

"Etta?"

"Yes?" Etta replied.

"Thank you for the ring. I realize I haven't taken the time to say that. I don't know what I would have done without it."

Etta smiled. "That ring is very special, Orah. It belonged to someone who you remind me of."

"You gave it to me before you even knew me," Orah replied, trying not to appear too shocked.

Etta shook her head. "It didn't matter. I knew *who* you are."

Orah was left feeling baffled while she watched Etta close the doors behind her. Nothing the housekeeper said made any sense but her exhaustion battled against her mind, taking control of her thoughts. Settling into the pillows, she finally allowed herself the rest she needed, while wondering what Etta could have possibly been referring to.

Chapter 21

Roan paced the hallway next to the kitchen—Jes still hadn't returned. Ms. Perri assured him Orah was settled and asleep, but he couldn't handle the thought of her up there with how much pain she was likely in. His pacing grew frantic and he sighed, deciding to check on what was taking so long.

He turned toward the side door when it flew open and Jes stood in the doorway breathing as though he ran to the manor. "I'm so sorry!" Jes yelled. The large bag in his hand clinked as he threw up the other hand. "There were two Godlings that had each somehow broken a bone minutes before I arrived."

Roan's irritation vanished. "Thank you for waiting that long. I was about to come check on you."

"How is she?" Jes asked.

"Ms. Perri says that she's asleep. We haven't heard any noise up there so I'm assuming she still is," Roan replied.

"How bad is it?" Guilt flashed across Jes's face. Roan walked towards him, setting his hand on his shoulder for reassurance.

"She's pretty banged up. Apparently, that bruise we saw extends further and wraps around the top of her rib cage."

Jes's eyes widened and he shook his head. "I swear Roan, I didn't push her like in the training room. But I also didn't know the course would ward something like that."

"How different was it from what you've seen before?" Roan replied.

"Some elements were the same but there were some I've never seen before. Those rock arms Orah mentioned earlier, an odd firepit, and a wall like in the training room, but at the top of the wall was a door."

Roan's eyebrow crumbled. "What do you mean a door?"

"I mean an almost exact replica of that door in the garden. Like the doors she's warded in the training room. I couldn't make out whether or not it had the same engravings on it, but it was the same color," Jes said.

Roan wasn't sure what to make of all these doors and what connection they had to Orah. "How did she get hurt?"

"The platforms that usually appear on the side of the mountain, those arms were between each one. She was jumping from one and from what I could see, she miscalculated the jump. The arm slammed right into her side."

Roan winced. She may have an unknown power inside of her, but she was still mortal. A mortal who could easily die.

"But Roan." Jes's tone changed, something similar to pride and admiration. "She got back up. I thought the Fates were playing a trick on me. I watched her fall to the ground and have the air knocked out of her, but she got up and tried again."

Roan looked down the hall behind him while a smile crept to the side of his mouth. She was so damned stubborn she couldn't accept she had been injured. Turning back to Jes, he nodded. "What happened after that?" Jes shuffled his feet. Roan didn't like the change in his body language. "Jes?" he asked.

Jes sighed nervously. "I don't know what happened exactly. She stood up on that platform for a while. Finally, I thought she might turn back the way she had gone up, but I encouraged her not to. I watched her stand there staring at it. I might be wrong, but I think she started shaking slightly and then everything around me burst into flames. If I had been paying any less attention the flames would have engulfed me."

Roan's eyes widened and he stepped back. "What?"

"The entire course was engulfed. I barely made it to her, and the flames didn't let up until I was able to get her to calm down. Tume barely made it into the air as well. All three of us were just hovering over the course watching it. You might see some large bruises on her arms from how quickly and roughly I grabbed her."

"And you have no idea what happened?" Roan asked.

"She mentioned something about thinking and traumas?" Jes replied.

Roan's chest tightened and he thought back on the blurred memories he'd seen in Orah's mind. How quickly her tears fell before he'd even started. He wondered what the woman had gone through in her life. What horrible things had she witnessed to cause a reaction like that?

"We need to get those tonics up to her. Do you have everything she needs?" Roan said, choosing not to discuss Orah's own past behind her back.

"There's a very specific one for today to help heal her now and prevent any further damage. That's actually here in my pocket," Jes replied while his free hand patted his thigh. "The bag here is for all the tonics we'll need to continue her training and ensure this doesn't happen again."

The tightness in Roan's chest shifted to anger. "What do you mean continue her training? She could have died today, Jes."

"I'm very aware of that, Roan. She insisted though. She wants to learn this power of hers. We don't have a lot of time before your birthday or the challenge. She needs to be as prepared as she can be."

"She'll be home by then." Roan wouldn't discuss the alternative. He refused to accept that he would not have found a solution by that point.

Jes stepped forward, placing his hand on Roan's shoulder. "There is no way you can know that for sure."

Roan knew he was right. As much as he didn't want to admit it, he knew. "Let's go get her that tonic. We'll address the rest later."

Silently they walked toward the stairs. Roan braced himself for what they would find when they got to her room and hoped she was still asleep. He wasn't sure how that could be possible given the bruise he'd seen on her out at the stables. Reaching the top of the stairs Roan felt oddly nervous, but that was how Orah made him feel. As though he were dizzy and off balance anytime he was near her or walked in her general vicinity. He laughed nervously and glanced at a smiling Jes.

"She's not going to bite you." Jes knocked his shoulder against Roan's.

Roan suppressed his laugh while shaking his head. "Now we both know that's probably not true." Covering his mouth, Jes chuckled and nodded his head. They both knew just how fierce she was.

They approached her door and Roan knocked. Moments passed with no answer and his anxiety built. Possibilities rushed in his mind. She could have just been asleep, or something worse could have happened. Breathing out, he knocked a little more firmly and waited. Thirty seconds passed. Jes nodded at the door, instructing Roan to try and turn the handle. Roan gripped the handle and the door clicked open with ease. He let out a breath of relief.

Quietly they walked into the dark room. Heavy breathing came from the direction of the bed—Orah was asleep. He looked back at Jes and stepped back confused at why Jes's eyes were glued to the ceiling.

Quickly glancing back at Orah, Roan stopped dead in his tracks.

What is she wearing? He had no idea where she got the nightgown or why she had put it on. Maybe she was trying to tease him again. *Maybe she's trying to kill me and Fates, it's working.*

His eyes scanned her from head to toe, lingering on the too thin fabric along her chest. He shook his head and turned back to Jes, trying to hold in his laugh at how uncomfortable his Beskermer appeared; as though he had never seen a woman dressed that way in his life.

Roan walked up to the bed, making sure to keep his eyes above her neck. His heart beat rapidly against his chest and he tried to control his thoughts while he pulled the blanket over her. He almost had it fully pulled up to her chin when her eyes popped open and her hand grasped his wrist.

Roan's eyes widened. *Fates, she's strong!* He stared into the flecks of gold that looked as though they were on fire. Burning fear and anger radiated from her and barreled right into him. Peeling her fingers from his wrist he tried to calm her. "I promise I had no ill intention. I was trying to cover you again. The blanket slipped."

Cool embarrassment replaced her hot anger and she glanced down at herself. Roan covered her chest, to his own dismay, until the blanket was resting at the base of her neck. Wincing she shifted to look toward the balcony doors.

"Thank you," she said.

Roan could barely hear her whisper but felt the pain that came with the movement. Dropping his voice to a whisper, he gestured behind him. "Jes has the tonic for you. Are you doing alright?"

Orah grimaced, shifting in the bed. "Yes and no. The sleep helped, but my body is stiff. Like my muscles have locked up and I have to force them to move."

Jes approached them both and Roan stepped back, allowing him to move in front of her. Jes sat on the bed. "This won't taste great going down, but you should feel the effects almost immediately." Jes's voice was now soft and soothing. Jes may have been a hardass when training but he always took care of his own.

Orah shifted to move but froze and let out a gasp. Icy shots of pain collided into Roan like a blast and he rushed to the other side of the bed. Her eyes widened when he climbed onto the other side and made his way toward her.

"What are you doing?" she demanded. There was a layer of panic but also, to his amusement, intrigue under the pain while she stared at him.

"I'm going to help support you so you can sit up better. Don't tell me you don't need it either," Roan replied.

Her eyes darted to Roan then back to Jes. Jes offered her a smile then motioned to Roan with his hand. With a sigh she grimaced while she shifted again, nodding her head. Roan moved across the bed until he was seated next to her. His eyes widened briefly at the purple under the sheer fabric of the night gown. Shaking his head, he shifted his gaze, not wanting her to think he was staring at her body.

Gently he wrapped one arm around her for support while she braced against the other and they worked together until she was in a sitting position. The only sound that filled the room were her quiet sobs. The burning cold of her pain was almost enough to overwhelm Roan, but he kept his hold on her. Ensuring she knew he had her.

By the time she was sitting, her face had a sheen of sweat across it. The bed shifted from Jes moving closer now with the small vial in his hands.

"Okay, Orah. I need you to promise that no matter how bad this tastes that you'll finish it all," Jes said sternly.

Orah tensed against Roan. "Jes, I am not a child."

Roan coughed trying to hold in his laugh. She was underestimating the tonic. He certainly had the first time it was shoved down his own throat. He shivered thinking about the taste and her eyes shot to his.

"Is something funny?" she snapped.

Jes coughed and Roan smiled. "What? No—nothing funny here."

"Ready?" Jes held his lips in a tight line to push down his own smile.

Orah nodded her head. Jes pulled the small bottle out of his pocket popping off the cork. The smell hit Roan and he turned trying to hide his gag. Orah tensed against him. Turning his head back to her, he watched while she grabbed the bottle and threw back the tonic. Her body went stiff and Roan glanced at Jes who shook his head in response. They watched her, waiting to see if she was okay when she finally shivered against Roan and let out a breath.

"Jesus Christ, that was awful," she whispered. Roan laughed at the disgust in her whisper and she shifted in his arms glaring up at him. "If you're going to laugh then why don't you try it?" Roan opened his mouth to respond when her eyes widened, and she stared down at herself. "I can move!"

Wiggling out of Roan's arms, she twisted her upper body back and forth. "I'm still sore but I don't feel as stiff." Tears lined her eyes and she laid back against her pillow staring up at the ceiling with a smile.

Jes's eyes jumped back to the ceiling and it didn't take Roan much effort to understand why. Keeping his eyes on the wall across from him he hoped she would notice she was exposed again.

A sly tone came from her and she chuckled. "Have you guys never seen breasts before?"

The bed shifted while Jes jumped up, stumbling on his feet, and almost crashing to the ground. Clearing his throat, Jes kept his eyes upward. "I'm glad you're feeling better, Orah. I gathered enough tonics to last us a while for further training. Meet me at the stables tomorrow after you've finished your usual kitchen duties with Yohan." He glanced at her, offering her a smile before rushing back out of the room.

Now alone with Orah, Roan's curiosity had to be sated. "Are you going to tell me why you're wearing that tempting nightgown?" he asked.

She met his eyes. "It was Etta."

"What?" His shock was genuine. He almost didn't believe her.

"Yeah." Orah pulled the covers up to her chin then shook her head. "Well Etta and Lahana. Lahana must have bought the damn thing but Etta pulled it out of the closet for me. She said anything else in there would have rubbed or pushed against my injury and this was the best choice"

Roan ran his hand through his hair. "I think Etta's trying to kill me."

"What?" Orah asked.

"Nothing," he replied. He cleared his throat and studied her. She didn't seem to be in too much pain. He suspected her bruises would be pretty awful for a while. That was one thing the tonic couldn't clear up quickly. It could heal whatever injury was below the bruise, but the coloring of the skin had to clear up on its own.

Desperate to change the topic from that little night gown, he cleared his throat again. "How are you feeling now?"

Twisting left and right again she pulled her arms out from under the blanket and lifted them high above her head. "Good as new. I couldn't do this earlier. Etta had to help me get my shirt off before."

"Why the sudden change from Ms. Perri to Etta?" he asked.

"Why don't *you* call her Etta?" she replied.

The question shocked Roan and they made eye contact. He could have answered her, if he had a logical answer, but he didn't. "I used to. I'm not sure what happened but once I was made the Governing God I just kind of stopped," he admitted.

Shifting his hips away from her, he slid off the bed and walked toward the couch. "Etta, she was, well she was my mother away from home as a child. She was the housekeeper for my Uncle's palace, and I pestered her to no end. But when I became the Governing God, something inside me shifted. Like I couldn't justify calling her something so casual with the position she has in my household."

Orah sat up, pulling the blanket to her chin. He watched her knees under the blanket pull upwards then she rested her face against them. He smiled. She was listening and she was listening intently.

She cocked her head to the side. "But you call Yohan by his first name, and Kai. Why not Etta?"

It was a valid question. One that Etta asked Roan many times over the years. Struggling to answer, he looked down. "I don't know honestly. I love her and would do anything to help or protect her. Maybe it's all the formal training that was hammered into me growing up in my Father's palace. I'm not sure. Ms. Pe... Etta insists that I call her what I once did. Maybe I'll get there again. If I can get my own head out of the sand."

Orah's eyes narrowed and she lifted her chin from her knees "You sure it's not anything to do with her being a woman?"

"Excuse me?" Roan replied.

Blushing, Orah glanced down at the bed. "Never mind."

Standing from the couch, he walked toward the bed. "I need to make one thing clear, Orah. No man is better than a woman. There may be many in this land who feel this way, but I do not. I don't know why I have this weird block and formality with her, but I can assure you it has nothing to do with her being a woman."

"Well, there's no use in arguing over it," Orah said. Patting the mattress, she motioned for him to sit beside her.

Settling next to her, he sighed. "So, you're feeling better. You're enjoying a treat. Are you going to be getting up or staying cozy in bed the rest of the day?"

Her answering smack against his shoulder made him yelp and he stared at her shocked. "You just hit me."

"You were being mean." Her eyes sparkled.

He was readying to throw out a snarky response when the bedroom door flung open abruptly. They both jumped, finding a disheveled Jes in the doorway.

A pit settled in Roan's stomach and he stared at his Beskermer. "Everything okay?" Roan asked. He was trying to sound calm and collected but the concern on Jes's face made that difficult.

Jes's eyes darted to Orah, then he nodded. "Amada sent word."

"Did she have an answer?" Roan replied.

Jes shook his head. "I don't know. We just got a message that says she's sending someone to talk to us some more."

Rolling his eyes, Roan stood from the bed. "*Someone specific?*" He had to ask even though he knew the answer.

Orah turned toward Roan. "Moros?"

"Yes." Jes's abrupt answer cut Roan off. Confused, Roan watched Jes turn his back and leave the room. Unable to interpret the reaction, Roan turned back to Orah.

"I don't think we're going to have an uneventful evening," she sighed.

Orah laid back against her pillow, watching Roan shut the door behind him. Jes left the room in such a hurry that Roan claimed he needed to find out where he'd run off to. Groaning, she lifted the comforter and swung her legs off the bed. The tonic was helping with the overwhelming pain, but her body was still stiff. Each step she took toward the bathroom was strained.

If Moros wasn't expected to arrive soon, she would have stayed in bed, but nothing was going to stop her from being part of that conversation.

Taking a long and careful shower, Orah made sure to dress in something loose and comfortable before heading out of the room. Reaching the bottom of the stairs, she turned to walk to the kitchen but a knock at the door stopped her. Frantically she looked around, hoping someone was going to answer but she was alone in the quiet foyer. With a deep breath she glanced toward Roan's study doors then walked past them, reaching for the front door. Pulling it open, she found Moros standing in front of her with a wide, almost irritating grin.

"Mortal! You're still here!" he said with an excited squeal.

Her annoyance boiled beneath the surface while she stared at him, tempted to shut the door in his face. It would have been cathartic, but she thought Roan would have been livid if she did. It wasn't exactly great manners to send away the messenger possibly bearing their answers. With a sigh, she gestured for Moros to come in.

"The wards have been updated." Moros inspected the door frame while he walked in.

Orah shrugged. "There's been a pest problem lately."

Moros's turned toward her and the grin on his face widened. "Yes, I've heard. Tell me, how are the two rival brothers getting along?" he asked.

"As well as you'd expect." Roan's voice behind her caught her off guard and she turned to find him standing at the bottom of the stairs. Gracefully he stepped off the stairs, walking toward the sitting room. "I believe Amada sent you here with some information?" Roan said.

Moros glanced at Orah then back at Roan. "I guess." Flipping his long hair back over his shoulder he winked at Orah as he followed Roan into the other room.

With a wide grin, Moros plopped onto the couch. His eyes darted back and forth from Roan to the sitting room door. Orah couldn't help but pick up the odd behavior. Moros seemed nervous but she wasn't sure why.

Roan cleared his throat. "Well? What was Amada sending you with?"

Moros glanced at the sitting room door once more before sighing. A mask of indifference fell across his face. "She said you were asking about portals again. I thought you'd already gotten your answer." He looked down at his nails as if searching for some kind of flaw.

"You know just as well as I do that I asked her a much more specific question," Roan replied.

A glimmer of something Orah didn't like flashed in Moros's eyes. "Yes, I know, but I want to test something first before I give you her answer."

"Excuse me?" Roan replied.

Orah jumped back when Moros stood and walked toward where she was by the window. "I just have a theory that I need to test out." He placed his hands out in front of him as if inviting Orah to take them.

Stepping back, she shook her head. "I would rather not."

"Oh please. I promise I won't hurt you," Moros said.

Orah glanced at Roan. Panic was boiling to the surface. She didn't know if Moros would hurt her, but she didn't want to take any chances. "Roan?" her plea came out in a whimper.

There was a shift in the air and Roan stood. "What are you playing at Moros?" Roan walked toward where Moros slowly approached Orah. His eyes were lit with anger and a buzz electrified the air.

"I have a theory that I need to test. Roan, you know I'm not dangerous." Moros's too innocent tone set Orah on edge. Her body hummed while he drew closer.

"Moros, knock it off." Roan's previously annoyed tone shifted to anger. Orah's heartbeat quickened while she stepped back, bumping into the wall behind her.

"Back off," she demanded, not recognizing the tone in her own voice. The lights in the room flashed on and off. She watched in a daze; Roan was losing his temper like she was. Moros stopped for a moment and grinned, peering back at Roan. Roan opened his mouth to protest when Moros ran toward Orah.

"I said back off!" Orah screamed and every light in the room shut off.

Seconds passed and Orah braced for Moros to collide into her, but nothing happened. Her ears buzzed and sounds were far away while she tried to make out any shapes in the room. She could hear muffled noises, but she couldn't tell where or who they were coming from.

Sinking to the ground she pulled her knees to her chin. She didn't know why Roan wasn't bringing back the light. Her eyes widened and she couldn't push down the panic while she considered what Roan could be doing to want to keep the room so dark.

Several minutes passed but to Orah it felt like hours when hands on her shoulder startled her. Pulling her head from her knees she blinked at the voice she was hearing.

Lahana

"Orah." Lahana's voice was a whisper. Her hands held Orah's shoulder firmly. "Orah it's okay. You can bring the light back."

What?

The comment startled Orah and every light blinked on again. She looked up to find Roan standing a few feet from her with his mouth open in shock. Moros was on the ground attempting to stand but appeared to be fighting some invisible force, like the air itself was attacking him.

"There you go. That's good." Lahana was still behind Orah, rubbing her back in slow comforting circles. Orah's eyes fell to Lahana's but she glanced back, realizing she could barely hear what she assumed were very loud yells coming from Moros.

"Why can't I hear him?" Orah's voice still didn't sound like her own. It was monstrous. Almost like Roan had sounded with Marek.

Lahana smiled. "Well, you've got us in a wind barrier."

Shock rippled through Orah. "A what?" She turned to face Lahana, finding her with an amused, almost proud, grin on her face. Lahana pointed forward and Orah turned watching Roan attempt to walk toward them but was then thrown back when he got half an arm's length away.

"I'm doing this?" Orah said. *There is no way I'm doing this.*

"Yes, and as funny as it is to watch Moros repeatedly fall on his ass, I think you've made your point," Lahana replied. Lahana stood then offered Orah her hand.

"How did you get in?" Orah asked.

"My magic calls to the wind. For some reason you heard me and let me in. I couldn't see anything, but I could hear the wind in the house and followed."

"I made the *whole* house lose light?"

"Yes, but we can talk about that later. Take one deep breath in, thank the wind for its protection and then let it out," Lahana replied.

Keeping her eyes on Moros, Orah followed Lahana's instructions. Deep breath in. *Thank you wind and air for your protection.* Deep breath out.

Sounds flooded back and Orah held down her laugh at the shrieks coming from Moros. They stopped abruptly and he shot to his feet. He glared at Orah with anger swimming in his eyes. She was sure he would attack when a sly grin spread across his face and he pointed at Orah. "I *knew* it."

"What?" Orah replied, confused and also unable to hide her anger.

Keeping his eyes on her, Moros sat back down. "I knew there was something different about you. Tell me, Roan, how did you transfer some of your power to her?"

"I–" Roan paused then rubbed his jaw. "I didn't do anything."

Shocked, Orah watched Roan walk toward the couch and sit next to Moros.

"Interesting," Moros replied.

Lahana's hand on Orah's shoulder tightened and she leaned down as if to whisper.

"Let's sit down."

Orah jumped and stared at Lahana.

"The wind." Lahana's eyes widened. Orah could hear Lahana's voice clearly and yet, no sound came from her unmoving lips.

"Think of all the secrets we can keep." Lahana covered her mouth and looked over at Roan.

A breeze licked at Orah's fingertips and she took in a breath, feeling the wind play against her skin. Focusing on the guiding near teasing tingle in the air, Orah replied, *"I think I'm going to like this."*

Roan's eyebrows shot up and his eyes widened. Sighing, he leaned against the couch, running his hands through his hair. Orah bit back her laugh at his quiet curse.

Orah sat down on a chair opposite of Roan. "What do you mean I have Roan's power?" she asked Moros.

"Well, unless you know anyone else that can lose their temper and make every single light in the room shut off then please introduce me to them." Moros turned to Roan. "She somehow even picked up on that freaky voice trick you do."

"What's happening to me?" Orah asked. She didn't know whether to feel fear, excitement, or even anger.

Roan's expression shifted to concern, as did Moros's, surprisingly. "Orah, I have no idea, but this is why we need to get you home," Roan replied.

"Does Marek know?" Moros asked.

"Why are you asking me? He's *your* friend," Roan snapped.

"Friends don't tell each other everything," Moros snapped at Roan, "I bet there are *plenty* of things you and Orah don't know about one another."

As if in sync, both Roan and Orah cleared their throats, shifting in their seats.

"We need to get her home before Marek finds out more than he already knows. Or worse, before he tells my father. What did your mother say?" Roan replied.

Letting out an exaggerated sigh Moros leaned against the back of the couch. "She said there *could* be ways to adjust the portals we have but she's not certain." His hand flew up and pile of books and scrolls landed on the sitting room floor. Waving his hand toward the pile he continued, "She sent me with these, and claimed they all have some mention of portals. There are obviously more but she thought these would be the most helpful."

Roan and Orah stared at the books. "Thank you, Moros. I'm sure Orah's as eager as I am to start on some research." Standing, Roan brushed his legs. "Now I wish you a safe journey home."

Moros grinned, his eyes moved toward the sitting room door. "Oh. I thought I'd *stay* the night and enjoy your little city before heading home tomorrow." Laughing at Roan's obvious discomfort, Moros stood. "Don't worry, I wasn't planning on staying *here*. I'll get a room in the city center." His eyes twinkled with delight, but his eyes hadn't moved away from where they gazed behind Orah. Slowly and curiously, Orah turned right as Jes darted out the front door.

Chapter 22

Orah wasn't sure how, but Lahana somehow convinced Roan to allow Moros to dinner—an event that only she was excited about. Standing at the sitting room window, Orah watched the pair ride off in the carriage to get Moros a room in the city center before dinner.

"Those two always get into trouble when they're together." Roan said.

"I wouldn't have thought that they liked each other."

"Moros is an interesting person. He's either the most annoying bastard you'll ever come across or he's the funniest bastard you'll ever spend time with," he replied.

"Were you both once close?" Orah noticed the hurt tone Roan had earlier. It felt a bit too personal for there to not be any history between the two.

Roan sighed. "I don't know if close is the right word. But we once had more trust between one another than we do now."

Nodding, she turned away from the window, feeling no need to pry into his past. "So, how are we going to kill time between now and dinner?"

"Care for a little reading?" Roan asked.

Her heartbeat quickened and she nodded enthusiastically. There was almost no situation where she would decline a book and she hadn't been in the library in days. Curling up with a book sounded like the best way to burn time.

When they walked into the library Orah's breath loosened. She couldn't seem to get used to the beauty of the room. Spinning around slowly she took it in. The tall bookshelves, the smell, the way the windows casted the most perfect light across the entire room. Roan's laugh pulled her back to reality and she turned to face him.

"What's so funny?" she asked.

Shrugging, he sat down. "Nothing's funny. Watching you made me happy. That was a good sound."

Unsure how to respond she turned away from him instead. With a sigh she took in all the books again. "I don't know what to read."

"We could try some of the ones that Amada sent?"

"Oh! That's a great idea." she smiled back. "Where are they?"

"Etta brought them in when Lahana was convincing me to invite Moros to join us for dinner." Roan pointed to the table in the corner and Orah made her way over. There were a handful of books and scrolls all piled on top of each other. Some small, some large, and a large assortment of the scrolls. Picking up one of the books she frowned.

"Why is The First Queen in this pile?"

Roan's head snapped from where he was staring off in the distance. "What?"

Holding up the book, Orah waved it. "The First Queen. The first book I read here. It's in this pile."

"You rarely pick up after yourself. Maybe you left it there." he replied while he leaned back against the couch.

Scowling, Orah shook her head then turned back to the table. After a few moments of consideration she grabbed 3 scrolls and 2 of the books then made her way over to him. "I don't think I can read most of these so I'll need the spectacles. Can you read all these?"

She laid the pile in front of him and he carefully inspected each one. Nodding, he smiled, "I might struggle with two of the three scrolls but I think I've got it."

Orah curiously looked at the pile. Unless her eyes were playing tricks on her, they all appeared to be written in different languages. Glancing back at him she couldn't help but ask her question. "How many languages can you speak and or read in?"

"Oh that's a good question." His eyes sparkled and he grinned back at her. "I honestly can't count at this point. I can read more than I can comfortably speak."

"How did you know that language I was speaking when I first arrived?" It had been a question she'd wanted answered for weeks now. She hadn't spoken French again, well, neither had he...

The grin on his face faltered and he stared across the room. "My mother." he murmured.

"How did she know it?"

With a sigh he stood and walked toward a bookshelf tucked under the stairs, as if it were meant to be hidden. "I'm not sure how she knew it but she loved it. My father hates it. Thinks it *sounds like gibberish* but my mother, my mother spoke it to us any chance she got." He disappeared while he crouched behind the bookshelf. She could hear him rummaging and when he appeared again he had a large stack of books in his arms. "While I don't know how she found out about it, I know she taught herself and wrote everything down." With a loud thud he placed the books on the table. Orah stared in wonder, biting back her tears when she saw they were all written in French.

"She wrote these?"

"Yes. She wanted the language to live on even after she was gone." His eyes lined with tears but he quickly wiped them away. "Orah."

"Yes?"

"How did you know this language? You said it wasn't your native tongue either."

Orah stared at the books in front of her. Her chest tightened at the question. He had just shared something with her. She shivered, she should have felt fine sharing with him, but yet sharing that part of her past felt akin to clawing off her own skin. Taking a deep breath she kept her eyes on the books while she answered.

"My mother, she was born in the country where the language is from."

"France." Roan replied.

Smiling, Orah nodded. "Yes, you remember. She spent a lot of time there as a child and her family moved to where I was born when she was a teenager. She was fluent and taught me. I bought my chateau in the country as a way to—I guess feel close to her again." She blinked back the tears lining her eyes, turning her head so that he couldn't see. There were more reasons why she ended up in France. Why she bought the chateau. Why she was who she was. But she couldn't get into that.

"I understand wanting to be close to someone. Even if they may not deserve it." Roan said.

His observation hit her in the chest. He'd walked through her memories. She was very aware of what she hadn't allowed him to see but the observation was a little too on the nose.

Leaning against the table, he crossed his arms. "As a young boy I tried to be close with my father. He's a hard man to try and do that with. I did everything I could to make him proud. I might have constantly argued with him but I wanted to be close with him. I wanted to understand him." Pushing off the desk he sighed and went back to the couch. "I guess even now I still want to. A small part of me hopes it would help me understand why he is the way that he is. Or at least understand the parts that I don't already know about."

The air tensed with his last sentence while he stared off into the distance. Orah observed him. In the weeks she'd been in his home she'd noticed the habit when he was lost in a thought he didn't want to share. It made her wonder how often she likely did the same thing.

"I get that. I tried for so long to understand my mother. Understand why she did the things she did and eventually I gave up. Going to France, I guess, was my way of accepting I'll never have the answers I want but I can take her memory and make something new out of it." Orah replied.

She had to hold back her laugh. She didn't even believe the words coming out of her mouth. She could have been a top student if there had ever been a class in bullshit 101. She had spent her life covering up the ugly with the presentable truth.

Shaking his head, he patted the couch cushion next to him. "Well, no point in chasing unattainable parents. Want to start reading?"

Scoffing she grabbed the pile, setting it down where he gestured and sat on the other side of them. Her hands moved to grab the spectacles when she remembered she'd forgotten them. A jingling noise rang in her ear and she glanced up to find Roan holding the spectacles with a large grin on his face.

"Looking for these?" he asked.

Snatching them out of his hand, she stuck her tongue out. "Yes."

His nostrils flared and his eyes landed on her lips. "Careful what you do with that tongue, Orah."

The only response she was able to give was to blink repeatedly while he continued staring at her lips. *He really needs to stop doing that.* Something, possibly a nymph, took control of her when she smirked and stared at his own mouth. "Is that a threat?" she teased.

The books between them flew to the floor before he was practically on top of her, pinning her against the arm of the couch. Their lips were now so close if she tilted her chin they would have touched.

"I don't make threats, Orah. At least not threats I don't intend to follow through with." Roan replied, pushing his body against hers. They held their gazes while their chests moved against each other. Subtly he shifted his hips and she smiled, feeling exactly what he was trying to conceal.

She stared into his eyes, knowing how easily she could kiss him. She wanted to kiss him. She wanted to wrap her arms around his neck and lock his study doors so they couldn't be bothered.

"Then don't make threats." she replied.

He let out a low groan and she bit her lip, waiting for his response. His eyes locked on hers then he slowly looked lower, scanning her neck and lips. Her hands shook with anticipation, unsure of what he would do next when a voice cleared at the library doorway.

As quickly as he'd pounced on her, Roan flew to the other side of the couch. Orah knew she was blushing when she turned and made eye contact with Jes.

"Yohan wants to know if we will be eating dinner in the dining room or kitchen." Jes said with a smirk.

Roan crossed his legs uncomfortably and shifted further down the couch. Jes's eyes darted to Orah. Orah shrugged, trying to hide her own smile.

A few seconds passed before Roan responded, clearing his throat. "Uh. The dining room. Tell Yohan we'll eat in the dining room."

"I'll make sure the message is conveyed." Jes turned to walk out of the room before turning back with a wicked grin. "Do I need to ward this room so you both aren't allowed in here at the same time?"

Orah didn't expect the book Roan threw at the back of Jes's head in response. She held back her laugh while Jes yelped, turning back to Roan with a scowl. "Do you need to fight off all that frustration, Roan? Why don't you stand and face me like a man."

Orah's hand covered her mouth while she tried to cover her gasp at the obvious mocking of Roan's current *situation*. She couldn't bring herself to make eye contact with him while she watched Jes stand at the door for a moment before winking and walking back out of the room.

The tension in the room thickened but she kept her eyes on the floor. The couch shifted and she found Roan sitting next to her again. A sly smile spread on his lips and his hand moved toward her face. Gently, he tucked a piece of hair behind her ear before he leaned forward and kissed her cheek.

"Too many nosey people in this house." he whispered while he pulled away.

Her hand moved to where his lips had been while she watched him stand from the couch. Placing his hand out for her to take, he pulled her up. "Better go get ready for dinner."

The only response Orah could give was a nod. He gestured for her to walk ahead and she didn't look back at him, but she knew his eyes were on her. Her body hummed, loudly protesting and screaming at her to question why she was leaving and not staying behind. Cursing softly, she reminded herself she couldn't cross that line with him and rushed to the stairs.

✴

Orah stared at the plate of dessert Xade placed in front of her and considered whether or not she could stomach eating it. Dinner had gone well, considering the awkward tension between Moros and Jes.

Moros let out a content sigh next to her. He had been poking and prodding Jes all night and Orah wasn't sure what to think of it. She didn't expect someone to be able to get under Jes's skin so skillfully. Lahana, however, thought it was hilarious and continued to remind Jes to loosen up a bit more.

Roan groaned, standing from his seat. "Well, despite my reservations, I think dinner was a success."

"Success?" Moros yelled drunkenly. "I say that was *fun*."

Jes shifted in his chair and stared at Moros. "Fun for who? You?"

With a grin Moros grabbed his wine glass and sipped from it. Not once breaking his eye contact with Jes. "Yes, actually. I had a great time."

The room fell silent while the two stared each other down. Unable to handle the tension, Orah cleared her throat and stood. "If you would excuse me, I'm going to the library to read what Amada sent."

Jes's attention turned to her then towards Roan and he smirked. "Reading alone or with a companion tonight?"

Moros sat taller at the obvious accusation. Orah opened her mouth to answer before Roan put up his hand. "I will be joining Orah in the library. I also want to read what Amada sent."

"Are you sure you'll be productive? You both seemed a little distracted earlier." Jes snorted out. A loud thump came from under the table and Jes yelped, bending down to rub his ankle. "What was that for?" His eyes went to Lahana and she smiled sweetly.

"Mind your business Jesiel." Lahana snapped.

Moros moved to stand next to Orah but almost knocked her down with his flailing limbs. "Fates." he yelped and hiccupped while he swayed on his feet. Orah rushed to steady him. She wasn't sure how he was going to get himself back to his room in the city in that condition.

"I'll get him back to the city." Jes said with a sigh.

"Why thank you handsome." Moros grinned and winked. Or tried to wink. He was too drunk to do it successfully and slowly blinked each eye one at a time. Roan grimaced at the awkward compliment then shook his head and stepped out of Jes's way. They all watched Jes drag Moros out of the dining room and to the hall.

The silence in the room was near palpable when Roan turned to Lahana. "Would you like to join us in the library?"

With a grin she glanced between him and Orah. "Why? Do you need a chaperone?"

"Absolutely not." Orah scoffed.

"Whatever you say." Lahana's smile widened and she stood. "But sure, why not? I have nothing better to do tonight. Fawn's not expecting me until tomorrow anyways."

"You're going back?" Orah couldn't hide her sadness.

"Not for the type of visit I would want. I'm actually Roan's official invitation deliverer."

"Would you please explain what is happening with a bit more context?" Roan replied.

Lahana rolled her eyes. "Fawn knows several of the well-known mortals. She's great with people and has been an advocate for better God and mortal relationships. We're spending the next couple weeks going to each Region to hand deliver an invitation to Roan's birthday to all the important mortals."

Orah nodded in response. The tactic was actually impressive, having the Governing God's sister hand deliver invitations to his party. "Are you going to be safe?" Orah asked.

Lahana's eyebrows crumbled with confusion. "What? Of course we are. I mean if I were going on behalf of Marek that would probably be a different answer, but people respect Roan. Especially the mortals."

Roan shifted next to Orah, as though he were uncomfortable with Lahana's proud tone. Something similar to pride warmed inside of Orah and she stared at him. He had never treated her any differently than anyone else in the house. She couldn't imagine how people like her were possibly treated in other Regions.

"Well." Lahana placed one hand on her hip and motioned to the door with the other. "Let's get reading."

Smiling, Orah nodded and walked toward the library. She and Roan had been distracted earlier and she was rather excited to read one of the books Amada sent. She didn't know what she was going to find but she wanted to get her hands on as many books as she could while she was still in their world.

Lahana walked up beside her, placing her arm through Orah's. "So." Lahana glanced back at Roan. "What's going on with you and my brother?"

"Excuse me?" Orah yelled her response then quickly snapped her mouth shut.

"Don't act innocent. You both have been glancing at each other all night. Roan seems rather flustered as well."

Orah blushed. "Oh. We—" Her hands tingled while she thought about how close they had been before dinner. The feeling of him against her. His hands in her hair.

"Gods! Orah!" Lahana jumped a couple inches off the ground and pointed in front of them. To the small fire now burning a hole in the carpet - again.

"Shit!" Orah scrambled over to the fire, stomping on it with her foot. Roan was behind her in an instant. His concerned voice sent shivers down her spine.

"What just happened?" he asked.

"Orah lit the carpet on fire, that's what happened." Lahana glared at Orah, but Orah could see in her eyes that she knew what just happened. Cocking her head to the side, Lahana grinned. "Feeling a little hot, Orah?"

Orah felt like her cheeks were going to light on fire. Staring down at the carpet, she shook her head. The floor was once again mending itself, as if her outburst hadn't happened. Glancing up she found Roan staring at the carpet muttering a curse under his breath.

"I've never seen it do that before." He lifted his eyes. She couldn't interpret the expression in his eyes but it felt as though he was peering into her soul.

Lahana cleared her throat next to Orah and they both turned to face her. "Well, now that Orah has shown off, I guess we should go read." Lahana motioned for them to walk in front of her.

Rolling her eyes, Orah glanced at Lahana then walked through Roan's study doors. She could feel him close behind her and her hands shook at the tingling buzz building across her palms. She had to get herself under control when she was around him. *These outbursts certainly aren't helping.*

Making sure to keep her distance from Roan, Orah picked up the spectacles and one of the books from Amada. Surveying the room, she picked one of the large armchairs in the middle of the room. Roan seemed to understand the hint and sat down on the couch they had been on earlier. Lahana chose the chair next to Orah and they all fell silent while they began to read.

Time slowed while they read, and while Orah was enthralled in her book, she wasn't finding anything specific about portal magic. Her book - **Portals: A History** at first glance looked like it would provide a lot of useful information but it was so far unhelpful. She felt a little as though she were on a high learning about the different portals in each Region and how long scholars believed they had been around. But enthralling, almost addictive history and helpful history were two different things.

With a sigh, she set the book on her lap. Lahana wasn't reading any longer and she lazily bounced around the room thumbing through Roan's collection. Roan, on the other hand, looked as though he had completely drowned out the world. Jerking suddenly, his eyes met Orah's.

"Lahana." His tone was serious.

Instantly, Lahana froze. "What did you find?" she asked.

He stood and walked toward Orah's seat in the center of the room. The near panicked but almost sick expression on his face made her want to shrink back into the chair. Staring down at her, he whispered. "I can't believe I haven't thought about this."

"What?" Lahana rushed across the room. "What haven't you thought about, Roan?"

Orah looked at Lahana, seeing how worried she was about her brother. Rightfully so, he wasn't acting right.

"Shadus." Roan murmured.

Orah's eyebrows rose and she glanced at Lahana again, unsure if she had heard him right.

Lahana's eyes widened. "Shadus."

They both obviously knew what they were referring to, but Orah was very much in the dark. Trying to suppress her irritation, she cleared her throat. "Is anyone going to enlighten me and explain why you keep saying that?"

"What did that book tell you about the portals in Shadus?" Roan asked while picking up the book from her lap.

"That there are only two. The one to travel there between regions and the one that souls enter through." Orah replied.

Roan stared at her while she finished her sentence. "The portal souls enter through is powerful. Where the portals in the city center can only have two or three people go through at a time, I've seen the one in Shadus welcome hundreds of souls at once."

"*Hundreds?*" Orah gaped.

With a nod, he smiled. She didn't have to ask to know what he was thinking. He was amused by what she had latched onto from all that he had said. But hundreds of souls at once was both terrifying and fascinating.

His eyes moved to Lahana and his smile tilted to a frown. "I know where we have to go."

"You can't possibly think that taking Orah to Shadus is going to be helpful." Lahana replied. "We don't even know all of the monsters that lurk there, Roan. What if the wrong monster gets a whiff of her power and reports to Father?"

"The monsters in Shadus are loyal to Aeron. I'm not worried about her presence being reported to Father."

"You and I both know that you can't say that confidently."

Roan crossed his arms over his chest. "We don't know that for certain. Just because we haven't ever seen what's in the depths doesn't mean that the stories are true."

Scoffing, Lahana mimicked his movement. "You're telling me that in all the years Aeron brought you down there you never once saw anything that should make you second guess taking Orah there?"

Shaking his head, Roan stared out the library windows. "I asked him plenty of times to take me further into the depths but he refused to. He said there are things there I wasn't yet ready to see."

Silence settled over the room. Deciding she didn't like when people spoke as if she weren't in the room, Orah stood and stretched. "So I guess we're going to Shadus then?"

Lahana jolted and turned. "Orah." Her tone was stern but soft as though she were scolding a child.

Orah lifted her hand and shook her head. "No, I want to go. I want to get home." She glanced at Roan. His entire body stiffened but his eyes remained focused on the window.

Quietly he spoke, his voice sounding far away. "We'll leave first thing tomorrow morning. I'll meet you at the stables." Without turning to look at either of the women, he walked out of the room.

Orah watched after him then turned to Lahana, unsure of what to say next.

"Orah." Lahana approached her, grabbing her arm. "Please be careful."

"I will be." Orah knew she didn't sound confident but she wasn't sure how else to respond.

Nodding, Lahana released her hold on Orah's arm then smiled. "Now, we didn't finish our conversation earlier."

Orah's body shivered with embarrassment and she couldn't control her eyes darting to the couch she and Roan had sat on earlier. Lahana's eyes lit up while she followed Orah's gaze. "I *knew* something happened in here! Something also happened at the bar last night too." Orah's mouth opened to respond but Lahana stopped her. "You don't need to make up any excuses, Orah. You're adults. Just tell me why you both seem inclined to not let it go any farther."

Moving back to the chair she'd been on when they'd first come into the library, Lahana set her feet on the table in front of it. With a sigh, Orah sat back in her own chair and stared at the ceiling. "It's not that I'm not attracted to him. I just—" Suddenly, Orah was aware she wasn't just talking to anyone about Roan. She was talking to his sister. "I don't know if I should have this conversation with you."

Throwing her head back, Lahana laughed. "Trust me, if you start giving me too many details I will make you stop."

They stared at each other for a moment before Orah decided she may as well be honest. "I don't get close to people. I don't have relationships or strong feelings. I keep it casual. That's how I am."

"What does that have to do with why you won't take advantage of what Roan obviously wants to offer?"

"God, I cannot believe I'm talking to you about this." Orah muttered. "Because it's been a while since I've been with someone."

She felt embarrassed at the admission. After losing her Father the idea of being close, in any way, with anyone felt uncomfortable – almost suffocating. Something as simple as casual sex had been uninteresting to her for months.

"Also – I can feel there's something more with Roan. Something intense and almost scary but also strangely familiar. I can't let myself have that when I'm trying to get home." Orah admitted.

Lahana gave an almost lazy shrug. "Okay, but I bet Roan could do just physical."

"It's not a matter of whether or not *he* could. It's a matter of whether or not *I* can. But to your point I don't think he could either. Not based on the conversations we've had."

"Yeah but Roan's probably just pent up. As far as I know he hasn't been with someone since he lost the last challenge and took over Nacht."

"What!" Orah yelled. "He said that was over fifty years ago!"

Lahana laughed. "You just said it's been awhile for yourself!"

Leaning back against her chair, Orah chuckled. "Yeah but fifty years?"

"Oh I know. He was very popular with women before, but once he threw the challenge he decided he would just live like Aeron and not have any children."

"Well, don't you have any kind of prevention to avoid having children?"

"Of course we do. How do you think Gods space their children so far apart? No, Roan just decided if he were to rule over Death he didn't want to subject someone to spending a life in Shadus with him."

Orah looked at the doors leading to the study, feeling a twinge of sadness. In Roan's own way he'd isolated himself as much as she had. "Do the Gods of Death never have children?" she asked.

"No, there have been a handful who have. It's been rare, but it happens."

"But Roan decided he doesn't want them?"

"I don't think it's a matter of whether or not he wants them. While he thinks it's beautiful, he also thinks Shadus is a sad place. He doesn't want someone to fall in love with him and be subjected to spending their life there surrounded by death."

Thinking of her own strange connection to death, Orah stared at the ceiling. "Interesting."

Lahana's tone shifted to something playful. "You guys could just have fun, you know that, right?"

"I know, but it's a line I don't think we should cross." Orah replied.

"Alright, I get it." Standing, Lahana stretched "Fates, I'm tired. I'm heading upstairs, you coming up anytime soon?"

Orah shook her head. "I think I'm going to read this a little longer then I'll be up."

Lahana leaned over reading the book title. "I was forced to read that by my tutors. I don't think I ever imagined someone would read it for fun."

Scrunching up her nose Orah threw up her middle finger.

Lahana's eyes widened and she laughed. "You are so much fun. Goodnight, Orah."

"Goodnight, Lahana."

Lahana skipped out of the room and Orah couldn't help but admire her. Even when having uncomfortable conversations about her brother, or dealing with all the stress Orah had brought them, her positivity hadn't ever faltered. Orah wondered what Fawn was like for Lahana to be so enamored by her. She smiled, hoping she would have the opportunity to meet her soon then nestled further into her chair and dove back into her book.

The clock in Roan's office chimed loudly, startling Orah. Pulling her nose from her book her eyes burned and she counted the bells. Ten, eleven, twelve.

Jerking back against the chair she gazed down at the book startled by how late it had gotten. Stretching, she set the book on the table in front of her and pushed up out of the chair. Her body groaned in protest. It may have felt like days ago that she was on the obstacle course but in reality it had been less than 12 hours. She knew her injuries were almost fully healed, thanks to the tonic, but the bruises were still tender.

She walked toward the study, turning back to admire the library before heading to bed. She had to get to sleep or she was going to have a hard time waking up to meet Roan. Nerves flipped in her stomach at the thought of going to Shadus.

She didn't know if the concepts of Heaven and Hell she'd been taught growing up were real, but where they were going felt as though she were taking a volunteer trip to Hell.

Walking out of the study, she moved toward the stairs. As if in protest, her throat felt parched and she turned down the hall to the kitchen instead, needing to quench the sudden thirst. Walking down the hall she turned into the kitchen and rummaged around for a glass. Very aware she was across from Jes's room and he was still complaining about her messing up his sleep, she tried to be as quiet as she could.

The sound of a door opening and closing across the hall made her jump and she rushed out of the kitchen to apologize to Jes for her noise. Coming out of the kitchen doorway, she found that there didn't appear to be anyone in the hall. Her eyes glanced to the side door and she gasped.

Standing in the doorway was Moros, staring at her with his mouth hanging open.

"What are you…"

A rush of cold air blew past her, interrupting her question. Suddenly she was pulled forward and she realized he was dragging her outside. Her feet hit the gravel in the courtyard and she turned to face him.

"Ssssh." He stopped her from speaking then looked back at the house with one finger over his mouth. "Follow me." He whispered. He turned and walked toward some trees and she eagerly followed close behind him.

When they were hidden behind a tree she stared at him. "What are you or should I say we doing?"

"Talk quieter please!" He replied frantically.

Lowering her voice she repeated herself. "What are you doing? Does Roan know you're still here?"

"Fates no. He would die if Roan knew."

"He?" She stared for a moment then her eyes widened with realization. She *had* heard Jes's bedroom door open but it hadn't been Jes opening it. "You were with Jes!"

"Sssssh!"

"Oh. My. God." Orah was sure her eyes were going to pop out of their sockets. She could see the signs now. His shirt was a bit disheveled. His hair was a mess, as though someone had run their hands in it. His cheeks red with a flush to them that was definitely not from any wine he'd consumed with dinner.

Grabbing her arm he pulled them further from the house. "Please be quieter."

"You and Jes?" She was shocked, remembering Roan's comment on how Jes would benefit from a lover to help his moods. "How long?"

Moros glanced back at the house and sighed. "Decades."

"WHAT."

"Orah, I swear to the Fates that if you don't be quieter I'm going to throw you off a cliff."

Stifling her laugh, she nodded her head. She could be quieter, if only to get more information out of him. "I'm sorry. I'm just in shock."

His panicked expression softened then he shook his head. With a sigh, he leaned against the tree behind him, sinking to the ground. Orah stepped back, surprised by the movement. From where she stood, he was no longer the cocky and slightly annoying man she'd encountered so far. He was certainly nothing like the man who had pushed her boundaries that afternoon either.

"Have you heard anything about Jes and his family?" he asked.

Something about the defeated way he sat felt familiar and Orah decided he only needed someone to listen. Setting herself down next to him, she nodded. "Yes, Jes told me that they're traditional and he doesn't speak to them."

"I think traditional is an understatement. But, yes, that's basically it. Jes has hidden who he is for so long that when we met he couldn't admit there was something there at first." Chuckling Moros leaned his head against the tree. "But like some love sick fool, I kept coming around—to Roan's absolute dismay. The more I came around, the more we spent time together, but always in private. In public Jes barely tolerates my presence."

"How long?"

"Since Roan took over Nacht. We met each other plenty of times before then but that night, fifty years ago, something snapped between us. The chemistry was undeniable."

"But if he doesn't speak to his family then why does he keep it secret? From what I've gathered I don't think Roan would care. He doesn't care about Lahana and Fawn."

Moros shrugged. "It doesn't have anything to do with our genders. It has everything to do with Roan's lack of trust in me. It's all justified mistrust, on both our parts, but combining Jes's internalized hate for himself and his desires and his loyalty to Roan, I'm his little secret."

"I had no idea."

"No one does. Jes hides it too well. The last few years I've been more brazen with pushing him in public but he's great at that mask he wears."

Orah felt dizzy from the sadness that hit her while she stared at him. She thought of Julian hating himself for who he loved. She thought of Lahana and how happy Fawn made her.

"I'm sorry."

Jumping, Moros glared at her. "What are you sorry for?"

"I just – I'm sorry you can't have your love in public."

"You're apologizing for Jes not accepting his feelings for me? Are you so unaware of yourself that you can't see the irony in that?"

"Excuse me?"

"Oh come on. You and Roan look at each other and I worry anyone in the room is going to get a very personal and intimate show."

Her mouth popped open and she smacked his shoulder. "Hey! You have no idea what you're talking about."

"I don't? Please, the glances you were both giving each other at dinner was enough to make me want to take Jes right at the table."

"Oh my god." Her cheeks burned and she leaned forward, covering her face with her hands. They had not been that obvious. Had they?

Chuckling he thumped his shoulder against hers. "I'm sorry for provoking you earlier."

"What?"

"I could feel your power simmering under the surface the first time I met you, but it's stronger now. For what it's worth I know I scared you and I'm sorry. I'm annoying and a bastard, but I had no intention of actually causing you any harm."

"Roan did say you're an annoying bastard." Orah replied.

"I'm sure he did."

Knowing not to push further, she leaned against the tree. The leaves of the trees swayed above them making the star appear as if they were waving down at them. Turning to him she breathed out. "Why Jes?"

"What?" He snapped.

"Why Jes? Why let it be a secret for so long?"

His answer came out in a quiet whisper. So quiet she wasn't sure she heard him at first. "Because I love him."

"Why?"

"Why wouldn't I? He's loyal, strong, brave, funny in his own way, and intuitive. Honestly, the list could go on. He makes me feel like the most beautiful and powerful God in the land. He encourages me to do well by my Region and people. Fates, I would probably do anything for him."

"Does he love you?" she bit her tongue as the question came out. She was doing her best not to judge but she didn't understand.

Moros let out a sigh. "He says he does. Do you know why he sleeps so close to that door?"

"Lahana said *he* says it's so he's near all the ground floor entrances. She thinks it's so he can sneak out."

Moros smiled a sly smile. "Jes stays with me at least twice a week. Once Roan has gone to bed, Jes slips out and takes the portal to my Region. I've spent the last fifty years sleeping in his arms as often as I can. Every night he's in my palace he whispers his love to me while I fall asleep in those large strong arms of his."

"Damn. I didn't know big bad Jes had a soft side."

"I think I might be the only one to have ever seen it. At least in that way." he replied with a laugh.

"I don't think I've ever loved anyone other than my parents so I can't say I understand why you're still around, but I can say that I respect that you are. Maybe for Jes it'll one day be the fuel to the courage he needs to admit his love publicly." Love was confusing and Orah spent her entire adult life avoiding getting close enough to someone to avoid any kind of similar situation.

"Thank you." Moros nodded his head, staring up at the stars. "Orah?"

"Yes?"

"Can you promise that you won't say anything to him? I don't want him to think that I betrayed his trust."

"Can you promise to never be a creepy dick to me again?"

His head snapped back to her. "I can try and keep that promise."

Smiling, she pulled her knees up under her chin while she watched the sky. "Then I can promise not to say anything to Jes."

"Where do you guys go from here? Any idea on how to get you home?"

Her chest tightened while she kept her eyes on the sky. She wasn't entirely sure how to answer him. Going to Shadus felt like grasping at straws but she didn't want to voice that. Roan was hopeful enough that they would find answers there.

Sighing, she glanced at Moros. "We're going to Shadus."

His eyes widened and he shook his head. His long dark hair rippled in waves with the movement. "Good luck."

Chapter 23

Pulling herself out of bed the next morning took every bit of willpower Orah had in her body. She and Moros sat on the lawn staring at the stars for at least an hour. When they were done, she walked him to the gate that led to the side patch and watched as he walked down to the city center.

Yawning, she walked down the stairs. Chills rushed down her spine while she considered what Shadus would be like. Would that familiar call of death call to her there? Her feet shuffled against the floor and she turned to walk down the hall, slamming right into Roan's back.

"Orah, do I need to wear a bell so you know where I am?" He turned around with an amused smile on his face.

"That's not necessary." She turned away from him to hide her embarrassed blush.

He chuckled and she glanced back at him. His eyes flared with the look of intention hidden in his eyes. Stepping aside, he motioned to the door. "Well, after you."

She glared at him and his amusement while she walked toward the door. When she passed the kitchen, Clarah stopped her to hand her a small brown sack.

"You're both leaving so early so I made sure to pack you something for breakfast," Clarah said.

"Thank you so much Clarah. You're always so thoughtful," Orah replied with a smile.

Clarah let out a little squeal before rushing back into the kitchen. Orah continued walking toward the stables, not able to ignore how close Roan followed behind her. Expecting Kai to be waiting with the chariot, she stepped back when he came out with only Nacht.

Part of her shock was how she had known it was Nacht Kai had saddled and not Tume. Observing the Pegasus, she nodded her head. The differences were small but they were there. Where Tume's wings were brilliantly black, Nacht's had a small purple tint to them when the light hit them at the right angle.

"Thank you, Kai." Roan stepped past her, taking the reins.

"Why can't we take the chariot?"

Roan's eyes narrowed and he grinned. "Were you wanting to take the portal?"

"I was assuming we'd be taking the portal," Orah replied.

"I prefer to fly into Shadus. I thought you'd like a little sightseeing of the land. You don't get to see its beauty going through a portal."

"Why can't I fly with Tume?" She stepped back, observing just how close they would have to sit to fly on Nacht.

"Because the journey is over two hours long. You might believe you're confident enough to fly for that long solo but we both know that's not true," Roan replied.

She glared at him and the accuracy in his observation. She knew he was right, but she didn't have to like it. She sighed. "How are you expecting me to sit?"

That gleam of intention in his eyes returned and he grinned. "You can sit on me however you'd like, Orah."

Her eyes widened and Kai cleared his throat beside Roan. Roan turned his body toward Kai but didn't take his eyes off Orah. "Kai, can you please comfort Orah and let her know the saddle you have on Nacht is plenty big enough for the both of us?" Winking, he pulled his gaze from Orah's.

Kai glanced at Orah nervously then at Roan before clearing his throat again. "Yes, Ms. Orah, what my Lord said. The saddle has more than enough space."

Letting out a breath, she glared at Roan. "Fine. But no funny business."

His hands lifted into the air and he grinned. "Me? *Never.*"

Crouching down, Roan cupped his hand and waited for Orah to approach. "I may look good for my age, Orah, but I can't sit in this position all day."

Shrugging, she approached him. "Guess you better work on that in your old age." He grinned wide while she stepped into his hand. With a wink, she threw her leg over the saddle and positioned herself in the seat.

Roan stood. "I'll take that advice into account." He turned to Kai, nodding his head. "Thank you, Kai. I'm not sure what time we'll be back tonight. If it's too late, I'll make sure Nacht is returned to his stable myself."

"Understood, my Lord," Kai replied while he bowed slightly.

Roan grabbed hold of the saddle and threw his leg over, seating himself behind Orah. He turned back to Kai and smiled. "One last thing, Kai."

Stepping back, Kai nodded. "Yes, my Lord?"

"Go take your wife out for the day," Roan stated. Kai chuckled and looked behind him. Orah followed his gaze, to the small cottage off in the back corner of the property.

"I'll make sure we both take the day off and enjoy each other's company."

"Good." Roan's arms wrapped around Orah as he grabbed the reins. Orah stiffened when they landed against her thighs. His thighs flexed while they wrapped around either side of her. His body was pushed right up against her and a very specific part of him pushed dangerously close to her backside.

Enough room, my ass.

He wiggled behind her and she froze in response. Leaning forward he sandwiched her against the front of the saddle and her backside pushed further against him. "Comfortable?"

His breath tickled her ear, and she couldn't control the shiver that ran through her. Her answer came out shaking and she cursed herself for how rattled she sounded.

"I'm perfectly comfortable."

Pushing further against her, his smile brushed against her ear. "Great."

His hands snapped the reins and she grabbed hold of his forearms when they launched into the sky. They flew into the clouds and she gasped, realizing she wasn't strapped in with any buckles.

"Where are the buckles?" she yelled over the wind.

"Don't worry, I've got you. I won't let you go." His arms tightened around her. She let out a breath of relief, unable to ignore the feeling of comfort from his hold.

Nacht completed his ascent and she watched in awe. She didn't know what direction they were flying but she could still see the city. From up in the sky the entire terrain mimicked the night sky. The sun had barely begun to rise and the lights on the ground sparkled like stars. Nacht banked to the left and she watched as the city lights disappeared in the distance.

While the sun rose Nacht dropped lower and they flew over several small towns. There were people outside, looking up at them and waving. "Are we still in your Region?"

"Yes, those are my people." Roan's tone was one of pride.

Orah smiled. "They seem to like you." She turned to look back at him and he smiled.

"I would hope so. I do my best to be likable."

Trying to ignore the heat of his body against hers she watched in awe while they flew over more purple-black mountains. Slowly the purple changed to lush green valleys. Turning to Roan, she pointed. "Still your region?"

"Yes, look at the mountains. Still purple and black," he replied, while pointing.

Staring off to the distance she saw what he was referring to. While they were far away, she could see the purple and black mountains. Her eyes surveyed to her right and she gasped when she saw blue. The only kind of blue that came from the ocean.

"That's water!" she yelled.

"Yes," Roan replied.

"You didn't say your region had a coast!"

His arms raised up and down, landing back on her thighs. As though he had lifted his shoulders into a shrug. "It's beautiful. Just didn't think to mention it. I have a home on the coast. I usually spend time there in the summer, but I've been a bit too preoccupied this year."

"I'm not sure if that's in reference to me or this party you've been planning."

His laugh rumbled against her back and he leaned down, pressing against her. "I'll just say my answer is yes."

Scoffing, she thumped his thigh with her fist. "You sure know how to avoid answering a question."

"You can blame the King of Gods for that skill."

Without meaning to, she leaned back against his chest. He was warm against her and his arms tightened around her waist. Trying to keep her mind off the heat against her backside she kept her eyes on the ocean. If she focused, she could almost smell it from up there. The salt. The sand. She imagined what lounging on the beach in the Land of Gods would be like. Sighing, she leaned forward and marveled at the beauty all around. The

Region of Nacht was truly beautiful. The dark mountains in the distance complimented the lush green fields they flew over. There were people all over the fields working and everyone stopped while they flew overhead. Not one person ignored their Governing God.

"Jes said that some of the mortals and Godlings in the guard are scared of you."

"I suppose they are."

"Why?"

"Jes didn't explain?"

"Yes, but it doesn't make sense. Is there something else I'm not being told? People aren't stupid and can put two and two together that the God of Death doesn't just take souls on a whim."

His hands tightened on the reins and his thighs flexed against hers again. "People believe I'm dangerous."

"Why?"

"Because rumors have started that I threw the last challenge. Because I have a temper. Because sixty years ago my temper destroyed part of the City of Kings."

Twisting to glance up at him, her eyes widened. "You did what?"

"I don't want to get into the details, but I lost my temper and destroyed a large portion of the palace along with the section of the city right below it. Just obliterated it in an instant. That show of power is partially why the rumors that I threw the last challenge started. It got out very quickly that the King's younger son had done the damage."

"But why did you throw the last challenge? What's the benefit of keeping your power hidden?"

Sighing his hand loosened on the reins. He stared down at her with her still leaning against his chest and smiled. "I'm sure you must know the answer, but I'll give you a small piece of it. I don't want to become like my Father. I wanted him to suffer, realizing that he placed his bets on the wrong son and there was nothing he could do to force me to beat Marek."

"So, it was for spite?"

"Partially, and partially for me to remind myself who I am. I don't care if people fear me. If I'm going to be the God of Death someday, people will fear me then too. I might as well allow it to happen before that day comes."

"Do you want to be the God of Death?"

"I've never known how to imagine any other kind of fate for myself."

Nodding, she admired the landscape in front of them. The steady rhythmic beat of his heart against her back pulled her away from the conversation he obviously didn't want to continue. The beating sounds and the repetitive motion of Nacht's wings weighed against her eyelids. She sighed; she shouldn't have stayed up so late with Moros. She should have slept more. Roan kept one hand on the reins but wrapped the other fully around her, pulling her closer to him. If she hadn't been so tired, she would have protested at how close she was pushed up against him, but the warmth was comforting. She smiled, thinking how his body was like a warm blanket against her back.

✴

"Orah. Orah, wake up," Roan whispered in her ear.

We're not flying. She jolted up. They were still seated on Nacht, Roan's arms still held her in place, but they were now in the middle of a lush green field.

"Where are we?"

"I stopped to take a break. We're about halfway there. We're in Spreng."

Whirling to look at him, her mouth popped open. "Where Fawn lives?"

"Yes, well at least we're in the Region. Fawn lives further East in Tuuli, the main city here."

"I didn't realize the Region was so close to yours."

Removing his arm from around her waist, he twisted backward and swung his leg over Nacht's backside. With a small groan, he hopped off and lifted his arms for her to slide into. Swinging her legs over, she winced.

His face twisted with concern. "Are you okay?"

"What? Oh, yes, just stiff," she replied. She motioned for him to step a little closer and gripped both of his arms while he slid her off the saddle. Her knees wobbled when she hit the ground and he kept his hold on her, keeping her from falling. She grimaced. "Sorry, I didn't think I'd still be so stiff."

"You don't have anything to apologize for. Honestly, I probably should have given you another day or so to rest."

"Do you have any tonics from Jes? He mentioned that I would take some today when we planned to go train."

Guilt flashed in his eyes and he shook his head. She sighed, "That's alright. I'm a big girl." Her stomach rumbled loudly, and his eyes widened with a responding grin.

"Honestly, I don't think I enjoy any other sound in the world like that one."

"What? My stomach?" she asked, too amused to be embarrassed.

"Yes, it gives away how you're feeling. The look of shock on your face every time it happens is priceless."

Scoffing, she turned away from him and walked around the other side of Nacht to the saddle bag. She pulled out the bag Clarah had handed her and the smell of fresh food made her stomach rumble louder.

"Oh, you be quiet," she scolded herself before turning back to face Roan.

He smiled wide. "See, gives you away."

"Will you be quiet? I don't have to share this with you."

His eyes narrowed on her. "You wouldn't dare."

Orah bit her lip, holding back her grin before her stomach rumbled once more. He snorted and she shook her head. "Where should we eat?"

He pointed off to the distance to a large willow tree. "Under there. We may be in the Region of Spring, but it's still summer and it's going to warm up soon."

Nodding her head, she walked toward the tree. Her breath stilled when she arrived in front of it. She hadn't noticed she was walking at an incline, but she could now see the tree sat at the top of a small hill. There was nothing around but large rolling fields of thick, tall grass. Off in the distance, she could make out meadows of wildflowers. The running sound of water told her they were close to some kind of river or spring. Two hummingbirds flew past her with a whirl and she twisted to watch them fly off. It was like being somewhere she had always dreamed of.

Roan walked up next to her. She glanced up and smiled at the grin on his lips. "I thought you would appreciate it. Nacht and I flew for a little while before I spotted this place," he said.

"It's beautiful."

He ducked under the long willow branches and sat down in the grass, patting the ground next to him. "I could easily take a nap in this grass. Depending on what Clarah packed, I might have to."

Smiling, she joined him and pulled open the bag. It was small but not tiny, to her own surprise. By the weight of it, she assumed Clarah had packed it full, but she wasn't sure what she'd find. Reaching her hand in she gasped and looked back at Roan. "This bag is huge on the inside!"

Leaning forward, he smiled. "I didn't realize she used a warded bag. She must have really packed us a meal."

"A warded bag?"

"Godlings and mortals use warded items. Gods do too, like the spectacles in the library, and that ring: they're warded to help read and understand languages you don't know."

"Interesting."

Trying to hide her smile, she pulled out the breakfast Clarah had packed. She couldn't seem to find the end of the food. Every time she put her hand into the bag she pulled out more. After several minutes, she observed a feast surrounding her and Roan. Muffins, breads, pastries, bacon, cheese, fruit, plates and utensils to eat with, cups, even a carafe of juice. At some point the breakfast food ended and she began pulling out jerkies and cured meats. As if Clarah expected them to go on a journey that was several days long. Finally, Orah was sure she'd reached the bottom of the bag when her hand wrapped around a vial at the bottom.

Gasping she pulled her hand out and shoved the vial in Roan's face. "Is this what I think it is?"

He leaned back a bit with a smile. "Looks like either Jes or Clarah thought ahead. Yes, that's one of the tonics Jes picked up for you."

Without hesitating, Orah popped off the top and threw the tonic back. A shiver ran through her when the taste of it hit her tongue. While it wasn't as bad as the day before, it was not pleasant either.

Roan laughed and shook his head. "I've never seen anyone take one of those so quickly. I've seen several hundred-year-old Gods whimper and moan before agreeing to a sip."

"Guess I'm tougher than them," she replied.

"I would agree. Should we eat?"

They both grabbed a plate and dished up what Clarah had prepared for them. Orah leaned back against the base of the tree and started her meal. Clarah had outdone herself with the delicacies. She let out a content sigh while she took a bite out of one of the pastries.

Admiring the hanging branches above, she felt an overwhelming feeling of peace. The wind blowing and the rich colors surrounding her made her believe she could have sat in that spot all day. Movement to her left pulled her gaze and she sat up. Roan jumped, seemingly aware of the movement as well and turned his head.

Across the field were a group of small animals Orah had never seen before. Narrowing her eyes, she realized they weren't animals. They were some sort of creature. Perhaps a foot or two tall with fur lining their body. They walked on two legs in a small group, focused on each other and hadn't appeared to notice the couple under the tree.

Turning her head to Roan, she gestured toward them. Scooting closer to her, Roan dropped his voice to a low whisper. "Brownies. They live out in the meadows and fields here in Spreng. They're mischievous little things. Best be quiet until they pass."

Together they observed the Brownies forage around the meadow. There were six of them, all with little sacks across their shoulders. Some Brownies grabbed flower petals or blades of grass, some pulled worms from the soil, and others just grabbed handfuls of dirt.

She wasn't sure how long they sat and watched the Brownies but eventually they stopped their foraging. She couldn't seem to pull her eyes from them while they crested over the hill, walking down toward the flower meadows behind the willow tree.

Sighing, Roan stretched and splayed out in the grass. His long arms were strewn lazily above his head and his eyes were closed. His breathing was slow and deep, and she wondered if he had actually fallen asleep. Her eyes slowly scanned his face. Those freckles. His sharp jaw. The small bit of stubble he hadn't shaved in a few days. Her eyes moved down to his muscled chest, his long torso, his strong legs. His dark skin against the brilliant green. The blond in his hair was more prominent out in the sun but the dark brown was still there. It was as though he were a work of art laying in the green grass.

"Enjoying the view?"

Jumping, her eyes shot to his and the large smile on his face. Clearing her throat, she looked down at the ground. She was sure she was going to overheat with how hot her cheeks now felt. She couldn't bring herself to respond to justify how blatantly she'd been objectifying him.

From the corner of her eye, she watched him while he pulled himself up from the ground, stretching again. His shirt untucked from his trousers slightly and she sucked in her gasp at the brief glimpse she got of his muscles. Turning her head, she tried to avoid staring.

I definitely do not need that image seared into my mind.

Staring at the ground, she willed herself to get a hold of her thoughts when two shoes came into view. Peering up, she found him standing over her with a smile still on his face.

"You can admire me, Orah. The Fates know I admire you." His eyes twinkled while they held their gaze.

Turning her head, she stood and brushed her legs. "As long as we both know admiring is not the same as acting on it."

She walked past him toward where Nacht now grazed in the meadow, but his hand flew out to grab her arm. Pulling her against his chest, he gripped her chin, titling it up so he could meet her eyes. "Remind me why we can't act on this again?"

Her breath slowed and their chests moved up and down in sync. He kept his grip on her chin with one hand while the other brushed up and down her arm slowly. Her thoughts were dizzy while wind whipped around them.

Not moving from his touch, she cleared her throat. "You're touching me without my permission again."

Both of his hands shot into the air and he took several steps backward. "What?" He appeared flustered now, as though he were trying to find the right words to respond.

Chuckling, she bent down and cleaned up their breakfast before responding. She could feel his building panic with each slow second she took to clear everything. Once she had it all packed back into the bag, she turned to face him again. His eyes were frantic and his cheeks a bright red. She had to hide her laugh. "You said that you wouldn't touch me without my permission. You've now touched me twice without my permission. Just barely and last night in the library."

"I –" Shaking his head he covered his face with his hands. "I'm sorry. You're right."

"And to answer your question, we can't act on this because it will make things messy. We're trying to get me home, Roan. I've explained this. We're forced to be near each other with me living in your home, but after today we should try and limit our contact. It's better for both of us."

"You want to limit our contact when we get back?" She turned her head to avoid the sadness that flashed across his eyes.

"Yes. If this portal isn't going to be able to get me home, then we need to stop finding ourselves in these situations."

She looked back over at him and he stood there seemingly frozen for a moment. Nodding his head, he finally turned and walked toward Nacht. She expected him to say something further. To joke or tease but he said nothing.

He said nothing when he crouched down, helping her back into the saddle. He said nothing when he lifted himself into the saddle behind her. His hands didn't rest against her thighs when they took flight again. She swallowed her comments and avoided the urge to rest against his chest again, sitting as straight as she could.

The Spring Region was beautiful and green. Every few miles they flew past a field of flowers. There were people there working in the fields like in Nacht, but no one turned upward to wave. If anything, they cowered and crouched as low to the ground as they could. Orah couldn't help but wonder if they believed Roan was his uncle, coming to collect their souls.

Eventually the silence between the two became unbearable and she looked up at him.

"Why is your Pegasus named after your region?"

Jumping at the sound of her voice, his laugh vibrated against her back. "I named him when I was a kid. Aeron gave him to me for my ninth birthday."

Her eyes widened. "So, he's almost three hundred years old too?"

"Yes, he's getting to be as much of an old man as I am," Roan replied while his hand landed lazily on her thigh.

Nacht's wings beat haphazardly beside them and Roan laughed again, reaching around Orah to stroke the Pegasus' mane. "You are a very beautiful and strong old man, Nacht."

Nacht let out a huff in acknowledgement and Orah tried not to laugh. The animals could really understand everything that was said. Orah leaned back without thinking and laid her head against Roan's chest again. His hand on her thigh flexed before relaxing again. "Tell me more about your world," he said.

"Why?"

"Because I saw interesting things in your memories. Interesting people too."

Tensing, she focused on the meadow beneath them. What could she tell him? What would interest a magical God of Night?

"We can fly there," she replied.

"I saw you in some odd carriage in your memories."

"That's a plane." She smiled then watched the clouds. "Planes can carry hundreds of people at one time, but this kind of flying is better than any flight I've ever taken."

"Who was that man in your memories?" Roan asked.

Her chest tightened. He had seen her Father and Julian and could likely be talking about either of them. One of them she was willing to talk about—the other was off limits.

Fixating on the cloud in front of her, she sighed. "You saw my friend Julian."

"You two seemed close."

She surprised herself when her voice came out quiet and shaky. "He's my best friend, or he was. I cut out almost everyone in my life a few months ago, he was one of them."

She jumped at the soft touch on her thigh. His hand lazily stroked up and down as though he was lost in his thoughts. She leaned back against him. "You saw him pick me up from the airport though. He showed up for me when I didn't deserve it."

His hand stilled and she looked up to find a puzzled expression on his face. "Why wouldn't you deserve that?"

"I cut him out. Completely stopped responding to him. We've been best friends for eight years and I disappeared like a ghost."

"Did he do something wrong?"

She blinked back the tears lining her eyes. "No."

His hand lazily rubbed her thigh again and he let out a sigh. "I almost pummeled Jes in my study the day the doors appeared."

Twisting, she stared at him. "What?"

"Yeah." He chuckled, shaking his head. "I wanted to throw him into a wall. I didn't outright threaten him, but I shut off the lights in the study and was ready to hurt him."

"Why?"

"Doesn't matter really. My point is Jes and I have been friends for over two hundred years. We've fought, with both our words and our fists. There have been times I can't stand being in the same room as him but he's still here. Do you really think your friend wouldn't have shown up for you?"

A lead-like weight settled in her chest and she watched the ground below them. "You're not wrong."

"How did you meet Julian?"

She smiled. He sure could redirect a conversation. "College—school. I left home and met him in a French class. We both were fluent but had the same idea to take what we thought would be an easy class as a break in our schedules. We were basically connected at the hip from the moment we met."

"Did you ever have a relationship?"

Her eyes widened and she threw her head back with a laugh. "Oh my god, no. Julian is *all* about the men. He's the brother I never had. I spent half of every summer break in France with him and his family. Once we both graduated, we took one trip a year to see each other. Me to him and him to me."

Roan's hand gripped her thigh. "Well based on those few facts I think I can confidently say he'll probably be there for you whenever you need him to be."

Relishing in his touch she nodded her head. He had no idea how right he was.

His chest pressed against her, then he spoke again. "How did you buy such a large house?"

Tears lined her eyes again and she blinked, trying to stop them. She opened her mouth to answer when an ice-cold chill ran down her spine.

"Death."

Orah jumped at the chilling voice that filled her ears. Death had always been this intuition in her life—it had never clearly spoken to her. The warm spring weather suddenly shifted to the familiar skin prickling cold and Roan's voice shifted from the lighthearted tone to something low and serious. His hand released her thigh. "We're in Shadus now."

Chapter 24

Orah couldn't bring herself to tell Roan she already knew they were in Shadus. To her own shock, Death had already said its quiet hello. She stared down at the gray ground below them. Tall mountainous spires covered the bleak terrain. Reminding Orah of stalagmites that had grown taller than naturally possible. With ease, Nacht weaved around each spire.

Captivated by the eerie terrain she sighed. "Does your uncle not have a city?"

Roan tensed against her and his chest moved up and down against her back. "Shadus is a very large region, close to the size of Erde, but there's only one city and it's not so much a city as it is a large mountain."

"What?" She couldn't imagine what he was describing but she could see that there were no towns as they flew over the bleak terrain. No fields, grass, or life existed there.

Nacht banked to the left and she couldn't help herself when she grabbed onto Roan's forearm. A mountain came into view and she stared in wonder. It was gray, the color reminding her of death, but somehow it also sparkled in the sunlight. All around the base of the mountain were vein-like vines that crawled toward the rock as though something were pulling the vines its way. Orah's eyes scanned the mountain from the base to the point, averting her gaze from the bright shining light coming from the very top.

A scream choked in her throat and she gripped Roan's forearm when Nacht suddenly headed straight for the side of the mountain. "Roan! We're going to crash!"

Chuckling, he let go of the reins and pointed. She had to squint to make out where a large archway was cut into the side of the mountain. Just beyond the archway, she could make out lights.

"That's Mirin," Roan whispered.

The familiar call of Death continued its shift from intuition to a silent call and she gripped Roan's forearm harder. With ease, Nacht descended to a large platform that jutted off the side of the mountain—as if it were made for landing.

She sat, unsure of what to say, observing the city in front of her. Buildings carved from the mountain itself curved along the sides in two half-moon shapes. At the very back sat a large, ominous building with a balcony off the front that hovered above the large cavern the city surrounded. People, or more so creatures, bustled about casually as if there was nothing significant about living in the city of Death.

Death hovered over the city, flowing out toward the balcony jutting from the mountain. Like an uncomfortable mist in the air. Peering up at Roan, she couldn't help but notice he didn't seem fazed by the city and the death that surrounded it. In all reality, it didn't bother her either. It was just—*there*.

A loud thud next to them made Orah jolt and she watched while a large woman with bat-like wings straightened on the platform. She eyed Orah and Roan then paused when she appeared to realize who Roan was. Sinking to her knees, she bowed her head low. "My Lord."

Roan made a kind of grunting sound of approval and she jumped back to her feet, rushing into the city.

"What was that?"

"Aeron keeps a tight hand on formality. I've been here enough that I guess she recognized me. That was how Marek expected you to greet him the first night you met."

"Oh. Will Aeron expect that from me today?" Orah's eyes lingered on the building at the back of the city.

Shrugging, Roan followed her gaze. "You came with me, so I'm not sure." Quickly, he swung himself off Nacht and helped her down. Tying Nacht's reins to a post, he motioned for her to follow him into the city. The inhabitants were a mixture of the most interesting creatures she'd ever seen. In Roan's city there was a balanced mix of God, Godling, and mortal. Mirin didn't appear as diverse.

"Is everyone here a Godling?" Orah asked.

"Mostly. Some are just creatures. Aeron opened Shadus as a place for the outcasts to come. Most everyone else in the land never travels here because of the death that surrounds it. But Aeron made it public knowledge any outcasts or unwelcomed are welcome here."

"He doesn't sound like a bad guy. Why are so many so scared of him?"

Turning to face her, an unsettling smile spread across his face. "You'll understand when you meet him."

The hairs on her arms stood but all she could do was nod her head. As they walked further into the city that prickling, cold feeling grew stronger. Every person they passed bowed low while Roan approached but they all stared curiously at her. She didn't understand how they knew who he was until she glanced up at him and gasped.

His freckles were lit in the dim light of the city and his starlight crown was on full display. He was making sure they knew who he was. No wonder they were giving her such curious looks. The son of the King of Gods, and suspected next God of Death, was walking casually with a mortal. A mortal who flew in basically sitting on his lap on his personal Pegasus.

The city street curved in a half circle in front of the buildings. From what Orah could tell, there were businesses on the lower levels and homes or apartments above. Reminding her of the cliff dwellings she'd once seen on a trip with her Father as a teenager.

The cavern in the middle of the city quietly called to them with a thrumming hum. Orah stared at it, while her feet moved toward the quiet siren song as if she no longer had control of her own movements. Her heart beat wildly the closer she got to the small wall surrounding the ledge of the cavern. Peering over, her chest tightened. The cavern was deep. She couldn't tell how deep but only a few torches spiraled down. The small slivers of light allowed her to see that there were different levels far below her but beyond that she couldn't make out what was on each level.

But the *sounds*.

They echoed louder the further she peered over the wall. Repetitive shivers ran down her spine while she sat, mesmerized by the wails, moans, snarls, and screams. If Hell did truly exist, Shadus must have been its entrance.

Death's quiet call pulled her further as though it were physically trying to speak to her but couldn't find its words, while she strained to get a better look into the depths. Suddenly hands gripped her shoulders, pulling her back.

"Fates, Orah! Were you planning on throwing yourself into the depths?" Roan yelled.

"What?" she replied, still thrown off by the radiating pull from the cavern.

"You were almost fully over that wall. I was halfway to the palace when I realized you were no longer next to me." Sighing he pushed her further back to the city street. "I should have warned you. The dead like to play tricks. They can probably sense there is something different about you."

"Oh." Death returned to its quiet, familiar hum while her heartbeat returned to normal and realization hit her. "OH."

His eyes widened and he nodded his head. "Yes. Please stay close to me."

She shook off her daze, glancing back at the cavern once more while they continued their walk. She made sure to keep right by his side when they approached the large building she'd observed when they landed. The building appeared to be carved from obsidian. No other building in the city was like it. Its black presence glistened as they drew closer. She wasn't able to shake off the unsettling feeling that flooded through her when they approached two large gates.

The towering gates were closed, and her stomach turned when she looked up at them. They were made of some kind of bone. Not human, they were too large to be human, but they were very much bone. Two decrepit creatures with tattered wings and only hollowed eyes on their faces stood in front of the gates, guarding them. Orah bit down her yelp when they both bowed low and somehow spoke, though they had no lips. "My Lord."

"My uncle should be expecting us." Roan nodded at their bow and they both stood. Looking up at the gate, they nodded their own heads while the doors slowly pulled open.

✳

Aeron's palace was massive and Orah didn't quite understand how they arrived at his throne room. Standing in the room, she let out a low whistle. Just like the exterior, the room appeared to be carved from obsidian. With the black rock glistening and echoes filling the chamber with each step she took.

In the middle of the room sat a throne made of bones—a throne Orah was trying to avoid staring at. Although, the city was beautiful, and while she felt slightly unsettled, she didn't feel uncomfortable. But she couldn't see Roan residing there as the next God of Death. Not the man who had a perfect view of his own lush, beautiful garden outside his window. Not the man that spun her around at the pub and laughed with her until they physically couldn't laugh any longer.

Gazing at the throne, she shook off the shivers that ran down her back. She tried, and failed, to imagine Roan sitting atop it. He was kind and while he would still keep Mirin as a place of sanctuary, she couldn't see him happily living somewhere surrounded by so much darkness and death. That wasn't Roan—he may have been the God of Night but he himself was light, goodness, and warmth.

Why has he assigned this fate to himself?

Lost in her thoughts the sound of footsteps startled her. She and Roan both turned toward the throne room doors. They flung open and an intense, ominous, yet familiar feeling filled the room. Orah's breath felt as though it was being pulled from her while she stared at the man that approached.

He looked like Roan but—different. His hair was a brilliant gold, but his caramel skin wasn't alive like Roan's—almost as though all the life in him had been drained. Taking pigments of his color with it. He was dressed head to toe in black and she couldn't hold back her gasps when she saw the lit freckles running across the bridge of his nose, just like Roan. Above his head hovered a crown of black shadows. As he walked further into the room his presence was overpowering and a heavy weight lingered in the air.

She made eye contact with him and a smile spread across his lips. Shaking her head, she tried to push down her quiet companion tugging at her, calling to her power, and the responding tingles at the tips of her fingers. She felt as though she were being watched by a predator and her body was responding as though she were in danger. Trying to control herself, she breathed in and out over and over again. Roan glanced at her, concern tight across his face. He shook his head like a silent attempt to tell her to get a handle of herself.

As if I'm not already trying to do that.

She shifted her focus back to his uncle, stepping back when she found him standing in front of her. "Interesting." Slowly he walked around Orah. Ice cold air swayed around them while he inspected her. "Roan said you were special."

Her fingers tingled, begging to reach out and play with his power calling to her lifelong companion.

She nodded. "He said you might be able to help me."

"Did he?" Aeron replied while he glanced at Roan. He continued his walk around her and her lungs tightened.

"*Listen.*" Finally finding its voice again, Death begged her quietly to pay attention. She shook her head, cursing its quiet call, commanding it to be silent. She stared back at Aeron; she understood why people were afraid of him now. It felt as though he was slowly sucking the life out of you when he was close.

"*Listen.*"

Orah jumped at the voice inside her head. Aeron stopped circling her and smiled wide, while stepping back. "Are you scared of me, Orah Clark?"

"How did you know my name?"

"My nephew told me." Aeron pointed to Roan.

Orah turned to Roan while he nodded in response. Aeron winked before walking toward Roan with his arms open. She watched stunned, while Aeron brought Roan into a tight hug.

Aeron's deep and comforting laugh echoed in the room. "My boy. Why did it take a mysterious mortal woman to get you to come visit?"

Roan's answering laugh made her smile while he wriggled out of his uncle's arms. "Sorry, uncle. You would have seen me at my party."

"Yes, but that's more official business. I've missed your company. I've been worried with the challenge drawing near. Are you preparing?"

Waving his hand dismissively, Roan nodded. "Yes, of course I have. Jes has been on my ass about that every single day. I'm making sure I'm ready."

Eyeing him with doubt, Aeron nodded. "I'll believe you—for now."

They both glanced back at Orah and Aeron smiled again then turned to walk toward his throne. Casually he sat and she couldn't refrain her shock that he was comfortable on a throne made of the dead. Aeron ran his hand along the arm of the throne. "Don't worry. I didn't kill them. This throne has been here for several thousand years. I'm not even sure who the bones came from."

"That's not any more comforting," Orah replied.

Aeron's eyes widened for a moment before nodding. "Roan said you speak your mind. I like it. Wanna give it a try? It looks cold but it stays surprisingly warm."

Stepping back she gaped at him, unsure how to respond. She glanced at the throne then swallowed her disgust. "I'd rather not disrespect the dead with my ass."

Roan let out a choked laugh. "The throne's missing out," Roan whispered and she snapped her head at him, glaring.

Giving her a wink, Roan walked toward the throne and motioned for her. Reluctantly, she followed until she was standing in front of Aeron. Aeron had an amused sparkle in his eyes and for the first time she noticed his eyes didn't resemble Roan's or either of his siblings. They were black. As black as his palace and the lit freckles across his cheeks made them look as though there were embers of silver fire burning inside his pupils.

Aeon leaned back in the throne. "Roan told me he had questions about the soul portal. I'm assuming this has something to do with you?"

Roan stepped forward, grasping Orah's hand with a reassuring squeeze. "Yes, that's correct. I didn't want to write it in my message, but Orah's not from here." Aeron's eyes darted to Orah's and a small grin formed at the corner of his mouth. Roan appeared to miss the quick glance and continued, "She somehow came through my garden door almost six weeks ago and I have no idea how to send her back. I asked Amada about traveling to the other worlds. The books she sent reminded me of the power of your soul portal."

Aeron's head turned to Roan then he stood. "My soul portal is for those that have passed, Roan, not the living."

"But how can you know? Have you ever tried?" Roan asked.

"Nothing can go through the portal on our side. Only souls passing through to either travel to the depths or to the Fates can."

Roan released Orah's hand and stepped closer to the throne. She had almost expected him to drop to his knees from the pleading tone in his voice. "Aeron, I've watched hundreds of souls go through that portal at one time. It's probably the best chance Orah has."

"Why do you want to send her away? Why not accept the gift the Fates have literally placed on your doorstep?"

Irritated she was once again being spoken about as if she were some prize, Orah stepped forward. "I'm not a gift that your *Fates* can deliver. I'm a person who has a life in my own world and Roan is trying to help me because I want to go home."

Aeron locked eyes with her and they stared at each other in silence.

"*Pay attention.*" Orah pushed down the quiet voice while Roan shifted uncomfortably next to her. Briefly, she worried she may have offended the God of Death. No matter what Roan and Jes may have tried to assure her of, in his presence, she had no doubt Aeron could collect any soul at any moment.

"*Listen.*"

Aeron jumped and narrowed his eyes. Cocking his head, he smiled. "Follow me."

"What?" Orah asked.

Nodding his head to Roan he walked away from the throne and past them. Roan nudged her shoulders, encouraging her to follow. They followed in silence while Aeron led them through his palace, stopping at a set of tall doors. The doors opened and Aeron stepped into an empty room. Motioning for Roan and Orah to follow, he waited just beyond the doors until Orah and Roan had joined him.

Orah yelped when suddenly the room shot upward. Looking up she found Roan and Aeron both grinning at her. Annoyed at their amusement, she shouted, "You could have warned me that the floor moved!"

"Yes, but your reaction was worth it." Roan's eyes twinkled briefly before he snapped his head up and gazed forward.

A few seconds later they came to an abrupt stop. There were no doors where they'd stopped. It was as though they'd appeared through a hole in the floor. The room they arrived in was bright and Orah squinted, trying to make out where they were.

Shaking off the shock of the light, she froze. The room radiated death. As though death was sitting above, waiting to pull an unexpecting victim in its grasp.

"*Welcome.*"

Her feet froze to the ground and she hesitated to walk any further. Roan tensed beside her, as though he was also not sure he wanted to walk further into the room.

"*Pay attention.*"

Orah's hands shook with how loudly Death called to her now. With a sigh, Aeron walked forward and motioned for them both to follow him again. Orah breathed out, then stepped forward. In front of them was a large portal, at least three times larger than the one in the city center in Iluna.

"*Judgement.*"

Death sang with a near giddy tune. A chill ran down Orah's back and she jumped at the invisible thread now pulling at her toward the portal. Her eyes watered while she fought the whispering song when a man and woman came from the shimmering light. With a bow they stopped in front of Aeron. The woman briefly looked up past Roan, as though he weren't in the room, and nodded at Orah.

"*What says Death?*"

Orah muttered a curse and begged the voice to silence itself. She nodded back at the woman then watched while Aeron surveyed the pair. Slowly, he nodded, and a bright light filled the room. The couple vanished and that thread loosened its grasp on Orah.

"*Judgment.*"

Orah nodded, acknowledging Death's call. A warm sense of understanding mixed with confusion settled over her. Glancing over at Roan, she breathed out.

"Where did they go?"

Roan's lowered voice made her jump, keeping his eye on the portal he shrugged. "To the Fates."

Aeron ushered them to the side and they stood for several minutes watching more people come through. With each person that came through the chill and call of death grew colder and louder. Orah thought that she should be scared, that she should have felt uncomfortable that death lingered there so comfortably but the more souls she watched the more comfortable she became.

"*Judgment. Judgment. Judgment.*"

That was until death called over and over again inside of her and an icy burst of air pulled Orah's breath. She watched, fighting back her screams when a winged creature came through the portal and black shadowed hands appeared from the pit, pulling it down to the depths.

"*Justice.*"

Orah stared at where the creature had disappeared, unsure how she hadn't noticed the opening to the cavern so close to them.

"You see, Orah, only the dead can come through this portal. No one can go through on our side. Living or dead," Aeron said.

She found Aeron staring at her, the look on his face was soft but stern. She let out an annoyed breath. "Have you ever tried?" She didn't want to be told something wasn't possible if no one had tried. She blinked away her tears at the fact they had somehow hit another dead end.

Aeron let out a long sigh before slowly lifting his right hand. Orah stepped back, unsure of what he was going to do.

"*Watch.*"

She stood, frozen, in shock when his skin withered away on his arm. What had previously appeared to be a normal hand was now replaced by a hand that appeared as though it were from a corpse.

Roan staggered backward. "How?"

To her surprise Aeron turned to Orah. "When my brother's wife died, I was here when her soul attempted to come through the portal. When I saw her, I panicked. I knew what her death would do to him. What it would do to all of us. I tried—" Choking on his words, he glanced at Roan again. "I tried to push her back. To send her soul back to her body but the portal and the Fates wouldn't allow it. The moment my hand went through the portal she went to the Fates and part of my soul went with her." Spinning his hand back and forth, he shrugged. "My hand is a physical reminder of my failure, but also that no living soul can enter this portal from our side."

A choked sound came out of Roan and he sank to the ground. "Why haven't you ever told me?"

Aeron rushed over, placing his hand on Roan's shoulder. "You already blame yourself. This was mine to carry."

The tears Orah had been fighting to hold back fell while she watched them. The moment was touching, but her frustration only selfishly cared for herself. She unknowingly built up a false hope that she would get home this way. Shaking her head, she began to pace the room. Feeling almost delirious with disappointment.

A strong hand gripped her arm and she looked up, expecting to find Roan, but made eye contact with Aeron. "I know you're disappointed, Orah. I wish I had better answers for you."

Shrugging off his touch, she wiped away her tears. "Thank you for showing me this."

He nodded and stepped back towards Roan – who now appeared to have composed himself again. Clearing his throat, Roan stared at the portal then at Orah. His eyes had a sad disappointed shining in them. "I guess we've got to start from scratch again. I'm sorry, Orah."

He turned toward the spot on the floor that they had arrived on and motioned for her to follow. "It's going to get late soon. We should probably begin our journey home."

Home—the word hit Orah like a block of ice on her chest. Staring at Roan's outstretched hand, she shook her head. She had told him that if Shadus didn't work that they had to keep their distance moving forward.

"If Aeron doesn't mind, I think I'll take his city's portal back to Illuna," she replied.

Stepping back, Roan stared at his uncle. Aeron glanced between them, confusion tight across his face. "If that's how you prefer to travel. You're more than welcome to use the Perambulate," Aeron responded.

Roan's expression shifted from shock to anger, but he nodded his head. "Fine. Let's get you to the portal and I'll see you when I get back to the house."

Silently, she nodded her head and stood a few inches from him. The floor flew back down and the tall doors at the bottom opened for them. In just the few seconds it had taken them to get down a few levels, Roan's irritation had built. The tension in the air was so thick one could cut it.

They moved through the palace quickly with Aeron accompanying them. Nerves fluttered in Orah's stomach at the thought of the awkward walk she was about to have with Roan. Not out of anything she thought Roan would say or do, more so anticipation for the silence that was likely to settle between the two of them. As if he could sense her nerves, Aeron stepped forward.

"Nephew, I haven't had a stroll in my city for a few days. I think I would like to escort your guest if you don't mind."

Roan's nostrils flared then he let out a breath. "Yes, that's fine. As long as it's fine with Orah."

Orah nodded. "I think that's alright."

With a grunt and a nod Roan bowed his head to Aeron and then looked at Orah. "I'll see you at the house."

The bustling sound of the city faded while Aeron and Orah stood by the palace gates, watching Roan walk away. She couldn't seem to get herself to move from where she stood until she watched Roan in the distance mount Nacht's saddle and take off into the sky.

Her silent companion sent an icy sensation through her and the hairs on her arm stood. She turned to find Aeron turning toward the opposite side of the city, gesturing for her to follow.

"*Go.*"

Still feeling frozen from watching Roan leave, she shook her head, silencing her invisible companion. Her power thrummed in protest to her silence and battered against her while she passed the edge of the sidewalk—near the cavern.

"*Please. One more peek.*"

Shaking her head, she cursed silently, remembering Roan's comment about the dead. She picked up her pace and caught up to Aeron's side. The people and creatures surrounding them briefly glanced their way. Aeron scoffed then smiled at her. Somehow, she could make out the amusement in his black eyes. She smiled back, wondering how often the people of Mirin saw their God walking with a mortal so casually.

"He cares about you," Aeron stated.

Not sure how to respond, her head snapped up to meet his gaze "What?"

"Roan, he cares about you. Can you not tell?"

"I think it's more of him desiring me because I won't let him have me."

Amusement flashed in his eyes again and he chuckled. "Orah, I've known him since he was a babe. If he didn't care about you, he would have sent you on your way weeks ago. He wouldn't be going to these lengths to try and help you."

"*Yes.*"

"*Oh, shut the fuck up,*" Orah silently commanded Death.

She didn't want to have this conversation right now. Not with Roan's uncle. She already had an uncomfortable conversation with Lahana. Trying to think of anything to avoid the conversation she allowed herself to ask a question she'd had since they'd arrived in Shadus.

"How do you know that other worlds exist?"

Stopping, Aeron laughed. "Well, I guess we're not talking about Roan then." Rubbing his hand over his face, he smiled. "Sometime, long ago, we could travel between worlds. Others could also travel here." He paused for a moment, seemingly lost in his thoughts before he cleared his throat and continued. "The knowledge of how to do this was lost but every now and then someone who was from here will pass and their soul will tell us of the other worlds."

Gasping, she stared at him. "So, there could be Gods even where I live? Practically immortal beings?"

He shrugged. "I think that depends on if where you're from has magic or not. If there's no magic then a God would age like a mortal but if a God somehow found themselves in another world that had magic then, yes, they would have their long lifetime."

She glanced around the city in front of her, unable to help but wonder if maybe that was how she came through the garden gate. If maybe at some point in time another God came through and left remnants of magic.

Admiring the eerie beauty of the city, she sighed. "Do you think Roan will be happy here?"

An unsettling quiet fell over them and Aeron continued walking. "Roan isn't meant to be the God of Death."

"How can you know that for sure?"

"Because I was. I know what it feels like for Death to beckon to you. To call you at any moment. To tempt you with its mysteries. I've spent hundreds of years with Roan and I don't think he's ever felt that."

"Death's call." Her quiet, life-long companion smiled within her. Sending a chill down her spine. She tried to hide her shock in her response. "Do you think Marek has?"

"Judgment—judgment calls to be heard."

Aeron stopped, his eyes widened while she fidgeted, trying to quiet the voice inside. His gaze lingered on her when he finally shrugged. "He could."

Orah stood for a moment, waiting for the quiet voice inside to say something but it remained silent. Trying to hold in her scoff at the irony of its silence, she sighed. "I hope Roan doesn't throw the next challenge."

Aeron stared past her and she followed his gaze to a large building behind her. "I hope not as well. Maybe he'll have something to fight for this time," he replied.

Shocked, she opened her mouth to respond but he shook his head and walked to the building. She followed while he pulled open the door. It was identical to the portal building in Illuna, but the room was empty, as though people had been expecting Aeron's presence. She glanced at him, then nervously looked at the portal.

"The last time Roan had me try one of these I saw a glimpse of home, but I couldn't get there," she admitted.

Shock flashed across Aeron's face. "You did?"

"Yes. I could see it but the closer I got the further away it felt. Finally, I screamed, 'I want to go home' and next thing I knew I was back with Roan." She breathed out, revealing what she had kept hidden for weeks. Shaking her head, she hoped Aeron wouldn't tell Roan.

"Interesting. Well today, right as you're about to walk through just think of the portal in Iluna, it'll get you back." Aeron's black eyes narrowed on her for a moment before he peered back at the portal. Slowly, they approached the thin blurred wall and he smiled at her as she stepped forward. "It was wonderful to meet you, Orah Clark. I hope I have the pleasure again." Shockingly, he dipped into a low bow and she watched, unsure what to say. The God of Death was bowing to her as if he respected her, or as though she somehow outranked him.

Shaking her head, she smiled, gathering the courage to respond. "It was wonderful to meet you as well."

"Not goodbye, not farewell."

She groaned at Death's quiet return and stepped forward to look back at Aeron one last time, intrigued by the show of respect he'd given her. Her power thrummed in her chest and she glanced through the glass doors that led out to the city streets. She stepped back, convinced the tendrils of shadows crawling from the edge of the cavern toward the building were only part of her imagination.

"Death calls to Death."

She froze watching the shadows grow closer. She shook her head and turned back to the portal. Letting out a breath she stepped through—thinking of Roan.

Chapter 25

Standing on the mat of the training room, Orah narrowed her eyes at Jes. Her body ached from him repeatedly throwing her down against the mat. Her temper was boiling and she was determined to beat him. Quickly he shifted his feet back and forth in a taunt and she let out a frustrated yell as she ran toward him. His hands grabbed hers and he flipped her so that her back was against his chest. He held her hands down, preventing her from getting out of his grip.

"You need to learn how to control your emotions, Orah. Your frustration is letting your guard down. Anyone can guess what you're going to do and stop you if you can't remain calm."

Fighting against his hold, she slammed her head against his chest.

He let out an amused grunt but tightened his grip on her. "I can say I didn't expect that, but I'm also not surprised."

She screamed and slammed her head against him again in response.

Laughing, he released his grip on her and spun her around to face him. "It's not always a bad thing to fight dirty but right now you need to get a handle on basics. Even something as simple as preventing me from grabbing you."

Rolling her eyes, she stared at him. They had been going around and around with this for close to a week since she'd returned from Shadus. Every day he reminded her to control her emotions and every day she ended up on her ass. Repeatedly.

The obstacle course was worse. It kept creating the same course as the first time he'd brought her there. She couldn't seem to get past the fourth platform, no matter how hard she tried. The day before she'd begged him to ward it like he did for his mortal guards and he not so kindly reminded her she was not one of his guards and the wards were doing it for a reason.

"Are you done living in your head?" Jes waved his hands in front of her face.

Shaking her head, she glared up at him. "I'm just contemplating how I'm going to kick your ass one day."

With a laugh he wiped the sweat from his brow. "I'd like to see that day come." Sighing, he walked to the other side of the training room, grabbing his cup of water. She followed close behind and they sat in silence trying to steady their breaths.

"Have you talked to him?" Jes asked.

She jumped at his question. She knew who he was talking about. She and Roan hadn't interacted much since they parted ways at Aeron's gates. They were friendly at dinner but other than that they'd been avoiding one another. They still ended up alone in the library for at least an hour each day, but they didn't speak beyond discussing what they'd researched about portals. They definitely made sure to sit on opposite sides of the room and keep to themselves as best as they could.

Orah glared at Jes. "Why do you care? You were very adamant about us not talking not that long ago." She didn't care to hide her annoyance. Jes had to make up his mind on whether or not he thought she was a danger to Roan.

Sighing, he shrugged. "I care because I care about you both, but I understand the need for boundaries."

She looked away, trying to conceal the expression on her face. Jes had no idea she knew about Moros and she was trying not to let it slip when they were together. She may not have understood Jes's choices, but she did understand it was a boundary he wasn't ready to address.

"I think we're done for today. I'm tired and the recruits want to go and celebrate passing their final course." He stretched wide and his wings flared out, almost hitting the walls behind him.

Orah smiled. "I'll meet you at the obstacle course tomorrow then?"

Nodding, he grinned. "You don't give up do you?"

She shrugged. "You said we didn't have a lot of time before the challenge. I want to be prepared. Aeron had no answers for us, and Roan and I haven't found anything new in the library so I'm preparing. Even if it hurts like hell."

Shaking his head, he walked towards the door and opened it, gesturing for her to walk through first. They walked silently to the bottom of the stairs and he looked toward Roan's study doors. They were open and his desk was empty. He was likely in the city center with his officials.

With a sigh, Jes glanced back at Orah. "You don't have to cross a line to continue being friends with him, you know. Roan's one of the greatest people you'll ever have the honor of being your friend."

She stared at the desk and her cheeks grew hot. "Jes, I don't know if I can just be friends with him. That's the problem."

With a nod, Jes walked down the hall to his room. She watched while he opened his door then turned to her again. "Just consider it." He walked into his room and she stood in the now empty foyer. The house was so quiet. Almost unsettlingly quiet, especially with Lahana away. She was expected to return soon but apparently the handing out of invitations to the mortals was going well.

The days were passing, and Roan's party was drawing closer. Soon the entire city was going to be diving into a week-long festival in preparation for the big day. That was one of the reasons why Roan was out of the house so often. He had been meeting with vendors and businesses since they'd returned to Shadus. All in preparation for the visitors from other Regions.

Orah breathed out and walked up the stairs. Dinner was approaching and she wanted to make sure she was washing up before going down to the kitchen. She rushed past Lahana's room and stopped in front of her doors with panic while she watched Roan walk out of his.

His head snapped up and they stared at each other. They had been alone in the library plenty of times since returning, but she had made sure they were never within several feet of one another. Their only conversations were discussing their research and the casual conversations around the others at dinner. But right then they both had a choice. They either ignored each other or acted like adults.

Clearing his throat, he nodded his head. Her eyes glanced at her bedroom door and he tensed. His hands flexed open and closed at his side. She couldn't help but stare at the odd movement when he cleared his throat again.

"Been having your ass handed to you by Jes?" he said.

"Excuse me?" She crossed her arms defensively.

"Everyone in this house could hear your curses and the colorful words you called him. I'm assuming those were each time he flipped you onto the mat." His eyes sparkled with amusement and she couldn't help her responding grin.

"I guess I'm predictable," she replied with a shrug.

Air rushed forward and her hair blew back behind her. She gasped, stepping back as he appeared in front of her. "You're anything but predictable, Orah." His hand lifted as though he were going to touch her face when he paused. Her knees weakened at the intoxicating heat from his hand hovering over her skin.

Her breathing slowed while her eyes met his. He pulled away and she jumped in anticipation of his touch but blinked, realizing she'd heard her door click open. Confused, she stared down to see his hand on the handle. He leaned forward. "I won't keep you from your shower," he whispered against her ear, holding her door open for her.

A wicked idea came to her and she looked up at him. She could invite him in. She could invite him to join her in the shower. She could get over herself and enjoy everything he had to offer.

Not everything.

She was sure that physically Roan would change her life, but there was so much more he could offer her. More that she wasn't quite sure she was ready for.

He cleared his throat, snapping her out of her thoughts. "Something on your mind?"

"Not particularly," she replied.

With each step he took closer to her she backed up until her back was fully pressed against the wall beside her door. He leaned down, whispering again, "Are you sure about that?"

She scowled with irritation until she realized what he was referring to. The hallway was lit but not from any light in the house. She was glowing like a candle again. His face shone in her light and his eyes slowly moved up and down her body.

"Just thinking about what it would be like to have company in the shower." She shrugged, trying to sound unbothered but as the words came out of her the light grew brighter.

His freckles sparkled as though they had been lit with a match and he stared at her lips. Leaning closer his hands rested against the wall on either side of her head. "And what exactly would *company* entail?"

She stared at his full lips, his sharp jaw, those eyes now wild with intention. She hadn't thought that far ahead and didn't know what it would mean. He leaned closer and his lower half now pressed against hers, pushing her firmly against the wall. Her chest tightened while he stared down at her. His eyes flared while she imaged her lips on his. His hands on hers. The hot water of a shower cascading over both of their naked bodies.

Staring at his lips, she gulped. Her body jumped inside begging her to move; to take action; to do anything. A sly smile spread across her lips and she slowly ran her hands up his chest. He stilled, a pulse between them jumped where their bodies were pressed together. Her eyes widened and she looked back up at him.

There's nothing wrong with physical. Lahana even said so. Nothing wrong with it at all.

"Fuck it," she whispered before wrapping her arms around his neck and pressing her lips against his.

Christ, his lips are soft.

The pulse between them jumped again and he froze. She opened her eyes to find his closed, but he didn't move. He didn't react. Maybe she had miscalculated. Maybe he was only teasing. *Oh God. What have I done?*

Suddenly, his eyes sprang open and he seemed to snap back to reality. He became unleashed. His lips claimed hers as though they belonged to him. His hands on either side of her head moved. One grabbing her hip, the other grasping her neck while he pulled his lips from hers and claimed her neck.

Gasping, she dug her nails into his back while his hand on her hips tucked up under the edge of her shirt. She jolted at his touch against her skin, sure that some kind of electric shock had just gone through her.

Roan was ravenous, moving his hand from her neck to the back of her head, tugging playfully on her hair. His lips found hers again and she let out a quiet appreciative groan. The obvious firm length of him pressed against her and her knees weakened. Suddenly, he pulled away.

Dropping his voice low, he stared at her lips. "I think your lips may become my addiction." The silver in his eyes swirled and he smiled before lifting her into his arms.

Gasping, she laughed, wrapping her legs around his waist while he walked them into her bedroom, slamming her door loudly behind them.

She ran her hands through his hair, kissing his neck as he led them to her bed.

Laying her down abruptly, she stared as he towered above her. She couldn't breathe, she couldn't think. Everything felt unmoving and yet alive and electric.

He smiled. "I think time has stopped for us, love." His eyes traveled up and down her body before he let out an appreciative groan. In an instant he towered over her then he was on top of her, pinning her to the bed. His lips collided with hers again and she wrapped her legs around his waist in response.

His hands moved while he kissed. They teased, they caressed, they explored all over her. She wiggled, silently begging him to remove the layers between them, to feel his skin against hers. Smiling against her lips, his hand slipped under her shirt again.

His touch made her head spin and she moaned against his lips. His fingers dug against her skin and he nipped her lip in approval.

"Yes," he mumbled against her. "Don't hold in those sounds."

Her legs shook in response to the enticing words he spoke. She would do anything he wanted her to. Anything to relieve the growing pressure inside of her.

Her hands frantically moved over his body trying to find a place to grip his clothes. Finding the edge of his shirt she tugged up, but his hand gripped her wrist. He pulled his lips from hers and shook his head. "Not yet. Right now, it's my turn."

She turned into a puddle at the words. She had no idea what he planned but she didn't care to ask. He had complete and total permission to do whatever he wished to her.

With a smile he pushed against the bed and stood. She sat up, leaning against her hands a bit in a daze. The loose shirt he was wearing was untucked from where her legs had been wrapped around him. His pants, well, they were struggling to keep his excitement hidden. He cleared his throat with a laugh and her head snapped back up to him. The look on his face....

He cares about you.

Panic hit her. Aeron's comment slammed into her mind. Roan wasn't just staring at her like he wanted her body. He was staring at her like he wanted more... like he wanted the parts of her she didn't know if she could give him.

She swallowed back a quiet sob and he tensed as if sensing her hesitation. Stepping away from the bed, he sighed. "Love, I just need you to make up your mind. I won't play games. If you don't want this, us, then just decide that."

Sitting up, she let out a shaky breath. "What if I just want something physical?"

She held back her reaction at the disappointment splayed across his face. Quickly, he replaced it with a mask of amusement and shrugged his shoulders. "If that's what you wanted."

"What if it turned into more?" she asked.

He drew closer, crouching beside the bed so they were now eye level. Looking down at her hands, he smiled. "May I?" She nodded nervously while he pulled her hand into his. Wrapping one hand around hers, he tilted her chin up with his other hand. "Would it be so bad if it turned into something more?"

Swallowing, she stared into his beautiful, enchanting eyes. The light of his freckles sparkled like they were dancing across his cheeks.

"But what if we find a way for me to go home?"

Pulling up their hands, he stared at them clasped together. Squeezing, he sighed. "Then I would think the Fates have played a cruel, beautiful joke on me." Her chest tightened and she pulled her hand, trying to unlink their connection, but he held his grip. "But I wasn't lying when I told you I would find a way to search every world until I found you again, Orah."

Slowly, he pressed his lips against the back of her hand. Her body burned as though it was going to catch on fire while she watched him lower their hands. Gently, he leaned forward, kissing the top of her forehead. A sound, almost like a sob, choked in her throat while he pulled away and stood again. Her anticipation for what was to come built to an agonizing speed. Smiling, he glanced toward the bedroom door then back down to her.

"Enjoy your shower, Orah."

Cold disappointment rushed over her. She went to ask him to stay but blinked, finding he had vanished in front of her. Sitting on the bed, she was unsure of what she had just started or worse... what she had just ended.

Cursing her inability to allow herself happiness, she climbed off the bed and angrily stripped off her clothes while walking to the bathroom. Her lips tingled, struggling to hold onto the memory of what his had felt like against hers. Tears lined her eyes while she turned on the shower to an icy cold and planted herself on the floor. Allowing that familiar angry numb to take over, she sobbed into her knees—wishing she could allow him in.

Standing by the wardpad of the obstacle course, Orah glared at Jes. "I don't want to today."

Jes's eyebrow raised comically and he shook his head. "I didn't think you had a choice."

Orah narrowed her eyes. "I always have a choice, Jesiel."

After crying herself to sleep the night before, she was tired of feeling like she stopped herself from achieving things or allowing people in. She hadn't gone down to dinner after Roan had left her room. She also hadn't gone down to the kitchen that morning like she usually did. In all reality, she just felt like she needed a break.

"I have a good feeling about today, Orah." Jes was trying to sound hopeful but part of her knew he was aware of what had happened between her and Roan.

I would think the Fates have played a cruel, beautiful joke on me.

She couldn't get what Roan had said out of her head. All night she replayed what happened. His kiss, the way his hand eagerly moved across her body, the warmth of him against her. The expression on his face when she panicked. His disappointment...

She replayed his comment through her mind in the shower, when she fell asleep, while she tossed and turned throughout the night, when she woke, the whole flight to the camp. Over and over again.

"Orah. Snap out of it for Fates sake," Jes said.

"I don't want to," she said, tightening her crossed arms against her chest.

"Please, for me. I feel like we might get a different course today," Jes replied with a smile.

His joking grin and the confidence was enough for Orah to approach the wardpad. They had been doing this for seven days and the course hadn't changed once. But perhaps he was right. Perhaps something would change.

Forcing herself to try, she pricked her finger, pressing the bead of blood against the pad.

The ground shook around them but she kept her back turned away from the course for as long as she could. She wasn't sure she could deal with any kind of disappointment if nothing was different. Next to her, Jes let out a small gasp and she turned around. Disappointment mingled with confusion rushed over her. The course appeared to be the same. The platforms were there, the spires were there, the odd pit of fire was there, and the wall with the door on top was there, but there were now two new doors. One on platform five and one at the last platform at the top of the mountain.

"It's like the course gave you a work around," Jes whispered.

"What makes you think I'll be able to open either of those doors? I haven't been able to yet," Orah snapped.

Shrugging, Jes glanced at her. "And you never will with that attitude." Clapping his hands, he grinned. "Come on. Get going."

With a sigh, Orah jogged toward the platforms. Just like always, she made it through one to five with no issues. Perhaps a lot of sweating and panting from the jumping but it wasn't too bad. Landing on platform five, she stared at the door. It looked as though it were made from the mountain itself. The handle was dark black, but the door had no engravings like the ones she had warded to appear at the house. Taking a deep breath in, she grabbed the handle, twisted, and pushed. The door groaned in protest but didn't budge.

She took a step back, inspecting the door. She could have tried jumping over it, but then she would have still had to figure out how to get through the other platforms. She glanced at Jes who waved his hands encouragingly.

She closed her eyes and thought about the top of the platform.

How badly she wanted to get there.

How she wanted to see what the course would pull from her and her magic.

Her hands hummed in response. Staring down at her palms, her eyes widened with excitement. She could possibly do it. All she had to do was believe in herself. Squaring her shoulders, she grabbed hold of the handle, bore down all of her weight, and pushed.

Nothing.

Absolutely nothing.

The door didn't even budge. She let out a scream of frustration and sank to her knees.

"What have I said about that temper?" Jes yelled from the ground.

Rolling her eyes, she threw her hand up and showed him just what she thought of his advice with her middle finger. His responding laugh was loud, and she smiled. At least she'd lightened the mood a bit.

She wasn't sure how long she tried to get the door open. At some point Jes left, informing her he had some things in the main part of the camp he had to address and that he would return later. She watched him walk through the archway then turned back to the door.

She had done better with controlling her emotions, but she still couldn't get the damned door to open. Sweat soaked her shirt from the constant pushing and shoving, mingled with the stifling summer heat. Her hands had a constant buzz and she thought of the rope of light she'd made appear before.

She stared at her palms, imagining how the rope felt in her hands then threw both hands in the direction of the door. She jumped, letting out a shocked scream when long tree-like branches shot forward instead of the rope she was expecting. The branches were similar to what Lahana had done to Marek's arms, but they were separate from her arms. Almost like they were thick rope branches she could control.

Smiling, at the surprise she threw out her hands and the branches wrapped around the handle and the frame of the door. The solid door groaned while the branches crept along its impenetrable surface. Perhaps she just needed an extra boost. Letting out a scream, she pushed the branches against the door.

A cracking sound echoed across the course, but the door didn't open. Her eyes widened with rage and she pushed harder. Her arms shook with the power and might she threw into the branches but still the door didn't move. The only response was the mocking cracking sounds of the rock.

She briefly considered giving up when an idea came to her. If she could make branches appear then she could use them to get to the other platforms. She didn't need a stupid door.

Narrowing her eyes, she shook her hands and the branches on the door withered away. She thought of the platform she knew was just beyond the door and threw her hands out again. The ground below shook and she stepped back while eight solid tree trunks rose from the ground to the edge of each platform. Conveniently placed just beyond the reach of the rock cylinders.

Orah peered back at the archway, hoping Jes had returned to see her accomplishment, but found only Tume, lazily grazing on the grass. With a triumphant "humph", Orah glanced at the trunk next to her then leapt. Her balance wobbled a bit and she steadied herself before feeling confident to continue.

Holding her head high, she leapt to the next trunk, right beside platform six. Letting out a proud cry when she made it safely. Up and up she went until she reached the top of the mountain. Amazed at herself, she twirled around the platform bolstered with pride.

Her hair whipped from a gust of wind and she looked up to find Jes hovering above her.

His eyes were wide and he stared at the new additions to the course. "How in the Fates did you do that?" he asked, pointing at the trunks.

"I improvised," Orah replied.

The weeks dragged on and Orah continued to improvise at the obstacle course and in her sparring with Jes. She was learning to control her emotions better and to Jes's delight, they had discovered she was pretty quick on her feet when she focused.

In the training room, her leg swiped under Jes's feet and he crashed to the ground with a loud thud. He'd underestimated her and she had distracted him with a small burst of light in the corner of the room.

He didn't know she had started sneaking off to the obstacle course before the sun rose over the last several weeks. Not only was she practicing her magic when training with him, but she was also doing it whenever she was alone. Discovering the light bursts the night before while in the bath. Once she'd figured it out, she spent most of the night putting on her own silent firework show.

Jes jolted to his feet and whirled around. She couldn't mask the triumph on her face as his eyes narrowed. "You played dirty," he said, but he also couldn't hide the pride in his voice.

"I didn't, I outsmarted you." She placed her hands on her hips then looked toward the small bursts of light exploding in the corner of the room.

He grinned. "When did you learn that little trick?"

"Last night."

He let out a quiet laugh then shook his head. "Orah, you're really something." He gestured for her to follow him and she watched, confused, as he walked toward the door.

"Where are we going?" she asked.

"Roan's study. He's got a bottle of good whiskey in there. We're celebrating you getting me off my feet."

Smiling wide, she skipped after him. The accomplishment was almost enough to make her cry. She didn't know if she would ever truly be able to protect herself in a real fight, but Jes was over twice her size and she had gotten him down. If she kept practicing, she could likely take anyone down.

Roan's office door was closed when they approached, and she paused. She didn't think he was home. His party was less than two weeks away now and he'd hardly been at the manor. They'd both kept their distance after what happened in her room. That didn't stop the overwhelming sense of guilt she felt whenever she thought about it. She had never meant to lead him on or play games. Or even worse, to hurt him.

"I don't need whiskey," Orah whispered, stepping away from the door.

Jes shook his head. "He's not going to bite. I bet he'll want to celebrate with us too. Come on." Jes grabbed her arm, pulling her behind him as he swung Roan's study door open.

"Excuse me." Roan peered up from his desk looking rather annoyed. His expression softened when he made eye contact with Orah then he glanced at Jes. "Is there a reason you two sweaty people have burst into my study?"

Beaming, Jes held up Orah's arm. "Orah just knocked me on my ass."

The desk rattled as Roan stood. "What?"

"Yup. She was like a trickster brownie playing a prank, but she got me. Threw some light bursts at the corner of the room, I thought something was about to catch on fire then she swiped her legs under mine and down I went."

Cocking his head, Roan smiled at Orah. "Light bursts?"

"I've been practicing my magic. Figured it out last night," Orah whispered, keeping her eyes on the carpet.

"Will you show me?"

She looked up to find both of their eyes on her, watching her eagerly. She swallowed, trying to push down the nerves sticking in her throat. "Uh sure."

Turning her back from them, she focused on the opposite corner of the room. She thought of the light and the images she'd been thinking of when they had appeared the night before.

Warm summers as a child.

Firework celebrations.

Sparklers.

Her Mother and Father laughing.

Mom's laugh.

Little tiny bursts of light appeared in the corner. To her shock they were more like fireworks than they had before. Some even had color to them.

She turned back and found Roan and Jes with large smiles on their faces. Roan crossed the room and stood in front of the light. She worried he would be burned and gasped when he stuck his hand into the middle of the light and smiled wider.

"Orah, this isn't just light bursts. This is starlight."

"What?" she asked.

Jes turned back to her, looking as shocked as she felt. Focusing her eyes, she could see it now. The light was like the stars Roan made appear the first day she'd arrived, but instead of blinking softly they were bursting over and over.

Suddenly she blurted out. "I'm not making planets explode, am I?"

Jes stumbled back against the desk and barked out a laugh, shaking his head. Roan smiled, shaking his head as well. "No you've made this all on your own. No innocent worlds have been harmed." He walked back toward his desk and bent down to open a drawer. "I'm assuming Jes was coming in for this?" he asked pulling out an intricate bottle full of amber liquid.

"Thought this type of celebration deserved the good stuff," Jes replied.

Roan made eye contact with Orah while he poured them each a small amount in the glasses he pulled out with the bottle. "I think you're right," Roan said, handing Orah her drink. Holding their gazes, they clinked their glasses to her success, but Orah was sure starlight twinkled in her eyes while she looked into Roan's.

Chapter 26

Roan leaned against the doorway of the side door, watching Orah slink off to the stables. She had certainly been practicing her magic by the way she held her hand out in front of her, using the light from her palm to guide the way. The sun hadn't yet risen but he knew where she was going.

She had been sneaking out for weeks now before she thought anyone else in the house was awake to go to the camp. He assumed she was leaning on the hope that anyone at the camp wouldn't think twice about the black Pegasus landing each morning and that their fear of Roan wouldn't bring them to investigate.

Roan just happened to be up with his balcony doors open a few weeks prior when he noticed the black dot of Tume shooting into the sky. With her display of starlight the night before, he was able to put together that she was practicing on her own. He didn't necessarily want to spy on her, but he was curious enough to see what she was doing at the camp to have improved in so little time.

He watched as Tume launched into the sky and as quickly and quietly as he could, he rushed into the stables to saddle Nacht. They were only a few minutes behind when they ascended, making their way to the camp. If they were fast, they would be able to surprise Orah before she warded the course.

Nacht's wings beat furiously while they raced to keep up. The city below was beginning to wake up and the early risers had their lights on. A few people stepped out of their homes and looked up, noticing Roan in the sky. With a smile he knew they couldn't see, he waved back. He would have done anything to protect his people. Even if that meant protecting them from himself.

Nacht turned toward the camp and Roan watched Orah and Tume descend. Pulling on the reins, he slowed Nacht a bit so they didn't startle Orah while they made their descent. The benefit of being the Governing God meant that he could land in his own guard camp whenever he wanted. Steering Nacht to the main gates, they landed quietly.

Two young guards, whom Roan assumed had just finished their final tests, stood at attention. They both glanced toward the course then to Roan. They must have seen Orah and assumed it was Roan. Putting his hand up, he stopped them from speaking and pressed his finger to his lips in a silent command. Nervously they glanced at one another and bowed while he handed Nacht's reins to them and walked toward the course.

The sun was barely cresting in the sky when he reached the archway. Tume made a startled noise when he walked past her grazing in the grass.

"Just me, girl," he whispered, placing his hand gently on her neck. She looked back behind her and he followed her gaze. Right in front of the wardpad was Orah and she appeared to be stretching. Roan observed the course, noticing it didn't look like anything specific. According to Jes, when Orah warded the course it was something Jes had never seen before.

Roan was enamored at the ease of Orah's movements with each stretch. He hadn't let himself stare at her for that long in weeks. Not after her bedroom. Not really since their picnic before Shadus.

Her long legs stretched out in front of her and he watched the muscles in her back stretch. She looked like she'd gotten stronger in the time she'd been training Jes. Nothing that shocked Roan. Jes could help anyone strengthen their body.

She let out a sigh and released her stretch, staring up at the sky with a smile.

He covered his mouth to muffle his gasp when brilliant green grass grew around where she was seated. Just like the grass in the meadow under the willow. Lazily she laid down in it and watched the sky.

Every time Roan believed he understood her power, she surprised him. Nothing specific was tied to her. It was just straight unfiltered power pulling from every magic source he was aware of.

With another sigh, she stood and brushed dirt off her legs. The grass disappeared as quickly as it had appeared, and she turned to the ward pad.

Smiling to himself, he stepped out of the shadows of the archway and cleared his throat.

"You really think I wouldn't know if someone was taking my personal Pegasus every morning?" he asked.

Jumping, she screamed and turned back to face him. Her fear barreled into him like a wave but then he was immediately hit with a wave of anger. "Are you spying on me?"

Her question was accusatory, and he chuckled. "I can't spy when you're in the camp for *my* guards. I know you've assumed they think you flying in is me flying in." Her arms crossed against her chest and she glared at him. "Unfortunately for you, I've blown your cover this morning."

Her eyes widened and she glanced at the archway in shock, understanding now that he had come from the main gate. Her rage burned hotter and she lifted her leg in a little stomp. Roan smiled. She hadn't done that in weeks.

He walked closer to her. "You've been practicing your magic here."

She tensed but held her glare. As if she were challenging him. "Yes, and?" The defiance in her voice. He loved it.

"I want to see what you've got."

"Excuse me?"

"I want to see what you can do. Let's play a game, a challenge if you will, one on one."

His stomach flipped with nerves he knew weren't his own and she looked him up and down slowly. Her eyes widened while she took that he was dressed to train. He knew exactly what he was doing when he woke up that morning. He'd kept his distance for weeks, allowing her the boundaries and respect she requested. He had no intention of breaking that, but he had every intention of finding out how deep her power went.

"You'll kick my ass." She swallowed as her eyes lingered on his body.

"I'm not asking to spar with you. You can do that all you want with Jes. I want to see what you can do with your magic" Roan replied.

A thick, hot emotion rolled over him and he had to compose himself before moving forward. She didn't know she couldn't hide her attraction to him. It almost killed him every time they were close to one another and he had pushed her more than he should have with his teasing.

"Fine," she agreed, crossing her arms over her chest.

As he approached, she sounded as though she were trying to control her breathing. Together, they turned the knob and pricked their fingers. Staring at each other they placed the small beads of blood onto the pad.

The ground shook around them, but Roan couldn't pull his eyes from hers. Finally, she let out a sigh and turned. Her gasp was too startled for him to ignore, and he turned eyes widening in wonder at the course in front of them.

The floating platforms a short distance away were separated by large spires which moved in an upward motion, coming from the ground. Appearing as though they were there to knock down whomever would be trying to get to each platform.

The platforms themselves seemed to cascade up in a straight row, then scatter sporadically. At the top of the mountain was the last platform, beside it, large spires were splayed across the ground. Each one shorter than the last until only one sat just above the ground.

Beyond the last spire sat an odd pit of flames, followed by a tall wall for scaling. Beyond the wall laid more platforms. Only these ones moved in the air, back and forth. Finally, at the other end of the course, Roan could see a white flag speared into the top of the mountain. Waving in the wind, calling for its victor.

Roan's smile was unavoidable. None of what he observed felt like it was designed for him or his magic. He had been in the course plenty of times in his life, and only a few of the obstacles before him had ever appeared. Turning his head back to Orah, he found her staring at him with a wicked grin.

"First one to grab that flag wins?" she challenged.

"Are you competitive, Orah?" he asked, glancing to where she appeared to be bouncing with anticipation. Maybe she had taught herself more than he'd given her credit for.

"Afraid to lose, Roan?" she replied. Her taunt sparked something inside of him and his own grin widened.

"On three," he said.

Squaring her shoulders, she positioned herself as if she were going to sprint forward.

"One. Two." He paused to look at her once more when she winked.

"Three!" she screamed.

In a mad dash, she raced toward the platforms ahead of them. He paused for a moment marveling at her speed. Watching while she jumped over each platform, throwing out walls of rock to block the spires coming from the ground. Appearing as though she were creating her own bridge to keep herself from being hit.

Shaking his head, he rushed after her. He could watch her win all day, but he knew beating her was going to be more entertaining.

She underestimated how fast he was, letting out a yell of frustration when he leapt over her, throwing a wall of starlight out to block her. Holding back his smile, he ran up the rock bridge she'd created. When he reached the scattered platforms he glanced back to see her hand, now on fire, shooting out from the wall he'd created, slicing it down the middle. She stepped out, starlight now showering around her and her eyes glistening as though they had caught on fire.

He smiled at her rage, knowing he had provoked her just the right amount. Peering back at the platforms, he jumped from each one with ease. This part of the course was meant to challenge her power, not his.

He reached the spires that cascaded downwards but fell back when she swung past him on a rope of light. Sticking her tongue out, she flung her free hand towards the next spire and he watched the rope wrap around it while she continued swinging. Laughing, he shook his head, unable not to compare her to one of the small animals in Zumner that swung from tree branches.

While she swung, she glanced back, giving him a cocky grin. He smiled in response; she was taunting him. With a snap of his fingers, the sunlight above them turned black while her collision with one of the spires echoed throughout the course.

Throwing out his hand, he created his own platforms of solid starlight and descended to the ground. He had to hold in his laugh at her curses but watched in awe as her body began to glow and the sunlight slowly faded back.

She stood on the second to last spire, with death in her eyes while blood dripped from her nose. Roan winced, opening his mouth to apologize, but her interrupting middle finger stopped him. His eyes widened with amusement.

Hopping off his platform, he rushed to the pit of fire and stopped. He didn't have any idea how to get over it. The hole in the ground wasn't large, but the fire itself was at least a foot taller than him. He couldn't go around it, there were walls blocking any chance to do that, but going over it wasn't an option either. Taking a deep breath in, he let it out slowly then blinked when a drop of water hit his cheek. He glanced up at the clear blue sky and cocked his head. It shouldn't have been raining.

Behind him, a laugh ran a chill down his spine, and he glanced back to find Orah. With a wink, she snapped her fingers and rain poured down from the cloudless sky. Roan yelped, ducking down but watched in pride as the fire extinguished and she rushed past him.

Her power was admirable, and he couldn't help but wonder if perhaps letting her win would be worth it. She was certainly working hard enough to earn her victory. With a smile, he shook off the thought and raced after her. Knowing he was faster and had scaled walls like it for most of his life.

She let out a shriek while he grew closer and ran as fast as her long legs could take her. He was close enough now he could have grabbed her if he had reached out, but he held back. She hit the wall and that rope of hers flung from her hand again.

"That's cheating!" he yelled, rearing back, and taking a running start at the wall.

Her scream of frustration when he passed made him laugh and he barely made it to the top from the distraction. Looking down he watched her swing on her rope, glaring at him. Placing both of her feet against the wall she began her climb.

The end was so close and all he had to do was figure out how the moving platforms worked. If he miscalculated it would be a very long and painful fall to the ground.

The platform in front of him appeared to be stable and he stepped onto it. He let out his own yelp of shock as it aggressively slid to the right. Another platform in front of him rushed to the left and he jumped for it. Barely making it, he teetered on his feet. He had to allow himself more time with the next one.

A grunt behind him whirled him around and he found Orah standing on the platform he'd just jumped from.

She had a wicked gleam in her eye while she stared at him. "You should give up now, Roan."

"Why? I'm ahead of you."

Shrugging, she grinned. "But not for long."

He watched equally enamored and shocked while she threw out her hand and branches formed between their two platforms. The platforms shook and groaned as if they fought to break the hold the branches had on them. She stepped across, seemingly unbothered by what she'd done, while she kept her eyes on Roan's. In a moment she was close enough to him that he could look down into her sparkling brown eyes.

"That was impressive." He said with a smile.

"Just watch this then," She winked and her hand flew out in front of her again. Solid platforms of light appeared in the spaces where the moving platforms didn't reach, and she took off.

"That's cheating, again!" he yelled, running after her.

Again, she underestimated his speed, and he caught her right before she reached her last three platforms of light. Considering his options, he knew he shouldn't use his powers he kept hidden, but he still tapped his foot against the platform. Her last three cracked loudly in response, crashing to the ground.

"Hey!" Her eyes burned, but it wasn't anger, no, it was closer to admiration. Or perhaps he was feeling his own emotions.

"No. Cheating," he said calmly.

They held their eye contact. The platforms whirling past threw her dark hair up into the wide. The longer they sat saying nothing, not pulling their contact, the further the world seemed to still.

Either of them could have won, but they didn't move. They hadn't been this close in weeks. Not since her bedroom. She strained her neck to look up at him and her chest pushed against his. He could feel each breath she took and felt he had stopped breathing while he stared down at her.

The sheer determination painted across her face.

The way her hair whipped wildly in the wind.

He didn't care about winning anymore.

No, he only wanted time to stop so they didn't lose the moment. Just them, together, with no other distraction around them. No stress about what they could and couldn't allow themselves to have. Just them there, together, and no pain of what could happen if she got home.

She swallowed and he pulled himself from his thoughts. He had been staring at her lips. His tingled at the realization, remembering how hers had felt against his. The way she tasted. Fates, he'd thought about her taste every night for weeks.

Without his control his arms wrapped around her waist, pulling her closer. Gasping, her hair wrapped around her face and she slowly nodded her head. His eyes widened, understanding what she was silently saying.

Permission.

His knees felt weak below him while he stared at her lips for a second longer, hoping he wasn't about to be woken from a cruel dream. He tightened his hold on her waist and in one gentle movement brought his lips against hers.

Time stopped.

The air stilled.

The world caught on fire.

Their lips collided and she pushed into him, wrapping her arms around his neck. Pulling her closer, he wrapped his free hand in her hair at the back of her head. Their mouths moved in sync just like before. As though they recognized each other and had found what they'd lost. Sound disappeared as their hands moved in a frenzy over one another.

He couldn't get enough of her.

Her taste.

Her smell.

The small sounds coming from her with each kiss.

His heart felt like it would burst from his chest when she pulled away, gasping hard. He didn't want to stop. He moved, ravenously, to her neck, biting and licking while her hands clawed at his back. He would have her right there if she let him. He didn't care who might have shown up.

Warmth covered his body and he glanced down to see she was glowing. Like the sun itself had filled her with its light. Light so warm he could feel it from his head to his toes. Smiling, he leaned down to kiss her again, but she turned her face and his kiss landed on her cheek. Confused, he peered back at her, finding an unfamiliar gleam in her eyes.

"I'm sorry," she whispered

He didn't know what she was apologizing for until he realized the warm feeling by his feet was her rope wrapped around his ankle. The world tilted to the side and he crashed to the platform they'd been standing on. He watched in shock as she turned the handle to a door that hadn't been there before. Flinging it open, she screamed triumphantly.

He couldn't keep his eyes off her while she walked through the door and her screams of success now came from the top of the mountain near the white flag. Where another open door now sat. With a wink, she picked up the flag and waved it above her head.

Pulling himself to his feet, he stared at her in shock. He didn't know what she had just done and a part of him felt that he should have been upset but he could only feel pride.

She'd just opened a door.

Chapter 27

That kiss

Orah hadn't been able to get the thought out of her head. All day it ran around and around. They kissed. Boy, did they kiss. She thought she was going to melt on that platform with the way his hands moved over her body.

She didn't have a single care in the world of what he planned to do to her out in the open. She was completely ready to let whatever he desired to happen. That was until he started kissing her neck and she watched the door rise from the platform.

The hum and warmth from the door felt as though it were calling to her and all thoughts of what Roan was doing stopped. She could only focus on one thing. That door. Getting that door to open. Getting to wherever that door was trying to lead her.

He left her in the course while he returned to gather Nacht. He also chose not to fly next to her. She worried he was upset, thinking that her agreement to his touch and kiss had been a trick, but it hadn't been. She was sure he didn't want anything more in the world than to kiss him again in that moment.

She'd expected him to follow her back to the manor but instead he and Nacht turned toward the city center. She wasn't sure if it was duty or avoidance that he went that way. The party was only 8 days away. Until that morning, she had honestly barely seen him since the night in his study with Jes.

Once she got back to the house she went about her day in almost a daze. Clarah kept asking her if she was okay, probably because she was lost in her thoughts all morning — as much as she was now.

"Orah, you might actually make me die of old age." Jes's annoyed tone brought her to reality and she looked back at him. She had been staring at the door on the fifth platform for a while, but she didn't feel any need to try and open it. She had already opened a door that day, unknown to him.

She, very conveniently, made sure not to tell him about her and Roan's encounter earlier. She didn't want a lecture of her becoming a distraction again.

The course had the same obstacles as it had for weeks. Despite her finding workarounds, Jes had been adamant she get through the fifth platform using the door the course provided her. He claimed as impressive as her improvised magic was that the door was there for a reason.

Rolling her eyes, she pushed against the door but nothing happened. Usually, it groaned or shook a bit, but it did nothing. And she didn't even care.

I opened a door today.

It hadn't even taken her much effort. The moment she saw it she knew she would open it. Not like before, where her body had hummed in hope. No, earlier her body knew that she would get it open.

"Orah! Will you please focus?" Jes yelled.

Orah's eyes glanced to the ground where she found Jes standing a few feet below her. Usually, he watched from the wardpad but she guessed she'd been standing there long enough that he was pretty annoyed now.

"Well?" His hands gestured to the door in front of her.

"It won't open," she stated.

He stepped back and his eyes widened. "Excuse me?"

"What? I've tried."

She jumped, having to keep herself from falling off the platform when he launched into the air and landed next to her. "Open the godsdamned door, Orah," he ordered.

"I already told you it won't."

He stood over her, as though he were trying to intimidate her. She didn't have to deal with his attitude. She didn't have to tell him she'd already done what he was asking.

"Orah."

"Jesiel."

Rolling his eyes, he ran his hand over his short hair. With a shrug, she waved her hand and a small staircase of rock appeared to her left. He jumped back into the air and landed on the top step.

"Don't you dare give up today."

"Jes, move out of my way."

Crossing his arms in front of himself, he glared. "No."

"I could make you. I could knock you right off that staircase and onto your ass." She glared back at him. The power she'd felt all day from opening that door was making her more confident than she should have felt.

Laughing he threw his head back. "Oh please. I'd like to see you try."

Without thinking she threw her hand out and her rope shot toward him. She expected it to wrap around his ankle but instead he caught it and tugged. She let out a scream while she stumbled, slipping off the platform. Holding on to the rope with all her strength she glared while he held her, dangling in the air.

"I told you that your temper gives you away."

"Fuck you." Her body felt hot while she stared at him. That anger she rarely let out boiled closer to the surface. How dare he think he could control her when she said she was done for the day?

His eyes twinkled and he grinned. "Oh, you wish you could."

With a wink he let go of the rope and she screamed while she fell through the air. She prepared herself to hit the ground but instead she landed in his arms.

Smiling down at her, he shrugged. "Ready to start again?"

She frowned up at him. "Put me down." She wasn't expecting him to drop her but that was exactly what he did. She landed on her tailbone, hitting the ground with a loud thump. Trying to compose her pride she stood and glared at him. "What's your problem today? Why are you so annoyed?"

He stepped closer. "I'm tired of standing here, week after week, watching you play pretend that you've unlocked that power. You've figured out some of it yes, but we both know you haven't fully unlocked it. To do that you'd have to actually face things about yourself that you're unwilling to face."

"Watch yourself Jesiel." Her anger boiled higher and she bit her tongue. He had no idea what she knew about him. What she could say.

He scoffed. "Why? What are you going to do? Attack me in a predictable fit of rage? Fates, you and Roan are practically meant for each other. You both wear your emotions right on your sleeves but you both hide everything important about yourself."

Her feet warmed and she looked down to see a small ring of fire circling her now. She shook her head. "You have no idea what you're talking about."

"I don't?" He stalked around the outside of the circle with an arrogance that pulled at the quiet building anger inside of her. He gave her an almost sickening grin. "Please tell me Orah, what don't I know? Oh, poor little mortal girl had a hard life. She's scared to love someone. She's scared to let anyone in. She's scared to accept who she is."

Tears lined her eyes and the fire built up near her calves. "Jes stop it."

He let out a low laugh. "Why? Am I pushing you too hard? You only seem to really show real power when you've been pushed. When you can't let those walls you've so carefully crafted get in the way."

Swallowing, she stared up at the sky, not allowing herself to cry. "Jes. Stop."

To her own shock he stepped through the fire circle, standing so close he was practically standing on her toes. "Or what Orah? I don't believe you'll do anything. You're too scared of who you are to actually protect yourself."

Her eyes widened and her anger engulfed her. "I'm too scared of myself!" She couldn't hold back the words as they spilled out in a scream. "Jes, why don't we go take a portal to Moros and see who, between the two of us, are more scared of themselves." The fire circle extinguished around them and he stared at her.

The air grew thick and he took a step back, shaking his head. "What did you just say?"

Her rage had full control while she stalked closer to him. "You are a bastard. I hope you know that, Jesiel Keita. You poke and prod at how I need to face who I am and yet you've kept Moros your dirty little secret for five decades."

His eyes narrowed and his hands grabbed her wrists, pinning them to her sides. He had her trapped, but she didn't care. She had hit her mark.

"You have no idea what you're talking about Orah," Jes seethed.

Scoffing, she shook her head and laughed. "I know *everything* Jes. I know he loves you but you're too much of a coward to admit that you love him too."

Abruptly releasing her hands, Jes turned away from her. His response was almost a whisper. "I tell him I love him each time I see him. I tell him I love him every night he falls asleep in my arms. I have never, in my long life, loved anyone in the way that I love that man."

She blinked while she stared at him. Her chest moved up and down and her anger slowly cooled. Standing in silence they didn't say a word for a while. It was as though neither of them had the fight in them to try. Finally, she shook her head and spoke. "Why won't you love him publicly? What do you hate so much about yourself that you can't let yourself have love?"

Slowly he turned back to face her, and she covered her mouth to hide her shock. Tears ran down his face. "What if publicly admitting my love hurts him? What if it puts a target on his back and I can't protect him anymore? I'm not just no one Orah. I'm the Beskermer to one of, if not the, strongest God in the last millennia. When Roan wins this challenge, that means I'm the Beskermer to the King. The *King*. Acknowledging him as mine could put him in danger."

"Wouldn't your position also mean you will have the power to protect him?" she asked.

"That's what he always says. I think it's wishful thinking. Despite what he may have told you or what you may believe yourself, I don't hate myself for loving him. Loving him the last fifty years has made me the best version of myself that I've ever been."

Orah's chest seized. She hadn't intended to attack him. She hadn't meant to do this…

They sat in an awkward silence for a few moments before he sighed and walked toward her. "Apparently you know one of my best kept secrets. I think I'm owed one of yours. What prevents you from truly trusting yourself Orah? From allowing yourself the power to actually protect yourself?"

"I can't." The tears she'd been holding back hit the ground. Her chest felt heavy with the building panic engulfing her. She grasped at her throat as if the open air had formed suffocating walls and she could no longer breathe.

"Orah, you can. It's just me and you here. No one will hurt you."

She turned back to him while her sobs pulled from her chest. He didn't know how right he'd been that whole time. How much she kept hidden. How much she worked to stay buried. He didn't know how heavy it all was.

"I'm the reason my mother is dead." The words tumbled out before she could stop them. She had never repeated it out loud to anyone. Her own dirty little secret.

"What?" Shock flashed across his face—the look she always avoided allowing someone to give her.

With a sigh she sank to the ground, covering her face with her hands. "My mother, she, well she had an illness in her head. Do you have those here?"

The gravel shifted next to her as he sat and placed his hand on her shoulder. "Yes, we do."

She let out a shaking breath and nodded her head. "Yeah, well she didn't just have an illness in her head, but she also had severe addictions. It's one of the reasons I've been so adamant that I'm not going to have an issue with those tonics you've been giving me. Between the addiction and the illness, she became a living monster. I don't know if I can handle going into too many details right now, but my childhood was dark. I think dark is probably an understatement. My mother would lose sense of herself, becoming this unfamiliar beast and I was her prey."

Tears fell between her fingers and she tried to manage a full breath between her sobs. Jes's hand didn't move from its place on her back, like he was attempting to keep her grounded. Breathing out, she continued.

"When she had these episodes there was almost no way to reach her. Nothing I said, no matter how hard I fought her did any good. And boy did I fight her. I argued. I pushed. I demanded she treat me right. That she saw how wrong and awful she was being, but it didn't do any good. It got to a point where she started to smack me, not fully beat me, but when she got frustrated, she'd smack me hard on the arm or against the back of my head. When I was sixteen, I told her if she ever hit me again that I would hit her back. I warned her. I warned her." Jes's hand squeezed Orah's shoulder and the sobs continued to tumble from her.

"I warned her not to do it again, but she did. We got in one of our fights and she raised her hand to hit me and it was like I became possessed. Before she could hit me, I slapped her right across the face and told her I hated her.

Then without saying another word I grabbed my keys and walked out the door. I didn't care that she followed me to the front porch and screamed at me that I was no longer her daughter. That I was no longer allowed back home. I didn't care as I walked with my head down past my neighbors. I just walked. I walked until I found a park and then I sat on the ground and didn't move for hours. When I finally got home the police and ambulance were there and Dad was frantically pacing the front lawn and I knew. I didn't even have to ask to know. She had downed an entire bottle of her pills within minutes of me leaving and overdosed. Dad got a call from a neighbor who heard her screaming at me and he found her when he got home. My temper, my inability to keep myself in check pushed my mother to that point. It was my fault."

Orah let out a shaky breath before glancing back at Jes. He was still crying but this time she knew it was from her story. Sitting straighter she focused on the obstacle course. "I'm so scared of this power because the last time I protected myself, someone I loved but also hated died. It's also why I haven't allowed myself to go further with Roan. My parents' love for each other allowed awful things to happen to me. My father was blind in his love and couldn't stop the abuse I lived through. I can't allow myself to open that part of myself. The part that will love but also protect. I can't hurt someone else. I can't be blinded by my love for someone."

Jes moved his hand in comforting circles against her back. Neither spoke for a while as the tears and sobs tumbled out of Orah. She couldn't remember the last time she'd allowed herself to cry like that.

Finally, with a sigh he removed his hand and stood. "Orah, your mother's choices were her own. You were a child, and she chose to take herself from you. You did not force her to do that."

"I don't feel like it's not my fault," she said, wiping her tears away from her cheeks.

His eyes softened and a small assuring smile tilted his lips up. "I know you don't. Maybe someday you'll understand that it wasn't."

Putting his hand forward he gestured for her to take it and slowly lifted her off the ground. With a sigh he glanced at the course then back to her. "I think we've both said enough today and you're probably as tired as I am now. We should head back."

She opened her mouth to apologize but stopped herself. It didn't feel right in the moment, so she nodded instead. "We have both said enough."

His cadence seemed to shift abruptly, and he smiled softly. "Also, I need to confess something."

Her eyes widened. "What?"

"I've been filling those tonic vials with water for two weeks now," he replied with a shrug.

Her mouth popped open and she scrambled to find the words to sling at him in response. He let out a loud chuckle and walked toward Tume. Laughing, Orah shook her head and rushed to catch up to him.

When she reached Tume, the Pegasus looked at Orah with concern and her hoof kicked against the ground anxiously. "It's alright, I'm okay," Orah whispered, lightly running her hand down Tume's mane.

Jes moved to help her up on the saddle but she shook her head. Placing her hand on the ground she pulled it upwards and a small dirt step appeared.

He stared at the step for a moment then shook his head. "I'm not even going to ask."

With a smile, Orah stepped up and went to swing her leg over the saddle when a large body slammed into the ground in front of them. Alarmed, she stepped back beside Jes and watched in shock, as a man, at least a head taller than Jes with almost identical wings stood. The ground around him was fractured and he cocked his head to the side while a smile spread across his face.

"Where's Roan?"

Jes stared at the man, his eyes narrowing. "He's not here."

The man turned to observe the obstacle course, his eyes stopping at the door on the fifth platform, then back at Jes. Slowly, he turned his head to Orah. "Interesting."

Without saying another word his wings flared out behind him and he launched back into the air.

Jes's eyes widened and he turned to Orah. "We have to go. Now."

"Who was that?"

"That was my cousin Arno." Jes lifts Orah up onto the saddle so quickly she couldn't

even protest. "He's also Marek's Beskermer."

An ominous feeling settled over Orah and she looked up at the sky. "Marek's here."

Her whisper wasn't a question but more of a statement. Jes tapped Tume on the neck and nodded his head. Together he and Tume launched into the sky. Orah's stomach dropped with anticipation while they raced to make it back to the manor.

Tume followed Jes as he landed on the front lawn. The three figures standing in front of the manor had caught their attention and something told Orah that Roan was one of them. Tume kicked up the dirt around her as she landed. Orah's stomach tightened when her eyes connected with Marek's and that predatory grin of his. Standing close behind Marek was Jes's cousin Arno.

Marek wasn't a small man, neither were Roan or Jes, but Arno made all three of them seem small. He towered over Marek, his dark skin seeming to glisten in the sun and his golden eyes narrowed on Orah. His long, dreaded hair cascaded down his back and his wings, likely as long as Jes was tall, sat at attention behind him. He was beautiful and utterly terrifying. Keeping his eyes on Orah, Arno smiled then leaned down to Marek and whispered.

Roan turned to Orah and Jes. The fear in his eyes ran Orah's blood cold. Roan shook his head at Jes. She didn't know what it meant, but knew it wasn't good. Jes quickly helped her off Tume and they slowly approached the men. Roan stood in front of the house as if to keep Marek from coming inside.

"Orah, you're still here." Marek grinned then bowed sarcastically. "I thought my brother ran you off the last time I was here. If I remember correctly there was a bag and you were leaving."

"I decided to stay," Orah replied.

Roan stepped forward and his voice dropped to that low gravelly sound. "Why are you here Marek?"

Marek's grin shifted and his face hardened as he turned his head to Roan. "I thought I told you that Father wasn't going to warn you again."

"I don't know what you're talking about."

Stepping forward Marek cocked his head. "You were never a good liar, little brother. Father felt another shift in power this morning. He tracked it to you and your guard camp. Curious that Arno found Orah there instead of you."

Orah's heart jumped and she forced herself to steady her breathing. Glancing at Roan she shook her head. *The door*. It had just appeared behind him. She hadn't questioned where it came from. Roan shook his head then looked back at his brother.

Marek studied their interaction and that smile returned to his face. "You know, I could finally tell him about her. I'm sure he'd be interested to know more about this strange mortal you've let live with you the last few months. Maybe I could take her now, let him meet her."

The ground around them shook. Roan's voice dropped lower. "You're not taking her anywhere."

Marek's eyes surveyed Orah's body as if contemplating how he would grab her. Glancing back at Arno, he whispered before Arno nodded his head and stepped forward.

The ground shook once more, and a large crack split the lawn between where Orah stood with Roan and Jes and where Marek and Arno stood. Marek's eyes widened and he stared at his brother. Shaking his head, he glanced back at the city center then back to Roan. "It would be a shame for you to lose your temper the day before your people begin their celebrations in your honor." Marek grinned at Orah. "I won't take her *today*. I'll give you the week to enjoy yourself. Next time I return, I'll have Father with me."

Arno's wings snapped out to the side of him and he launched himself into the sky. Where Marek stood, a bright burst of light blinded Orah. When it dissipated, Marek was nowhere to be seen. She turned to Roan. The silver in his eyes burned like fire and she wasn't sure if he realized his crown was on display.

Jes cleared his throat and they both turned to face him. Stepping back, Orah didn't expect the anger on Jes's face. He pointed between the two of them and in a low voice he spoke. "You two are going to tell me what happened and you're going to tell me. Now."

Roan glanced at Orah and she suddenly felt like a child being reprimanded. Sighing, Roan stepped forward. "Orah has been sneaking off before the sun rises to train at the camp."

Jes rolled his eyes and crossed his arms against his chest. "I knew that."

Orah scoffed. Apparently, she hadn't been as sneaky as she thought she'd been. Roan answered her scoff with a wink then turned back at Jes. "I followed her this morning. I challenged her to an obstacle race. When we were both almost at the finish line, we—" He glanced at her nervously.

Orah sighed, there was nothing wrong with what they did. Clearing her throat, she stepped forward. "We kissed. When we were kissing a door appeared from nowhere and I opened it."

Jes stepped back and his eyes widened. "What do you mean it appeared?"

"It wasn't there when we started; there were no doors on the entire course. At some point during our kiss, it appeared behind Roan and I opened it. But not just opened it. I walked through it and it took me to another door at the end of the obstacle."

Jes shook his head. "Your father knows about her."

The ground shook again. "You can't know that," Roan replied.

"Roan stop the denial. We need to get her home. Soon."

Panic clawed at Orah and she looked back to where Marek had been standing. Where the lawn had now mended itself and the crack was gone. She turned back to Roan and Jes wondering if they'd noticed but stepped back to find Roan standing in front of her. His hands lifted toward her face and he softly tucked a piece of hair behind her ear. Sadness danced in his eyes. "I'll figure out how to get her home."

Jes nodded and walked toward the house, pausing for a moment. Orah watched his shoulder sag and he turned back to them. "Roan—you and Orah need to talk."

Stepping back, anger replaced her previous panic while she connected what he was referring to. How dare he try and reveal her secret when she'd kept his. "Jes." His name came out as a plea on her lips.

She couldn't do that with Roan. Telling him was going to change everything.

"Orah, there are things you need to face. If we cannot get you home before next week then you need to have full access to that power. Roan, there are things you've kept from Orah. She needs to know them. She needs to know what she's up against."

Neither Orah nor Roan spoke while they watched Jes shoot up to the sky and disappear into the clouds. A thick silence settled over them and they stood on the lawn inches from each other. She resisted the urge to reach out for his hand. To try and distract them both from the conversation they'd both been avoiding.

Sighing, he walked toward the house. She looked back at the city again and where Marek had stood. There were flowers now lingering where the crack formed. As if the house itself were trying to replace the moment with something beautiful. With a sigh, she turned back and followed Roan inside.

Orah followed Roan into his study and he shut the doors behind him. Expecting him to sit down at his desk, she was startled when he kept walking toward the library. He turned back and smiled at her. "We have more privacy in here."

Nodding, she followed behind him. He walked toward the couch they had been on the night Moros brought the books. She paused for a moment, trying to decide whether she should sit next to him. His eyes met hers and the look in his took the breath from her. He was scared. As though he were as apprehensive and nervous as she felt. She realized then; it was possible they both had been holding things inside themselves for far too long.

Letting out a breath, she walked to the couch, placing herself beside him. So close their knees were touching each other. A smile spread on his face and his hand rested on her knee. Her eyes lingered on his hand and the warmth there. The familiar warmth she'd felt every time his hands touched her. Maybe she'd been wrong all along. Maybe she should have let him sooner.

"Jes says we need to talk. Usually that means Jes knows there is something that needs to be talked about." Roan let out a nervous laugh. "I know I haven't been fully honest with you Orah. I've kept things secret and hidden. I've told myself it's been to protect you, but I think it's been more to protect myself."

Shaking her head, she chuckled. "I think I've been keeping things inside for so long for the same reason. Jes said that in order for me to unlock this power I need to face things."

"I need you to help me with something." Her stomach sank with the weight of what she was about to ask. But, if there was anyone who could help her right now, it was Roan. "I need you to walk through my memories and help me break down those walls."

Roan's hand squeezed the knee he held. "Are you sure?" he asked.

Orah closed her eyes. "I'm sure. I need to face who I am and what I've kept hidden for so long."

Roan stared at her in silence for several minutes. She started to question whether or not she should have asked him when he cleared his throat. "Do you understand what you're asking me?"

"Yes," she confirmed.

Shaking his head, he grabbed her hands. "Orah, I don't know if you do. Your mind—it built those walls for a reason. Breaking them down will be very painful."

"I understand that, Roan. I built them for a reason but now they need to come down. I *need* them down," she said, pulling her hands from his and placing them on her lap.

"I don't think we'll be able to get them all down right now. I think we should focus on the ones that feel the most important to unlock the part of yourself you've been trying to reach."

She let out a breath of relief. She could do that. She could let her mind guide her to the most important memories. The ones that held her back the most.

Nodding, she met his eyes once more and smiled at the emotion in his eyes. It reminded her of warmth, safety, and kindness. It reminded her of love.

She turned her body, so she was fully facing him now while he laid his hands on her lap and wiggled his fingers, inviting her hands to lay against his. Closing her eyes once more, she prepared herself for what she was about to let go of. What she was about to face.

"You can do this." His whisper of encouragement pulled her eyes open once more and she nodded her head in response.

"I can do this," she whispered, laying her hands on his, she let the flood of emotions wash over her. The library and reality slipped away from her, enveloping her in a haze. She fell further into the haze, while off in the distance she could make out a blurred wall. The sounds behind the wall Orah recognized immediately – Mom and Dad.

Chapter 28

Roan couldn't stop the emotions that consumed him when Orah's memories appeared. The last time they had done this he hadn't known her. He hadn't known her goodness—her fierceness. He didn't have the sheer admiration for her he now had. All those months ago she was a stranger in his home, and he hadn't felt how he felt now.

Her memories took them to a blurred wall – the emotion behind it shocked Roan. He'd expected something dark and painful, but this felt light, happy, but with a heavy layer of grief. To his surprise, Orah appeared beside him. This didn't usually happen when he was in someone's memories. He was usually a fly on the wall, but he had also never really done anything like this before.

She smiled at him sadly then nodded her head toward the wall. He watched, mesmerized and with bated breath while she tugged on the wall and it dropped to the ground like a curtain.

Silence settled over them while they stood, watching whom Roan assumed to be young Orah, with her parents in a modest home. Her mother brushed her hair at a table and her father moved about tidying up their kitchen. They were all laughing, and Roan's eyes fell to the bags by the door on the side of the room. Quickly the memory shifted to them walking out of a set of doors holding their bags and getting into one of those self-driven carriages he'd seen in her memories before.

Fast flashes of memories of the family traveling rushed past him. They visit small towns, what appeared to possibly be family, large palaces, and lots of laughter and smiles. Mingled in with the laughter and love, however, were also memories of her parents arguing. Near constant arguing, no matter where they went on their travels.

Her mother laid on the ground sobbing while her father begged the woman to get into the carriage. The near hysterical wail her mother let out echoed in the air and Orah flinched. Holding her hands to her ears, Orah tried desperately to drown out the sounds.

Her mother's frantic wails faded into the distance and the next memory was them back at home. Where Orah's mother laid in a small bed where some kind of lit box with moving portraits sat in front of her. At the foot of the bed was Orah, blocking the box while tears ran down her face.

She begged her mother to get up. She begged her mother to take her to school. But she didn't seem to register Orah was there.

As if Orah were a ghost in the room screaming to be heard.

Roan watched, angry and heartbroken while Orah learned how to care for herself. Dress herself, feed herself, and learn every other task for her basic needs. Tasks she should never have had to learn so young.

But still, every day Orah went to her mother's room and every day her mother didn't move.

Roan's anger boiled while he watched feeling helpless that she was all alone.

Where was her father?

His thoughts of her father threw them forward in her memories and Roan watched while the man walked through the front door of their home. Her mother, who had previously appeared so ghost-like, now resembled a monster. Her voice was unrecognizable, and she screamed at the man. An almost black and eerie emotion flew out of her as she pointed to Orah. Throwing out accusations on the young child, as if as a child Orah spent her days tormenting the adult. Her father stared down at Orah disapprovingly, shaking his head. Small, innocent, and quiet Orah watched while he ushered his wife back to her room and called Orah to his.

In his room, the man's voice was kind, but also sad. Obviously, a man who he himself didn't know what to do with their life and circumstances. He looked at his daughter with love then scolded her, telling her she had to respect her mother and to stop arguing with the woman. That Orah needed to do as she was told. How much easier it would be if she *just stopped arguing*.

With tears running down her cheeks, Orah argued her mother was lying. She begged her father to listen, begged him to do anything, to stop the madness. But he shook his head—she had to respect her mother.

Roan's chest ached and he choked back his sobs while memory after memory of Orah and her mother played out in front of him.

The older Orah got, the worse her mother was. Roan couldn't push down the horror he felt while he listened to her mother scream awful, disgusting things at her daughter.

Telling Orah, who couldn't be more than twelve, that she should have died as an infant. That the woman's life would have been so much simpler if Orah had never existed. Calling Orah horrendous names and making up stories about her and even her father. Going as far as throwing objects at Orah and then demanding the child pick up the mess.

And Orah did it.

She took the abuse.

With each passing memory Roan watched Orah numb herself to the anger and the hate. Watched her pull inwards and push down her emotions.

She should never hold back who she is.

Confusingly in the middle of all the chaos her mother seemed as though she could become two separate people. Conflicting memories appeared of Orah and her mother laughing together hours before her mother suddenly shifted, turning into an unrecognizable monster. In public Orah stared at her mother with disgust while the woman painted an image of herself to all that would listen.

But Orah never spoke up.

She only listened.

She listened while knowing the truth.

The memories slowly faded, and Roan glanced to his side, finding Orah standing next to him again. Tears stained her cheeks and she glanced at him. "I kept her secrets. From everyone. It got worse the older I got." she whispered.

As though on cue another blurred wall appeared. This time Roan could feel all those dark heavy feelings he'd felt in her memories before. His stomach dropped. "Are you sure?" he asked, not sure if even he was able to witness what lay beyond the wall.

She refused to meet his gaze, but she nodded in response. Lifting her hands, she gripped the wall – again as though it were a curtain but this one didn't fall easily. She had to use both hands while she pulled it to the ground. The wall fell with a heavy thud, as though it were made of heavy velvet.

New memories appeared and Roan saw Orah, now a teenager, sitting in a small room with an older woman sitting across from her. Roan didn't recognize the woman, but the feeling of empowerment radiated from her. She explained some condition of the mind to Orah. Telling Orah her mother had this condition. With a firm, yet gentle expression, she told Orah she was not required to do everything her mother requested.

She gave Orah the permission to stand up for herself.

More memories appeared, causing Roan's stomach to sink low. Orah was screaming at her mother. Rage radiated off her, flowing out with the words leaving her lips. She held some kind of small bottle and screamed at her mother to stop taking whatever was inside. Her screams, while angry, were obvious pleas from a child – begging their parent to listen.

Her mother's eyes narrowed but Roan couldn't make sense of the emotion. It was as though the woman had somehow made it so she didn't even know how she felt. When she spoke, her voice was a monstrous sound, but also slurred. Reminding Roan of those in the city who let their love of their drink and tonics go too far.

The fights between Orah and her Mother became more volatile the further Orah's memories pulled her and Roan. And Roan watched, tense and sickened, as her mother slapped Orah over and over again.

Memory after memory.

Never more than one hard slap, but hard enough it rattled Orah each time.

But no matter how angry it made Orah, no matter how much it hurt, or how betrayed she felt, she never fought back. She stood, stoic and silent as her mother's stinging touch bit against her skin.

Roan wasn't sure how much more he could watch but he knew he had to be there for Orah. He had to give her the support she desperately craved. The safety she begged for and never received. He could do that. He would be that for her.

The older Orah grew the more her Father appeared to believe her. Mixed with the sickening memories of her fights with her Mother were happy and light memories with her Father. When she wasn't isolating herself, she seemed to have spent every spare moment with her Father. Out of the house, eating in restaurants, watching those moving portraits on lit walls in front of them. Roan felt a sense of responsibility from Orah's father and that the man believed he was doing his best given his circumstances.

Roan choked down his scoff watching the man justify to Orah why he stayed. Why he didn't take Orah far away from the abuse.

The man should have done more.

He should have protected her.

At the same time her fights with her mother grew more violent and explosive while Orah continued to isolate herself. Roan held back his emotions, watching her bury herself in books with her back against her bedroom door while her mother wailed behind the frame like a shrieking monster. He hadn't realized her love of books went deeper than a love of stories.

They kept her safe.

They kept her sane.

From what Roan could see, Orah kept any friends an arm's length away. Never inviting anyone over. Never allowing anyone inside her house of horrors. Around her peers she kept a beautifully and painfully crafted mask on her face.

Never drawing attention.

Never allowing questions to be asked.

Throughout it all a sense of love and duty obviously confused Orah, but the older she grew, her anger grew alongside her. Roan's stomach turned at the warm, almost poisonous anger that bled from Orah any moment she was around her mother. He hadn't ever seen her let out that anger. He hadn't even realized it was there.

He shook his head and his tears fell once more while Orah held up what she believed to be her duties as a child. He watched while Orah led her half-naked mother back into the house. The woman was so far gone and numb, mumbling incoherent curses and insults while her daughter led her to the safety of her tiny room of chaos.

Orah's memories faded and he stood, holding down his pride when one overpowering memory came into view. Orah sat screaming at her mother—informing the woman if she were to ever lay a hand on Orah again that Orah would hit back. Orah's eyes burned with the fiery passion Roan had come to crave.

That was the Orah he knew. The one who would never back down from a fight.

Suddenly, another thick, blurred wall appeared in front of him. Shaking his head, he turned to find Orah standing inches from him. Her emotions ran off her like a flooded street unable to keep up with the storm. Heavy grief, anger, agony, and guilt poured from her. She breathed out a shaky breath, lifting her hand but her hand shook—she didn't seem able to still it. She choked on a sob and shook her head. Roan rushed to her, lifting his hand to help but she shook her head once more.

"I have to do these myself," she muttered.

Nodding, he watched while she pulled up her other hand and tugged on the wall.

But it didn't fall like the previous two. It remained towering over them in an almost sinister manner.

Letting out a breath, she lifted her hands again and pulled using her legs to bring her entire body down. A crack echoed in the air and the wall fell, but not like before. This time the wall crashed and they both ducked trying to avoid being hit by the debris.

Blinking while the dust settled, Roan held his breath. The feeling of the memory was recognizable. He'd felt something similar 60 years prior.

Orah stood in the kitchen of her home while her mother approached her. She had an almost mocking grin on her face while the woman yelled at Orah incoherently. Orah shook her head, not understanding what her mother was upset about.

Her mother's eyes flared at the amusement on her daughter's face and she pointed at Orah screaming that Orah was ungrateful and disrespectful. Orah's smile stayed plastered on her face and she leaned against her kitchen counter casually.

Her mother's rage built and she threw out as many insults as she could. Over and over - coming up with the most disgusting things she could. Orah stared at her and let out an amused laugh.

The noise set her mother into an untamable rage and she lifted her hand to strike. Roan held his breath, sure the woman would inflict some damage. To his own shock, Orah's hand met her mother's cheek before her mother's strike could land.

Roan's eyes widened and he held in his cheer of pride when suddenly a heavy emotion fell over the memory.

Orah's mother's eyes were wide and she held a hand to her cheek while Orah stared at her.

Slowly, Orah spoke. "I. Hate. You."

Roan's stomach turned from Orah's anger while she turned, grabbing a pair of keys, then walked toward the front door.

Her mother's own rage built, and Roan worried he was going to be sick by how thick and poisonous it was. She followed Orah out of the house screaming at the top of her lungs. Somehow the mortal woman didn't look like a person anymore. She looked as though she had been possessed by something from the depths of Shadus. She screamed at Orah. Threatening if Orah left she would not come back and even worse – she was no longer her daughter.

Orah didn't look back though, she kept walking. She passed a neighbor standing on their lawn staring at her in shock, but Orah didn't seem to fully register they were there. Keeping her eyes on the ground she walked.

And walked.

And walked.

Until she found a grassy park and then she sat.

The day seemed to rush past, but she didn't move. She didn't make a sound. There were no emotions coming from her – just numbness.

Roan expected tears, but they didn't fall. It was as though she had frozen in time and the world went on without a care for the girl alone in the park.

When the sun began to set, Orah stood forcing herself back to her house and the beast waiting for her return. When she arrived those odd carriages were in front of her house but each one had some kind of flashing light on top. Her father paced the lawn and then looked up as she approached. His eyes widened and he ran frantically to her.

Scoffing, Orah shook her head. "The bitch finally did it."

Roan didn't know what she was referring to until her Father approached with tears lining his eyes. Grabbing Orah, he pulled her into a hug, whispering how sorry he was. When he pulled away, he peered back at the house then to her, explaining her mother had taken pills and overdosed.

She had taken her own life.

Orah didn't respond, she only blinked and stared at the house. Numbness still had its grasp on her while she kept her eyes on a large carriage pulling away from the home. She brushed her Father's hands away from her and walked quietly to the house.

She said nothing when she walked past the guards in uniform.

She said nothing as she walked up the stairs to her Mother's bedroom.

With a sigh she sat on the small bed and looked around the room. The single bed in the corner had an indent in the mattress from the years of someone laying there for hours – never moving – never leaving. The room itself was piled high with clothing and junk. The only clean part of the small chaotic room was a small walkway from the door to the bed.

Finally, Orah's numbness broke, replaced by grief and anger. Then her tears fell.

She sobbed silently in that small dirty room, but no one came to comfort her.

No one even seemed to hear her.

No one seemed to care about the girl whose heart had just changed forever.

When the tears had run their course, she surveyed the room, whispering quietly, "I'm sorry."

Roan's head swam with the guilt hitting him. His chest tightened—she thought her Mother's death was her fault.

He looked over to his side while the memory faded away and found Orah crumpled on the ground. No emotions were coming from her and he realized she was making herself numb.

Never again.

He quickly pulled them out of her mind, shaking his head and physically pulling his hands from hers. Her memories faded and they returned to reality in the library. She blinked, staring at him. The tears staining his own face appeared to take her by surprise.

They sat in silence in the room they both found comfort in while she tried to steady her breathing.

"You think your mother's death is your fault," Roan finally spoke. He stared at her, shocked by the revelation. She had no idea how strongly he related to the exact feeling.

Nodding, she looked down at her hands. "It was. I pushed her. I let my temper get the best of me. It was my job to protect her. I kept her secrets for so long. I should have just walked away."

Roan's hand grabbed hers. "Orah, she was your *mother*. It was her job to protect you. Hers and your fathers." He couldn't hide the disgust in his voice when he mentioned her Father. Roan knew she loved the man, and it was obvious he adored her, but he could have done so much more.

Orah jumped, pulling her hand from his and her stare hardened. "My dad did the best he could. Yes, he failed me. Over and over again he failed me, but he protected me to the best of his abilities. He let his love for *her* blind him and allow too much pain to go on."

"Is this why you've never allowed yourself to fall in love?" It wasn't even a question. Roan had known this from the moment he'd first walked through her memories. She never allowed herself to develop true intimacy with anyone. She kept a fine line between physically intimacy and emotional.

She sighed. "Yes. Love is dangerous and people get hurt because of it. People allow and do stupid things because of love and I've refused to let myself be one of them."

Roan let out his own sigh and leaned against the couch"Are you alright?"

The atmosphere in the room shifted and he looked back over to her. She was staring at the ground now, her head hung as though she had no strength to keep it up. Blinking back his tears again he realized she was making herself numb.

"Love?"

Snapping her head up she stared at him for a moment before a rush of emotions settled over them. "I don't know." Her response was whispered with a layer of pain within her words.

He grabbed her hand again, understanding all she wasn't able to say. "Will you be alright?"

She blinked a few times while keeping her eyes on his before she turned away to look around the library. He bit back his emotions. He needed to get a larger library if only to provide her with her own never-ending sanctuary.

She nodded her head and a light air emotion almost similar to relief came from her.

"I'll be okay. I think I'll be okay."

"We didn't go through everything." He assured her, squeezing her hand while he spoke.

Her voice dropped low while she gave her own responding squeeze. "I know. I can't expect to unpack all of my trauma in one go." Letting out a chuckle she smiled at him.

Fates, what he would do to make sure a smile never left her face. What he would do to bring light into her eyes and remove every bad memory and experience she'd ever had. But he couldn't—all of those dark hidden parts of her shaped who she was and he would have never changed anything about her.

His own head spun while he let out a sigh. It was time for him to be open. "Did your father change after your mother's death?"

Her eyebrows crumbled and she cocked her head. "I mean, he felt a lot of guilt. He never voiced it until I was an adult, but I knew he felt it. He made an active effort to spend as much time as possible with me after she died. He tried to get me to stay and go to school near home but didn't stop me when I left the state. He helped me move into my first apartment in Boston. Literally carried every box I owned at the time and unpacked my place himself. He loved her but I think her death was a relief that he was finally free too."

She leaned back against the couch. Roan tried to cool his anger toward the man he would never meet. He couldn't judge what someone did. He didn't even know what he would do or allow for love.

Clearing his throat, he focused on the ceiling above. "I asked because my father changed after my mother's death. She made him good, well as good as someone like him can be. She balanced him and his temper— his moods. She was a literal light wherever she went and when she died it destroyed him. He was hard when I was a child, but he wasn't evil. Or I never would have considered him that way but when she died. He—He changed."

"What happened to her that caused him to change so drastically? Aeron said that he knew her death would impact everyone," Orah asked.

Roan kept his eyes on the ceiling. "Aeron said that because he was thinking of the love he had for her. What Aeron didn't know was that my father killed my mother." Orah gasped and her hand squeezed his. The response somehow bolstered Roan's confidence and he finally revealed the secret he'd never voiced aloud.

"He killed her, and it was my fault."

Chapter 29

Orah stared at Roan—sure she hadn't heard him right. There was no way they both somehow felt responsible for their Mothers' deaths. "What did you say?"

"My mother's death *was* actually my fault, Orah," Roan replied, finally pulling his gaze from where he'd had it fixed above them.

"I don't understand."

Tears fell from her eyes unexpectedly. He wouldn't have gotten his Mother in a situation where she would have been killed. He wouldn't. Not the man who had done nothing but try and protect her. He wouldn't allow someone he loved to get hurt.

Silently, Roan stood and crossed the room. Orah watched him pace, a habit he regularly did when he was remembering something he didn't want to. As though moving helped him gather his thoughts.

"Sixty years ago, I was in Erde. I'd just come home from a forced extended visit to Aeron and I was fed up. Aeron was pushing me to start prepping for the first challenge. He was so convinced I would win. Something about how I don't *hear* the call of death and he was sure I was meant to be king. But I didn't want to do a challenge. I didn't want to go against Marek. I was so fucking tired. The moment I got back to the palace I went to find my father."

He leaned against a table across from her, his eyes focused on the small hidden bookshelf by the stairs. The bookshelf with his Mother's books. "I decided I was going to petition him to cancel the challenges. I didn't care if Aeron thought I had the power, I just wanted it all to be over. Marek and I have been compared our whole lives and I just wanted to be *me*. My father laughed in my face when I made my petition. He told me he couldn't decide anything and if I really had an issue I should go to the Fates. The way he laughed set me on edge and so I called him a coward." Roan grimaced.

"That was a mistake. I could feel his rage as he stood and glared at me. He told me if I was so confident to call the King a coward then I should be confident enough to actually face him. So, I did. My stupid, young, arrogant self threw out a blast of power forgetting my power can't touch him."

"What do you mean it can't touch him?" Orah interjected.

"I'm not sure. It's something between every parent and child with powers. Something, I'm guessing, to do with the fact that as a child I come from him. He can't touch me with his power and my power can't touch him."

"But you and Marek?"

He smirked. "Oh, siblings can wreak havoc on one another but parents and children can't do a thing. I seemed to forget that important and well-known piece of knowledge when I threw out my power, but it wasn't just my power. I'd been slowly showing signs of having Kingly power. It was pure, untethered, and unbound power I threw at him. I watched in horror as it bounced off him and took out a wall behind him. I knew I was going to die at that moment. He had every intention of killing me when he threw out his own, stronger blast of power at me. What I hadn't expected was my mother. She screamed when he threw his hand out and stepped right between us. The killing blow meant for me went right through her." He choked on a sob. Tears were now running down his face and Orah jumped to her feet, running to him. Bringing her hands to his face she brushed away the tears.

"I also hadn't known Lahana was hiding behind a tapestry in the room. She saw everything. I'll never—" The choked sound came from him again and he turned his face out of Orah's hands. "I'll never forget the sound she made. As long as I live, it will haunt me. She ran to our mother's body and held her while she wailed. My father sat there staring at my mother. There was an obvious shift in the air the moment he changed to the man I know now. I could feel a shift in me too." He paused for a moment. The lights in the room flickered around them before he shivered then continued. "I don't remember much. I remember my rage. My vision blurring. Lahana says I lit up as though the sun had speared through me. Followed by half of the throne room and the part of the palace it's in exploding. Along with the section of the city below the palace. Somehow, no one was killed. That's what I remember clearly. I didn't want to hurt anyone but him." Roan's lips upturned to a sad smile. "The rumors are that the people below felt something, similar to a warning. Telling them they needed to go. Godlings and mortals believe it was the King, protecting his people from me. But Lahana believes it was me, protecting them from myself."

Roan's hands moved toward Orah's face and he brushed away the tears falling down her cheeks. "Marek only saw my temper flare and the explosion. He believes I'm the reason why our mother is dead. He thinks I killed her. And while his assumption of who's to blame for his death is correct, I've never told him who actually made the killing blow."

"Lahana hasn't ever told him?" Orah asked, leaning into his touch.

"Lahana and Marek's relationship has always been strained. The moment he so easily turned on me and assumed that I'd killed our mother she decided she wanted nothing to do with him. They don't interact with one another beyond royal duties. I say I moved into this home when I became the Governing God fifty years ago but that's not true. Lahana and I left the city immediately after and came here. Aeron let us move into the manor and we lived here for ten years as his guests. Once I took the Region after the challenge, I started making it *my* home. I grew to love the people and the city and didn't want to rule from some inaccessible palace out in the distance."

Orah watched him. His hand still rested against her cheek, but he was staring out the window – at his city. The sadness that had been in his eyes was now replaced with pride. She smiled, lifting her hand and placing it against his chest. Right over his heart.

She wanted to be supportive to be there for him, but she had questions. "But I don't understand. The challenge? The first one. If you destroyed so much of the city, then how did your father not know you would win?"

Pulling his eyes from the window, he smiled and ran his thumb across her jaw. "That was the thing. I begged him to make me the God of Death. He knew I didn't want to be King. He thought me winning meant I was going to be forced into an existence I didn't want. That I would be forced to learn from him. He thought I would win, and my punishment would be becoming King. He didn't expect me to throw the challenge."

"You said before he doesn't want you to win because it would mean he had placed his bets on the wrong son, and he doesn't like to be wrong."

"That's what he wants people to believe publicly and it's also partly true. He's been so sure Marek would win and he's practically announced it since

Marek was a child. Me winning means he's made a fool of himself but me winning also means I live a life he knows I don't want."

Orah understood him better now. He was just as scared of himself as she was of herself. Her hand brushed his cheek and he smiled at the touch. Her chest felt heavy while she looked at him. His beauty had always caught her attention, but it was now something otherworldly. She felt like she could lose the moment in time at any second and slowly brushed her fingers across his lips then up his cheek. He shivered, closing his eyes, and offering her a soft smile.

Her feet moved in response before she could decide what she wanted to do next. Staring at his full lips she lifted herself up and brushed hers against his.

The air in the room shifted to something heavy and his eyes flew open. In an instant his arms wrapped around her waist, flipping her so she was now leaning against the table.

Their lips moved against each other, but not like they had at the course earlier that morning. These kisses were softer, gentler, guided by the emotions and secrets they'd just shared.

Every wall she'd carefully crafted when interacting with him tumbled down. Orah wasn't sure how to process being kissed this way. The way it felt as though he were taking away every bad memory with each brush of his lips. As though every kiss were healing every broken part of herself, repairing them with something new. Something she'd never felt before.

Only they existed in that moment. The soft caresses of their lips against one another muted out everything else in existence.

Grabbing her backside, he lifted her so she was now sitting on top of the table. His kisses become firmer then. A silent request for more. She wrapped her legs around his waist in approval, groaning when he pushed his hips against her.

The brush of him so close to her. The heat between the two of them was intoxicating and she wanted more. Pulling him closer, she moved her lips across his, replacing her soft kisses with her own desire. Tasting him, learning him, exploring every kiss he offered her.

Disappointment pulled her out of her frenzy when he pulled back. Smiling he leaned down, kissing her neck then whispering in her ear. "I can feel how you desire me, Orah."

Grinning he pulled his lips from her neck, kissing down to her shoulder, then further to her collarbone. She shivered at the touch, but her mind couldn't ignore what he'd said.

Feel?

He kissed lower, running his lips against the neckline of her shirt and she shivered again. Still unable to pull the comment away from her she pushed against his chest, pulling him from his kisses. "What do you mean you can *feel* how I want you?"

His eyes widened and he stared at her. She glared back at the shocked expression on his face. She wouldn't have questioned anything if he had been touching her skin when he'd said it. But neither of them had removed any clothing. There was no way he could feel any kind of physical reaction other than how eagerly she kissed him.

Clearing his throat, he let out an awkward laugh. "One of the many secrets I've kept. I can feel people's emotions."

Her legs dropped from around his waist. "What?"

Every moment from the last several months crossed her mind. Her cheeks burned while she thought of all the times he had teased her when she had been in the middle of her indecent thoughts about him.

Stepping backward he placed his hands in his pockets and smiled a teasing smile. "Surprise?"

"Surprise?" she hopped off the table. She couldn't even hide her embarrassment—he already knew what she was feeling. "You couldn't have told me that before? Not once in the last almost three months you couldn't have mentioned it?"

"You're not wrong," he replied with a wince. "It's not something I'm *supposed* to be able to do. It's another one of my Father's gifts. Or more so gifts of the King. It's how I knew he meant to kill me that day." His eyes twinkled and he grinned. "It's also how I've known you've wanted me pretty much from the first day you've been here." Slowly, he approached her again, brushing hair away from her face. "I tease and jest, Orah, but everything I feel for you is real."

She stared at him unsure of how to respond.

She was tired.

She was dizzy.

She was also angry.

"What else have you kept from me?" she pleaded.

He stepped back, shaking his head. "What?"

"Power – the depths of your power. What else have you kept hidden?"

He froze in his place while the room chilled around them. She shivered from the cold. It crept down her entire body while he kept his eyes on her.

The lights in the room went black and she pressed up against the table. Her heart pounded in repetitive beats. The only sound she could hear was the frantic beating of her heart while her eyes tried and failed to scan the darkened room.

"Boo."

She screamed and returned to her position on top of the table. "Roan! Knock it off."

Suddenly she was blinded by a bright light. She closed her eyes briefly then pulled them open. Roan stood in front of her holding a ball of light with a wicked grin on his face. She scowled but found herself stuck to the table. Her eyes widened and she looked back at him.

He grinned. "There's a lot that I can do, love." He casually tossed the ball of light into his other palm. "I can make light."

The light vanished and his low, spine-chilling voice echoed in the room. "I can take light."

Her breathing felt difficult, but she wasn't scared—no, she was feeling something entirely different.

A hand brushed the back of her neck, and she yelled, unable to see where he was. His warm breath tickled her ear. "I can force obedience. I can create. I can destroy."

Her chest moved up and down with anticipation. The room was pitch black, not even his usual lit freckles shone in the darkness. Her eyes scanned the room. She couldn't hear him, but she could feel him circling where she was frozen on the table.

His hand suddenly grabbed a handful of her hair and he yanked her head backward. She let out a low groan while his lips brushed against hers. "I can do whatever you what me to do, love."

She bit back her moan at the devastating tug he had on her.

He smiled against her lips. "There's so much more I could show you."

She swallowed. The anticipation almost drove her mad.

Nodding her head, she whispered, "Yes."

He smiled against her neck, pulling her hair again. "Yes, what, love?"

"Show me."

Her body loosened and she blinked, coming back to reality, and understanding she could move from where she still sat atop the table. She whirled around trying to find him in the dark. Slowly his freckles began to sparkle on his cheeks and she smiled.

His responding grin scrunched up his now lit nose. Her legs shook beneath her while she took him in. Breathing out, she chuckled. "While that was freaky, you still didn't answer the question."

He shrugged. "I promise I'm not keeping secrets. I'll show you everything in time."

She slid off the table. The lights in the room faded back on while she made her approach. He stood frozen in place; his eyes locked on hers until she was standing in front of him.

She smiled up at him while her body thrashed inside begging her to make a move. Begging her for more.

As if on cue, a knock at the doorway made them both jump and they found Jes in the doorway. He grinned at them and how closely they were standing. "I take it you talked?"

Roan winked at Orah. "Yes. We both learned some interesting things about each other today."

She laughed, shaking her head. How could he have made such an intense afternoon sound so casual? Nothing about what had just happened between the two of them had been casual.

Jes stepped into the room and looked at the books. The expression on his face was serious and stern. Concerned, Orah turned to Roan knowing now that he could sense emotions, she couldn't help but panic while she watched him tense.

"What is it?" Roan asked.

Jes sighed. "I have confirmation Marek told your father about Orah. I trust your gut feeling that we need to do something before your birthday."

Roan's hand found Orah's and he squeezed it. "After dinner. After dinner we'll come back in here, everyone in the house, and we'll all search for an answer. There has to be one here. Somewhere."

Jes nodded. "I'll let Etta and Kai know to join us tonight. Yohan also let me know dinner should be done within the hour." Shooting a glance at Orah, Jes smiled then turned out of the room.

Looking down at their hands then up at Roan, Orah sighed. "I guess we better go get ready for dinner."

"Want any company?" he said with a grin.

Her stomach dropped low and a pulling pressure pushed inside of her. "As tempting as that sounds, I don't think either of us will want to leave that room in under an hour if I invite you in."

Pulling her closer to him, he wrapped his arms around her waist and smiled. "You're not wrong there. I intend to take my time with you when you allow me to." Tightening his hold around her he leaned down, kissing her softly.

Her knees weakened at the touch of their lips. His promise of his intention played in circles in her mind. She didn't know if she was going to be able to leave that room with what they'd now started. His lips felt intoxicating and she could only think about how she could spend days kissing him without losing interest. Pulling away with a smile he brushed his fingers against her lips.

"I might be able to feel your emotions Orah, but what I would give to hear the indecent thoughts that run through your mind."

Chapter 30

Orah sat in her bathroom looking at herself in the mirror, thinking of how long they had continued kissing before finally pulling themselves apart from each other. He had followed her upstairs and she nearly invited him into her room, but they both agreed Yohan and Jes would have been cross with them if they missed dinner.

She laughed and lightly rubbed her fingers against her lips— imagining what his felt like against hers.

Shaking her head, she snapped herself out of her trance and placed her brush on the vanity. Deciding to be brave, she finally stared at her reflection in the mirror. Her chest felt lighter, but her head felt dizzy after going through her memories. The reflection staring back at her was and wasn't someone she recognized. She hadn't seen this version of herself in a long time—perhaps never.

She looked lighter, less tense, and her eyes actually appeared alive. She knew they hadn't gone far enough into all her pain to release everything, but it had been a good start.

A knock on her door startled her and she moved to check who it was. Part of her hoped it was Roan and he had decided they could skip dinner—just for that night. Smiling at the thought, she pulled open the door and stepped back in shock.

Lahana squealed, jumping up and down while they made eye contact. To her own surprise, Orah let out a similar squeal and rushed into Lahana's arms. She had been gone for weeks and Orah didn't expect to see her until right before Roan's party. Pulling themselves apart, Lahana looked Orah up and down.

"Orah! You look good! You look so much stronger than the last time I saw you!"

Grinning, Orah did a small spin in place. She'd been admiring the muscles she'd developed since working with Jes every day. Combined with the humming power inside of her, she felt as though she could now take on anything.

Facing Lahana again, Orah stopped spinning and glanced down at the small envelope in her hands. Cocking her head to the side, Orah pointed. "What's that?"

"I'm pretty sure the assumption is that you were going to attend the party, but I told Roan as his mortal ambassador and deliverer of invitations that I was hand delivering you one of your own," Lahana replied, passing it to Orah.

Staring at the dark blue envelope in her hands, Orah fought back her tears. She didn't understand why her emotions had come on so strongly, but the gesture hit her hard. Looking back up at Lahana, she smiled but then her eyes widened in shock at the next sentence that left her lips.

"Roan and I kissed. A lot."

Lahana's eyes widened along with Orah's, before glancing down the hall to Roan's room. "Inside. Now!" she demanded. Pushing against Orah's shoulders she shoved her back into her room, slamming the door behind them. "Start talking." Lahana's smile widened with each breath she took.

Orah stared at her nervously. "It first happened a few weeks ago. Then again this morning. Then again about an hour ago."

"Oh Fates! Finally!" Lahana clapped her hands together and danced a little dance where she stood. "You two have been killing us all with your tension. I can't believe it!"

Orah watched Lahana celebrate for a moment. "There's something else," she finally said, needing to tell Lahana more.

Lahana stopped her dance instantly and snapped her head toward Orah. "Is it going to ruin this moment?"

"Nope. I also got a door open and walked through it," Orah replied, coyly.

"Orah! Look at you!" Lahana cheered. Pulling Orah into a tight hug, Lahana squealed while she shook Orah about. Orah laughed and strained against Lahana's tight hold. The Goddess was much stronger than Orah had given her credit for.

"Jes said your magic has grown. Show me."

Ready to impress her, Orah waved her hand. Grass began growing on every surface of her bedroom followed by bright flowers. Lahana's eyes glistened and she waved her own hand. Her flowers joined Orah's, covering the entire room. The scent alone was overpowering while they both spun around the room laughing.

With a sigh, Lahana snapped her fingers and their little game of magic disappeared. "Orah, I'm so proud of you." She said, sniffling back the tears lining her eyes.

Unsure of how to respond to the compliment, Orah looked down at the ground. "Thank you."

Lahana grabbed Orah's hand and tugged her toward the bedroom doors. "Come downstairs, there's someone I want you to meet." Pulling Orah down the stairs in a mad dash they stopped at the open sitting room doors. Sitting on the couch was a small woman. Her size surprised Orah. While Lahana wasn't much taller than Orah, the woman on the couch was several inches shorter than both of them. Her warm tanned skin seemed to warm the room, complimenting her dark red hair that was cut in a short, bobbed style. The woman gazed lovingly at Lahana and Orah couldn't help but smile at how similar the women's green eyes were.

"Orah, this is Fawn." Lahana beamed walking Orah over to her partner.

Fawn smiled and stood from the couch, holding her hand out to grasp Orah's. "Orah, I've heard so much about you." Fawn's voice was comforting and Orah immediately knew she liked her. She felt warm and kind, but also somehow like she could keep anyone levelheaded. Orah chuckled, it was likely why Lahana was so drawn to the woman.

Smiling, Orah nodded her head. "Fawn, it is wonderful to meet you."

Lahana let out a cheerful squeal and hopped in place. "I have lived in this house for six decades dealing with two very grumpy men. I cannot tell you both how happy I am to have more women walking these halls."

Orah snorted at the comment which in turn made Lahana and Fawn laugh. Orah smiled as

Lahana led them all to the couch, listening contently to Lahana prattle on and on about her and Fawn's travels.

Every mortal they delivered an invitation to had agreed to come to Roan's party. They had all heard of his kindness to mortals and believed he was worth attending what was bound to be a rather unusual evening.

A soft knock at the door pulled their attention from the conversation and they all turned

to find Roan standing in the doorway with a smile. "Dinner's ready."

Lahana's eyes bounced between Roan and Orah. She beamed, then grabbed Fawn's hand, ushering her out of the room but not before she gave Orah a wink while she passed.

Chuckling, Roan watched as his sister walked away. "Lahana gave you your invitation?"

"Yes, thank you," Orah replied quietly.

"Don't thank me. She's the one who realized none of us have officially invited you. We all just assumed if we haven't gotten you home by then that you'll be here." An awkward tension fell between them at the mention of Orah going home.

Clearing her throat, she motioned to the kitchen. "I'm assuming we're eating in the kitchen tonight?"

He nodded his head then silently followed her as she walked down the hall. Everyone settled around the table while Yohan and Xade brought out platters of food. The room quickly filled with sounds of eating and chatter. Jes and Fawn, to Orah's surprise, were comfortable and friendly with one another, as though they were familiar with each other. Jes asked how Fawn's mother was and Fawn asked how the training of the recruits was going at the camp. The only other person Orah had seen Jes interact with at a meal was Moros and he had obviously not been so casual.

Chuckling to herself, she sipped on her wine, listening to the happy conversations filling the room. She didn't feel any need to be an active part that evening. Something about the warmth of the kitchen, the casual comfort of the conversation, and the hearty home cooked meal made her want to observe so she'd never forget the moment in time.

Nudging her with his elbow, Roan leaned toward her, whispering, "You're awfully quiet tonight."

Shrugging, she took another sip of her wine. "I'm just enjoying everyone being together."

He smiled and sat up straighter, admiring his family. "Yeah, it is really nice."

The meal and happy chatter dragged on, to no one's complaint, and they eventually ended up eating the dessert Xade prepared right from the pan. Fawn had mumbled in disbelief at how informal everything was in the

Gods of Nyte's home. She laughed, with a mouth full of chocolate cake, at how shocked her Mother would have been to see them all eating out of a pan around a modest table.

Roan had let out a loud, hearty laugh at the shock and informed Fawn that her Mother was welcome to join a casual meal whenever she'd liked.

Once the cake pan was picked clean, Roan stood abruptly and the atmosphere in the room shifted. Clearing his throat, he looked down at Orah then to each person around the table. "My father knows about Orah," he finally said.

Lahana let out a startled gasp, making Orah jump. Fawn squeezed Lahana's hand tight. Letting out a breath, Lahana shook her head. "Way to bring down the fun, Roany."

Roan's lip tilted to an amused smile while his eyes lingered on Orah. "I'm asking all of you, if you are willing, to spend the night in the library with me to try and find any mentions of adjusting portals so we can get her home. Preferably before my birthday."

Lahana's eyes widened and she opened her mouth, but Roan stopped her, putting up his hand. "As much as I would like for her to join us for the party, I don't know what he will do. Marek has all but confirmed they will be back after this next week and by 'they', I mean him and Father." A choked sound escaped Lahana's lips.

Clearing his throat, Roan glanced at Yohan and his family. "I know tomorrow the city festivities begin and I know you have a stand to sell your goods. I don't want to keep you up too late but if you all are willing to help, even for an hour I would be eternally grateful."

Orah couldn't help her responding smile to the sound of Yohan's thick accent. "Roan, it would be an honor to help get our Orah home."

Yohan's claim on her filled a hidden hole inside of her and she quickly looked down at the table, hoping to avoid tears from falling. Roan's hand landed on her shoulder and he squeezed softly. "I need to know if there are any more powerful portals, we might not know about that we can try and use to get her home. The Perambulate didn't work. The soul portal in Shadus isn't an option. But, in my gut I can feel those aren't our only options."

Everyone at the table jumped when Etta cleared her throat. "What about the one in the palace?"

Roan stared down at her, shaking his head. "Etta. One – my Father's personal portal is *His*. Two –- I'm trying to avoid him from getting his hands on her. I can't just take her to Erde."

Shaking her head, Etta looked out the window behind her. "Not your Father's palace, Aeron's—the Governing God portal."

Roan's eyes widened. "Excuse me?"

It wasn't Etta who responded to the question, but to Orah's surprise, Fawn. "You don't know about your own portal? The Governing God portal? Everyone has one in their palace. They can travel anywhere you can think of; you don't need to think of the Perambulate in another Region like you do with the ones in the cities." Lahana glanced at Fawn with a confused look. Fawn shrugged. "I thought you would have known with Roan being a Governing God. Roan, how didn't you know about this?"

Orah's eyes snapped to Jes, who now sat as still as a statue. Her eyes widened. There was no way he didn't know about Moros's portal—not after fifty years.

Jes's eyes widened and he shook his head. He looked like he was going to be sick. Orah glared at him. Roan's eyes were on Fawn, having no inclination about the interaction happening silently.

Narrowing her eyes at Jes, Orah mouthed her disapproval.

Bastard.

Jes's eyes widened again and he bit his lip. She wasn't sure if that was from offense or amusement before his eyes darted up to Roan again.

Roan cleared his throat and Orah looked up to find him staring out the window behind Etta. It was dark now, but there didn't have to be light for Orah to know where they were both looking. They were looking out to where Aeron's palace sat beyond the city.

Finally speaking, Roan's voice was barely audible. "I never moved into the palace once I took over the region and Aeron never told me about any special portal. I've always either flown on Nacht or used the Perambulate to travel. Etta, where is it in the palace?"

"Aeron's study," Etta whispered.

Roan tensed then nodded. Glancing at Jes for a moment he turned his attention to Orah. "I guess we're not spending the night in the library."

Orah's stomach sank, some untouchable thing lingered in the air, as if nodding its head in approval that they had discovered something significant. So significant Orah likely would be going home.

The sound of Jes's chair pulling away from the table pulled Orah's eyes from Roan's. A sad look flashed across his face before he tucked his chin down then walked out of the kitchen. Orah felt frozen in her chair listening to the soft sounds of the side door opening then closing.

Kai stood abruptly and nodded. "I guess I'll go help Jes get Tume and Nacht ready." Stopping in front of Orah, he grabbed her hands gently. "It's been a pleasure knowing you, Orah. A real pleasure."

One by one every person at the table stood and offered Orah their goodbyes. Everyone in that room could feel what Orah could. They all somehow knew this was a final farewell. By the time Lahana approached, her tears were running down both of their faces.

Standing, Orah rushed into Lahana's arms. The women crumpled around each other, shaking, and gripping each other as if they would never let go. Orah believed her heart would burst when Lahana finally pulled away.

"For what it's worth I would have loved to have you as a sister," Lahana whispered through the wind.

Orah choked on her sob, not fully understanding what Lahana meant *"I would have loved to have had a sister,"* she returned through the wind, despite her confusion.

Lahana nodded her head while Fawn walked behind her, grabbing her arm, and guiding them out of the kitchen. While they disappeared around the corner, Orah turned to observe the now quiet room. Roan and Etta were all who remained.

Orah's heart sank when she made eye contact with Etta. They had grown close since Etta's help after her injury at the obstacle course. The housekeeper was a woman of few words and often came across stern and cold but for Orah, she'd become a source of comfort. Not by conversation, but through Etta's quiet sometimes unseen actions. A smile when passing in the hallway, warm towels after a rough training session, even being Orah's willing guinea pig when she'd spent hours working on new foods in the kitchen.

As if she were running through the same quiet exchanges they've had, Etta smiled and held her hands out to Orah. Orah bit back her sob and took the calloused warm hands, squeezing them tightly.

"I don't say goodbye." Etta returned Orah's tight squeeze. "I don't believe in goodbyes." Releasing Orah's hands, Etta pulled her into a hug and held her tight. Somehow not being forced to say the words felt right for Orah. A silent agreement between them, one even distance or time couldn't break.

Finally, Etta released her hold then placed Orah's hands in Roan's. Sternly she looked up at her Governing God. "You take care of her," she ordered.

Roan smiled at the command then nodded his head. They kept a firm grasp on each other's hands while they walked Etta out of the room. Without saying a word, Roan pulled Orah toward the kitchen door and outside into the courtyard. Orah could make out Jes in the distance with the Pegasus and her heart ached. Planting her feet firmly on the ground she halted their movement. "What if I don't want to go?" Admitting what was going through her mind felt like both a relief and a shock.

Letting out a sad sigh his eyes traveled toward the stables then out to the city. "I need you safe, Orah. I need to know he can't find you."

He didn't let her respond as he tugged on her hands again, continuing to guide them toward the stables. Jes looked at them both sadly when they approached and let out a quiet breath.

Words felt bitter on Orah's tongue. She didn't know what to say. She didn't know how to fight against the gnawing panic rising to the surface. All she could do was silently obey when Roan crouched to help her into Tume's saddle.

The melancholy group exchanged no words amongst them while they took to the sky. Orah held in a shaky breath looking down at the city below her while they flew toward the palace. She hadn't been wrong when she'd first flown over it, wondering how beautiful it would look at night. The city was alive in the dark, just as it was intended to be. The buildings twinkled, the mountains blended in with the sky disappearing entirely once the sun set, and the people who bustled about on the ground somehow looked like shooting stars.

Orah blinked back the tears lining her eyes. She knew, deep inside, she knew she would never see the enchanting city again.

The flight to Aeron's palace only took a few minutes. Orah wasn't shocked when they drew closer, noticing the palace appeared to be built from similar material as the one in Shadus. She couldn't help but wonder, however, which one was built first. The only difference between the two was the palace now in front of her also sparkled in the night, like all the buildings in the Region did. As though anything built there had to shine in the night.

Tume followed Jes and Nacht as they landed on a large balcony overlooking a barren field. Orah stared at the field mesmerized. It was the only time in the three months she'd been there when she'd thought a piece of Roan's region looked sad and unloved.

Roan cleared his throat. "Aeron did something years ago that prevents anything from being grown in front of this palace. I'm not sure why but he preferred it this way. It also deters the citizens from trying to settle the land in front of the palace."

Orah stared out at the field, nodding her head, unable to admit out loud how she related to creating a space of isolation. Letting out a huff, Tume lowered herself and Orah slid out of the saddle landing with a soft thud.

She gazed up at the black ominous palace. It felt cold. It felt unwelcoming. The perfect escape for someone determined to live a life of solitude.

Roan stared up at the palace before sighing then advancing toward two towering double doors that led inside. The doors opened on their own, silently welcoming their Governing God through the threshold.

Their footsteps echoed throughout the hall while they followed Roan. They all had yet to speak. Not one of them could find the words to break the tension, knowing what was about to happen.

Orah took in their surroundings while they walked. Every wall in the palace was either the dark obsidian or covered with an equally dark tapestry. The halls were unnaturally cold. Despite being aware the building had been empty for decades, for Orah, the cold felt as though the very center of the house sent the chill outwards to combat any chance of warmth.

She lost track of her directions when Roan suddenly stopped in front of a very tall door.

"I hate this room," he whispered.

Orah's eyes were fixated on the door while her body hummed in response. She shook her hands, trying to ignore the feeling of recognition coursing through here. "What happened here?" she asked.

Roan shook his head, placing his hands on the door. "Nothing that harmed me. Just too many memories as a child being in here and being told by Aeron what my duties would be as the God of Death and Nyte. Then as I got older being lectured by him that I needed to do more to fight for my birthright and to not allow myself to be stuck here." He let out a quiet breath while his hand gripped the handle. The door pushed open at his command followed by an odd burst of warm air, coming from the room.

"That's not right," Jes whispered.

Roan shrugged, moving to walk into the room when Jes placed his hand out. Pushing Roan behind him, Jes entered the room. Orah and Roan stood in silence, watching the door, waiting for Jes to come back. Several minutes passed and Orah's heart raced with panic when his head finally came from behind the door.

"All clear. Come on."

Squeezing Orah's hand, Roan led her into the room. She walked in twisting her head back and forth, trying to take in the massive room. It was almost as large as Roan's library with books scattering every surface, including the large black desk sitting in the middle of the room. Orah's eyes scanned the room trying to find any sign of a portal when her eyes fell to a tapestry behind the desk.

There was a warm buzz pulling at her and her eyes widened.

"Found a door behind that. I'd bet that's the portal." Jes's voice pulled Orah from her trance and she nodded her head.

Somehow, she knew he wasn't wrong. Her body pulled to the buzz coming from the tapestry. She let out a breath, squeezed Roan's hand, and stepped forward.

The closer she grew to the tapestry the more electric the buzz felt. Her hands tingled and her heart beat wildly inside her chest. As though the portal itself were calling to her. Even if she wanted to, she couldn't push down the reaction she was feeling inside.

It was how she'd felt when the door appeared in the training room.

It was how she'd felt that morning at the obstacle course when the door appeared behind Roan.

She was being called to it and her power begged for her to respond.

Releasing Roan's hand, she placed her hand on the hidden door handle and pulled. With a loud groan, the door opened. She held her breath at the electric shock that ran from her palm and throughout her body.

Peeking through the door she found a small room and a framed doorway covered by a curtain. Every part of her body felt alive while she stepped inside. She was sure every hair on her body stood. Her eyes were focused on the door when hands gripped her shoulders softly. Glancing up, she found Roan standing over her, staring at the doorway.

Moving her eyes behind him, she found Jes standing outside the door. Slowly, he nodded his head and smiled. She tilted her head, motioning for him to join, but he shook his in response. Tilting his chin down he mouthed *goodbye*.

Orah blinked and held in her gasp, watching him pull the door shut and leaving her alone with Roan.

She looked back at the curtain then shook her head. "Roan, I don't know if I can."

Moving her hair from her shoulder, Roan leaned down, kissing the crook of her neck. The contact sent electric shocks down her spine and she clenched her fists. Leaning up he whispered against her ear. "I know you can. I believe in you."

Softly pushing against her shoulders, he moved her forward. He didn't let go and didn't allow her to look back at him. Her breathing felt heavy from the panic gripping her heart. She didn't want to move her feet, but she couldn't bring herself to stop. She couldn't bring herself to fight against his grip on her.

Stopping them in front of the curtain he whispered against her ear again. "Now, just pull that curtain down like you did those walls earlier."

She tensed at the mention of her memories. That couldn't have been that same day. Could it have been? Her body had been begging her for sleep from the exhaustion, but she'd refused to give in. Maybe she hadn't learned anything by pulling them down when she was ignoring the lingering pain like she'd always had.

Keeping his lips close to her he kept his voice in a whisper. "Just grab hold of the curtain." Lifting her hand, he guided her to grab onto the dark fabric. "And pull."

She let out a gasp and he kept his hand on hers while he ripped the curtain from the frame. Bright brilliant light filled the room, and she turned her head from the shock.

Roan kissed her neck. "Look up," he coaxed.

Nervously she did as he asked then pushed back against him, trying to run from what she saw. The portal was just like the one in the city center, but it was smaller, only meant for one person at a time. She moved her head to look up at Roan, but he shook his head, not allowing her to. In that moment, she wasn't sure if it was to protect her heart or his.

She let out a shaky sigh, before focusing on the now shifting portal. She shook her head. No. No. It couldn't possibly already know where she had to go.

She took a panicked step back, gripping Roan's arm. "Roan, no. Not now."

"Love, you have to." The pet name grabbed hold of her heart and she shook her head.

"I can't." Her voice cracked.

Gently kissing her neck, he wrapped an arm around her. "We didn't get too messy, Orah. A few kisses. A bit of trauma sharing. We made sure to keep it clean."

She let out a laugh at his jokes while tears lined her eyes. She didn't want to go. They had just started. The living power inside of her buzzed and thrashed, begging her not to leave him.

"I just found you," she whispered.

She didn't have to be looking at him to know the responding sound he'd made was a choked sob. Moving his arm from her waist he squeezed her shoulder, placing a kiss on the top of her head. "I make this promise to you now, Orah; I will find you. I will go through every portal in my world until one leads me back to you. This isn't goodbye."

"What if it takes you longer than you want and you find me as an old woman?"

His smile rustled the top of her hair and his laugh vibrated against her back. "You will never be older than me. I will have you as you are now or as you will be 30 years from now. It doesn't matter—I will find you again."

Forcing his hands off her shoulders she turned to face him. "I can't go without knowing your full name." She laughed again. How ironic it was that he had known her name for weeks, but she'd never thought until that moment to ask him his.

He nodded his head. "My name is Roan Cael Durel and I will find you again, Orah Clark."

She gave him a sad smile in response. "Roan Cael Durel, I will be waiting for you." She tried to memorize his beautiful face. His full lips. His scattered freckles. His hair, always tousled by him running his hands through it, but somehow always perfect. He smiled while she observed him, then glanced back behind her and his eyes widened.

Twisting around she let out a yelp, pushing back against his chest. "Fates." His whisper was the only sound in the room while they stood and stared at a perfect view of her chateau.

Shaking her head, she looked back up at him—one last time. "I think I could have loved you, Roan Durel. I think I could have loved you more than I've ever allowed myself to love."

A single tear ran down his face. "I think I could have loved you too."

His hands gripped her shoulders then she gasped when he pushed her forward and she fell into the portal.

Her chateau looked as though it were just a few feet away. Picturesque and calling out for her to return. Her heart tugged and her power screamed at her to go back.

Go back.

Go back.

Go back.

Over and over her power screamed and her tears ran down her face. Falling through the portal she closed her eyes, picturing what could have been and the love she may have just left behind.

She imagined Roan lifting her into the air, laughing at the pub.

She saw nights sleeping in his arms.

She saw him winning the challenge—becoming the King.

She saw herself by his side.

Her body felt on fire and she threw up her hands, screaming his name. She didn't want to go back to the chateau.

She wanted to go *home.*

Chapter 31

Roan's tears blurred his vision while he watched Orah and her chateau fade into the distance. He had done it. He'd gotten her home. Startled by a knock on the door, Roan turned to find Jes standing under the door frame.

"I heard," Jes whispered, approaching Roan.

Roan nodded his head. He was sure his heart had just broken. It was similar to when he'd watched Lahana cradling their mother's lifeless body. Honestly, it was worse than that moment. The grief was like a knife slicing him open.

Roan looked back at the portal shaking his head. He should have told her the truth. He should have told her how he actually felt. He should have found a way to keep her safe—with him. Pushing down his grief he spoke. "We need to find a way to block this portal so no one can try and follow her." Turning back to face Jes, he cocked his head to the side in confusion at the look on his Beskermer's eyes.

Jes's eyes were wide and his mouth hung open. Panicked, Roan twisted back around. He shook his head in shock, unable to hold back the sob that came from him while he watched Orah casually walk out of the portal.

"Hey stranger." She grinned widely.

Time stood still. She was back. How was she back?

He pushed down his responding panic of what this now meant and instead he ran to her. Wrapping his arms around her legs he lifted her off the ground, spinning her in the air. The sound of her laugh filled him from head to toe while he looked up at her bright smile.

"How?" he asked, setting her gently back on the ground.

Glancing back at the doorway, she shrugged. "It didn't work. Like last time I saw my chateau, but then I was falling back to your world."

"Are you okay?" He took her in. She seemed too calm compared to how she'd reacted when the city center portal had failed.

"I'll be okay," she replied.

Jes cleared his throat and they both turned to face him. "What do we do now? We probably have about a week until your Father shows up."

Roan sighed. "I don't think he'll come to the party. I don't even think he'll come right after the party. I think he's going to make us sweat and sit on the edge of our seats waiting for him to show up."

Jes nodded then looked at Orah with a curious look on his face. Roan could have pushed down his own elation to get a better sense of Jes's emotions in the moment but all that mattered was that Orah was there. Looking down, Roan smiled, finding her hand wrapped around his. He hadn't realized she was also staring at him or that she had taken his hand.

"Let's get you back home." Jes gave Orah another curious look before turning and walking out of the room.

They all walked silently through the empty palace. Despite the warm comfort of Orah's hand in his, Roan couldn't stop how on edge his body felt in the palace. Aeron had never made Roan feel unwelcomed there. Roan had never been in danger, but the building never felt like home. It had always had that uncomfortable chill no matter how many fires were lit or how many people filled its halls. Shivering, Roan tried to ignore the chill while they approached the balcony doors.

The doors opened for him making Nacht and Tume jump while the group walked out into the crisp night air. They approached Tume and Orah gripped his hand hesitantly. Smiling, he gave her a squeeze, helping her up onto the saddle.

"I'm not going anywhere," he whispered assuredly while he buckled the straps.

Usually, she waved off his help, but she was being rather willing. Smiling, he looked up at her again and found her staring down at him. She appeared almost as though she were in a daze and he stared back, worried something may have actually happened in the portal. Shaking his head, he patted Tume's neck then climbed into his saddle on Nacht.

The flight back to the manor was just as quiet as the flight to the palace but Roan made sure to fly right beside Orah. Jes kept glancing back at her every minute or so as if he also couldn't believe she was there.

When they arrived at the house Jes offered to take the animals back to the stable and Orah eagerly pulled Roan toward the house.

His heart beat hard with anticipation and wonder over why she was so eager to get inside

but he would go wherever she took him. He would do whatever she asked of him.

They walked past the sitting room, passing Fawn gently rubbing Lahana's back. Lahana jumped up with her mouth hanging open, staring at Orah. Orah, however, didn't seem to notice while she tugged Roan up the stairs.

"Later," Roan whispered, shaking his head, discouraging his sister from following.

Lahana glanced at Fawn then quietly closed the sitting room doors. Orah's pace quickened while she tugged him down the hall. He expected her to stop in front of her room but instead she led them both to his.

Finally, she spoke, pointing to his doors. "I want to see your room."

"What?" he asked.

"I haven't seen your room yet. The whole time I've been here I haven't seen inside of it. I want to see it, please." He couldn't understand the emotion coming off of her. It wasn't arousal, it wasn't desire, it wasn't fear, or even curiosity. He couldn't place it and that was enough to peak his own interest.

Without breaking their gaze, he slowly turned the handle and pushed the doors open. Orah gasped while she walked into the room.

Many would probably have said Roan's bedroom was rather large. He knew the bed in the middle of the room certainly was. At night, it was as though you were in the sky with black velvet curtains around the four-post bed and a deep blue, almost black, comforter across the mattress. The wards had slowly adjusted over the sixty years the room had been his to make the walls look like the night sky as well. During the day it looked like the room was painted black, but in the night small sparkling lights twinkled on the walls.

Orah stepped further into the room and stopped when she passed the archway that led to the bathroom. He smiled, knowing she had spotted the large tub sitting in the middle of the marble floor. Grinning, she walked into the bathroom, flicking her finger, inviting him to follow.

Gulping, he took a deep breath. He had been with plenty of women in his life. This moment with her was no different. At least that was what he was telling himself as he followed her taunting invitation.

Everything slowed while he watched her. She didn't take her eyes off him as she pulled off her top and threw it to the floor. Bending, she grabbed the waist of her pants and just as slowly pulled them down her legs.

Standing in only her undergarments she stared at him. Her emotions hot and wild. Almost as if they could burn him from where he stood. He smiled, noticing the goose flesh on her skin while her chest slowly moved up and down.

He couldn't help but take her in. She was exquisite. Every curve of her body was a work of art. From her full breasts, to the soft curves of her hips and stomach, all the way down to her agonizingly long legs.

Turning, she bent to turn on the tub and he was sure he had died from the sight. He bit his lip, restraining himself from rushing up behind her and removing the last two very thin layers from her body. His eyes flared when she straightened and smiled at him.

Her eyes moved up and down his body slowly, feeling like both a taunt and a dare. A dare he was happily going to take.

Holding her gaze, he pulled off his shirt with the same teasing slowness she had done with hers. Her breath slowed and her chest rose while she stared at him. He couldn't keep his eyes from her breasts with each breath she took. He could barely wait to get his hands on her.

Grinning, he pulled his trousers off and she jumped back, eyes widening. He smiled, unable to hide his appreciation of her gawking. Now totally bare in front of her, he paused while her eyes scanned him fully. Once she'd taken all of him in, she smiled then turned to shut off the tub. He couldn't ignore his body's responding twitch from the sight of her bending down. How easily it would have been for him to remove those thin layers.

She turned back to face him, and his breath stopped while she pulled off her bra, flinging it across the room. Her breasts shifted softly with the movement and his eyes widened. Still keeping her eyes on his she pulled off her panties then straightened herself.

The air in the room stilled around them while they stood in silence staring at each other. The moment felt more intimate than any moment Roan had previously had with anyone.

Slowly he moved to touch her when she stopped him, placing her hands on his chest.

"Only a bath."

He shook his head, trying to fight off the daze he was in. "Just a bath?"

She nodded her head nervously then looked down at the water. "I don't want what we're starting to go too fast, Roan. Trust me when I say all I want is for you to take me right now but—I think we need to go slower. Just a bath tonight and if you'll have me, I'd like to sleep next to you as well."

He couldn't ignore the quick disappointment he felt, but he nodded. "I can take this as slow as you want to take it. I'm in no rush."

Smiling she turned and stepped into the tub, letting out a quiet hiss while she sunk into the deep water. "Oh my god." Her eyes rolled to the back of her head while she dunked herself under the water. "I don't think I've ever been in a tub this large or deep before." She splayed out in the water lazily and he sat for a moment, watching her. Appreciating her beauty. Popping up she grinned. "Are you going to join me or just watch me?"

"Is just watching an option?" He smiled. He could have easily sat and watched her until she was done. He would have been completely content with that option.

"Please join me," she replied, motioning with her finger.

Let out a sigh he reminded himself of his own self-control and stepped into the water.

"Fuck!" His foot flew out from the water. "How are you in there right now and not burning alive?" His toes yelled at him in protest and anger as to why he had just willingly stuck them in scalding water.

She shrugged. "I think it feels wonderful."

Shaking his head, he braved the hot water, wincing while he lowered himself. "I think you might be a creature from the depths of Shadus."

Her eyes widened and she splashed water then let out a playful scream when he came after her. His arms wrapped around her waist and he held her in place against the edge of the tub. Laughing, she wiggled and kicked, trying to get away from him but his grip tightened. She stilled and he pushed himself against her backside, holding the front of her in place against the tub. Gripping her chin with his free hand, he tilted her face back toward his. Her wriggling stopped and she stared back at him.

He looked down at her lips and smiled knowing he could kiss them every day for the rest of his life and never tire of their soft addicting touch.

She wiggled slightly, pushing him against her backside. So close to where he wanted to be but yet so far at the same time. She stared back into his eyes, lifting her chin a little more until their lips touched.

His fingers dug into her soft stomach and he let himself get lost in the kiss. His legs opened hers and he pressed right up against her, letting her feel just how much he appreciated the kiss. She moaned at the teasing pressure.

Her mouth was hot against his and he wanted more.

He pulled back and flipped her, so she was facing him, pushing her back against the tub again. Her bare skin against his was almost unbearable while he kissed her. Needing more. Craving more.

Wrapping her legs around his waist he groaned. He was so close to her, feeling the heat between her thighs. His body begged him to push forward. To slip himself inside.

He pulled back, shaking his head. They were taking this slow. He could do that.

His hand gripped that long dark hair of hers and he tugged, exposing her neck. Gasping, her nails dug into his back while he slowly licked up her neck. Her legs shook against him while he nibbled and teased the sensitive spot. His own legs trembled beneath him and he bit down on her neck. Gasping, she thrust her hips forward and he groaned. Sure, he was going to melt from how close she had just come to his tip.

Pulling away he pushed back, before taking a deep breath. "You said slow." Moving away from her, he laid back, dunking his head in the water. He felt dizzy from the kiss and the heat and steam of the water wasn't helping. When he sat back up, he found her staring at him with her mouth slightly open. Looking down, he smiled, he hadn't considered how exposed he was by laying back like that.

Slowly her eyes met his and she smiled, biting her lower lip. "Yes. Slow."

She backed up until she was on the opposite side of the tub and they sat, facing each other. Both trying to steady their breathing. Roan ran his hands over the surface of the water while it cooled to a comfortable temperature.

Letting out a sigh, he smiled at her. "Come here."

She pulled her eyes from the twinkling walls of his room. "Why?"

"I want to wash your hair," he replied.

Her confusion and curiosity traveled across the warm water while she made her way to him slowly. He spun his finger as a way to tell her to turn her back to him and she followed the request. He sucked in his breath when her backside brushed up against him. He had just started calming down and the brush of her against him was not helping.

She chuckled, wiggling against him a little more and he grinned. Her chuckle turned to a gasp when he grabbed a handful of her hair again and jerked her head back.

"No wiggling," he whispered against her ear while his hands rubbed the side of her ribs in slow teasing movements. Swallowing loudly, she nodded her head, and he released his grip.

He took his time washing her hair. The pine scented soap complimented her, and she let out groans of appreciation while his fingers slowly scrubbed against her scalp.

He watched while his hands moved through the thick layers. It had captivated him from the first moment he'd seen her. How dark it looked in the dimly lit bathroom but how much red it had when she was in the sun. He marveled in the feeling of how thick and soft it was.

Her head tilted back against his chest while his fingers moved from her scalp down to her shoulders. His hands moved as if on instinct and he pushed gently against the tense muscles below her neck. She stiffened, digging her fingers into his calves under the water.

"Just relax," he whispered while his fingers worked her tense shoulders.

She never relaxed based on how tight her muscles were. He tried not to push too hard while he worked until her body relaxed against his. He moved almost in a trance while her breathing turned heavier. Stopping, he looked over her shoulder to see her eyes slowly closing.

He kissed the top of her head. "Don't fall asleep yet." She startled at the sound of his voice. "Just lay back and rinse out your hair then we can go to bed."

She nodded then pushed away from him and laid back. Lazily she ran her hand through her hair, and he watched while the soap rinsed out. Admiring her body as if were artwork while she floated in the water with the soap flowing out around her. Her breasts barely peaked out above the water and he held back the urge to cup them both in his hands.

"All done," she said, sitting up from the water.

Walking out of the tub, Roan grabbed two towels, wrapping one around his waist he motioned for her stand. He wrapped the towel under her arms and without warning placed one arm under her knees then the other around her shoulders, picking her up out of the tub.

"I can walk, you know," she said with a gasp.

"Yes, but carrying you is so much more fun," he replied with a teasing wink.

She rolled her eyes before resting her head against his chest. The walk to his bed wasn't far and he set her down gently. Laying back she let out a long sigh. "Your bed is much softer than mine."

"Like sleeping on a cloud." He smiled, then walked into his closet.

He had to find clothes for them both. If he didn't, he wasn't sure he would be able to keep his hands off her. Dressing quickly, he threw on a loose shirt and pants then grabbed another loose shirt for her.

She was almost asleep when he walked out of the closet and tossed the shirt in her direction. "You need clothes."

Groaning, she sat up. "Why?"

His eyes fell to the towel that had slipped slightly, now exposing her upper thigh.

"Because if that towel comes off, I don't think I'll be able to keep my hands off of you. With your permission of course." He said the last sentence with a wink and crossed to the other side of the bed.

He didn't have to look up to know a blush had formed across her cheeks. He sat, with his back turned, listening to the rustling of the towel being replaced by his shirt. Only turning back to face her when the sounds stopped.

She slid off the bed briefly, pulling back the covers. A happy content sound came from her when she climbed back in and laid her head on the pillow.

Lying down, he turned to face her, propping himself up on his elbow. She turned to look at him and smiled. "I might sleep in here from now on."

He caressed her arm slowly, smiling back at her. "You can sleep in here all day, every day, if you would like."

While Orah shifted closer to him, Roan adjusted his position, allowing her to nestle into the crook of his arm. Roan stared down to where she laid against him, taken back by how perfectly they fit together. As if she had been made for that spot.

Continuing to run his hand across her arm, he listened as her breathing slowed, growing heavy and deep. He didn't care how slow she wanted to take things, but he knew he couldn't let her sleep in another room ever again. Something about her being on the other side of the wall now felt wrong when she felt so right lying beside him.

He admired how peaceful she was in her sleep. The constant tension she seemed to carry around was relaxed, perhaps for the first time since he'd known her. She snuggled closer while her hand gripped his shirt as if she were trying to pull him closer. Smiling, he wrapped his arm around her, holding her tight.

He muffled his gasp with his free hand when her body warmed against his and the room filled with soft candle light. She was glowing and what had started as a dim light quickly grew brighter. He stared in wonder at the light while the room brightened. It almost looked as though sunlight had filled the space around them and his heart swelled in admiration.

His logical side told him he should have been worried or concerned that a seemingly mortal woman had so much power, but he didn't run his life solely on logic. Nothing about Orah was ordinary or *normal*. She was this living force since the moment she had slammed into his back three months prior. If anything, all of her gifts and power made sense for a woman who didn't take "no" for an answer. It was as if her power improvised ways for her to get around obstacles in her path and he found it pretty inspiring.

Slowly the light in the room faded and the twinkling lights in his room flicked back on. He ran his hand through her dark hair, shaking his head with amusement. The warmth and light had dried her hair completely. You wouldn't have known she had just come out of a bath.

Smiling, he pulled her closer. He didn't know what had happened at Aeron's palace or why the portal didn't work, but he was going to worry about that in the morning. Right now, he was going to fall asleep holding her, believing he would never have to let her go again.

Chapter 32

Orah woke up in Roan's bed alone, the spot where he'd been beside her was now cold, telling her he'd been gone for at least an hour. She blinked at the sunlight peeking through his open curtain. She'd slept in later than she had in months. She briefly wondered if the massage Roan had given her in the tub had been some kind of spell. She couldn't remember the last time she had slept so deeply.

Her cheeks heated while her thoughts went back to the night before. How brazenly she had stripped off her clothes. How breathtaking he'd looked while he'd stripped off his. She shivered at the thought. The restraint it had taken for her to not rush to him and grab hold of him had almost been painful but taking things slow felt like the right choice.

Not like we haven't been taking it slow for months.

But it felt right. She hadn't allowed herself to accept wanting him until yesterday. She hadn't allowed herself to really consider what was happening between them.

Shaking her head, she pulled off the covers and stood. His room was huge. She couldn't comprehend how much space it occupied on that side of the manor. His bed could have easily fit six people and felt how she imagined a cloud would have felt like. Despite its large size, they had slept holding each other for most of the night. At some point she remembered pulling away from him, but she didn't stray too far. She could feel his warmth next to her all night.

Taking one last look around his room she walked toward the bedroom doors to dress before going downstairs. It was the first day of the week-long celebrations in Iluna and the first day of preparing the manor for the party. She was determined to be as helpful as she could.

Quietly closing the door behind her she turned and walked to hers but paused when she locked eyes with Lahana.

Standing outside her bedroom, Lahana stared at Orah. Her eyes widened while she looked Orah up and down. In an instant, she was in front of Orah, pulling her into the bedroom.

Shutting Orah's doors behind them, Lahana grinned. "Did you and Roan?"

Orah blushed. "No. Just a bath together and then I slept in his bed."

Lahana walked past Orah into the room and sat down on the bed. "I thought for sure you were leaving last night. There was this buzz in the air that seemed to confirm it."

Orah casually walked into the closet, making sure not to look at Lahana. "I don't know what happened. I could see it more clearly than the other two times but when I was almost there I was thrown backwards."

Orah rummaged through her clothes while Lahana sighed loudly. "Well at least you got a bath out of it." Orah smiled at the grin in Lahana's voice that was followed by a loud laugh. "I honestly don't want any more details than that. My brother's intimate life can remain private."

Deciding on her outfit, Orah slipped it over her head then stepped out of the closet. Lahana's eyes lit up and she smiled. "You're wearing Roan's favorite color."

Startled, Orah looked down at her dress. It was simple and long with open sleeves connecting at her wrists then again at her elbows, but the color had been what caught her attention. A dark, almost black navy blue that reminded her of the color of Roan's comforter.

Orah shrugged. "I liked the color."

Lahana slid off the bed. "This week is going to be so much fun. Yohan is going to be out in the city center all week with a stand to sell his goods. Clarah too! I'm hoping she makes a good purse full of coins selling those baked goods of hers. Etta is going to be running around readying the house for the party so we better not get in her way. Roan is likely going to be in the city center most days interacting with the people and the festivities. Jes will be hovering over him grumpily." She stopped to catch a breath and her grin widened. "And *we* are going to have some fun."

Laughing, Orah nodded her head while she walked into the bathroom to fix her hair. Lahana followed, leaning against the doorframe patiently while Orah pulled her hair back into a braid. Sighing, Lahana stared at her. "I wish I had hair like yours."

Surprised, Orah observed Lahana's reflection in the mirror, focusing on her long golden hair. "Your hair is beautiful, Lahana."

"I know but—" Lahana's eyes moved toward the floor then back to Orah. "Your hair reminds me of my mother's. She didn't have the bits of auburn in it that you do but it was dark and beautiful. She used to let me spend hours as a child brushing and playing with it. My golden hair is all from my Father. I just wish I had more of her in me."

Setting her brush down, Orah pulled Lahana into a hug. "From what Roan has told me about her I think everything about you is a part of her. Roan said she lit up a room when she walked in and she definitely passed that to you."

Hugging Orah tightly, Lahana nodded her head. "Roan told you then."

"Yes. I'm glad you both have each other after experiencing something like that."

Lahana sniffed while she wiped away tears that ran down her cheeks. "That was 60 years ago, and I do miss her, but let's not let today be a sad day."

Grabbing Orah's hand once again, Lahana pulled her out the door, meeting Fawn in the hallway. Fawn and Orah smiled and nodded at each other while Lahana grabbed Fawn's hand and dragged them all down the stairs.

They all collided with Roan when they hit the bottom of the stairs and Lahana let out a frustrated yell. "Roany! Why in the Fates were you just standing there?"

Roan shook his head. "I was walking up to my bedroom." His eyes darted to Orah's. "But I see you've already found who I was going to fetch."

A mischievous grin formed across Lahana's face. "Caught her sneaking out in one of your shirts. So much for being private."

Orah gasped and glared. Lahana's only response was a wink as she pulled Fawn down the hall to the kitchen.

"You look beautiful," Roan whispered. She didn't notice how closely he'd gotten to her in the few seconds she was focused on Lahana. Slowly his hand caressed her arm. His touch leaving a buzz on her skin.

"Thank you," she replied.

Smiling, he offered his arm for her to take and they walked to the kitchen. "I was helping Yohan set up this morning. I felt I needed to with how willing he had been to stay late last night. I didn't mean to leave you alone."

Her knees trembled with how softly he spoke. "It's alright."

Stopping in front of the kitchen, he brushed her cheek softly. "No more sleeping in separate beds."

"What?"

Smiling, he leaned down, kissing her forehead softly. "After last night I don't think I can sleep without you next to me. So, we either sleep in your room every night or mine. Your choice."

She could feel Lahana's inquisitive eyes on them from the kitchen. Panic began to claw at her and she took a step back. "I—"

Roan's eyes traveled toward his sister before he pulled the kitchen door shut. His hands gripped Orah's. "I'm not asking for anything more than to sleep next to you, love. I will take this as slow as you want. If this is too fast, then forget I said anything."

Tightening her hands around his she breathed through her panic. She knew what she wanted when she went through that portal. She knew what she had imagined. What she had seen. Swallowing, she nodded. "Your room. The bed is bigger."

"My room it is then," he replied, running a finger over her lips.

Her breathing became erratic as he leaned down to kiss. Their lips had almost touched when the door she hadn't realized she was leaning against opened. Stumbling backwards against Jes, Orah yelped.

"Is this how it's going to be with you two now?" Jes groaned.

Orah's eyes snapped up to find Jes rolling his, followed by a sly wink. Gripping her arms, Jes lifted Orah upwards while Roan held her hands, steadying her.

"Dunno. Maybe we'll just keep surprising you," Roan replied to Jes with a shrug.

Jes let out a groan while they stepped back into the hall. Once he'd shut his door the air shifted slightly. "I was coming to find you. The message to Amada was delivered this morning," Jes said solemnly.

"What message?" Orah demanded.

Roan's expression hardened. "I had a message sent this morning when I left to help Yohan. I asked for any further information about other portals in our world."

The hallway shrunk around Orah while the air felt sucked from her lungs. "You're still trying to send me home."

Clearing his throat, it was Jes who answered. "Of course he is, Orah. You're still in danger. The King knows about you now. He knows Roan cares about you. You will be his next target, especially with the challenge coming up."

"It didn't work last night," Orah replied.

Roan's hand found hers, giving her a reassuring squeeze. "I will keep searching for a way to keep you safe until the very last minute. Don't forget my promise. It won't be a final goodbye," he promised.

Despite the conviction in Roan's voice, Orah felt sick knowing he was still determined to send her away. Knowing it was only because he cared, she nodded her head in response. Roan tightened his hold on her hand, leading her into the kitchen.

After finishing their meal, Roan stood. "I want everyone to have fun this week. Enjoy the city, the treats, the music, and the fun. I know we're all on edge with what's been going on but let's let loose a little for the next few days." He gave the group a boyish smile as he finished his proclamation.

With a squeal, Lahana grabbed Fawn's hand, pulling her out of the kitchen. Jes shook his head with amusement before following them out of the kitchen. Now alone once more, Orah turned to Roan.

"How many guests do you expect for your party?" she asked, curious to know how many people would be filling the manor in only a few days.

"Anywhere between one hundred to one hundred and fifty. We still have some who haven't confirmed whether or not they'll be here."

Orah's mouth opened in shock. "Where in the house is this party going to be?" His wasn't small by any means, but she had yet to see any room that could hold such an event.

Roan smiled. "Follow me."

Now needing her curiosity sated, she didn't question while they left the kitchen. Walking past the stairs, he stopped at an empty wall beside the sitting room doors. Orah's eyebrows rose.

"I'm confused."

Orah turned at the echoing footsteps behind them, finding Etta approaching. The housekeeper had a peculiar grin on her face. Clearing her throat, Etta smiled at Orah. "As the keeper of this house, I control the wards. I also help Roan close up any rooms he doesn't use often."

"Use often?" Orah asked.

Stepping back, she gasped when a wardpad appeared on the wall beside the sitting room. Roan gave her an eager responding smile while Etta pricked her finger. The wall shook softly as two large double doors appeared. Roan's eyes twinkled before pushing them open.

Orah gasped again when a spacious room came into view. Stepping into the room, she marveled at the grand ceilings nearing the height in the library. Across from her, a wall of windows stretched the length of the room. She thought back on the image of the front of the manor. The identical windows on each side. One the library, and one she hadn't realized had been this room.

Spinning in place, she imagined the marbled floors of the room echoing the sounds of guests dancing. A room this grand, this beautiful would have no issue fitting over one hundred people.

"I had no idea this has been here the whole time." Orah said, continuing her dazed spin.

"I have little to no use for it every day. I have Etta keep it concealed, but we keep it maintained. It's why I didn't want to have the party at Aeron's palace. It would have taken twice as long to prepare to receive guests," Roan replied.

Orah stopped spinning. "Guests? Are people going to be staying here this week?"

Etta let out a loud laugh. "Fates, the fact Roan has let you stay here for so long was enough of a miracle. No one is staying here. Just guests the night of the party. Guests I'm sure *he'll* push out the moment he's ready for the night to end."

Letting out a loud laugh, Roan nodded his head. "No other guests but my favorite one. Oh, and Fawn, but she's in Lahana's room so she's no bother."

Turning her head to hide her blush, Orah admired the room. Her imagination ran as she imagined a live band, beautiful dresses, and dancing the night away. The kind of night she'd read about all her life. Roan's hand found hers and he pulled her against him. The room disappeared around them while he guided her toward the center of the room, spinning them around slowly.

"I'm going to be obligated to entertain my guests the night of the party but this is my official request that you save at least one dance for me." His hand rested against her lower back. Their feet moved effortlessly against the marbled floor. She didn't understand how they moved so flawlessly together, but she never wanted it to stop. Nodding her head, she wrapped her arms around his neck. "I think I can schedule you in."

His eyes sparkled with amusement and he bent down placing a gentle kiss against her lips.

Her knees weakened while she leaned against him for support. His hands tightened around her lower back. Keeping their lips against each other, they somehow still moved gracefully across the room. Lost in the calming storm of his kiss, Orah didn't care to leave the room for the rest of the day.

Etta's clearing throat pulled them away from each other. Orah bit down her laugh. While Etta appeared stern, there was a soft look in her eyes while she glanced between Roan and Orah.

"I do have work to do in here, Roan. As much as you two are enjoying yourself I'm going to request that you leave me to my duties."

Orah looked back at Roan as he shrugged his shoulders and gave her a quick wink. "You're right, my apologies." Removing his hands from her waist, he stopped their dancing and pulled her toward the large double doors. Before they walked away, he turned back to Etta.

"Please don't work too hard. We have help coming in to do the set up and make sure everything is running smoothly. Make sure that you and Kai enjoy the festivities as well, please."

Scoffing Etta crossed her arms. "I will enjoy the festivities once I know this home is running at its best."

Orah held in her laugh at Roan's responding smile to Etta's stern response. He nodded his head then walked out of the room, pulling Orah with him. They walked hand in hand out the front door and toward the now lively city. Even from the hill Orah could hear the laughter and music coming from the city center. Her heart swelled from the show of celebration and love for Roan. Something told her the number of people she could now see on the streets were not all from Iluna but from all over his Region.

Tightening his grip on her hand he smiled down at her. "Let's go have some fun."

Turning over in the warm comforter, Orah wrapped her arm around Roan's chest and opened her eyes slowly. The sun slowly lit the room, telling her it was almost time to get up for the large city hosted breakfast being held in Roan's honor.

The last four days Orah had been dragged through the Iluna to meet the merchants and citizens of Roan's Region. Every place they visited they were met with love and excitement. She'd expected to spend most of her time with Lahana but instead Roan had made sure she was right by his side. Never leaving her for more than a few minutes at a time.

She let out a content sigh from how magical the time with him had felt when Roan's sleepy voice rumbled against her cheek.

"We don't have to go to this breakfast."

Her head shook against his chest. "No, I want to."

His hand lazily stroked her bare skin and she jumped at the touch. They hadn't taken things farther than kisses and light touches, but her control slipped more each night they laid down in his bed.

"Are you sure?" he asked. His hand slipped down her back and she stilled while his fingers casually drifted lower.

"I mean—"

His responding laugh shook her on his chest and his fingers traveled lower until his hand rested teasingly at her lower back.

"We don't have to go. We could stay in bed." His hand gripped her rear as he flipped her back onto her back. "We could kiss."

His lips found hers and she groaned against the heat of his mouth while his hand moved out from under her, resting on her lower stomach. Pulling his lips from hers, he kissed her neck, her collarbone, between her breasts, trailing his kisses until he stopped above her navel.

"There are many places I've yet to kiss you, love."

Letting out a moan, Orah nodded her head. "Yes, there are."

He smiled against her stomach and twirled his finger lazily on her upper thigh. "We really don't have to get up. I'm the Governing God. I can cancel the whole thing."

Pulled from his erotic trance, she sat up abruptly. "You can't cancel!"

His eyes stared at her breasts now in front of his face. "Well, that's where I think you're wrong."

His eyes narrowed and he moved toward her, but she shirked his touch. "Roan—Lahana planned this entire thing."

Groaning, he laid back against the bed. "I know. I won't do that to her." Leaning up on his elbow he looked over at Orah. "Just know all I'm going to think about today is your naked body in this bed and the kisses you stopped me from giving you."

Holding her lips tight to hide her smile, she shook her head. "I should have never let you convince me to skip pajamas after our bath last night."

His eyes flared. "I convinced you? If I remember it correctly you refused to put anything on because you were *too comfortable*."

Grabbing the pillow behind her, she threw it at him. "I think your old age is messing with your memory."

The bed shifted as he moved to grab her, but she hopped off the bed quickly, shaking her head again. "We need to get ready."

He smiled at her then nodded his head before swinging his legs off the bed and walking into his closet. She followed close behind, taking a moment to admire him from behind.

From the moment they agreed for her to sleep in his room, the manor appeared to have listened and to both of their surprises provided a door from his closet that led into hers.

Walking through the door she winked at him while she closed it behind her, knowing he preferred her to keep it open when she dressed. He let out a disappointed laugh behind the door as she turned to find her outfit.

They were readying for a breakfast held in Roan's honor. A breakfast Lahana had been planning for several weeks and Orah wanted to ensure she was presentable to be on the Governing God's arm the whole day. Shifting through her outfits, she found a long sleeved, dark green dress then walked into her bathroom.

Running her brush through her hair she smiled at herself. With the festivities happening she hadn't been training with Jes all week. Not that he was wanting to train either. She had caught several glimpses of Moros in the city and she knew they were both off together while Roan was preoccupied. Shaking her head at their continued sneaking around, she admired her reflection in the mirror.

With all the rest her face looked full and she looked, well, great. She hadn't realized how lifeless she had been for months and even after she had arrived in Roan's world. All those months of isolation, all those months of hiding, and she never noticed how empty she'd looked. She shook her head. Julian's concern at the airport had been valid.

Her heart tugged at the thought of her friend. He would have loved the week she'd had. All the shopping with Lahana. All the interesting people and foods. All the interesting *men*. She let out a quiet laugh at how giddy Julian would have been to admire the men in Comas. Looking back in the mirror she let out a yelp at the reflection of Roan leaning against the doorway.

Her hand flew to her chest. "You scared the shit out of me."

A wide smile spread across his face and he shook his head. "That mouth of yours."

Something about the way he responded made her knees tremble. Knowing he could sense what she was feeling she wasn't shocked when he quickly crossed the room, wrapping his arms around her waist. Slowly he ran his fingers over her lips, not once taking his eyes from hers.

"You know, we don't have to go to breakfast."

Swallowing back her desire she stared into his eyes. "It's your duty to go and accept this celebration from your people." Knowing the words were straight out of Jes's mouth she had to bite back her chuckle.

"I'd rather spend the whole day with you and that mouth of yours."

Her knees shook while she cleared her throat. "No distractions." Pushing him away softly she straightened herself. "I've been told by Jes too many times that I'm a distraction. I don't want to prove him right."

Laughing, Roan stepped away, motioning toward her door. "We definitely don't want to upset our good friend Jesiel."

Passing him she smiled. "Plus, Lahana would likely kill both of us. I'm more scared of her than Jes honestly."

Roan nodded his head. "I'm definitely more scared of Lahana than Jes."

Holding each other's hands, they left the house walking toward the city center. Roan's people greeted them as they passed, smiling brightly at Orah as much as Roan. She certainly had received interesting looks at the beginning of the week when he'd walked through the tents and canopies holding her hand, but as the days dragged on the people became eager to know her.

For her, it felt odd knowing in the back of her mind Roan was still finding a way to get her home. His people appeared to be overjoyed that their Governing God was with someone and it felt almost cruel to get their hopes up.

They hadn't yet heard back from Amada, but Roan had assured Orah they would. Even if it wasn't until the night of his party, which his aunt confirmed she'd be in attendance for.

After walking through the city streets for a few minutes they arrived at the large park where his breakfast was being held. Looking around the park, Orah couldn't help but feel a bit emotional. Lahana had obviously put thought and time into planning the gathering. You could see her attention and love in the details. Small groves of flowers surrounded the entire park, each one a different shade of blue. Each table had a different bouquet of flowers, all also in Roan's favorite colors. Two trees in the middle of the park looked as though they had sprung from thin air with a banner in the middle that comically read:

HAPPY BIRTHDAY ROANY!

Roan let out an annoyed sigh while they passed under the banner but Orah beamed. He was loved, much more than he even gave himself credit for. As they walked toward the crowd his people all turned in his direction and cheered his name loudly.

His hand tightened in Orah's and somehow, she could sense how nervous he was. Like an odd twist in her stomach but it wasn't her own. Smiling up at him she squeezed his hand, reassuring him. "They love you."

He shook his head and whispered. "I don't think I'll ever understand why."

Looking out at the smiling people then back at him, she squeezed his hand again. "I do."

Chapter 33

Orah let out a laugh at Fawn's joke, trying desperately not to spit out her juice. Clarah's responding gasp made Lahana laugh and soon the four women found themself hysterical in Lahana's room.

Holding her stomach, Lahana shook her head. "Why haven't we all had a women's only breakfast before?"

Clarah blushed. "I think we should do it more often."

Orah smiled, appreciating the moment. After they'd returned from Roan's breakfast the day before, Lahana announced only the women in the house were allowed to join the exclusive breakfast in her bedroom. Etta, to no one's surprise, declined the invitation due to readying the house, and it had taken a lot of pushing to get Clarah to agree as well.

Thankfully, Lahana was very persuasive.

Orah let out a sigh, leaning against Lahana's couch. Clara giggled quietly, shaking her head. "I can't wait for the party. Father's beside himself that His Lord won't allow him to cook."

"Roan," Lahana interjected.

Clarah blushed. "Yes, Roan." Lahana smiled, nodding her approval while Clarah continued. "His—Roan—had custom outfits made for us! Did you know that Orah?"

Orah smiled at Clarah's excitement thinking how right it was that Roan was doting on his staff. As Clarah mentioned, Roan had very firmly informed Yohan he was not allowed to cook for his birthday. Yohan had countered, claiming it was his right as head chef and they'd come to a compromise; Yohan picked the caterer and was allowed to make Roan his birthday cake.

Orah laughed at the argument the two men had several weeks before in the kitchen and how excitedly Clarah pushed her father to accept Roan's decision. It was only right that the three were treated to outfits and a night of fun. They all deserved it.

Pulling herself from her thoughts, Orah looked over at Clarah, listening while she described the gown she'd had made for her and the matching suits she'd commissioned for her father and brother. Imagining how beautiful they'd all look, Orah's eyes widened suddenly with realization.

"I don't have a dress!" Orah yelled.

Standing suddenly, she looked toward Lahana's bedroom door. "Oh my God. I didn't think about a dress." She smacked her head, panicking when Lahana let out a chuckle. "I've taken care of it."

Orah glanced down at where Lahana sat casually. "What do you mean you've taken care of it?"

Lahana grinned. "Don't worry about it, Orah. You'll look amazing."

"Lahana I—"

Lahana shook her head to stop Orah when suddenly a loud, abrasive knock came from her door. Lahana rolled her eyes. Standing, she moved toward the door but suddenly it flung open and Jes stepped into the room.

"Excuse me!" Lahana shouted, placing her hand on her hip. "What makes you think you can just barge into my bedroom?"

Jes's eyes moved from Lahana's, focusing on Orah. Orah felt herself shrink down against the couch, unsure of what was going on but suddenly feeling sick with anxiety and concern.

"Roan's room now," Jes ordered.

Lahana scoffed. "I am not going anywhere with you, Jesiel Keita, unless you tell me what is going on."

Before Jes could respond Orah caught movement behind him where Roan stood. Stepping into the room, Roan looked at the women apologetically. "I'm sorry, Fawn, Clarah, I need to speak with my sister and Orah."

Fawn gave an understanding nod and turned to Clarah, whispering quietly.

Lahana scoffed again and begrudgingly followed her brother out of the room. Passing Jes, Orah paused for a moment. He was cold but also hot. He felt—anxious.

Shaking her head, she followed close behind Lahana until they were all in Roan's room.

"What is going on?" Lahana demanded, sitting down on the couch by the balcony.

"Amada's on her way," Roan said.

Orah stared at Roan while a quiet gasp brushed against her lips. "What?" Her chest tightened with panic.

"I don't know why but we just received word. She said she needed to speak with me and my *guest*."

Crossing the room, Orah sat on the edge of the bed, pulling her knees to her chin. Amada must have found something then to want to come in person two whole days before the party.

Orah's response was a whisper so quiet she wasn't sure how Roan heard her. "When will she arrive?"

Shaking his head, Roan stared at her for a moment before answering. "She just said this evening. No idea when."

Sighing, Lahana leaned against the back of Roan's couch. "Well, why did Jes have to barge into my room so aggressively?" She shot a glance at Jes then back at Roan.

Shrugging, Jes stepped forward. "It was important information, but also, I need to speak with Orah."

Roan's brow crumbled with confusion and he turned to face Jes. "Why?"

Jes's eyes narrowed on Orah and her stomach sank. "That's between me and her."

Shaking his head, Roan stepped forward. "Anything you have to say to her you can say in front of myself or Lahana."

Something in the way Jes was looking at Orah told her that he did not want Roan to be part of whatever conversation he was looking to have. Clearing her throat, she slid off the bed and placed her hand on Roan's shoulder. "No, it's fine. Jes won't do anything to hurt me."

Nodding his head, Jes stared at her. "I'll be in my room." He turned without saying another word and walked out the door.

"And I thought he couldn't get any stranger," Lahana whispered, while she stood and followed him.

Roan turned to Orah. "Do I get to know what this is about between you and Jes?"

She shook her head. "No, you do not."

She herself wasn't sure what Jes wanted to talk about but she was curious enough now to want to find out.

Sighing, Roan nodded his head, allowing her to exit the room. She gave him a quick kiss on the cheek and rushed down the hall.

Her heart felt like it would burst from anticipation when she knocked on Jes's door. She hadn't once dared to look inside the room in the months she had been there. It was an almost unspoken rule in the house that no one went in there. She was even sure Etta was only allowed in Jes's study but not his room. Moros might have been the only soul besides Jes to have stepped foot in there in at least fifty years.

Jes's door opened quietly and he pulled her inside. She stumbled through the doorway and took in the room. It felt lighter than she'd thought it would have. In the corner sat a large bed with a wooden headboard, as if Jes had taken the trunk of a tree and placed it behind his mattress. On the wall adjacent to the bed was a large fireplace with a roaring fire burning.

Looking around, Orah admired how cozy the space felt, unlike the way Jes presented himself.

Clearing his throat, she turned to find Jes sitting on an armchair to the right of her. Tilting his head, he pointed to the matching armchair across from him.

She stared at him for a moment then placed her hand on her hip. "Why did you pull me out of bed? So we can sit in your giant armchairs and chat?"

He shook his head but said nothing. Again, he tilted his head toward the armchair. Obviously unwilling to speak until she sat.

Sighing, she walked over to the chair and sunk down.

He glanced around his bedroom for a moment then sighed. "What happened at Aeron's palace?"

"What?"

He leaned forward, placing his hands on his knees, and narrowing his eyes. "You heard what I asked. What happened at Aeron's palace?"

Trying to deflect his question she shrugged. "Which one?"

The air in the room shifted and she could almost taste his irritation. "Stop playing games, Orah."

Averting her eyes, she looked around his room. A small chest on the table next to his bed grabbed her attention and she looked back at him. "That chest isn't yours. It's Moros'."

Pausing, he stared at her. "How in the Fates did you know that?"

She wasn't sure how she knew but the chest didn't feel like Jes. Something about it was cold—like winter. "Intuition."

Jes shook his head and stood. "Orah, I'm only going to ask this once, because I respect you. Because I don't even want to ask this, but I have a duty to Roan. Are you here to harm him?"

She blinked back her shock while she watched him cross the room.

How *dare* he? After all, they had been through. All that they both had shared. After all this time he still thought she was a threat? He still thought she was there to bait and betray Roan?

Laughing in disbelief, she shook her head. "I can't believe you."

Approaching the chest, he picked it up softly and then returned to his chair. She kept her eyes on him while he opened the chest slowly and pulled out something she couldn't see behind the chest lid. With a sigh, he held it up. In his hand was a beautiful ice sculpture that was somehow not melting from the heat of his hand. But it wasn't just any sculpture, it was a sculpture of a winged man embracing another man. It was Jes holding Moros.

"Moros gave this to me twenty-five years ago. He made it and warded it to never melt." Jes looked up from the sculpture and narrowed his eyes at Orah. "I've only ever known two people other in my life with *intuition* like yours. One is the man you've been sleeping next to for the last week, and the other is his father." Setting the sculpture down he kept his eyes on her. "So please forgive me if I'm still feeling a bit concerned about you. Tell me what happened at Aeron's palace."

Orah stared at the ice sculpture, shaking her head. "Nothing happened, Jesiel. I saw my chateau, but when I stepped through the portal to go back it felt as though it slipped right through my fingers."

"I don't believe you," Jes replied.

Jumping back shocked, her eyes locked with his. "You weren't even in the room."

"Yes, but you seem to forget that uncomfortable talent Roan says I have I can feel you're not telling the truth. Not all of it at least."

The air in the room felt thick, making breathing difficult while they stared at each other. She didn't know how to keep deflecting his questions. She honestly didn't know what the answer to his question was supposed to be. She wasn't sure what had happened in the portal. She could feel the chateau at her fingertips. She could see it clearly but then all she could think about was Roan and then there he was, standing just beyond the doorway with tears running down his face. She had to get to him. She had to tell him she was okay.

Shaking off her thoughts she let out a sigh. "Jes, the portal didn't work. I don't know why, but it didn't. One moment the chateau was there the next I could see Roan in the doorway. Then I was moving towards him instead."

Shaking his head, Jes rubbed his jaw. "What happened to not letting things get messy?"

Her eyes glanced at the floor and she swallowed. Jes wasn't wrong, she had let lines cross between her and Roan. "I honestly don't know," she admitted.

His chair groaned and she looked up to see him slowly stand. "I'm not going to judge you for allowing yourself to enjoy his company. The Fates know he's been too lonely for too long, but I am worried about what this distraction means for him."

Rolling her eyes, she sighed. "There you go with the distraction nonsense again. I'm not a distraction."

"You seem to think that, but what happens in a few days when his father shows up and grabs you? Do you think he'll be able to focus on the challenge that's only a month away? Do you think he'll be able to let himself use all of his power to ensure our world doesn't get a King like Marek?" His eyes narrowed and a heavy tension settled between them. "You and I both know the answer to those questions. He will rip this world apart to get you back. He will turn himself into the very thing he's avoided becoming."

She couldn't bring herself to respond. She knew he wasn't wrong. She had become Roan's weakness and Marek had taken it upon himself to tell their Father about her. Tears lined her eyes and she spoke in a whisper. "I'll go back, I will. If we find a way to go I will."

Shaking his head, Jes stared into his fireplace. "I don't think you can guarantee that Orah."

The tension in the room lessened and they sat in silence staring at the hypnotizing flames. At some point, he returned to his chair and leaned back, twirling the ice sculpture in his hands.

Watching him, she sighed. "I saw Moros a few times this week."

Sitting straighter he set the sculpture down. "And?"

"And he had a large smile on his face each time. I hope you two have been enjoying yourselves."

A shy smile formed at the corner of his mouth and he looked back at his sculpture.

"We've been here the whole time whenever the house has been empty. It's been nice to have so many days in a row together."

She nodded then turned, observing the room. She wasn't sure how she hadn't noticed before, but she could now see little remnants of Moros everywhere. A small painting of snow-covered woods with a large palace in the distance hung on the wall above his bed. Dark gray towels hung in the bathroom and a pine mingled with firewood scent seemed to linger in the air. The chest sitting on the table in front of them. The thick jacket hanging on the back of the door. Small little bits of the man Jes loved scattered lovingly around the room.

Finally standing, Orah looked at Jes once more. "I promise I'm not here to harm him. I didn't come here intentionally. I didn't mean to feel what I feel for him. I was only trying to restart my life, but I fell into his."

She turned away, not allowing Jes to respond while she walked out of the room. Her heart hurt from the accusations he'd thrown at her, but she understood. Jesiel would do anything to protect those he loved. She couldn't fault him for that.

The day ticked by slowly while they waited for Amada's arrival. Orah laid against the chair in the library, staring at the pages of the book she'd been trying to read for over an hour when a loud knock on the door startled her.

Looking around the room, she watched Jes rush out in a flash.

She had come into the library first but slowly everyone followed. Roan sat on the chair next to her and nodded his head. Somehow, he knew who was at the door—Amada.

They both watched the doorway until Jes walked back in with a beautiful woman following behind him.

She looked so much like Moros but instead of his dark hair, hers was blonde like Lahana's. Her skin was the same color as Roan and his siblings, and her eyes were the same blue as Marek's. She was taller than Orah had expected and she carried herself with a level of grace Orah had never witnessed in someone before.

Jes moved to stand behind Roan and Amada bowed her head. "Nephew."

Orah held her breath, as Roan stood then held out his hands. "Auntie," he said with a smile.

They pulled each other into an embrace and Lahana rushed from where she sat next to Fawn to join them. Orah watched the familial reunion and smiled to herself.

Pulling away from their embrace, Amada's eyes turned to Orah. "This is your guest."

Orah blinked then stood, bowing her head. "My name is Orah."

A bright smile scrunched up the corners of Amada's eyes while she nodded. "It's nice to meet you Orah. Moros mentioned Roan has had a guest in the last few months. I can see why he has chosen to invite you into his home."

Roan cleared his throat and the two women looked over to him gesturing to one of the chairs across from him. Amada nodded at the request and they all sat quietly. Her eyes glanced over to Jes and Orah couldn't help but notice how still he'd gone. She wondered briefly if Amada knew about her son's lover.

Amada's soft expression became serious. "You want to know more about portals. Something tells me Orah is the reason why."

"I'm not from here." Orah sighed.

Amada nodded. "I assumed as much."

"How did you know?"

She grinned. "Goddess of Wisdom."

Orah's cheeks warmed from her embarrassment and she looked over to Roan, finding him on the edge of his seat, staring at his aunt. "I know you said world traveling magic has been lost and you believe it used to be connected to our portals. We've tried a few to get Orah home but none have worked. Do you have any answers or knowledge of any other portals that could get her back to her world?"

Amada shook her head sadly. "I'm sorry, Roan. What I've already told you is where my knowledge ends. I may be the Goddess of Wisdom, but I don't know everything."

Roan let out a defeated sigh while sinking against the back of his chair. Holding up her hand, Amada sat straighter. "But I didn't come all this way to disappoint you. I found several mentions of portals, but they were followed by histories of the Fates and Kings. I wanted to tell you in person that from what I can gather the only two places you could get your answers are from your Father or the Fates."

Lahana's gasp was the only sound in the large room while they all stared at the Goddess of Wisdom.

Roan shook his head. "No, that can't be right. You know I can't go to him. He knows about Orah, if he finds out she's not from this world…" He threw an alarmed look at Orah then leaned against his knees, placing his face in his hands. "I don't want to imagine what he'll do to her."

Orah kept her eyes on Roan, trying to ignore the painful pulse in her chest. She knew—somehow she knew—the pain she felt wasn't her own.

Suddenly Jes stepped out from behind Roan's chair, clearing his throat. "Then we need to go to the Fates. It's the only other option."

Shaking his head, Roan straightened, and his eyes found Orah's. "What if they refuse our request?"

Amada answered, while shaking her head. "I don't think they will. Something has shifted in the air and I know they can feel it. It's been building for months. How long has Orah been here?"

Orah's eyes pulled from Roan's and she stared at Amada. She felt uneasy processing what the Goddess had said. There wasn't a possibility she had caused such a disturbance that the Fates would know about her. Was there?

Trying to calm her unease she cleared her throat. "I've been here for three months."

"Three months. It's been almost three months to the day since the air changed. Orah, I think the Fates will be very eager to meet you," Amada replied.

Roan turned to Jes. "Jes, take the portal from Aeron's palace and go to Tiid. You won't be able to get past the gates but let them know the God of Nyte and his guest have requested an audience with Eon. For tomorrow."

Jes gasped. "Tomorrow? Are you sure?"

Roan stood. "I have two days until my birthday. Marek has all but promised he and Father will be here within days after that. We need an answer, and we need to get Orah home."

Nodding, Jes looked over at Orah nervously before turning to walk out of the room. Orah sat, frozen in her seat, listening to the sound of the front door opening. Turning her head, she watched out of the library windows while Jes launched himself into the sky and flew toward Aeron's palace.

She didn't know what to think. She didn't know what she felt. Her frozen state didn't seem to catch anyone else's attention in the room as a heavy silence fell over everyone.

Pulling her eyes from the window, Orah found Amada still staring at her and Roan with an odd smile on her face. Her eyes caught Orah's and she shook her head, as though embarrassed she'd be caught staring.

"I hope my arriving so early isn't a problem. My room in the city center won't be ready until tomorrow. Would you allow me to stay for one night?" Amada asked, clearing her throat.

Roan smiled at his aunt. "Of course. Let's go find Ms. Perri and get a room ready. Honestly, she probably has one ready as a precaution with the party so soon."

Laughing, Amada grabbed hold of the arm Roan offered her and they walked side-by-side out of the room.

Leaning against her chair Orah watched them walk out of the room. She still felt frozen and unsteady. Looking back at Lahana she shook her head. "The Fates?"

Lahana let out a quiet sigh. "I didn't think it would go this far."

Orah sat unmoving in her chair staring out the large library windows until Roan. Etta had in fact readied a few guest rooms on the off chance that they would be needed. That hadn't surprised Orah considering how well-prepared Etta was.

Standing in front of her, Roan gestured to her chair. A silent request to sit with her.

Nodding her head, Orah stood while Roan sat where she'd just been, and she silently climbed onto his lap. She curled herself up while his arms wrapped around hers. Breathing his scent in the world disappeared as they all sat in silence waiting for Jes to return.

Roan's hand lazily ran along Orah's arm when Jes finally stepped through the library doors, looking a bit disgruntled. "We didn't think about how I would be getting *back* from Tiid."

Stifling her laugh, Orah straightened on Roan's lap, watching Jes stomp across the floor then sinking down into the chair beside Lahana. "I had to fly to Veturs and convince Moros to let me use his palace portal."

Orah bit her lip and glanced at him. He shook his head sternly in response. The look was enough to make Orah's toes curl from fear. She was sure Jes had to be *very* convincing to get Moros to help out.

Roan leaned forward, tightening his arms around Orah's waist. "I definitely didn't think that through. Sorry. Did you get an answer?"

Jes nodded his head. "Yes, surprisingly. The guards at the gate had me wait and in just a few minutes they returned with an answer from Eon. They agreed to the meeting. Tomorrow afternoon. They asked that you fly in and over the gates right to Tyme."

"Tyme?" Orah asked.

"Yes, that's the main city in Tiid. Tyme is the only place visitors are allowed to go. I'm surprised they want us to fly in, but I'll follow whatever instructions we've been given," Roan replied.

Sighing, Lahana sank into her chair. "I hope that this is the right choice."

Roan pulled Orah against him. "It's better than going to Father."

Tapping her arm slightly, he moved to stand and Orah slid off his lap. Grabbing her hand, he pulled her silently out of the library while Lahana and Jes followed close behind them.

The group solemnly parted ways with Jes at the bottom of the stairs and continued their walk upwards. Not one of them had the desire to speak. Not one of them knew what to say. All Orah knew was none of them were going to sleep well that night.

Chapter 34

Orah tossed in bed, unable to shake off the nervousness that was in Jes's voice when he'd relayed his message in the library. Frustratedly, she threw off the comforter and stared up at the black canopy. Her hands lightly brushed the now empty spot where Roan had been when she'd first fallen asleep—or tried to sleep.

Turning over toward the balcony, she sighed when she spotted him looking out at the garden. Sliding off the bed, she walked toward him. The crisp autumn air brushed her skin as she walked up behind him. "Can't sleep?"

He jumped at the sound of her voice. "I've never been to Tiid. Definitely never been to Tyme and I've never requested an audience with Eon. Honestly, I half expected Jes to come back with a no. I guess I'm feeling a bit nervous."

Motioning for her to come over, she rushed into his open arms. He pulled her against him while she leaned back against his chest and looked out over the garden. The sun was barely rising, and the garden door glowed in the background. His chin rested against the top of her head and they stood there watching the sky brighten slowly.

Staring at the garden door her chest felt tight and uneasy. Her voice shook while she forced herself to ask what was on her mind. "Do you think I'll be leaving today?"

His chin slowly moved left to right on top of her head. "No, I don't. I think we might get some answers, but the Fates are known for being obscure."

She couldn't stop the relief she felt from his response. She knew something needed to happen before his Father came, but she didn't feel ready for what that would entail.

Staring back at the garden, she pulled his arms up and kissed his hands. His fingers flexed from the contact and he let out a sad sigh. "I don't know if we've had enough time, love."

Her stomach flipped at the pet name and she squeezed his hands. Choking back her emotions, she shook her head. "You promised to find me, remember?"

His responding chuckle rumbled against her back and he tightened his hold on her. "I did. Didn't I?"

She smiled. "Yes, and even if I'm old and wrinkled."

His chest shook against her back harder than before while he laughed. Kissing the top of her head, she felt his smile tousle her hair. "I'll have you as you are now, or as you are in thirty years."

Blinking back her tears, she kept her eyes on the garden door. Her body hummed the longer she stared at it, trying to avoid the inevitable truth neither she nor Roan wanted to admit. Blinking, she stared at the door unsure if what she was seeing was real. The door appeared to be glowing as though it were calling out to her to pay attention.

She shook her head and shifted to face Roan. Placing her hand on his face she caressed his lips. "Whatever we learn today. Whatever happens, we'll be okay. You'll be okay. If I do get back, you have to promise me you won't throw the challenge."

Tensing he pulled her hand away. "You can't make me promise that Orah."

"Roan. Your world cannot have Marek as a king. We both know that. They need *you*."

Shaking his head, he pushed away from her. "You have no idea what you're talking about. I'm dangerous Orah. I have a temper. I could destroy an entire city if I wanted to. I could snap my fingers and this entire house could vanish."

"But you know that. You're not hiding it. You're not pretending you don't have the power. You know you wouldn't do that," she said, approaching him slowly.

Averting his eyes, he turned his head. "I could have killed people the day my mother died."

"But you didn't. Despite what the rumors are you and I both know it was you who warned those people to get out of their homes. Not your father."

"You believe I'm better than I actually am."

"You just believe too little of yourself." she took his hands gently and pulled him back toward her.

Pulling her hands to his lips he smiled against them. "Orah, I will do my best to win the challenge. I will do my best to control my temper. If I win then I will also do my best to be a good King."

She stared into his silvery-blue eyes and considered his words. He hadn't promised anything, but she thought perhaps he genuinely couldn't. Perhaps there was a chance Marek would beat him fairly.

Shrugging, she smiled at him. "I guess I'll accept that."

He chuckled. His eyes moved upward toward the sky and he turned back into his room. "It's a long flight and we'll need to take a break in between. We should get dressed and head out."

She followed him into the closet where he silently turned his back while looking for something to wear. Glancing at him briefly, she walked through the adjoining door to her own closet. Something felt off, as though he needed time alone. She rummaged through her closet for a moment, picking out her outfit.

Walking out of her closet, she grabbed the jacket she'd purchased from a vendor earlier that week with Lahana and walked out her bedroom door.

The foyer was empty when she reached the bottom of the stairs. Turning, she looked at the ballroom doors and smiled. Etta had been in there every day readying the room. The party was in two days and Orah was sure Etta was going to surprise them all.

Sighing, she turned and walked toward the kitchen. To her surprise she found the room also empty. Shrugging, she grabbed a muffin from the counter, then headed back out the door. She was almost to the side door when Jes's bedroom opened.

"Good morning," she said.

Nodding, he sprinted into the kitchen and came back with his own muffin and some fruit.

Side by side they walked out to the stables. Orah felt fidgety and irritated that he was also acting odd, just like Roan. Feeling fed up, she turned to him.

"Why are you and Roan being weird this morning?"

"Roan's acting weird?" Jes asked, seemingly surprised.

"Yes, and you are too. Is there something neither of you are telling me? Should I be concerned with where we're going?"

"Roan hasn't told you?" Jes asked.

Her heart raced in response and she glanced over at the side door. "Told me what?"

With a sigh, Jes motioned for her to keep walking. "The Fates are where our dead go. Well, they can go to Shadus or to the Fates."

Gasping, she looked up at him, remembering what she had seen in Shadus with Aeron and the souls disappearing with the bright light. "Aeron sends them to the Fates?"

Shaking his head, he looked toward the stables. "Not exactly. I think it's more so of what or who the person was in their life. When they cross the river and pass through the portal into Shadus they're either sent to the depths or up to the Fates. The reason why we can only go to Tyme as visitors is because the dead live beyond the city."

"What's the river? There was no river at the top of the mountain."

"I'm not sure. It's mostly myth and legend really. You only know when you die, but essentially all the dead meet the ferryman at the river with their coin. Handing their coin to the ferryman is how their souls cross through the portal into Shadus. It's said that the journey to the portal is a journey on a barge across a river."

Her eyes widened while she listened to his explanation. "We have myths about that in my world. It's called the river Styx. The Ferryman guides the boat to the Underworld and a God of Death called Hades." Shaking her head, she laughed. "So much of what I was taught seems to pull straight from your world."

Jes shrugged. "We told you we can control elements of the other worlds. Or at least the Governing Gods and King can. Not sure how any of it works but it would make sense if elements of our history have made it to other worlds."

Orah let out a breath of disbelief as they approached the stables. Kai came out with a smile, leading an already saddled Nacht. "I can grab Tume if you'd like. I just figured with how long of a flight it is that you might prefer to just take one."

"Just Nacht is fine, Kai." Jumping, Orah turned around to find Roan standing directly behind her. Her eyebrows crumbled while she stared at him. She had no idea how he had approached her so quietly.

Kai smiled, nodding his head, and walked back into the stable.

"I can ride Tume for that long you know." She stared at Roan, crossing her arms.

"I know. I just like how close we sit when we ride together." His wink pulled a scoff from Jes. Orah let out an annoyed groan. There was no doubt in her mind he was going to make jokes like that for their entire journey.

Shaking her head, she approached Nacht. Usually, the Pegasus was more weary around her than Tume was but he huffed at her in approval. Waving her hand, a small step of dirt rose from the ground and she quickly mounted the saddle. Roan followed closed behind and they all took one final look at the manor before shooting up to the sky.

Wrapping her jacket around herself, she shivered. It was much colder in the clouds now the summer heat was quickly cooling. Roan's arms wrapped around her, pulling her against him. "Get as close as you want, love. I'll keep you warm." His whisper against her neck only made her shiver harder. Digging her fingers into his arms, she did her best to avoid looking up at him.

The clouds were low, but she could still see Roan's Region below them as they flew. The green trees and grass were changing color with the season. To her surprise, the dark mountains hadn't changed, but the bright purples, blues, and dark black contrasting against the yellows, reds, and oranges of autumn was breathtaking.

Slowly her shivering stopped, likely from Roan's warmth against her back. Leaning against Roan she sighed, marveling at his world.

They flew for about two hours before taking a break. The sun had risen fully and from what Roan had told her, they were on the edge of his Region by the border of Moros's Region.

Glancing a look at Jes, she winked at him before turning back to her lunch in front of her.

Kai and Clarah had made sure to pack Nacht's saddle bag and they all were leaning against yellowed trees eating their fruit and jerky.

Sighing contently, Orah breathed in the smell of the fruit in her hand. She hadn't asked what it was called but its taste reminded her of a blend of pear and peach from back home. She still hadn't gotten used to how flavorful the food was in the Land of Gods. Everything tasted ten times better than in her world. She considered, once again, whether or not she would be able to leave just for the food alone.

Poking her side softly, Roan smiled at her. "Something on your mind?"

"Sensing my emotions?" she asked.

Jes stopped eating his jerky midbite and stared at her. "What did you just ask him?"

With a shrug she stood. "Roan told me he can sense people's emotions. Or more so he let it slip and I called him out on it."

Jes glared at Roan and Orah stumbled back in shock when the piece of jerky he had been eating smacked into Roan's face. "Why would you tell anyone that?" Jes almost yelled.

With a look of disgust, Roan wiped his face where the jerky landed. "I can share whatever I like with whomever I like, Jes."

Glaring at each other for a moment, Jes finally cracked and let out a laugh. "After keeping a secret for decades, it takes one mortal woman for you to give it up." With a sigh, he looked over at Orah. "At least now you know why he teases you so incessantly."

Grinning, Roan stood and tossed the half-eaten jerky into Jes's lap. "If you throw your food at my face again, I'll beat your ass." Winking he walked over to Nacht, placing the remnants from their small meal back in the saddle bag.

Orah choked back her laugh at the glare Jes gave her while she passed him, following Roan. She and Roan settled themselves into the saddle watching Jes grumble and pull himself up off the ground.

Once they were settled, they launched back up to the sky. Quickly the brisk fall air turned cold and frigid. Orah watched the landscape below change from autumn colors to whisps of whites and silvers.

"Veturs—Moros's Region," Roan whispered into her ear.

"Why is it so much colder here? Is it winter all year long?" Orah asked, trying to avoid her head turning toward Jes.

"No, it's just a lot colder in the winter. It might feel bitterly cold right now but once winter has fully settled on the land, you'll know."

Shivering, she hugged herself tightly and nestled against Roan. Letting go of the reins he wrapped both of his arms around her.

"You shouldn't let go," she said through chattering teeth.

"Nacht knows what he's doing. You're shivering so hard I'm genuinely worried you might fall off."

Nodding her head, she pushed against him further, trying to steal some of his heat. She tried to think of warm thoughts. The sun. Summer days on the beach. Outdoor swimming pools and afternoons spent with friends.

Slowly her shivering stopped, and her body warmed.

"Fates." Roan's arms tightened around her. "Orah, you're warm."

Twisting to look back at him she smiled. "I just thought warm thoughts. That's all."

"Well, it worked. Now I'm warm." He kissed her forehead, brushing her cheek with his hand. "Thank you."

Grinning wide, she twisted back and watched while they flew over Veturs. Despite the cold, the landscape was magnificent. Snowcapped trees scattered the mountains they flew over. Mountains shining with a silver hue, just as Roan had told her. Gliding through the low winter clouds, a glittering city came into view. Orah gasped at the sight. Instinctively, her head snapped to Jes.

Moros's city appeared as though it were made of pure ice. His palace, a towering ice sculpture on the hill glistened in the sun. His city scattered out beneath the palace. Each building shining like glass against the mountain, were all topped with a layer of snow.

"It looks magical," Orah whispered, unable to take her eyes off the crystal palace.

"It really is. Many assume Kall would be bleak and unwelcoming, but you probably won't find warmer or more cozy homes in the Region." Roan tightened his hold on her as if he were now trying to soak up her own warmth.

Sneaking a glance at Jes, Orah smiled sadly. His eyes were locked onto the ice palace, while his hands balled into tight fists. A small tug of hope pulled at her and she wondered if he would ever be able to tell Roan about his love.

"What are you thinking about?" Roan's voice startled her.

"Nothing," she replied quickly.

"I could feel sadness. Are you okay?"

Panic gripped her and she muddled through her mind trying to come up with an answer. She didn't want to lie, but she also couldn't reveal Jes's secret. "I just—I thought about how you said you and Moros used to trust each other more than you do now. Made me sad you guys don't have that anymore."

It wasn't a complete lie. She believed whatever happened between the cousins was the reason why Jes kept things so hidden.

Staring down at her, Roan's eyebrow briefly raised then he turned to look at the palace as they flew overhead. "Some things are meant to happen. Mine and his relationship changing was one of them."

Her stomach tightened with a feeling of disgust. Shaking her head, she breathed out, trying to shake it off then she glanced at Jes again.

He was staring at her and Roan now and she couldn't help but wonder what he could and couldn't hear up in the wind and clouds. Trying to change the subject, she lightly caressed her hand over Roan's arm around her.

"I have a question."

She didn't have to look up at him to hear the smile accompanying his response. "I'm happy to oblige."

"It's a bit morbid." Nerves flipped in her stomach while she considered what she was about to ask. The closer they got to Tiid the more she couldn't stop thinking about what Jes had said and her knowledge of what had happened to Roan's mother.

"I'll answer as truthfully as I can," Roan replied stiffly.

"I've been thinking about what you said happened to your mother and how it changed your father." His arms dropped from around her waist and his hands gripped the reins again. "I don't understand why he's held onto it for so long. I know it was an accident. Hell, I've obviously struggled with my mother's death and my part in it all but how did it instantly make him shift to who he is now?"

Resting his head against hers, Roan let out a breath. "I understand what you mean. My Father is over one thousand years old. Sixty years since her death probably feels like only a handful of years to him. But he didn't just kill his wife. He killed his fate bound."

"His what?"

"Fate bound." Straightening, he let go of the reins and wrapped his arms around her again. "It's said to be rare, but I don't think it is. Fate bound is a kind of love where you're connected to your love at an almost cellular level. It's said the Fates bless the love or marriage and the two souls remain connected. There are many stories and legends about how a fate bound can turn an evil man good, how a fate bound will know when their love has died, and even that only two equal in power and might can be fate bound."

Rubbing her arm softly, he kissed the top of her head again. "Because many believe it's rare, many stories have been created about epic loves and the power of fate's binding. Some I'm not sure of but some I believe. I think when he accidentally killed her, the piece of his soul that was connected to hers was severed and he lost her goodness. That thread of balance she held between them snapped and his tether to any kind of good snapped with it. I don't think it's something anyone could come back from."

Her heart ached and she stared down at the hand caressing her arm. "Why don't you think it's rare?"

"I've seen too many great loves to think it's rare. Etta and Kai. Yohan and his wife. Fates, even Lahana and Fawn."

Gasping, she looked up at him. "Lahana and Fawn?"

A slight grin tilted the corners of his lips up and he nodded. "They have to figure it out themselves but there's something there. I can feel it."

Shaking her head, she stared at him. "How do they *figure* it out?"

His arm tightened around her and that look of intention flashed in his eyes. "It depends on the couple. For some, it's a moment they experience together that they've never had with another. For others, they know immediately. Then there's the more common experience of the binding pulling into place the first time they lay with one another."

She was sure she could hear her heart almost beat out of her chest while they stared at each other. Gulping, she looked away quickly. "Oh. But Lahana and Fawn have definitely…" Her cheeks warmed and she shook her head. "We shouldn't be talking about your sister like this."

He shrugged behind her and chuckled. "I'm not sure. Maybe they already know and they're keeping it private. It's not like those around the couple instantly know. Once the couple announces it the Fates will usually confirm with some fancy show of confirmation."

"What kind of show?"

"Again, that depends on the couple. For Lahana? I wouldn't be surprised if it started raining wildflowers."

Sighing, she leaned back against him and watched as they flew over large snow tipped mountains. Jes soared ahead then circled back a moment later. "I can see Tiid. We're almost there."

Roan tensed behind her and she straightened. Leaning forward, she tried to make out any kind of sign of the island. All around were clouds and she couldn't see anything below. Letting out a frustrated sigh she went to lean back against Roan when a small glint of gold caught her eye.

Nacht seemed to propel forward and the gold drew closer. Orah stared in wonder at the island that now took her breath away.

She'd expected an island in the ocean but Tiid—Tiid floated in the clouds.

Large golden gates and an accompanying fence lined the front half of the island. Beyond the gates, from what she could see, were only clouds.

Nacht ascended higher into the sky to avoid the gates and Jes followed close behind.

Orah's body hummed excitedly the closer they drew. She could feel her power pulsing inside of her while they flew over. She leaned further in the saddle trying desperately to see through the clouds.

"You're going to fall to your death if you don't sit back." Jumping, she looked back at Roan. His jaw was clenched, and she hadn't noticed how tightly his arm was wrapped around her waist. Leaning back against him, she grabbed onto his arm and squeezed it softly.

He shook from the touch as though she had just pulled him from his own trance with what was below them. "Sorry," he whispered against her ear.

Shivering at the soft tickle, she snuggled closer to him, straining her neck to try and see anything beyond the clouds.

"You're not going to see anything. The Fates have powerful magic. These clouds aren't normal clouds. They're meant to conceal the island."

Letting out a frustrated noise, she willed the island to come into view. She threw all of her focus out silently begging her powers to assist her.

Gasping, she thought she had actually done it when Roan chuckled behind her. "And that is Tyme, the only part of this island the Fates allow to be seen."

Sitting up again she focused on the city coming into view. It appeared angelic. Bright white buildings were everywhere with large rooftops of solid gold.

The clouds appeared to slowly dissipate as if acting like a stage curtain revealing the production for the first time.

Orah's body felt electric while she stared below her. Something about this city felt familiar and her power hummed in response.

Looking back at them, Jes descended and Nacht followed closely behind. Orah couldn't seem to catch her breath while they flew lower to the ground. They flew right over the rooftops and she couldn't hold back her gasp.

The buildings were even more magnificent up close. She didn't recognize the material but something about them felt as though actual angels had carved them.

A large building came into view and she looked up at Roan. "Is that where we're headed?"

Nodding his head, he kept his eyes focused on the building. "Yes. That's Eon's palace. The Palace of Fate. I've only seen drawings of it in textbooks. It's older than our entire world."

Orah stared at the building in disbelief. It was white but not quite as brilliantly white as the other buildings they flew past. Something about the slight difference in color told her what Roan had said was true.

She gulped back her nerves. She was about to step foot in a building likely older than both Roan's and her world combined.

Slowly, Jes banked slightly to the left then descended onto the grass of a large lawn in front of the palace. Orah looked up as Nacht settled in the grass and watched Two hooded figures in white cloaks approach.

"Roan Durel, Jesiel Keita, Orah Clark, welcome to Tyme." The taller of the two lifted their head.

Orah blinked, the person she now stared at was the most beautiful person she had ever seen. They didn't look either female or male but everything about them was beautiful. Their bright blue eyes softened while they made eye contact then bowed their head again. "Eon is expecting you."

Roan let out a grunt and slid off the saddle then quickly helped Orah down. Holding his hand out for hers, they quietly followed their guides inside.

Orah marveled while they walked. The air in Tyme felt overwhelming, as though she were breathing fresh air for the first time in her life. Her head whipped back and forth while she tried to desperately take in her surroundings as they walked up a long staircase leading to the palace doors.

She could hear music, laughter, and breathed in the taunting smells of fresh food being cooked beyond in the city. It felt like Paris when she'd visit with Julian. But somehow it felt lighter and more serene.

Sighing, she looked up at Roan, but he didn't seem to notice. He was holding her hand tightly and his jaw was clenched again. Orah glanced at Jes worried but he shook his head, discouraging her from saying anything.

Their guides stopped as the group reached the palace doors and watched them slowly pull open.

The palace beyond the doors was beautiful, reminding Orah of ancient ruins that had open courtyards. Walking in she noticed there was no roof in the main area. A small fountain sat in the middle of the room and the bubbling sounds of the water echoed back against the white marbled walls.

More hooded figures in white cloaks bustled about the palace. All kept their heads down, but a few paused and quickly glanced at the visitors—at Orah.

Marveling at the beauty, Orah didn't notice when they approached another set of doors. Tall golden doors with engravings of planets, the sun, the moon, and around the edges were engraved markings of ivy. Orah stared at the doors and her power hummed. They felt... familiar.

Roan let go of her hand, finally speaking. "Jes. The *doors*."

Lost in her own admiration she looked over. Jes's jaw was now also tight while he looked at her then the doors.

Sighing, she shrugged. "You two are always too serious. Just admire the beauty of them."

The beautiful golden doors pulled open and Orah was hit with a blast of warm welcoming air. Neither Roan nor Jes appeared to notice the quick shift in temperature. Orah's body felt light and the world melted away when she stepped foot into the room.

Standing in the middle of the room was a tall figure. Their back was turned but she could see they weren't wearing a hood. Their long white hair cascaded down their slender back, almost blending in with the white robes they wore.

Orah's feet pulled her towards the unknown person without a care until Roan's hand gripped her arm, pulling her back.

Annoyed, she twisted back to snap at him but stopped when they made eye contact. Slowly he shook his head and pointed to the spot beside him. Something in how serious he stared at her brought her back to her senses and she shuffled to where he'd asked.

The white-haired figure turned to face the group and Orah held back her gasp. If she had thought the person on the lawn was beautiful, she had been very wrong. The person now in front of her was beauty personified. Their white hair glowed against their tanned skin. Their eyes, shocking pale purple, seemed to swirl as though they were alive and separate from their body.

Smiling, they cocked their head to the side and looked amongst the small group. Orah's skin chilled and she felt exposed when their eyes landed on her, lingering for a while.

To her shock, Roan lowered to a bow next to her, grabbing her pant leg to pull her down with him. Without questioning she followed his lead and glanced to find Jes doing the same. Averting her eyes, she focused on the floor until Roan tapped her again to stand.

"Roan Cael Durel. I have to say I was pleasantly surprised when your Beskermer arrived last night requesting an audience." Their voice was light and alluring but held a power behind it that Orah could feel resonating deep inside of her.

Clearing his throat, Roan stepped forward, bowing his head again. "Eon. Thank you for agreeing to meet me so suddenly. I know it's not the usual procedure for a God to demand the Fate's time so abruptly."

Eon smiled at Roan, but their eyes glanced at Orah. "Orah. Come here please."

She stared at the Fate in front of her. For some reason she couldn't question how they knew her name but their voice, despite the power radiating from it, felt welcoming. Stepping forward, she walked past Roan, narrowly avoiding his arm that flung out to hold her back. When she was an arm's length away from Eon she looked up.

From where she had been standing, she hadn't realized just how tall the Fate was. At least close to Jes's height and she had to strain her neck to meet their eyes. Stopping herself from jumping, she kept eye contact as their hand shot out and grabbed her chin.

The Fate tilted her head left to right, as if inspecting her. "Not of this world but made from this world." Dropping her chin, Eon looked back over at Roan then back at Orah. "You two have questions."

Stepping back, Orah cleared her throat. She wasn't sure what to make of what the Fate had just said. She glanced back at Roan and he rushed toward her, grabbing her hand and then addressed the Fate. "It appears you already know Orah isn't from here. We came to ask if you know how to get her back? How to open a portal back to her world?"

Eon stared at Orah again and her power hummed in response. Something about the Fate felt familiar, but not a recent feeling. A feeling as though she had somehow always known this Fate or somehow had felt them before.

"Only the King's power has the key to unlock the door you're looking for." Eon pulled their eyes from Orah's, focusing once more on Roan. "The key lies with the King's power."

Tightening his grip on Orah's hand, Roan cleared his throat. "I'm not sure what that means. I can't take Orah to my Father. He knows—" He glanced at Orah then back at Eon. "He knows who she is to me."

A smile formed across Eon's lips. "Roan Durel—the only answer I have for you is what I've said. The key lies with the King's power. You may do what you'd like with that information."

"Eon, I don't know what that means. How can I help her if I don't know where to start?" Roan replied.

A kind look flashed across Eon's eyes and they smiled. "You have everything you need."

Orah's body suddenly warmed as though she were about to catch on fire. Looking at Roan she panicked for a moment, scared her power was unleashing when she realized the anger wasn't from her. She'd spent three months with Roan and had picked up when he was masking his temper pretty well, but his mask was slipping. Staring at Eon, Roan's hands flexed open and shut. A light in the room flashed off and on, so quickly Orah wasn't sure if anyone else noticed.

Taking a deep breath, Roan relaxed his hands and Orah's body cooled as rapidly as it had heated. Unsure of what to make of it she shook her head trying to steady her own breathing.

Roan bowed once more. "Thank you for your time today. I know you are very busy, and this was an abrupt meeting." Turning to walk out of the door he paused and stared out of the large windows looking out towards the city. He opened his mouth as if to speak when Eon interrupted.

"Roan, you know I cannot give you the full answer to the question you are about to ask." Eon approached Roan and placed their hand on his shoulder. "But I can tell you Leora Durel is whole and she finds no fault in you."

The room tilted and Orah felt as though the air had been knocked from her lungs while she listened to Eon speak.

Leora.

She felt unsteady on her feet while she tried to process what had been said. Now understanding why Roan and his siblings had looked at her so stunned when she'd first introduced herself. Chills ran down her spine and she looked over at Jes who appeared as though he wasn't breathing. Catching her gaze, he nodded his head before glancing at Roan.

Roan's back was still turned but his shoulders moved up and down. Orah's stomach tightened and a cold wave of grief ran through her.

Slowly, Roan turned to face Eon. Orah bit her lip, trying not to react to the tears now lining Roan's eyes. "Aeron said he tried to stop her."

Nodding, Eon tightened their grip on Roan's shoulder. "Your uncle's good intentions did not prevent her from being whole."

Silence fell over the room. Roan's eyes met Orah's and a sad smile appeared on his face.

"Leora, Orah, light." Two tears fell from his eyes and he blinked, pulling his gaze from hers.

Jes cleared his throat across the room. "I'm sure Eon must be busy, and we should head back. You've got a large celebration in your honor coming up, Roan."

Nodding, Roan stepped away from Eon and toward the golden doors. Looking them up and down he whispered something but Orah couldn't make out what it was. Eon's voice startled her, and she looked towards them.

"The first King admired those doors and had them replicated for the Palace of Kings in Erde. They're quite something aren't they?"

Turning, she expected Roan to look at Eon but instead he stared at her. "Yeah. Quite something."

Orah watched Roan and Jes leave the room and lingered back a moment, admiring the doors. Her fingers reached up to brush the engraved ivy. The engraved ivy that reminded her so much of her garden door. Her fingers were barely an inch from the engraving when she felt the warmth of someone beside her. She turned, knowing Eon was there before she met their eyes.

"The ivy is to acknowledge the first winner of the first challenge," Eon whispered, running their hand along the door. The ivy briefly appeared to light at the touch and Orah's fingertips buzzed in response.

Shaking her hands out in front of her she looked out the doors, finding Roan and Jes already nearing the entrance of the palace. Roan's head was down, obviously lost in his thoughts, and unaware Orah had lingered back.

"Thank you for your time today." She quickly bowed her head and ran after her companions.

Making it through the doors, she walked down the short steps leading away from the room, turning to head toward the entrance when she ran into a cloaked Fate. "Oh my god!" Orah whispered, hoping no one had seen the collision.

The mysterious Fate let out a quiet chuckle and Orah stepped backwards when her face came into view. At first Orah thought her eyes were playing tricks on her. Lahana had somehow snuck into the palace. She hadn't thought Lahana was even awake when they had left the manor.

Taking her in, Orah's eyes widened at what she saw. The same slightly dark skin as Lahana, the same wide smile, but the eyes and hair—the eyes were brilliantly blue and the hair dark and thick.

Orah's mouth popped open, her head snapped to the entrance as Roan stepped outside. Turning back to the Fate, she thought her heart would explode when Leora Durel softly touched her arm then shook her head. Slowly, Leora pulled her other hand out of a pocket in her cloak. In her hand lay a solid gold coin. Her eyes softened and she smiled at Orah, placing the coin in her palm. The same smile Orah had seen on Lahana's face yesterday.

Wrapping Orah's fingers around the coin, Leora spoke. "Threads of fate bound together. Coin hence proof of knot they tied. A deal once made. By oldest oath two souls entwined."

Blinking back her tears and confusion, Orah looked down at her hand then back up to find Leora gone. As quickly as she had appeared.

The coin felt heavy in Orah's hand but warm. The buzzing feeling intensified and she took a deep breath, trying to steady her heartbeat.

Guilt settled over her and she turned toward the entrance to where Roan was now standing looking around frantically for her. Even from a distance, she could somehow feel his panic.

Clearing her throat, she placed the coin in her pocket and hurried over to him.

Relief loosened the panic that wasn't her own when his eyes locked with hers. Rushing toward her he grabbed her hand, bringing it to his lips. "I thought you were gone."

His whisper tugged at her heart and she shook her head. "No sorry. Got lost in the beauty of this place."

Pulling her hand from his lips, he squeezed it hard, and pulled her toward the stairs back to the lawn where Nacht and Jes waited for them.

The hairs on the back of her neck stood and she glanced back inside the palace. Beyond the still-open palace doors stood Eon speaking to someone next to them. Both Fates turned to face Orah and she shook her head. Leora Durel's eyes watered as she looked at her son.

The two women met each other's gazes and Leora nodded her head at Orah. As if giving a blessing of love.

Roan shivered beside Orah and she turned to him. "Are you okay?" she asked.

Running his free hand through his hair he chuckled. "Yeah, just had an odd feeling. It was warm and familiar, but I can't place it."

Taking one last glimpse inside the palace, Orah wasn't surprised to find Eon and Leora gone. The coin warmed against her thigh and she resisted the urge to pull it out.

Jes's hands smacked against his thigh when they approached. "I thought Eon had tricked us and sent Orah home without us knowing."

Chuckling, Roan helped Orah onto the saddle. "Eon's answers may have been obscure and really unhelpful, but I don't think any of the Fates would stoop that low. Orah got distracted."

Jes glanced at Orah and they stared silently for a few seconds before he looked away. She knew he was somehow aware that wasn't what had happened. Deciding to get it over with, she cleared her throat and pulled the coin from her pocket.

"When I was leaving the room, a Fate handed this to me."

Snatching the coin out of her hand, Jes inspected it. His eyebrows bunched together, and he handed it to Roan. "Dunno where it's from. Looks like something from someone's coin purse but feels heavier."

Flipping it between his fingers, Roan inspected it. "Maybe the Fates have coins slightly different than ours?" Turning to Orah he handed it back. "Did the Fate say anything when they handed it to you? Was it Eon?"

Taking a deep breath, she shook her head. "Not Eon, but they did say something." Glancing between the two of them, she sighed then repeated what Roan's mother said.

Jes shook his head. "What in the Fates is that supposed to mean?"

Shrugging, Roan looked at the coin again. "I think I'm leaving here with more questions than I had when we arrived." Climbing into the saddle, he reached around and wrapped Orah's fingers around the coin in her hand. "If a Fate gave that to you then take care of it. It's said a gift from a Fate is a good omen."

Orah stared down at the coin before turning to the palace one more. The towering doors were closed now, but her power felt as though a warm thread was pulling at her.

Glancing at Roan she smiled softly. She wanted to tell him about his mother but somehow, she couldn't find the words to do so. She wondered if perhaps the coin was preventing her from revealing the secret. Perhaps Eon was doing it. Whatever reason prevented her from finding the words felt unfair to keep such a revelation from him.

Roan lightly tapped Nacht's side and they ascended into the air. Clouds quickly enveloped them the higher they climbed and the city of Tyme fell away into the distance. They flew in silence, all unable to face the pending future with Roan's party less than two days away.

Chapter 35

Groaning, Orah stood in her closet staring at the gowns in front of her. She only had a few hours until Roan's party and she had nothing to wear. Cursing herself, she kicked the ground. Lahana assured her she would have something for Orah, but she was nowhere to be seen. Sinking to the ground, Orah stared at her options.

The dress she'd worn for that ill-fated dinner with Marek, a haltered dark green dress, a lilac colored gown with long flowing sleeves that tightened at the wrists, and a simple black gown. While all options were beautiful, none of them felt right for Roan's party.

Leaning her head against the dresser in front of her, she sighed. Her frustration was likely due to the fact she had barely seen Roan since they'd returned from Tiid. Besides sleeping next to each other every night, they'd had almost no other interaction.

With the party only a few hours away, he had been in almost constant meetings with his officials and greeting arriving guests in the city center. Most of the day was focused on the mortal guests arriving in Iluna. Roan had a specific inn set up only for the mortals to stay in and had, according to Lahana, greeted each mortal personally. Her frustration cooled while she thought of his dedication to include people like her. People he felt shouldn't be underestimated and should be respected.

Smiling, she pulled herself from the floor and inspected the gowns again. The gown from the dinner with Marek was the closest to Roan's favorite color. She cocked her head while considering it. She could wear it, even with the negative memories. Turning her head, she looked at the black gown. It was simple but she thought the simplicity could be considered a statement.

Picking both gowns up she inspected each one. Neither felt right. She let out another frustrated sigh and walked out of the closet, determined to have words with Lahana. Fuming, she made her way to her bedroom door when it suddenly popped open and a beaming Lahana stepped in holding a gown in a protective bag.

"Please don't be too mad at me! The tailor surprised me with their own modifications on the sketches I provided them, which put the pick up behind." She grimaced as they made eye contact. Orah knew it was due to the scowl plastered across her face.

"You're cutting it really close, Lahana. I was about to come give you a piece of my mind. I almost wore the gown from the dinner with Marek!"

Frowning, Lahana shook her head. "Oh Fates no. We should burn that thing violently. I really did mean to tell you yesterday. I got distracted but I know that's no excuse." Lahana motioned for Orah to follow her into the closet.

Orah followed reluctantly and stared while Lahana hung the dress across from the closet door. Orah couldn't see any specific details of the gown other than it appeared to be long based on the size of the bag.

"Close your eyes," Lahana instructed.

"Lahana I don't want to close my eyes," Orah bit back.

Frowning, Lahana crossed her arms then stood in front of the dress. "Close your eyes or I'll make you wear that other one." With disgust, she pointed to the blue dress from the dinner with Marek.

Scoffing, Orah shut her eyes and listened intently to Lahana unzip the gown bag. After a few painful minutes of silence Lahana cleared her throat. "You can open them now."

Hesitantly Orah opened her eyes and gasped.

Hanging in front of her was an almost identical gown to the gown she'd seen in the window the night she and Roan had gone to the pub. It was the same beautiful burgundy color, but it was different. The neckline now dropped down in the way she would have picked at home. The previously long sleeves were now thick straps, stopping right at her shoulders, and to her surprise a long slit ran up the right side, stopping where she assumed would be the top of her thigh.

Shifting her gaze to Lahana, Orah choked on her words. "I—where—"

Lahana ran her hands across the gown. "Roan. He saw you admiring it in the window, but he had it tailored to the styles he's seen you wear in your memories." Lahana grinned back at Orah. "He told me he hasn't been able to stop thinking about the way you stopped to admire it and had a sketch done for the alterations for my tailor." Chuckling, she moved to stand beside Orah. "My tailor, however, disapproved of some of his changes and kept some of their personal preferences. Roan wanted the neckline to be lower and straps more like the blue dress you arrived in."

Orah chuckled. Slowly she walked up to the gown and ran her hands over it. It was almost unthinkable to put something so beautiful on. "I don't have the words to show my gratitude."

A mischievous grin flashed across Lahana's face. "It's not me who you should be showing gratitude to. Maybe your thanks to Roan won't require words."

Staring at her, Orah let out a laugh. "I'll be sure to share *all* the dirty details."

Squealing, Lahana covered her eyes. "No! Forget I said anything. I think I need to go stick my head in a boiling tub now."

Leaving the dress, Orah walked back over to Lahana and pulled her into a tight hug. "He may have come up with the idea, but you made sure it happened. Thank you." They sat in Orah's closet holding each other for a while. It may have been the night of Roan's party but something else lingered in the air. As if something life changing was going to happen. And Orah couldn't help but feel the need to hold Lahana as tightly as she could.

Lahana pulled herself from Orah's embrace. "I'm going to get ready. Wait till you see mine. I took inspiration from the fashion in your world." With a wink, she walked towards the closet doors. "Do you want me to wait for you before heading into the ballroom?"

"No, I'm a big girl. Go get beautiful and I'll see you down there. You and Fawn deserve a grand entrance that's not interrupted by having to wait for me."

Orah followed Lahana out of the room, closing the door behind her before turning back to inspect the bedroom. In the three months she had been in Roan's world, the room had become her home away from home. Even though she hadn't slept in there for over a week, it was still very much hers. Little things she'd collected throughout her time there were scattered about. Small trinkets from shopping, her smoke-stained shirt from the first day at the obstacle course with Jes, the sandals she'd been wearing the day she came through the garden door, books she'd brought up from the library and hadn't yet returned. It was as though the room had always been meant for her.

Glancing at her closet doors she considered going through the adjoining door to see what

Roan was up to but shook her head, deciding they didn't need to distract each other. She rushed into the closet and grabbed her gown before heading to the shower to rinse off. She didn't know how close it was to the party starting but based on the sounds downstairs she could tell preparations were fully underway.

After quickly scrubbing herself in the shower she hopped out, wrapping a towel around herself. Appreciating the magic of the house and the lack of steamed mirrors she smiled then immediately let out a scream when she spotted Roan's reflection in the mirror. Pressing her hand against her chest she turned to face him. "Fates, Roan, you scared me."

"Fates?" An amused smile spread across his lips. "I see you've fully acclimated then."

Embarrassed, she turned away from him, and back to the mirror. "I wasn't in my right mind. Someone decided to spy on me."

Almost too fast to detect he rushed across the room and wrapped his arms around her. "Not spy. Appreciate. Thoroughly." Placing a soft kiss on her neck he looked up at their reflection in the mirror.

Something about the image tugged on her heart. As though they'd been there before. Blinking and shaking her head she wiggled out of his arms. "You need to go get ready."

"I will. I promise." That intention filled stare returned to his eyes and his eyes lingered on the towel wrapped around her. "I came to ask for my birthday present."

"Your birthday present?"

"Yes. I came to request that tonight when we climb into my bed," he pulled her against him while he spoke. His hand lazily caressed her arm and he smiled. "I would very much like you to wear that little black nightgown again."

Her body warmed at his touch and she forced herself to make eye contact with him. "You'd like me to wear that nightgown? No other requests?"

With a shrug he released his hold on her. "Anything further will only happen with your permission."

She wasn't sure how to respond to his tease before he winked and grinned again. "I'll see you at the party."

Remembering to thank him for her gown she rushed out to her room to find it empty. She stared at the closet doors. Following him to his room felt like a very distracting idea and she sighed before returning to the bathroom.

Staring in the mirror she pulled open the drawers and got to work.

Standing in front of the mirror Orah admired herself. She had somehow managed to get her hair styled using warded tools she'd found in the drawers. The result was her hair now cascading down her back in loose curls.

Her burgundy dress hugged every curve of her body and she stared in disbelief. She didn't understand how either Roan or Lahana had managed to have a dress perfectly tailored for her. She turned to catch a glimpse at the back of the gown and smiled again. The open back had been a surprise and she wasn't mad about it, she felt a little more exposed than she'd thought she'd be, but not in a bad way.

She took herself in, admiring the work of art she was. It was likely she was going to turn heads at Roan's party, but there was only one person she cared about staring at her.

Breathing out a breath of relief she left her bedroom and walked out into the hall. The noise and loud sounds of voices downstairs caught her off guard immediately. Usually, the manor was almost eerily quiet. That night, however, the manor felt alive and bustling. A thrumming energy seemed to fill the halls as though the house itself was celebrating with everyone as well.

Nerves flipped in her stomach and she leaned against her door. "You can do this." Whispering to herself, she looked down the hall to the top of the stairs. A cold rush of air caught her breath and she almost let out a scream when a cold hand landed on her shoulder.

"Don't scream. We don't want the birthday boy rushing up to save his damsel." Scowling at Moros, she stomped her heeled shoe right into his foot. Holding back his own squeal he stepped back and glared at her.

"I'm nobody's damsel." Brushing her dress, she straightened, continuing to scowl. "What are you doing up here?"

Shrugging he looked her up and down. "Dunno. Saw you weren't downstairs and thought I'd come check. You're running fashionably late."

"I wasn't aware of what time it was."

His eyes glanced up briefly and he looked her over again. "Oh, don't apologize. There are going to be many appreciative eyes down there tonight. You look beautiful."

Taken back by the compliment she blinked at him. "Uh. Thank you?"

"No ill intention in the compliment, Orah. Very genuine." Waving his hand, he turned away and walked down the hall. "I'll see you down there."

The voices downstairs grew louder while she watched Moros walk away. Swallowing, she continued her breathing, trying to calm her nerves. She was going down there for Roan. Not to impress any Gods. Not to make friends. She was going down there for him.

Finally pushing off her door she straightened herself again and walked towards the stairs. She couldn't see anything other than the shadows of Roan's guests while they walked from the front door to the ballroom. Shadow after shadow crossed the foyer.

Letting out the breath she was holding she lifted her gown, hoping to avoid a clumsy entrance, and descended the stairs.

Trying to keep her eyes on her feet, she didn't notice the voices had suddenly stopped until she was down the stairs. Looking up her cheeks blushed, finding every person standing in the foyer staring at her. Unsure of why she was now the center of attention her eyes drifted to the suited figure standing at the bottom of the stairs.

Roan.

His eyes were focused solely on her. His chest moved up and down so slowly Orah worried he was actually having trouble breathing. Movement down by his legs grabbed her attention and she gasped watching how rapidly his hands shook at his sides.

Looking back at the people around him, she couldn't ignore her embarrassment. If anyone had wondered whether Roan felt something for his guest their questions had just been answered by his response to her arrival.

Slowly she finished her descent, walking up to him while she reached the bottom of the stairs. The world stilled while they stared at each other.

It was possible his guest's noise and chatter had resumed but she wasn't entirely sure. He was the only thing she could focus on.

Taking a slight step back, she admired him. He was in a dark suit tailored to fit him almost too perfectly. All the muscles in his body flexed while her eyes traced every inch of him. The light from the ballroom briefly caught his suit and she realized it was a dark blue, almost black color. His hair was slicked back but tousled a bit, likely from his habit of running his hands or fingers through it when he was nervous.

Beneath his suit jacket was a dark gray shirt in a collarless fashion that buttoned up to the base of his neck. His freckles shone brightly on his cheeks and his starlight crown was on full display.

He looked as she would imagine a God of Night to look.

Slowly her eyes traveled up his body again and she found him staring at her. His breathing appeared to have returned to normal and sound was certainly happening around them now.

Holding out his hands, he smiled at her. "You look beautiful, Orah."

Blushing, she took his hands. "You look beautiful as well, Roan."

"Beautiful? Not pretty?" Squeezing her hands, he winked.

She bit back her laugh, remembering her drunk blundering. "I mean pretty works too."

Trying to avoid staring at the people still coming in from the front door, she looked toward the ballroom. "I forgot to tell you happy birthday earlier."

"That's alright. People have been repeating it all night for some reason."

His joke caught her off guard and she laughed. "How odd."

Grinning, he pulled her against him. "I think I've had enough of welcoming my guests. Any late stragglers can come find me." Meeting his eyes, her chest felt tight and heavy. That odd lingering feeling in the air was still there but somehow thicker than earlier. She couldn't shake the nervous feeling still settled in her stomach and she glanced back up the stairs.

"Considering escaping?" His whisper was low, but she could hear the concern in his voice.

She shook her head. "No, just a weird feeling. That's all." Turning her head back to him she smiled "Let's get to your party."

With a smile he grabbed her hand and led her into the ball room. The music grew louder the closer they walked to the room, as did the sounds of voices and laughter. As they stepped into the room Orah shook her head in disbelief. The room itself was beautiful when Roan had first shown it to her days before but now it was magical.

Along the two side walls were tables with cloths of varying blues, purples, and blacks. On each table sat a centerpiece of what appeared to be bouquets of pure starlight. Orah's eyes moved upwards towards the ceiling that looked just like the night sky, as though Etta had possibly had the roof removed for the night.

Looking closely, Orah squinted, barely able to make out the outline of where the walls met the roof. She smiled; Etta had warded the illusion.

Orah observed the room and the people scattered about in groups. Some were seated at tables, some were standing, and some were dancing in the middle of the room to the music being played by the live band in the back.

An excited chill ran down Orah's spine. The energy in the room was fueling the excitement and she couldn't help but appreciate how electric and alive it felt.

Roan followed behind her silently while she walked into the room and all heads turned toward him. Orah, still watching while a few guests smiled at them both, nodding their heads. Others just stared at them, shaking their heads. Then there were the ones that didn't seem to notice Roan at all and only stared at Orah.

Orah's body buzzed in response and she cursed herself, forcing herself to not allow any outbursts on his big night.

Taking in her surroundings, she appreciated the diverse crowds. All around her were Gods, Godlings, and mortals. All mingling together, all seeming to enjoy themselves.

The Governing Gods were the easiest for Orah to pick out. Each had a female or male, winged Beskermer standing behind them. Orah made eye contact with Amada who bowed her head in greeting.

"Death."

Orah turned immediately before the bone chilling cold settled over her and found Aeron standing behind her.

"Orah, I told you I would enjoy meeting you again." He bowed while taking her hand. "It appears our host of honor is not the only one catching his guests' attention tonight."

"I think they're all likely focused on him," Orah replied nervously.

Behind Aeron, a large man with snow white wings shifted gently on his feet. Aeron noticed the movement and looked back at him, then shook his head. "Where are my manners? Orah, this is Nas, my Beskermer."

Bowing, Nas looked over at Orah. An odd feeling of confusion and intrigue rushed past Orah as Nas straightened his pose. "I apologize that I was unable to meet you and his Lord, Roan, when you came to Shadus. I was otherwise occupied in the depths."

Orah suppressed her shock, trying not to stare when Nas grabbed hold of Aeron's hand. Aeron met his eyes and a warm rush of joy and safety warmed Orah's body before quickly fading away.

Someone across the room called Aeron's name and he bowed his head, excusing himself quietly. Hand in hand, he and Nas walked over to the other side of the room.

Turning to Roan, Orah's mouth popped open. "Aeron and his Beskermer?"

Amusement flashed across Roan's. "Yes. Aeron may have chosen not to have children, but he isn't celibate. He and Nas became partners when I was a child. Apparently, they fought their attraction to one another for too long."

Smiling, Orah watched them approach the unknown God who called Aeron. Nas stood protectively behind Aeron, not once letting go of his hand. Every few minutes Aeron looked up at Nas lovingly before continuing his conversation. They appeared completely comfortable and completely in love.

Curiosity hit Orah. "Does your father have a Beskermer?" she asked.

The smile that had been on his face quickly shifted to a frown. Nodding, he glanced around the room. "He did. Part of why everyone is so on edge with him lately is because he relieved his Beskermer from his bond within hours of my mother's death." The air thickened and people around the room shifted uncomfortably. No conversation stopped but somehow everyone could feel the shift.

"Where is his Beskermer now?"

The air thickened further, and Roan glanced behind him, to the corner where Jes stood, watching him. "He's dead."

Glancing at Jes, Orah's stomach sank. "Your Father's Beskermer was Jes's father."

Roan nodded his head. "Yes. He died mysteriously a few months after my Father relieved him of his bond. No one knows what happened, but I have my suspicions."

He didn't have to provide any further explanations for Orah to know he suspected his Father was the cause for the death. Her stomach turned at the thought. She didn't know very much about the Beskermer bonds, but she imagined killing your Beskermer was not something people would willingly accept.

Shaking his head, Roan looked up to the other side of the room. Following his gaze, Orah spotted a tall woman waving at him, beckoning him to her. "That's Aila, our Governing Goddess of Guerra. She probably wants to see if I've heard anything more about the challenge. The Goddess of War always likes to talk strategy." Pulling Orah's hand to his lips, he looked into her eyes. "I promise I'll be back for you. Don't get yourself into too much trouble."

She watched him walk away until he reached Aila, who slapped him hard on the back and they both let out loud laughs that echoed throughout the room.

Shaking her head, Orah glanced around the room trying to find Lahana or Clarah. Her eyes fell on Lahana standing with a group of who Orah believed were mortals. Orah's mouth hung open while she took in the Goddess.

Lahana was wearing a dark green dress that had two *very* high slits running up both of her legs. The neckline was in a halter fashion tied at the base of her neck. The fabric across her chest looked as though it could have slipped at any moment. Her long blond hair was woven in a thick braid, lying to the side. She looked incredible but also very out of place amongst the conservative outfits every other Goddess wore.

"*I can feel you staring at me.*" Slowly she looked away from the group she was gathered with and winked at Orah.

Remembering their little secret, Orah smiled. "*You took inspiration from my world?*"

Lahana spun in her place. "*Oh yes, but my tailor didn't make the slits on my dress as high as I requested, so I took scissors to it and made them the height I wanted.*"

Focusing on her dress, Orah laughed, noticing small frays of fabric up near her thighs. "*What were Fawn's thoughts on the outfit?*"

Smiling wider, Lahana glanced to her right. Orah followed her gaze and smiled. Fawn was in an almost identical dress, but it was a reddish-orange color, almost like flames.

"*She was completely onboard with making a statement tonight. Her mother almost fell over when she saw us, but we got her to calm down,*" Lahana replied.

Lahana's eyes motioned towards the woman sitting next to Fawn. She could be her daughter's twin. She had the same dark red hair but long instead of short like Fawn's. She was wearing green like Lahana, but lighter like new trees in the spring. Behind her was a woman with white and gray peppered wings, likely her Beskermer. Fawn made eye contact with Orah and pointed, leaning to whisper in her mother's ear. The Goddess of Spring looked up at Orah and smiled wide.

Orah jumped back in shock at the flowers now blooming on the ground in front of her then quickly disappeared.

"*She likes you.*"

Lahana's voice in the wind startled Orah. She looked up from where the flowers had been and smiled back at Lahana's response. Suddenly Lahana's eyes widened and she pointed behind Orah. Whirling around, Orah let out a yelp when she found Marek standing a few inches away from her.

"Orah." His voice was low, almost as though he had been drinking. His hand moved to grab Orah but her own snapped up to stop him. Wincing at the hold she had on his wrist, he grinned. "Very strong for a mortal."

"What do you want?" Her heart beat frantically and she looked over to where Roan was with Aila. Only, he wasn't at the table any more. Both he and Aila were nowhere to be found.

Not wanting to keep her eyes off Marek for very long, Orah turned back to him.

Flexing against her hold, he cocked his head. "Can't a man ask a woman for a dance?"

"I'm not dancing with you." Her body hummed in response, confirming her stance. She could feel her power rising to the surface, ready to throw whatever she needed at him.

"Tell me Orah, look around you. What do you see?" He smiled sheepishly while she glanced around and gasped at the people now staring at them. A few looked at her as though she were a threat and looked worriedly at Marek.

Remembering what Roan had told her about Marek's ability for people to instantly trust him, she looked back at him. "They think I'm going to hurt you." Releasing her hold on his wrist, she tried to calm the pulse coursing throughout her body.

That predatory grin spread across his face and he nodded. "Yes, they do. I think you should agree to my request for a dance," he yelled out the last two words, causing more heads to turn their way. "It would cause quite a stir if Roan's guest so rudely denied his brother, who also just so happens to be the son of the King. I remember you don't really follow usual protocol, but it would be considered disrespectful to decline the *honor* of my dance."

Groaning at his logic, she nodded. "One dance."

His grin somehow spread wider and he set out his hand for her to take. Sighing, she placed her hand in his, allowing him to guide her to the dance floor. Couples around them lined up while the band started the slow melody and Orah desperately searched for Roan.

"You're not going to find him. Aila *conveniently* distracted him in his study."

Snapping her head back to Marek, she glared. She held her mask while her chest tightened, and her mind raced through what that could mean. Marek stepped closer, as though he were about to embrace her and leaned down to whisper in her ear. "Don't worry, just distraction of words. Based on how my little brother looks at you, I don't think Aila would get very far even if she wanted to."

Orah let out a sigh of relief while the couples surrounding them drew closer to one another. The men wrapped one arm around the women's waists and clasped their free hand. Marek grinned and grabbed Orah's hand first. Slowly, he looked down at her waist then back up to her. His arm moved to wrap around her, but she stopped him.

The whisps of flames in her hand bit at her fingertips while she glared at him. Wincing, he stared down at the small flames then smiled at her. "I would control that temper, Orah." His eyes darted to the left. "Our very own emotional Goddess of Sommer, Zira, will not be happy to see a mortal with power that rivals her own."

Following his gaze, Orah found a woman seated at a table surrounded by people wearing varying shades of blues, reds, and oranges. Zira's head turned to Orah's briefly, as if she could sense Orah's stare. Quickly Orah extinguished the flames licking at her fingers. Scrunching her eyebrows, Zira held her gaze with Orah for a moment before shrugging and returning her attention to the people seated around her.

Marek's eyes flared and he smiled. "You may be able to use your little tricks on me when no one is here but anyone seeing the power you have tonight could likely start a war. We wouldn't want to cause that kind of disturbance on our dear Roan's special night."

The music picked up and the couples around them began to move. Marek stared down at Orah's waist again. Holding up his hand, he grinned while he hovered his hand over her waist while his eyes lingered on hers. She scoffed. He very obviously believed the teasing touch was in any way tempting.

Rolling her eyes, she allowed him to take the lead and they joined the others in the dance.

"You're an interesting mortal, Orah." Grinning, he tightened his grip on her hand and flung her out into a spin then quickly pulled her back to him. "You and I could have so much fun, you know. I can sense a darkness in you. Something you hide."

A sick feeling rolled in her stomach and she pulled against his grip, prompting him to hold her hand tighter. She scowled up at him. "I don't want to have anything with you."

Smiling, he pulled her against him. "You don't have to want anything. That's what could make it so much fun."

Her eyes flared with rage and she tried to wiggle out of his hold. His hands wrapped around her waist and he stared down at her chest. "This dress is borderline inappropriate. My brother should be more careful with how he dresses his plaything."

Gasping, she pushed against him again but still couldn't seem to loosen his hold on her. His grip on her waist somehow tightened against her and her stomach sank. Trying to keep herself composed, she shivered as an icy breeze blew her hair against her bare back and a cold hand gripped her shoulder. Marek's grin fell and he narrowed his eyes at the person standing behind her.

"Mind if I cut in?" Jumping at the sound of Moros's voice, she looked back. The irritation pulled enough of Marek's attention that she was finally able to pull herself out of his grip. She glanced back at Moros then threw a taunting grin at Marek.

"Not at all," she replied.

Marek's palm lit briefly as he glared at Moros. "Cousin—we were just about to have some fun."

"Yes, but now I want a chance for my own shot at it." Moros winked at Orah and grabbed her hand, pulling her into a dance before Marek could respond.

Keeping her eyes off Marek, Orah breathed out a breath of relief and looked up at Moros. The God of Wintur was in a sleek gray suit and she could barely see his stark white tattoos beneath the collar of his shirt. His long dark hair was pulled back. She smiled. He was rather handsome, and something told her he was trying to look his best for Jes like she had wanted to feel for Roan.

Moros's eyes darted behind Orah and he scowled. "We might have to stumble our way through two dances before Marek lets this go."

"Thank you."

His shoulders lifted up and down in a soft shrug. "Marek likes to think he can do what he wants. I try to cut in whenever I can."

"Are you really his friend?"

"I think I'm more of his watcher. Someone has to make sure he doesn't destroy everything and everyone he touches."

Moros's eyes drifted back behind Orah where she knew that Marek still stood. A sad look flashed in Moros's eyes then he looked back at her and smiled. Suddenly her opinion of Moros changed. He was annoying and a bit arrogant, but he wasn't bad. If he was so determined to prevent Marek's dark side from having its way, then she could see why Jes was drawn to him. Meeting his eyes, guilt consumed her. She had promised him she wouldn't say anything to Jes.

Before she could stop herself, she blurted out her confession. "Jes knows that I know."

His smile faltered and he glanced behind her. Slowly the smile crept back up and he nodded. "I know. He told me. He also told me he only knows because he was being an ass and pushed you too hard. Something about an argument and him dangling you in the air by a rope?"

Scoffing, she looked to where his eyes had gone and found Jes leaning against a wall, staring at them. "Something like that."

Chapter 36

Moros and Orah danced for three songs before he gave her the all-clear that Marek had turned his attention away from them. Bowing sarcastically at the ending of the final song, Moros smiled at her. "It was a pleasure, Orah."

Orah returned her own sarcastic bow. "I'm surprised to say I agree. Thank you, Moros."

Flipping back his long ponytail, he shrugged then glanced back to where Jes still stood, staring at them. "I've got to go attend to other matters." With a little skip he winked as he discreetly walked toward his lover.

Laughing at how nonchalantly Moros skipped away, Orah looked around the ballroom. Marek, to her relief, was nowhere to be seen, but neither was Roan. Sighing with disappointment she made eye contact with Clarah sitting at a table with Yohan.

Smiling, Orah crossed the room to join them.

"Orah!" Clarah beamed sitting straighter when Orah sat down next to her.

"Are you not dancing?" Orah asked.

"I've been dancing all night. Father looked disgruntled so I just joined him."

Orah held back her laugh when she looked over to find Yohan disapprovingly picking at his small plate of food. "Something wrong with the food, Yohan?"

The cook frowned. "There's nothing *wrong* with it per se. Just not up to the quality I believe My Lord deserves." His thick accent made his disappointment seem far worse than he likely felt and Orah smiled.

"Yohan, Roan only barred you from cooking so you could enjoy the evening. Not so you could spend the evening critiquing the food."

Yohan let out an unamused laugh and shook his head. "All I know is my cake will most certainly be the highlight this evening."

"I'm confident it will be, Yohan."

Orah shivered in response to the voice behind her and the warm hand now on her shoulder. Twisting, she found Roan smiling at his cook.

Yohan sat a bit straighter then nodded his head. "Only the best for you My Lord."

"I'll echo Orah's sentiments. The best thing for me, on *my* birthday, is that you enjoy yourself. Please stop fussing," Roan replied.

Clarah grinned mischievously at her father while Roan spoke and Orah held back her laugh. There was something amusing but also admirable about the way Roan spoke in the moment. He could have been stern with Yohan but instead he was kind and empathetic.

Shrugging, Yohan smiled at his daughter. "Clarah, my love, care to show your old father some new moves?"

Clarah let out a squeal before hopping up and grabbing her father's hand, pulling him to the dance floor. Orah watched them go with a smile. Roan cleared his throat behind her, and she looked back up at him again.

"I'm sorry for leaving you for so long."

"It's alright."

Shaking his head, he knelt so they were eye level. "No, it's not. Jes told me Marek cornered you."

Orah looked around the room, trying to see if Marek had returned to the ballroom but found no sign of him. An uneasy warning settled in her stomach and she shivered, trying to shake the feeling off.

"I dealt with him. Moros also helped bat him away."

Roan's face softened while he brushed a hand across her cheek. "I shouldn't have allowed myself to be distracted. Aila ended up revealing Marek sent her my way. I'm sorry."

"Roan, I'm fine. I promise."

She leaned into his affectionate touch and admired him. His crown still hovered above his head, but his freckles were a little less bright than they'd been when she'd encountered him on the stairs. His silvery blue eyes looked happy, as though he were enjoying himself, but he also looked tired and she was sure she saw a glimmer of worry as well.

"I haven't had a chance to thank you for this gown," she said, trying to shift the conversation.

He grinned. "I should be thanking you for wearing it."

"I didn't think I'd been so obvious when I was admiring it that night."

"I don't know how you thought you were being subtle. You were frozen in your spot and I knew you wanted it. I hope the adjustments I had Lahana's tailor make were okay."

"They're perfect."

He kissed her forehead. "Good. I promised you a dance."

Orah smiled while he grabbed hold of her hands and pulled them both away from the table. There were more people dancing now than when she'd been on the dance floor with Marek. They passed Kai spinning Etta, whose usual stern expression was replaced with one of glee and joy. At the edge of the dancefloor, Orah caught sight of Xade holding the hand of a young girl. Both of them had a sheepish grin on their faces as they whispered to one another.

For Orah, the alive electric feeling pulsing throughout the room was stronger now. As though everyone was waiting with anticipation for something to happen.

Expecting the same soft music that had been playing all night she let out a yelp when the band began playing something more upbeat and almost wild. Everyone on the dance floor let out cheers at the lively beat and Orah listened. The music sounded familiar. As though it danced around her, calling her to move.

Looking up at the stage, she focused on the band for the first time. Eyes widening, she snapped her head up to Roan. "This is the band from our night at the pub!"

His eyes sparkled while he nodded. "I personally requested them for entertainment tonight. Did you think I would expect a slow dance? I like you dancing when you're free, Orah. Not stifled slow movements."

Her cheeks warmed while the music pulsed through her. Leaning into him, she tilted her hair back, letting the sounds and the beat call to her. All around them Roan's guests clapped their hands and began dancing. Those that had been dancing to the slower music were now fused together. Orah's eyes widened while she watched a Beskermer grind against a God's leg.

Roan's whisper tickled her ear. "When Gods let loose, they really let loose." Grabbing her hands, he spun her out in front of him, yelling over the band. "Let loose Orah!"

Grinning, she let go of his hands and threw her own into the air. The music now felt as much a part of her as the blood pulsing in her veins. As though there were invisible tethers of sound slowing wrapping around her body, controlling her movement. Orah tilted her head back and let out a laugh.

She couldn't help but feel free and unleashed in the moment. The music, the happy faces surrounding her, how safe she felt, how secure she felt. As though nothing could ever bring her down from the high.

Roan approached behind her, flipping her forward and pulling her against him again. The smell of him and the heat of the bodies surrounding them was intoxicating. Wrapping her arms around his neck, she moved her hips against him, taunting him, calling for him.

His eyes widened and he smiled, moving his hips against hers. The music entangled them while they moved dangerously and tauntingly against each other.

Staring into his eyes, Orah couldn't hold back her smile. The music drowned out everything other than them. Roan's hands wrapped around her waist and he hoisted her so she was now straddling his thigh.

"Let loose, love," he whispered into her ear.

The responding shiver that ran down her back was almost too much for her to handle but she did as he asked. His hands held her in place while she ground against his thigh. The near electric shocks now barreling down her spine with each twist of her hips drove her mad. Their breathing became synced while she kept her eyes on him.

Each movement, each time he moved his thigh with her hips became addicting. Orah no longer cared if they were in the middle of a crowded room. She no longer cared about keeping control or holding anything in. All she cared about was him. The near labored sound of his breath and the heat radiating from his hands wrapped around her waist.

His hands gripped her, and she let out a yelp when he hoisted her into the air, just like their first night out. His head tilted back with his loud laugh and she smiled. That sound. It was all she could hear. A sound she knew she would be able to find even in a crowd of a thousand people.

Staring up at her, he tightened his hold on her waist. Her body felt on fire, like she would combust in mere seconds. Out of the corner of her eye she noticed his guests all standing, staring up at her in shock. Shaking her head, she glanced back down at him, realizing the room was now silent, not even the band's music filled the space.

Roan hadn't seemed to notice yet, he still held her above him in a trance. "Roan," she whispered, hoping his guests couldn't hear her.

Roan stared at her with admiration. "Orah, you're glowing," he whispered as he gently set her back on the ground.

Looking down at herself she jerked, seeing what he was referring to. Her body was glowing again and the room that had been slightly dim before, was now bright—as though they were standing in the afternoon sun.

Blinking, she took a slow and steady breath trying to calm herself when a flash of movement in the corner of the room caught her eye. She made eye contact with Marek who grinned back with his predatory grin.

As quickly as he'd appeared in her vision he disappeared, and she looked back down at herself. The light was now dimming but everyone in the room still stared. Suddenly, Jes stepped out from behind a column and clapped his hands.

Tall champagne-like glasses appeared on every table in the room and in every standing guest's hand. Orah jumped back at the glass now in her own hand when Jes's voice filled the room. "Let's make a toast to our Governing God of Nyte, Roan! And the starlight he's just shared with his guest!"

Everyone in the room glanced back and forth between themselves, obviously unsure of what to believe based on what they'd seen. That was until Moros stepped out from behind the same column Jes had been behind and clapped his hands in response. "To Roan!"

Roan's guests continued to exchange their confused expressions. Orah's chest tightened, unsure how to address what they had all clearly seen from her. The sound of a chair scraping echoed in the room and Orah turned to find Lahana standing and raising her glass.

"To Roan!" Lahana cheered.

The band's music picked back up to a lively but milder tune and every glass in the room finally lifted in unison. Roan's guests' apprehensive expressions remained on their faces as the sounds of their toasts filled the room. "To Roan! Happy Birthday!" echoed throughout the room.

As if on cue, Yohan appeared through the ballroom doors with a large caking on a rolling tray. Looking back at Roan, Orah smiled, partially from relief but also joy. Despite how nerve racking it had been trying to distract so many people, Roan still deserved to be celebrated.

Roan blushed and he softly clinked his glass against Orah's. Jes approached them both, winking before Yohan stopped in front of Roan with the cake. His guest's cheers grew louder while everyone in the room called for Roan to cut his cake.

Out of habit, Orah clapped, yelling out, "Make a wish!"

Jes turned to her. His eyebrow couldn't have raised any higher if he had tried. "A wish?"

"Why not?" she replied, trying to ignore the obvious blush she felt on her cheeks.

Roan stared at her for a moment before grinning. "Yeah. Why not?" Closing his eyes, he let out a breath and then a small sword of starlight appeared at his side.

Everyone, Orah included, gasped at the show of power while he casually sliced into the cake. Once he pulled the sword from the cake the cheers began again, and Yohan stepped in front of Roan dishing up slices for anyone who wanted one.

Roan pulled Orah aside, leaning her against a column. "Whatever Jes said means nothing. I hope you know that light was all you."

"I know."

Despite how much pride and admiration he had in his voice she didn't feel relief with the knowledge. Every guest in the room now looked at her with an odd smile and she felt sick to her stomach. Letting go of her control hadn't been a good idea. She didn't truly believe Roan would be able to stop the rumors this night would now likely start.

Roan's hand gripped her chin and he leaned forward to kiss her. Orah smiled, ready for the kiss then grew aware they were in a crowded room and quickly turned her face away. The sound of his face colliding into the column behind him made her grimace. Covering her mouth to quiet her laugh she shook her head. "I'm so sorry."

He rubbed his nose. "It's my own fault, but Fates that hurt."

They both looked out at the people around them and choked on their laughs. If anyone had seen Roan's ungraceful collision with the column, no one was making it known.

Sighing, Orah leaned against the column right as an older gentleman approached Roan. She nodded to alert Roan someone was approaching and he turned to meet them.

The man smiled at Orah. "Roan, on behalf of the mortals I would like to thank you for hosting us the last two days and for the wonderful evening."

Orah tried her best not to blatantly stare at the man while he talked. He appeared to be maybe in his 50s; his hair was gray with little bits of dark brown peppered throughout. His face, while weathered, was kind and as though he was a man who carried a plethora of knowledge with him.

Roan smiled, before gripping Orah's hand and pulling her forward. "Anders, I would like you to meet my guest and friend, Orah." Anders nodded his head softly, his eyes lingering on Orah a moment before drifting back to Roan. "Orah, I would like you to meet Anders. He's one of the smartest and most cunning men you'll ever meet." Anders scoffed, but Roan continued, "He's also a good friend and a man who can help anyone out, as long as you know how to ask."

Anders lightly smacked Roan on the shoulder and shook his head. "This old man gives me too much credit. It's wonderful to meet you Orah. I hope I'm not overstepping when I say that Roan has found himself a very beautiful friend."

Orah blushed in response. Roan grinned back at Anders. "I could counter that old man comment with something sarcastic, but I won't because you're right, she is beautiful."

Orah glanced at Roan and the wide smile on his face sent her heart into a frantic response. Anders' loud yawn pulled their eyes apart.

"Apologies." Anders laughed. "You Gods may know how to party all night, but old mortal men like me need some sleep." He said the last part with a wink and Orah chuckled. She may not have been close to Anders' age, but he wasn't wrong. She could suddenly feel how long of a night it had been.

Roan observed the room then nodded. The cake had brought the electric buzz of the party down. Most of his guests were now sitting picking at their plates or conversing amongst each other. Looking back at Orah she caught the intention in his eyes. She bit back her lip realizing he had no plans to end the night anytime soon—at least not with her.

Clearing his throat, Roan stepped out to the middle of the room. "I want to thank everyone for coming tonight. It has meant the world to me. It's getting late and I can see I'm probably not the only one here who's feeling the long night. I think we're going to wrap up now if that's okay with you all."

A few drunk Godlings in the corner of the room protested but everyone else nodded or mumbled in agreement. Roan pointed to the ballroom doors. "I'd like to thank you all personally for coming, if you'll follow me to the front doors, please."

His guests began to gather their things or to find the groups they'd arrived with. Taking advantage of the few free minutes, Roan rushed to Orah. Leaning down to whisper he caressed her arm. "This shouldn't take very long. I'll meet you upstairs." Kissing her forehead, he dropped his voice lower. "I hope to find you in a certain black nightgown when I get up there."

Orah gasped and moved to smack his shoulder but he was too quick for her. Laughing, she watched him saunter out of the room, followed by a line of his guests.

Sighing, she walked toward the door. Turning, she admired the ballroom behind her. It was a mess, and she was sure Etta was going to be beside herself fretting over everything the next morning, but it was also evidence of how alive the night had been. An electric buzz zapped through her as though the house was somehow agreeing. Smiling, she picked up the long skirts of her dress and headed up the stairs.

Lahana and Fawn raced past her giggling while they rushed toward Lahana's door. Pausing, Orah decided to avoid the hallway for a moment to give the women privacy. Instead, she made her way to the stairs leading to the roof. She knew Roan underestimated how long it would take him to say goodbye and Orah wasn't ready to sleep yet.

Pushing open the roof door, she gasped at the brisk rush of autumn air. Rubbing her arms, she walked toward the chairs. The sky was just as alive as the house felt and she couldn't help but wonder how much of it was Roan. He'd been light and free all night, as though any stress he'd had in the weeks leading up to the party had just melted away.

Turning, Orah watched the lines of people walking out toward the city center. She was sure the majority of his guests would be going to the Perambulate to return to their homes in other Regions or returning to rooms in the inns in the city. But something told her the night wasn't over for many of them and the city wasn't quite settling down for the night.

Breathing out, her eyes moved back up at the sky. The stars twinkled above her, reminding her of the freckles on Roan's face. She smiled at the thought and how much she'd come to love those freckles.

A sound by the door pulled her away from her thoughts and her heart stopped as she watched a figure step out from the shadows.

Marek's grin was somehow worse than she'd seen so far. "I told you that dress was borderline inappropriate." His eyes lingered on her chest while he bit his bottom lip.

Crossing her arms to cover herself, she scowled at him. "You sound drunk. Go back to your room in the city."

Scoffing, he flicked his finger and disappeared. Panic engulfed her while she tried to locate where he could have possibly gone. A cold brush of air moved her hair against her back, and she whirled around as he stepped out from the shadows behind her.

"Get away from me," she demanded, stepping back, and bumping into the chairs.

"I bet you didn't know I could do that." He neared her, and she looked down at the shadows now covering the lower half of him. "Even Roan doesn't know. It's rather new but also rather useful." The shadows enveloped her legs and she cried out, realizing she could no longer move.

Stepping closer, his hand gripped her chin. "I meant it earlier when I said we could have so much fun." Slowly his thumb caressed her lips. "Just imagine the noises I could pull from you."

Rage replaced Orah's panic and her body hummed in response. The shock of his appearance was wearing off and now she was angry. Wiggling, she pulled her arms out from the shadows that had been slowly creeping up her body. "Take your hands off me." He hadn't yet noticed part of her was free and she wasn't quite ready to reveal her freedom.

Shaking his head, his grip on her chin tightened. "No, Orah. A *God* is *speaking*."

Abruptly his hand threw her head to the side. Trying to hide her groan from the unexpected movement, she watched while he took a step back. His hands flexed at his sides and he bit his lip while his eyes scanned her from head to toe.

A sour taste coated the inside of her mouth and she knew, deep down she knew, it was not from the fear mingled rage she felt. Her body recoiled at the realization of the things he was thinking of. The things he would very likely do to her if she didn't get herself away from him.

She thought of her training with Jes and tried to control the temper boiling inside of her. She didn't want—no, she couldn't give herself away when he obviously believed he had control of the situation.

His eyes lingered on her chest and she used his distraction to move her hand as quickly and discreetly as possible. From the corner of her eye, she could see the bright light forming in her palm and flicked her wrist out to wrap her rope around his ankle.

His eyes darted down the moment her rope flew out. She smiled, believing she had the upper hand when to her surprise a shadowed hand appeared, barreling into the middle of the stomach.

She doubled over in shock while her rope fell to the ground, disappearing in front of her. Holding her arm to her stomach, her eyes met his. He stood over her now and that sour taste in her mouth grew thicker.

"Did you really think you could trick me by using light magic?" His eyes glowed and she looked down to see his palms were lit as well. Genuine fear flooded through her when two large hands of light flew out toward her. One grabbing the back of her neck and the other wrapping around her throat.

Her eyes widened and she tried but failed to make a sound. He smiled, as though the power had taken almost no effort and moved until he was mere inches from her face. His physical hands caressed her cheek, wiping away the tears she couldn't control.

"No need to be scared Orah." He lowered his voice as though he were trying to be comforting but there was something else layered beneath. Something evil. Something unnatural.

Orah's tears fell faster now, but she couldn't move. His shadows held her in place and his hand on her throat held her still, preventing her from looking away from him while his hand slowly traveled down her neck and toward her chest. She tried but failed to shake her head away and his hand of light tightened its grasp on her neck.

Her gasp choked in her throat and she silently begged herself to move, to fight, to do anything but she couldn't. She was frozen. She was so frustratingly frozen.

He smiled while he tightened his grasp further and she closed her eyes. He was choking her, and she realized she would die if she fought back.

Perhaps she was meant to die. Perhaps that's what she'd been feeling all evening. Perhaps things had been too good. Perhaps it was what she deserved. Her familiar cold friend clawed inside of her while its cold grasp gripped her at the same tightness his hands now held her.

"Open your eyes Orah," Marek coaxed.

Blinking back her tears she opened her eyes. If he were going to kill her. If he were going to do whatever it was that he had planned. Then she would not be afraid.

His hand stopped above the neckline of her dress and he smiled at her. "You know my Father said I could have you when I come back with Him. Too bad He wasn't here tonight. I might just have to ask for forgiveness rather than permission."

Her power screamed at her to fight but she couldn't bring herself to move. What was the point? Rage, that was and wasn't her own, battered inside of her while her power thrashed and fought as though it were trying to claw at her skin. She couldn't breathe through his grip, but she closed her eyes.

Jes told her this power was hers. Jes told her she needed to learn how to control it.

Marek let out a scoff and his hand of light tightened its grip on her throat. She let out a whimper from the pain and tried to bring herself out of the paralyzed fear she was frozen in.

She needed help.

Opening her eyes again she glared at Marek. The sour taste felt as though she were trying to swallow clay and he sneered at her, but he didn't know about her little secret.

"*Lahana.*"

"*Lahana. I need Roan.*"

"*I need help.*"

Keeping her eyes on Marek, Orah called to the wind, unsure if Lahana could hear her but she had to do something. Anything.

"*Help please.*"

"*Roan.*"

"*I need Roan,*" she begged.

Marek pulled her head back with the hand of light at the base of her neck. He brought his hand to the neckline of her dress and she cried out when a small knife of light appeared.

"Forcibly taking these things off is so much more fun." His eyes burned with evil amusement.

Trying to breathe through his crushing grip, she cried out again as his hand came down, slicing open her dress.

"*Roan—please.*"

The tears ran down her face while she threw out her desperate plea to the wind. Marek's knife disappeared in his palm and his hand moved to pull open the frayed fabrics of her gown right as the roof door slammed open. Orah's stomach slipped and the sour taste in her throat was replaced with something hot and scalding.

Rage.

A large figure landed next to where Marek held her. Her eyes darted to the door as Roan stepped out. His rage lingered like a heavy mist in the air.

Hot.

Wild.

Untamable.

Keeping his eyes on his brother, Roan flicked his pinky and Marek's grip on Orah was ripped away while he flew across the roof.

Chapter 37

Jes, the figure next to Orah, scooped her up, pulling her back toward the roof door as Marek's grip was ripped away. She watched in horror and fascination while every light in the sky, the city, and surrounding the house blinked off.

Every light but Roan.

Starlight seeped from his every pore. The crown at the top of his head was lit, appearing to be on fire as he approached his brother.

Orah struggled to breathe through his rage while she watched. Marek held out his hands in a silent plea for mercy when Roan's pinky flicked again, and Marek let out a terrified scream as he flew off the roof, crashing loudly on the ground. Roan didn't look back while he waved his hand, and a descending staircase of starlight appeared.

Staring at the sight in front of her, Orah pushed herself out of Jes's arms. Frantically, she looked back at him. "You have to go down there. You have to help him."

Jes moved to stand in front of her, putting up his hands. "Our Beskermer bond called to me Orah. Yours and mine. That's why we're here and while my Beskermer bond with him is screaming at me to go help him, my brotherly bond is commanding me to stay and keep the one he loves safe."

She stared at him, trying to comprehend what he had just said. Pushing back the questions now running rampant in her head, she focused on Roan's light descending down the stairs.

Shoving Jes to the side, she rushed to the edge of the roof.

"Where is Arno?" Roan's voice had shifted to that low, gravely, almost monster-like tone.

"Why is he asking about Arno?" Orah whispered, keeping her eyes on Roan.

Jes stood next to her, conveniently blocking access to the staircase. "A Beskermer cannot attack a Governing God unless that Governing God has attacked their bonded. He's trying to make sure Arno doesn't attack and very likely kill him."

Orah shook her head and gasped when her eyes traveled to where Marek had landed. Roan had thrown him so hard the earth cracked beneath him.

Marek appeared as though he was struggling to get up, but he grinned at his brother, spitting what Orah could only assume was blood beside him. "I told him he couldn't come tonight. That I didn't *need* him."

Jes let out a quiet breath of relief, but Orah couldn't pull her eyes away from the brothers. She watched while Roan approached Marek. The grass he stepped on withered away, as though his rage was poisoning the earth.

"What made you think you could touch her?" Roan demanded.

Her heart sank as Marek stood, glancing her way. "Someone has to."

His arrogant shrug enraged her, and she shoved Jes, trying to get him to allow her down the stairs. Jes shook his head, grabbing her arm. "You will stay here." He was talking to her, but his eyes were solely focused on Roan.

Scowling, she ripped her arm from him. "Roan needs me."

Jes pulled his eyes from his Governing God and glared at her. "Orah, if you go down there right now, Marek will make a grab for you. I can see it in his eyes; he's baiting you. If he goes for you, Roan will kill him. We can't let Marek push him that far."

The world paused at Jes's words. Thick, almost suffocating tension surrounded them, and she looked back down to the ground, where Marek and Roan now stood an arm's length from each other. Neither spoke, but a low, invisible hum pulsed between them. Orah's own power thrashed inside of her. Begging her to let it out. Cursing, she smacked the edge of the roof. What was the point of her power if she froze up when she needed it most?

She shook her head, not allowing herself to go down that thought path when Marek finally spoke again. "It's too bad Father couldn't make it tonight. He would have been very interested in your mortal's little magic trick. Shame, I couldn't make her glow like that when I had my hands on her."

Somehow not surprised at his arrogance, Orah watched the ground shake beneath the brothers. The grass under Roan's feet caught fire. For several moments, the only sounds were the clattering of the chairs shaking on the roof next to her.

Abruptly the fire around Roan's feet extinguished, and he shrugged. "I didn't want Father here anyway."

Marek's eyes glanced at Orah briefly, then back to his brother. Marek appeared unphased, almost bored, but Orah could see that it was a mask. Roan's small display of power had scared him.

"Happy birthday, Roan. I'll be back another day to claim my party favor," Marek said, keeping his eyes on Orah.

Roan's hands balled into fists, and he moved to attack Marek, but a thick cloud of shadows came between them, blocking Roan. By the time the shadows dispersed, Marek was gone.

Beside Orah, Jes whistled low. "I didn't know he could do that."

"It's how he surprised me up here." Shame greeted her while she watched the ground where Roan seemed to be collecting himself. Sighing, she walked to the chairs and sank down. "I should have been more alert with how he'd acted in the ballroom. I should have expected something from him."

Jes knelt in front of her, placing a hand on her knee. "Orah this is not your fault. You were surprised. Even though it's been weeks, we really haven't been training for that long. Please don't blame yourself."

She kept her eyes on Jes, not needing to look up to know Roan had joined them on the roof again. The thrumming hum of his presence had told her he was there. Despite how she'd felt so many emotions from others that night, she couldn't understand how she felt his worry and anger. It was hot, like it wanted to burn right through her.

Clearing his throat, Jes stood and without saying a word he launched into the sky, leaving her alone with Roan.

Her heart tightened when she finally looked up at Roan. She hadn't realized all the lights had returned to the sky and the city behind him. He was still glowing but not like before. The light coming from him now reminded her of the first day in the sitting room, when he'd shown her his power for the first time.

She shifted to stand but he rushed to her, kneeling. He placed his hands on both sides of her face and stared at her. His eyes scanned her up and down, surveying the damage from his brother. Grimacing, he stared at her neck and she knew she had some kind of mark from the hand that had gripped her.

Sickening anger flipped her stomach when his eyes landed on her chest and the now torn neckline of her gown. "I should have killed him." His voice still didn't sound like his. He sounded far away. So far away.

"No, you shouldn't have." She laid her hand on his forearm and squeezed tight. "I'll be okay. I promise."

Shaking his head, he brushed his finger against her lips. "I'm so sorry, Orah." Tears lined his eyes while he stared at her neck. The chill of his shame washed over her.

It wasn't his fault.

It wasn't hers either.

"Roan, please. I'll be okay," she repeated.

"You shouldn't have to be okay," he whispered. "I will kill him if he touches you again."

"Not if I kill him first." The conviction in her own tone shocked her but she knew she meant it.

A smile formed on Roan's lips and he stood, offering his hand to help her up. When she made it to her feet she looked out over the edge of the roof, where the stairs had been then back to him.

"You barely flicked your pinky and threw him from here."

"I told you I hold back. I wouldn't have known if Jes hadn't heard you. I thought his Beskermer bond to you was figurative. I guess it's more literal than we realized."

Without thinking she blurted out what was on her mind. "Jes said you love me."

"He did?" Roan replied, jumping back a step.

"Yes. He said that while his Beskermer bond was telling him to go and help you with Marck, that his brotherly bond was telling him to protect the one you love."

Roan's eyes moved up to the sky then out to the city. Orah panicked, thinking she may have misspoken when he let out a sigh. "Fifty years ago, when I became the God of Nyte, I decided I would live a life of solitude. If I were to become the God of Death then I didn't want anyone to be forced to live a life surrounded by death and tragedy." Turning, he leaned against the edge of the roof to face her. "I kept that decision. I didn't pursue anyone. I didn't even allow myself to fulfill purely physical needs. I couldn't let someone get close. Then three months ago you walked right into me."

The world stopped and she swallowed back a gasp.

"The Fates like to play jokes, I guess. Having this wonderful, strong, beautiful, feisty, and confident woman literally walk right into my life. I knew I wanted you from the moment I first saw you. I knew I wanted to know you past any physical desires. I walked through your memories. I saw the pain you fight through every day and I knew I wanted to know more."

With a sigh he pushed up off the roof and stood in front of her. She held her breath as his hand touched her cheek. Letting out a quiet laugh he shook his head. "I think I started falling in love with you at The Burning Boar when you threw back that ale like it was water. Then when you told me you were leaving, I knew I was falling for you because of the piece of my heart I felt die in that moment. But I knew without a doubt I loved you when you wrapped that light of rope around my ankle just to beat me in the obstacle course." He pulled his gaze from her lips and stared into her eyes. "Orah, I have spent three hundred years walking through life alone and empty until you walked into it. It's crazy to admit I love you after such a short amount of time, but I do. I love you." He chuckled. "I'm unsteady when you're near me. I feel as though I can't breathe but also like I'm taking my first breath every time I see you. You are everything I haven't realized I've been looking for."

Orah's heart beat at such a speed she was dizzy while she tried to process what he was telling her. What he was confessing. Grabbing her hands, his smile grew. "I love how you always pick up the most obscure bit of information you're given. I love the scowl you get on your face when you're engulfed in your books. I love watching you cook in the kitchen and how everything you cook somehow ends up all over you." His eyes shone with starlight. "I love that somehow you have gotten a magically warded house to not pick up after you. I love your determination and your will to keep going. I love that you fight for yourself and for your life. I love your light and your darkness. I love your bravery and your strength. I love you."

Words stuck in her throat. Something deep inside of her screamed for her to speak but she couldn't. She opened her mouth to respond but nothing happened. Not even a noise came from her.

Roan nodded his head. "You don't have to love me, Orah. I hope you know that."

That thing inside of her battered inside. She had to say something. He had to know. She forced the words to form. "I lied at Aeron's palace when I said I thought I could love you."

Shock flashed across his face and he stepped back. Putting up her hands she prompted him to wait and allow her to finish. "I thought I could love you when you first showed me your library. Seeing the love you put into it made me realize you were someone worth knowing."

Panic surrounded her, clawing up her throat but she pushed it down. She could do this. She could do this. "The first time I really heard you laugh—at The Burning Boar, I thought again that I could love you. I wanted to bottle up the sound and play it over and over the moment I heard it. When you held me that night, after the portal failed, I knew I could love you. Your kindness. Your warmth." Her voice shook the more she revealed everything she'd kept hidden from him and even from herself. "When you took me up to the meadow in the mountain, and again when we went to Shadus, there was no doubt in my mind that I could love you. The way you admired your city and the world below us. The wonder and pride in your eyes told me you were definitely worth loving." Finally, she met his eyes and choked back a sob. Tears ran down his face and he looked like he was holding his breath. "When we went to Aeron's palace—" A wall inside her blocked her from finishing the thought. Her panic clawed at her. Steadying her breathing she kept her gaze on him. She could admit this. "When we went to Aeron's palace, I saw the portal and I knew. Right then, I knew I loved you. I love you, Roan. In a way I've never loved another person before."

Silence fell between them as she finished her confession. All the feelings she'd refused to accept. All the things she'd pushed down and shoved away, unwilling to face. Her lower lip shook while she held back the sobs trying to escape.

He seemed shocked. He appeared unable to form his own words. She turned her head from him, but his hands cupped her face and he pulled her toward him.

Their lips collided and somehow the world stilled further. Sounds stopped. Her breathing stopped.

They were all that existed. All that mattered.

Their kissing became frantic, hungry, as if they had never kissed before. His hands ran over her body; gripping her; pulling her against him.

She was lost in him. Utterly lost in the madness and unexplainable intoxication of his touch, his kiss. So lost she wasn't sure how she would ever be found again.

The screaming thing inside of her yelled louder, begging for her to listen. She groaned, pushing her body against him, hungry for more, inviting him to take what he wanted. The small noises of approval coming from him almost undid her completely.

She let out a quiet moan, wrapping her hands around his neck, savoring the feeling of him against her. Softly, he grabbed her thighs, lifting her into the air. She smiled against his lips, wrapping her legs around his waist in response.

Holding her tightly, he started to walk. She pulled away to see they were heading toward the door to the stairs. With a smile, he nipped her ear. "I won't drop you."

Falling into the safety of his hold, she laid her head against his neck while he walked them down the flight of stairs, holding her firmly.

She savored the warmth of him when she found them now standing in front of his bedroom door. A look of intention flared in his eyes and he kissed her, pushing her against the door frame.

His room quietly called to them and slowly his hands pulled from around her waist while he pushed the door open.

Anticipated tension pulled between them and he stared into her eyes while setting her on the ground. In the distance, she could see the edges of his bed. She smiled, imagining it as this living thing calling to them, inviting them to take the step they've been holding themselves back from.

Her eyes met his—it was different between them now. It was no longer about going slow. It was no longer about holding back.

With a smile, she grabbed his shirt and dragged him further into his room. His responding grunt of approval weakened her knees while she slowly unbuttoned his suit jacket. Her breath felt tight and hot while she slowly pulled it off of him.

His eyes hadn't left hers since she grabbed his shirt, and she was sure his breathing was just as labored as her own. She stared at his shirt, undoing each button with agonizingly slow movements but he remained patient and unmoving.

Pulling his arms through the sleeves, she marveled at him. His muscled body shone with his starlight. His broad shoulders flexed slightly while she ran her hand down his torso. She smiled knowing she could have easily spent the whole night only touching his skin. Learning each part of him, memorizing every inch of him.

Her hand brushing against the waistline of his trousers appeared to be his undoing and he grabbed her wrist. His eyes flared and he smiled. "My turn."

The promise in his tone set her on fire and she nodded her head. His hands moved to pull down her dress, but he stopped. His excited look shifted quickly to anger and he stared down at the rip on the neckline then to her neck.

He stepped back. "Are you sure?"

Her hands shook as her fingers brushed against the now tender skin around her neck. She didn't understand why everything inside of her was choosing to ignore what had happened on the roof. Perhaps it was a shock. Perhaps something else was at play. Perhaps she would wake up in the morning and it would all hit her at once. But it didn't matter. She looked up at him, knowing if she wanted everything to stop at that moment he would. Of course, he would. She had always been safe with him.

He stared at her nervously and the hot tension of his arousal called to her. She pulled her fingers from her neck and nodded her head. "Yes."

Her confirmation seemed to be the words unlocking a caged beast and he pounced. She couldn't hold in her gasp when his hands grabbed hold of the sliced neckline and in one movement, he tore her dress in half—exposing her completely.

She had expected slow movements, like her own, but that had been so much better.

Slipping the torn dress off her he stared down at her bare chest. "You're magnificent Orah."

She chuckled. "I was just thinking the same thing about you."

With a smile, he pulled her to him. The touch of their skin against each other pulled a moan from both their throats. Wrapping his hands in her hair, he pulled her in for another kiss.

Their bodies being so close and bare against each other created another frenzy while they kissed and clawed at one another. Her hands moved to remove his belt, but he stopped her. Cupping her backside, he lifted her again and walked them to his bed.

Setting her on the bed, he stared down at her. "Say it again." His voice was low and quiet. His eyes lined with tears while she stared up at him, knowing what he was requesting.

Her heart hammered against her chest. Something about the moment felt more real and intense than the declaration she'd made on the roof. That beating pulse inside of her stopped, as if waiting in suspense for her to speak.

Shifting to her knees she cupped his face and admired him. Roan—the beautiful man in front of her. The man who had just as much anger, pain, guilt, and darkness inside of himself as she did. Brushing his hair with her other hand, she stared into his silvery blue eyes.

"Roan Cael Durel. I love you. I love every part of you. The light and the dark parts. I see who you are. I know you."

The doors in the room shook violently in response to her words. Jumping, her chest tightened as though her heart would explode and she blinked back her shock from the jolt. The bed began to shake in response, the doors in the room rattled harder, and despite knowing she should feel scared—she felt no fear.

His eyes glistened and a smile titled the corner of his lips. "Threads of fate, bound together."

Orah startled at what his mother had told her. She tried to tell him who had said the words to her but her own words failed her, as though some strong magic prevented her from revealing this crucial truth to him. Finally, she only smiled and nodded while she admired him.

Holding their eye contact he leaned down, pushing her further up onto the bed. She watched full of anticipation while he unbuckled his pants, his look of intention now hot and overwhelming.

The loud clatter of his trousers hitting the floor caused her skin to prickle and she watched while he slowly crawled up the bed to her. The emotions between them were now almost too much to handle and tears ran down the sides of her face. An expression of concern flashed in his eyes and he wiped away the tears.

"Good tears. Very good tears," she managed to say through the emotions now overwhelming her.

With an understanding nod he leaned down, kissing her again, long and hard. Wrapping her arms around his neck, she pulled him closer. Closing her eyes, she kissed him back. Every time she'd imagined being in his bed flashed through her mind. Every imagined encounter. Every fantasy she had let herself dream of for months raced around her but somehow this moment was better than anything she had been able to come up with.

Wrapping her legs around his waist again she felt him twitch in response against her. She smiled and shifted her hips to open her legs wider for him. Pulling his lips from hers, his hand brushed her hair behind her ear. "We can still stop. If you want to, I'll stop," he whispered.

Shaking her head, she pulled him down with her legs to rest him right against her—all he had to do was shift slightly.

"I want you and only you," she replied.

His hand cupped her face while he brushed his fingers against her lips. "I'm yours. I've always been yours. Now and forever, love."

Shifting her hips, she moved toward him, ready for him, but he pulled back. Pushing away from the bed, he sat up while his eyes scanned her body.

"Not yet." The promise leaving his lips shivered against her skin. There was so much said in only two words, and she couldn't wait to see what he had planned.

His lips upturned as he leaned back down, kissing her forehead while his hands trailed along her skin, leaving a burning trail in their wake.

"Jesus, Roan," Orah gasped.

He laughed. "You've said that word before. I have no idea what it means."

Biting down her responding laugh, she shook her head. Words bubbled in her throat to respond, but instead came a low moan when his hands brushed down her stomach. Gripping the blankets beside her, she forced herself to meet his eyes.

"Do you like that?" he asked, moving his hands across her lower stomach.

"Hmm."

His hands stopped. "That's not an answer."

Pulling at the sheets, she tried to will the words, but his hands resumed their descent. Taking away any ability she had to respond, even if she had wanted to.

"There are so many things I want to do to you, Orah," he said, placing a kiss just below her navel. "There are so many spots on your body I want to learn."

",” Orah groaned.

"That is my name," he replied, smiling against her skin.

"I—" Her thoughts and response paused at the jolt of sensation from his fingers moving lower.

"You what?" he asked, slowly running his fingers against her, teasing her.

"More." She struggled to gasp.

"As you wish," he said with a smile, before sliding his fingers deep inside of her.

"Oh god." Orah's hand gripped the sheet tighter, while the stars twinkling on the bedroom walls blurred from the ecstasy of his touch.

His fingers moved inside her at an agonizing pace. Not quite fast, but just enough that she was sure she would go insane from the pleasure. His free hand ran up her stomach, stopping between her breasts.

"I love these," he whispered, before cupping one firmly.

His fingers continued moving inside her, their pace quickening with her breaths. Orah threw her hand back against the pillow, marveling at her body's response to him. Her breaths quickened further, growing with the pressure building low in her stomach.

"Roan. I'm—" She couldn't finish her sentence before his head dipped lower and his mouth claimed her, sucking against her most sensitive spot while his fingers moved faster. The pleasure was too much. Orah's vision blurred as she screamed out his name while his tongue moved in circles.

Shaking from the release, she stared up at the canopy above her, unsure if she could move. The bed shifted slightly, and she glanced up, finding Roan leaning over her.

"You're beautiful," he whispered, smiling down at her.

Suddenly feeling exposed, she blushed. Bringing a responding twinkle of mischief into Roan's eyes.

Her eyes traveled between them, where he sat patiently waiting. The image of his body's response to her trembled her legs. Shifting forward, she reached between them, grasping him tightly.

"Fates," he whispered in response.

He pulsed in her hands and she tightened her grip. "I want to play with you," she teased.

So many months she'd dreamed of touching him; of tasting him. Now she was there, in the moment, questioning whether the feeling of him in her hands was truly only a dream.

"Love," he groaned, pushing his hips forward, sliding himself in and out of her grip.

"Tell me what you want," Orah coaxed.

"I want you," he replied, pulling her hand away from him while he gently laid it above her head.

Anticipation rushed through Orah and she shifted, opening her legs for him. Gripping her hips, he slowly slid inside of her. She let out a gasp while her nails dug into his back. Thoughts and any ability to respond escaped her while the house shook around them.

She let out a shaky breath, sure she would burst into flames with each thrust he made. Shifting her hips to keep in pace with him, she stared up at him. Tears ran down the corner of her eyes while she reveled in the feeling of him, of them, together. His pace quickened and she held onto him tighter—unwilling to let him go.

She was lost in the intensity of how they felt together when suddenly he pulled away and sat back, motioning for her to climb onto him. Desire slammed into her while she stared at him and his body's response to her. His desire for her.

Sitting up, she crawled over to him and climbed onto his lap. His body shook while she lowered herself onto him and he let out a quiet breath. He pulsed inside of her and she shook, almost lost in her own pleasure.

She stared down at him, moving up and down slowly. His eyes flared each time she lifted up then slid back down the length of him. Soon their pace quickened again, and her hands tangled in his hair while she rose and fell onto him. Again and again.

He rested his hand on her lower back while she moved and the other gripped the back of her head. Pulling her down, he kissed her, their tongues tangled with one another and she quickened her pace. The pressure from the pleasure was nearly too much, but she wanted—she needed more.

As if understanding his hand pulled from her hair and both hands fell to her hips. He smiled while lifting his hips, guiding her up and down.

Her breasts brushed against him softly and his eyes moved from hers. Removing one hand from her hip she watched with anticipation as he cupped one breast and slowly brought it to his mouth. Trying to keep with their pace, her knees weakened at the sensation of his mouth and her body shook from the pleasure. Again, every door in the room shook violently as the building pressure finally released and she shuddered against him.

:asure filled his eyes, but he didn't remove his mouth from her ‗‗‗‗ ile he watched her climax slowly. She wasn't sure she'd catch her breath but after a few moments she composed herself only for him to quickly flip her to her stomach and lift her hips.

Her body tightened with anticipation again while his hand slowly ran down her spine. She bit down on the pillow below her head—sure she would go insane from the wait.

"I love you," he whispered, running his hand along her back. She looked back to respond when he placed both hands on her hips and thrusted into her.

Letting out a scream of both shock and pleasure, she gripped the pillow. Before had been intimate and raw but what he did now was wild and passionate.

This was what her fantasies had been.

He shifted one of his hands from her hips and grabbed her shoulder, slamming against her in wild frantic movements. She briefly registered that she was screaming his name as he pulled her against him—filling her with each thrust.

Gripping the pillows harder she screamed out again. The pressure built, hot and heavy. She was sure she would die from the pleasure.

His hand released its hold of her shoulder and he reached around, caressing between her thighs. The shock of his hand on the sensitive spot jolted through her and she screamed out again. He let out a low groan, holding her tight while he quickened his pace, moving his fingers against the nerves in teasing erotic motions.

The building pressure crested higher while his fingers played and teased her until she couldn't stand it any longer. Her body spasmed and she called out his name with her release. His fingers dug into her hips in response while he thrusted deep, shaking against her until his own climax slowed.

She breathed against the pillows unable to move while he remained behind her, keeping them connected. Neither of them dared to move. Neither of them dared to speak. The only sounds in the were the sounds of their breathing. She stared at the bed in a daze and considered never allowing them to separate from each other when he finally pulled from her and laid down beside her.

Her breath was shaky and uneven as she flipped over and laid against his chest. She could hear his heart beating as quickly as hers and she looked up to find him staring at the black canopy above them with a smile on his face. Reveling in the moment her eyes began to drift shut when a thought hit her.

"We didn't use protection." She sat up. Birth control—prevention hadn't once crossed her mind in the time she'd been in his world. But now...

"I take a tonic every day. I have for fifty years. We're protected," he replied with a tone of amusement.

She stared at him, still unable to ignore her panic. "Are you sure? You said you haven't had anything with anyone for all this time. Why take a tonic?"

He sat up. "That's valid but I'm not lying, Orah. I take it as a precaution. I'm only a man, you know. I'm aware that despite my conviction in my decision, I could slip up and I've wanted to be sure I'm always protected."

"I don't know if I want children." Turning away from him she tried to hide her embarrassment at what she just admitted.

Chuckling, he laid back against the pillow. "I don't know if I do either and we don't have to make that kind of decision anytime soon." She stared at him, unsure how to change the subject when he motioned for her to lay against him. She let out a relieved sigh and laid back down. Her body hummed while the beat of his heart acted as her own lullaby.

His arms pulled her tighter against his body and her body grew heavy from the now immediate demand for sleep. Her eyes drifted closed while she fell asleep to his whisper. "I've got you, love."

At some point in her sleep, she turned to her side and the bed shifted, followed by the quiet sound of his door opening then closing. But she was too sleepy to look up and snuggled back into the blanket, sure he would return soon.

CHAPTER 38

Orah woke with her cheek on Roan's chest again. She wasn't sure how long he had been gone when he'd left the room but all she cared about was that he was back next to her. His arm tightened around her and she shifted, resting her leg onto his. The feeling of his bare skin against hers almost set her on fire again and she smiled.

"Good morning." His chest rumbled with the sound of his voice and she glanced up. He looked like he had been awake for a while. Smiling down at her, his hand moved back and forth against her bare skin.

Shifting, she pulled the blanket up around her and sat up. "Good morning."

"Oh, don't cover up for me. Please." His eyes flared and he tugged on the blanket softly.

Grinning, she allowed him to pull it off of her, exposing her naked body to him. He sat up and moved so he was in front of her. Crawling up to her he smiled, his arousal was hot while it brushed against her. "We could stay in bed all day." Kissing her neck his hands traveled down brushing her ribs. "We don't have to get up yet." His hands moved to cup her exposed breast.

"Yes—we could," she replied with a gasp.

A delighted expression flashed across his face and he twirled his thumb against her nipple. Biting back a moan, she gripped the blanket. His eyes sparkled while he lowered his mouth onto her, never breaking eye contact. Her back arched against him from the pleasure and she grabbed hold of the sheets, desperate to hold onto something to help keep her from losing sense of reality. Keeping his eyes on her, he shifted, settling himself right between her thighs. His tongue moved against her nipple in playful movements and she smiled down at him.

Leaning back down against the pillow she looked down at him. His other hand lazily traced up and down her body. She shook in response and closed her eyes. She would likely never leave the bed if he kept that up. His chuckle of approval vibrated against her skin and her eyes flung open as he pushed himself inside of her again.

They had ended the night frantic and wild but that morning he moved as though he intended to take his time. Each thrust was almost agonizing, and she wrapped her arms around his neck, trying to pull him closer to him. They made barely any sound other than the sounds of their breaths.

Pulling away from her breast, his lips found hers again and they moved in sync. Every thrust and kiss felt as though their bodies were remembering lifetimes of rhythms. Lifetimes of moments just like this.

Wrapping her legs around his waist she shook while his movement quickened. Her tears slowly fell while she watched him. It was like a dream. Like at any moment he would disappear, and she would find herself alone in the world again.

Soon his own tears hit her cheeks and she cupped his face, knowing he was feeling the same emotions she was. She'd had sex in her life, she'd had hot, heavy moments, but she had never had what they were experiencing. She'd never had true intimacy.

She hadn't realized the pressure building inside until she let out an involuntary gasp and arched her back against him. Intense waves of release crashed over her and she dug her nails into his back, holding back her screams. Letting out a loud groan, his hands gripped the pillow next to her and he thrusted deeper with his own release.

Again, they laid together, unwilling to move until their breathing slowed. Softly, he kissed her neck and she winced. She didn't need a mirror to know that she was bruised from Marek and it was likely pretty bad with how Roan's kiss had felt.

"I love you," he whispered

The words hit her heart and she choked back a cry. "I love you too."

Removing her arms from around his neck, she brushed a hand through his hair. The freckles under his eyes lit softly. "You really are beautiful." She didn't think she would ever stop admiring his beauty.

Finally pulling himself from her, he sat up. "As much as I want to stay in bed with you all day, we should probably get up." Placing his hand out for her to take, he helped her off the bed. "But first I want a shower."

at the intention behind his eyes, she followed him to her room. to him, while his tub was better than hers, her shower was better than his. He turned the water on quickly and smiled before pulling her in with him.

By the time they shut off the shower the water was cold, and they were both flushed. The shower wasn't anything quick and they had done very little washing of themselves. At least, washing up using the hot water. The hot water had been used for more kissing and touching.

Stepping out, Orah groaned in appreciation for the warm floors while she wrapped up in a towel. Roan followed close behind her. Finally looking at herself in the mirror she let out a gasp at what she saw. Her neck was purple with very clear finger marks wrapped around it.

The lights flicked on and off and she glanced at Roan, but he wouldn't meet her gaze. His eyes were focused on her neck. Touching his chest, she leaned up and kissed him softly. "I'm going to be okay."

Pulling his lips from hers, he shook his head. "I'll kill him. *I'll kill him.*"

"Roan. Please. I'm okay."

Still refusing to look at her, he grabbed her hands, pulling her to him. "I'll make sure he never lays a hand on you again. I promise, love."

Responding didn't feel right and she instead nodded her head while squeezing his hands. Pulling her into her closet, he silently left her alone in front of her clothes while he ventured into his own. She smiled, noticing he was sure not to close the conjoining door.

Looking around, she picked up the first outfit she could find—a coordinating shirt and pants set in a dark, almost plum purple. The shirt was long with a high neck. High enough that it mostly covered the bruise.

She stared at herself in the mirror, expecting the purple to make the bruise look worse but to her surprise it didn't. While her neck didn't look great, the purple somehow concealed the bruise slightly.

A glint of gold in the mirror pulled her attention and she looked to find the coin Roan's mother had given her. Without thinking, she grabbed it, tucking into her pocket. She felt that Leora had something to do with her and Roan realizing who they were to each other and having the coin close by felt... right.

Shaking her head, she walked back to the bathroom to brush her hair. Roan's throat clearing caught her attention and she looked over, finding him leaning against the wall by the bedroom door. "I think I could watch you get ready every day and never tire of it."

"I guess it takes very little to entertain a God," she replied.

Laughing he pulled her in for a kiss. His hands tenderly brushed the hair from her face and his eyes glistened while he looked into hers. She knew, despite the unspoken words, he was trying to avoid staring down at her neck.

The warmth in the room dipped quickly to a suffocating cold. Orah's heart beat rapidly and she looked at him. "Are you okay?"

Just as quickly as it had grown cold, the warmth in the room returned. Turning his head toward her, he shook his head. "Yes. Of course I am."

She didn't quite believe him but allowed him to pull her out the door and into the hall. The house still felt alive from the party the night before, but she couldn't help noticing how quiet it was again. While the house was usually quiet, this felt sadder. As though there was an odd layer of mourning from the house that it was empty again.

They reached the bottom of the stairs and a loud clatter echoed from the kitchen. Rushing toward the hall, they stopped right next to the dining room doors and found Lahana standing in the hallway staring at them. Her wide mischievous grin spread to her eyes and she squealed. "I swear to the Fates I don't want any details, but I *know*."

Roan tensed beside Orah and she wondered what his sister was referring to when she rushed toward the both of them. "You guys were *not* quiet. Fates, Fawn and I had to move to the other side of the house last night. Roan, way to put on a show and make the literal house shake. Fawn thought the ground was opening to swallow the city whole."

Blushing, Orah looked up at Roan, realizing Lahana was talking about their bedroom antics and not what they had learned about each other. Roan's eyes sparkled and he looked down at Orah, shaking his head. "I don't know what you're referring to."

Cocking her head to the side, Orah laughed. There was no possible way he hadn't felt the house shaking last night. The doors had been rattling so hard she'd wondered if they were going to fall off their hinges. His eyes flared and realization hit her. The shaking hadn't been him. It had been *her*.

ly response was a quick nod. Blinking, Orah looked back at ble to grasp what she'd just realized. She had done that. She had made the actual house shake.

She couldn't stop the blush that spread across her cheeks. She shook her head and laughed. "Okay, we can stop talking about our nighttime fun. I'm starving."

Lahana scoffed and turned back towards the kitchen. "I'm sure you are."

Letting go of Roan's hand, Orah chased after Lahana while she let out a squeal, running to the safety of the kitchen. Roan laughed, rushing after them both. Orah was focused only on Lahana and almost collided with Etta when she finally reached the kitchen doorway.

Etta stopped and smiled at Orah then glanced at Roan. "This house has been waiting for its Queen."

Before Orah could respond Etta walked out of the kitchen toward the ballroom. Orah turned and watched her, placing her hand on her now stinging heart. She wasn't sure if she had heard Etta correctly. That wasn't true—she had heard her right.

Roan wrapped his arms around Orah, whispering in her ear. "I have to agree with her."

Orah's eyes blurred and her body hummed in response. *Queen.*

Shaking off her shock, she pulled Roan's arms away from her waist and walked into the kitchen where Yohan and Clarah smiled at her. It appeared that everyone in the house was aware of what had occurred between her and Roan.

Roan motioned for her to sit at the table and she watched while he dished up the large breakfast spread Yohan had prepared. Next to Orah, Fawn grinned at her then winked. Orah put a finger to her lip, trying to hold in her laugh, and silently begging Fawn to not ask any questions.

After a few moments, Roan approached the table with two plates of food. The room soon filled with the happy sounds of laughter and everyone discussing the party.

Apparently, there was quite a lot that Orah had somehow missed but Lahana filled them in. Most of the Governing Gods were not surprised that the King wasn't there but all of them were shocked that he didn't at least try to appear for his own son's party. Aila had left abruptly after distracting Roan in the library, and to Orah's shock Moros supposedly left the party very drunk, having to be escorted out personally by Jes.

Orah's face crumpled while she tried to think back on what she'd seen when the party had ended. Could that have happened when she had gone up stairs? Is that possibly why Jes took so long to hear her cries for help?

Lahana let out a giggle recounting Moros's exit. "He absolutely refused to leave unless the *big bird* man walked him to his inn."

Orah covered her mouth and snorted. Roan and Lahana's heads snapped towards her and she tried to compose herself. "I'm sorry. I just think I'll call Jes the big bird man from now on."

Roan bit his lip to hold in his own laugh and nodded his head. Beside him Lahana's eyes darted back and forth between Orah and her brother before she spoke again, this time her voice dropping low and serious. "Now you two need to tell me what happened last night."

Jumping, Orah stared at Lahana whose eyes had fallen to her neck. Orah's hands moved to cover the bruise.

"Marek," Roan said quietly, while the fork in his hand bent from the force of his grip.

Lahana's eyes widened. "Did he?"

Shaking her head, Orah touched her neck again. "No. He tried –" Her stomach rolled at the thought of what he intended to do. Breathing out she forced herself to continue. "Jes heard me calling for help. I thought I was calling to you but apparently that Beskermer bond Jes made with me actually worked. He and Roan showed up right before Marek –" The words stuck in her throat again, unable to voice what Roan had narrowly stopped. Shaking her head, she looked over at Roan. "Roan wiggled his pinky finger and Marek went flying off the roof."

Fawn's mouth opened in surprise and Lahana shook her head. "We were both so drunk last night that I thought I imagined the lights going off. Orah I'm so sorry I didn't hear you."

Orah reached across the table, grasping Lahana's hands. "You didn't do anything wrong Lahana. Jes was meant to hear me, not you."

Lahana's eyes narrowed on Orah's. "It's not your fault either."

Orah swallowed her sob. Lahana's responding squeeze on her hands almost made her sick from the comfort. Orah looked up again to find Lahana staring at her brother. "Did you hurt him?" The fear in her voice was real and Orah knew it was not out of concern for Marek's safety.

Roan shook his head. "No, I wanted to kill him, but no. He has a new control on shadow magic, and he was able to use it to get away."

out, Lahana released Orah's hands and leaned against the back "You know he's going to be back."

Roan's still lingering anger was replaced by something Orah couldn't translate. He looked around the kitchen then nodded his head. "I know and he won't be alone."

Tension fell over the room and they all sat in silence for a moment. Orah's stomach flipped again and she glanced down at her half-eaten plate. Suddenly unable to finish it, she stood to dispose of the food and set the plate in the sink. Halfway to the sink the ground shook beneath her. The glasses in the cabinets shook violently and Roan jumped to his feet.

Lahana's eyes widened with sheer panic and she turned to Fawn. "Fawn—leave now."

Shaking her head, Fawn looked at Orah, obviously as confused as Orah was herself. "What? No."

The responding scream from Lahana startled Orah and her plate crashed to the ground, shattering.

"FAWN LEAVE NOW!"

Glancing at Orah once more, Fawn said nothing while she jumped up and rushed out of the kitchen. Orah's body hummed along with the violent shaking while she stood listening to the side door open and close. Orah's eyes went to the kitchen window and she watched Fawn take off toward the side path to the city.

Near the sink, Clarah whimpered and Roan turned to Yohan. "Yohan, take your children and go. Do not turn back. No matter what you see, feel, or hear. You take your family ,and you go home. Lock your doors and do not come out."

Yohan let out a grunt of acknowledgement and rushed Xade and Clarah out of the kitchen. Clarah's terrified expression flipped Orah's stomach again and she turned back to Roan.

The house was shaking so hard it now felt as though it would collapse around them. Etta burst through the kitchen doors, holding her chest, and staring at Roan. Orah hadn't seen her so unsteady. "What is going on?" she asked breathlessly while she observed the room.

Orah's power thrashed inside of her and the room tilted from the force. Leaning against the kitchen counter she breathed in and out, not able to understand what was happening. Looking down she jumped at the bright glowing light coming from her palms. Roan turned back to her then to Etta. "My Father is coming. Etta you need to leave now."

Shaking her head, Etta crossed her arms. "I'm not going anywhere."

The house shook harder and Roan moved to stand in front of her, gripping her shoulders. "Etta Perri, I am not asking you, I am telling you as your Governing God that you will leave this house and this property, now."

The room stilled for only a moment while Roan and Etta stared at each other. Orah was almost sure that Etta was going to attack him when she finally nodded her head. "Fine, but I'll be back."

Picking up the skirts of her dress, Etta then rushed out of the kitchen. Orah listened, once again, to the side door opening and closing loudly. Looking out the window she watched Etta run, meeting Kai at the stable doors. Together they rushed inside then exited the stables atop saddles on Nacht and Tume. Orah's heart hammered in her chest while she watched them launch to the sky and fly toward the city center.

Orah was so sure she was going to be sick. She looked over at Lahana who appeared to be sweating. Her eyes were still glued to the side path as if she could still see Fawn running off.

Orah's hands shook and she looked back over at Roan.

But he was gone.

Letting out a scream, Orah ran out of the kitchen and stopped in the hallway. She knew she hadn't heard the side door open again so she turned and ran down the foyer finding Roan standing in front of the door. His anger, fear, and power radiated off of him, so intensely Orah thought she could actually see it like waves of color in the light.

Turning to face her he smiled. Orah looked down, unable to ignore how hard his hands shook. "No matter what you see love, please promise me you'll stay inside."

Something in his tone set her alert and she shook her head. "No. No. You are not going out there."

Rushing to her, he grabbed her face. "Orah, please, stay here." Pulling her to him, he kissed her as if he were afraid he would lose her.

Tears built in Orah's eyes and she grabbed his shirt tightly, desperate to somehow keep him next to her. Finally pulling their lips apart, he smiled. "The King of Gods can have me, but he can never have you." Abruptly, he shoved her shoulders, pushing her away from him. She fell back and watched helplessly as he rushed out the front door. Clamoring to her feet, she ran to follow but Lahana appeared in front of her.

"Go in there and do not come out," Lahana yelled, shaking Orah's shoulders and pointing to the sitting room.

Orah stared at her in disbelief. "Why do I have to stay here but you can go?" It didn't feel right. It didn't feel real. Orah couldn't let either of them go out there.

Shaking her head, Lahana's voice dropped. The defeated tone in her voice brought tears to Orah's eyes. "He won't hurt me. Please, Orah, do as Roan said. Stay here."

In a flash, Lahana went out the door and Orah ran to follow but flew backwards from the wall of wind now blocking the exit. "NO!" Sinking to her knees she screamed.

She sat for a brief second in defeat before pulling herself to her feet. Running to the sitting room her knees almost gave out from the scene on the lawn. A tall man with bright golden hair walked up the path with rows of armored guards following him. Directly behind him were Marek and his Beskermer Arno, who towered ominously over both of the Gods. The man with golden hair approached Roan and Orah swallowed back bile at the smile that spread across his face. It was an almost identical smile to Roan's but something evil lurked beneath it.

The man—whom she assumed was the King spoke to Roan. The conversation looked tense, but Roan stood in an almost teasing stance. Orah wanted to hear what was being said, she wanted to be out there with him. Suddenly, the King glanced backwards at the group behind Him. Her eyes widened and she slammed her hands against the window when Marek stepped forward and slammed his fist into the side of Roan's head.

Chapter 39

Roan's heart cracked after he shoved Orah back and rushed out the door, slamming it shut behind him. He was more hopeful than sure the shock of his shove would keep her behind for a moment.

He turned forward and watched his Father and His guards approach from the city street. Behind them were lines of Pegasus harnessed to golden chariots. Roan's people ran inside for safety, slamming their front doors as He approached. No one dared to get in the way of the King of Gods' path.

Roan turned at the sound of the front door opening to find Lahana standing there staring at their Father. His brief panic that he hadn't distracted Orah enough subsided. His sister nodded her head. She didn't have to say what she had done; he already knew. She blocked Orah from being able to leave the house.

Near crippling relief hit him and he turned, watching his Father step onto the front lawn. Raw, untethered rage barreled right into Roan's chest. Stepping back, Roan grunted.

Shaking off the shock of the blow, Roan straightened and approached his Father, who had come with a small army. Marek stood behind their Father with a wild look of excitement. His eyes darted behind Roan and Roan's head snapped back to find Orah standing in the windows. *Fates, she looks like she's going to be sick.*

Letting out a shaky breath, Roan turned back to his Father, waiting until He stood a few feet away. The King's voice echoed in the air. "How dare you?"

Flicking off a small piece of lint from his shirt, Roan shrugged. "I'm not sure what you're referring to."

The King's anger barreled into Roan again while he glared. "Don't play stupid, boy. Do you really think I would show up on your doorstep with my guards if you hadn't done anything? You went to the Fates."

"Jealous Eon gave me an audience so willingly?" Roan replied with a sneer.

"What did you do?"

"I don't have the faintest idea of what you're referring to," Roan responded, with another unphased shrug.

Taking a moment, Roan looked at his Father, now noticing how drained He looked. As though He hadn't slept. Roan blinked with surprise. As the King of Gods his Father always looked full of life but now—now He appeared tired and aged.

"Stop playing stupid, Roan. How dare you interfere with the challenge. How dare you claim what is not yours."

Marek shifted excitedly behind his Father. Roan's fists tensed at his side. What he would have done to rip the smile off his brother's face.

His Father stepped closer. "How did you do it?"

Knowing he was baiting the King, Roan rolled his eyes again. "How did I do what?"

The arrogance finally pushed his Father over the edge, and He let out an annoyed groan. His hand flicked forward, and Marek stepped out from behind him. Roan stepped forward, ready to fight, but realized he couldn't move. Dark shadows appeared from the ground, holding his legs in place. Glancing back at Orah he watched her eyes widen. His head snapped forward just in time as Marek's fist collided with the side of his head. Roan fell to the ground from the force of the hit and groaned.

Lahana screamed next to Roan but their Father put up his hands. "I would suggest you stay out of it unless you want Arno here to go into the city and fetch Dagny's daughter."

Roan's stomach rolled and he looked at his sister. Tears ran down her face and she sank to the ground. Roan shook his head. *Marek told Him about Fawn.*

The shadows held Roan in place while his Father approached. Bending down, He looked up toward the window Orah had been in. "Seems your plaything decided she can't watch this."

✦

Orah watched in horror as Marek's fist connected with the side of Roan's head. Screaming, she pounded on the windows. She had to get out of the house.

Flying out of the room she tried the front door again, but the wind shoved her back. Letting out another scream, she ran to the side door but again, she couldn't get close. Desperately she ran up the stairs leading to the roof but almost flew backwards when another wall of wind pushed her away. Tears ran down her cheeks while she tried doors and windows all over the house but each one prevented her from leaving.

Roan forced himself to glance backward and sobbed in relief to find Orah no longer in the window. His Father's hand shot out, gripping Roan's chin, pulling him upward. "Tell me how you did it."

Grinning, Roan spit in His face. "I told you, I have no idea what you're talking about."

His Father's eyes flared with rage and the ground shook as he released Roan's chin. The sudden movement caught Roan off guard and his head slammed into the ground. The King may not have been able to hurt His son directly, but He could distract him enough that Roan could hurt himself.

Glancing at Marek, the King nodded, and Roan's brother's shadows pulled him upright. Struggling against their hold, Roan stared at Marek. "I'm going to kill you."

It was a threat and a promise—that was if Orah didn't do it first.

Marek glanced back at the house and grinned. "I could see my mark on her from here. Tell me, how did it feel to bed her knowing my hands have been on her first?"

Roan couldn't hold in the scream of rage that came from him as Marek landed another punch but this time to the middle of Roan's stomach. Lahana sobbed next to her brothers. "You're upsetting Na-na, Roany," Marek said, glancing over at their sobbing sister.

Marek's shadows crawled up Roan's body and he yelled. This must have been close to how Orah had felt the night before. Roan shook, not having felt so powerless in such a long time. Roan tried to steady his breathing and glared at his Father.

The King stepped forward. "Look at me, Roan, and tell me you don't know what I'm talking about. My power has been drained. I could feel it was here with you. What did Eon give you that allowed you to override the ascension?"

Roan's anger coursed through him as if trying desperately to break out of Marek's hold. Roan shook his head definitely. "Wouldn't you like to know?"

Groaning, his Father looked back at the house then at Roan. "Do I have to allow your brother to go fetch that mortal you have in there? He's been rather obsessed with her. I could see if letting him have her prompts you to finally be honest with me."

The mention of Orah enraged Roan and he let out another shout. The burst of power from his rage threw Marek's hold on him, forcing his shadows to wither and disappear into the ground.

Landing on his feet, Roan breathed in and out, trying to quell his boiling rage. He knew he couldn't attack his Father, but he also knew he couldn't give Him what He wanted either.

Straightening, Roan crossed his arms and smiled coyly. "She'll kill him if he tries to get close."

His Father's large grin spread across His face and He chuckled. "I would love to see her try."

Stepping closer, The King's eyes darted to Marek and Roan moved a fraction too slowly before the shadows grabbed hold of him again. This time, however, they were not just wrapping around the outside of his body. Roan thrashed and screamed as the shadows seeped into his pores, grabbing hold of his organs. Gasping at the unexpected pain he couldn't prepare himself when Marek's fist slammed into the side of his head again and Lahana let out another scream.

The world tilted to the side and Roan crashed to the ground. He had forgotten just how strong Marek was while small white dots formed in his vision. Marek let out a guttural laugh as his shadows grabbed hold of Roan's lungs and squeezed. Trying to let out a strangled breath, Roan looked up to find his Father smiling down at him. "Where is my power, Roan?"

Roan shook his head, refusing to answer. His Father was not going to get any information out of him there. The King would have to take Roan and torture him to get the answers He wanted.

Sighing, His father stood and nodded to Marek again.

Marek let out that evil laugh again and kicked Roan right in the side. Roan groaned at the impact but took the kick. Then the next one and the next one. With each kick Marek's shadows gripped Roan's organs tighter than before.

✻

Cursing Lahana, Orah rushed back to the sitting room and let out loud sobs when she found Roan

on the ground with Marek standing above him, kicking him repeatedly.

Roan was a God but Orah had felt Marek's strength. She knew that very few people could handle being beaten like that for long.

"Hurry."

Orah let out a choked cry at the silent voice of Death greeting her.

"No."

✻

Roan took each kick, refusing to allow either his Father or brother to get any answers. They would have to take him—or kill him.

"This can stop as soon as you decide to be honest with me, Roan!" His Father projected his voice over Lahana's screams and cries. "Just tell me what you did. What did Eon give you?"

Roan spat up blood, continuing to take Marek's kicks. He would not give his Father anything. Looking over at Lahana, he grimaced at the tears running down her cheeks. His heart lurched realizing his sister would watch him die that day.

Struggling to breathe, he let out a pained sigh. "Fine, I'll tell you."

His Father held up his hand, stopping Marek from landing his next blow. Roan smirked at his brother. "I'll tell you and only you."

Nodding, his Father leaned down and lifted Roan by the shirt. Staring up into his Father's golden-green eyes, Roan couldn't help but think of how much he hated the man.

"Wanna know my secret?" Roan whispered.

Letting out a frustrated sigh, the King rolled his eyes. "Roan, I really don't have all day."

Roan's voice cracked as he spoke. "Come closer." His Father's grip on his shirt tightened and he pulled His son closer. Smiling, Roan used the little strength he had left and whispered his answer. "Fuck you."

Rage flared in his Father's eyes and he dropped Roan back onto the ground then motioned for Marek to continue. Marek threw back his head with a laugh while his shadows released their hold. Roan breathed out in relief but was too weak to fight him. His organs felt heavy and weak and as though they were fighting to keep going.

✴

Orah shook her head, refusing to hear Death's quiet voice. She pushed down the call and watched while Marek stopped his kicking and their Father approached Roan. He appeared to be whispering to his son but from the distance Orah couldn't interpret either the King's or Roan's body language. Her eyes moved to where Lahana was crumbled on the ground near Roan, rocking back and forth. She couldn't hear anything but Orah knew that Lahana was screaming.

Frustrated tears lined Orah's eyes and she slammed her hands against the window.

Suddenly the King stood and Orah's stomach flipped, feeling his rage even while trapped inside the house. He motioned for Marek to come forward again and Orah choked on a sob as Marek grabbed Roan's arm, twisting it backwards.

Roan writhed on the ground and Lahana's screams finally broke through her own wind

walls. With a grin, Marek peered back at Orah while he dropped Roan's now disfigured arm.

Orah's own hot anger engulfed her while she stared at Marek and the King.

How *dare* they.

How *dare* they touch him.

Her hands shook and she stared out the window. Breathing in and out, she imagined a door in front of her. A large door to replace the windows. A large door to let her out.

Desperation overwhelmed her and she sobbed. "Please let me out. Please."

She begged the house, the wards, and her own power to help her. She had to get to Roan. She had to help him.

The house shook violently, and she glanced up with relief as the window shifted to the exact door she had been imagining. Surveying the room, she somehow knew the house had listened.

※

Releasing Roan's arm, Marek hopped up and down on his feet with sick excitement. "Gods. I've been wanting to do that for years." Cocking his head, he grinned. "Your mortal is back."

Nearly blinded by the now radiating pain in his arm, Roan couldn't turn to look but knew his brother wasn't lying by the sick, hungry look on his face. Laying against the ground, his chest sank in and out. Breathing was more difficult and each breath he took came out with a rattling sound.

The King appeared in front of Roan. "Marek, go get her but let's remind your brother what happens when he continues to be this stubborn."

Marek grinned back at Roan, lifting him by the collar of his shirt, he pulled him close and whispered, "I'll make sure you can hear her screams in Erde from here."

Roan's eyes widened in rage and the ground shook around them. Shaking his head, Marek whirled back his hand and then slammed his fist into the side of Roan's head again. The world tilted and Roan's eyes rolled to the back of his head. Marek released his hold on his brother and Roan slammed against the ground again, right as the sky suddenly darkened and the ground shook again.

A guttural near animalistic scream filled the air and a bolt of lightning came from the sky, hitting Marek, sending him backwards into the King's guards.

Orah.

Roan shook his head, unable to respond to his power's demand to do something. To do anything to stop what was about to happen. But all he could do was open his mouth as his whispered plea stuck in his throat.

"No."

Chapter 40

Orah kept her eyes on Roan's unmoving body while she grabbed the handle of the door and pulled it open. Her foot hit the lawn beneath her and the ground shook. Her body warmed and hummed while her power responded.

Finally allowing everything inside of her to awaken, she grinned at her targets.

The sky darkened to a stormy gray while thick bolts of lightning cracked in the sky. Looking at Marek, she smirked. Flicking out her hand, she unleashed her scream and a large lightning bolt crashed down, hitting him directly.

He flew backward into the line of guards and she laughed a gravely laugh. Her voice didn't sound like her own, but her power fluttered in response. She kept her eyes on Marek for a moment before they darted back to Roan.

"*Hurry.*"

Her rage was briefly replaced with panic and she ran, faster than she had ever ran before.

Stopping in front of Roan she let out a sob. Only his chest barely moved with the ragged breaths escaping his lips.

"*Not yet,*" Death whispered.

She knelt next to him and carefully lifted his head. The responding lifeless tilt jolted her heart. Tears ran down her cheeks and her eyes lifted to the King.

The God stared at her with a wide grin. Cocking His head, He stared up at the sky then back at her and His eyes narrowed. "There you are."

Burning rain showered down from dark clouds and rage exploded from Orah. A circle of fire surrounded her and Roan. "How could you? He's your son!" she screamed.

"I've got two of them," the King replied with a shrug.

Her eyes widened, and the fire protecting her and Roan grew higher. Out of the corner of her eye, Marek pulled himself to his feet. He glared at her as if he were ready to end her, but she threw out her hand. With a yell he flew back into the wall of guards. Everything inside of her pushed to hold him down. To keep him from being able to stand.

The King's smile widened further. "Interesting."

Orah's power battered inside of her again and she stared at the King. That sick evil smile was on His face—that smile that was but also wasn't Roan's. Orah's rage flipped to disgust and she realized the King was enjoying watching his son's life falter in front of Him.

The fire around her crawled even higher. Her body itself burst into white flames while she stared at the King. Throwing her hand out she moved to hit Him with a burst of flames but stopped when someone stepped out from behind Arno.

Blinking, her chest seized, and she shook her head.

Putting up his hands, Jes approached her slowly. "Orah, don't"

Orah couldn't comprehend what she was looking at while Jes drew closer. A strong wind blew past, extinguishing her flames. Staring down at Roan, she shook her head in disbelief—she was sure her shock hadn't prompted the flames to die down. Lahana's whimper beside her pulled her attention and the realization settled over her; the flames had been separating Lahana from her brother.

Lahana crawled up next to Orah. A push inside of Orah prompted her to gently lay Roan's head in his sister's lap while Orah kept her eyes on Jes.

"No. No. No." Lahana held Roan's limp body, shaking her head as her tears hit his cheeks.

"*Hurry.*"

Orah pushed back the quiet call, commanding it to silence itself. Standing, she looked at Jes and realization hit her.

Jes had left after Marek.

Jes hadn't been in the kitchen that morning.

Jes hadn't come rushing out of his room when they all felt the King's power.

Because Jes went to him.

Jes went to the King.

The scalding rain thickened, and tears hit Orah's cheeks. Wind blew around her as Jes approached. She shook her head again. "How—" The words choked in her throat. "How could you?"

He was only a few feet from her now, still holding up his hands. "Orah, calm down."

"HOW COULD YOU?!" The shock of his appearance withered away, and her rage returned. She threw her hands out again but he lurched forward, pinning them to her sides.

"Orah, you can't."

Lahana let out a loud sob. "He's not here. Roan come back."

"*Not yet.*"

Orah chose to believe Death this time, allowing it to keep her aware of Roan while she kept her eyes on Jes.

Her hands shook at her sides. "Let me go, Jesiel."

Her tears were hot and heavy, mixing with the onslaught of rain coming down on them. How could he? After all that he and Roan had been through. How could he?

Shaking her head, she shoved Jes away from her. He stumbled, falling to the ground and her hand flew back up while she screamed at him. "How could you?"

Nodding his head, he looked back at the King, then slowly to Roan's limp body on the ground, then back to Orah. "He's my King."

The words sliced Orah open and her eyes widened. The dirt on the ground picked up with the wind, circling around them. The King's hot rage rushed through Orah and He stared at his daughter.

"I told you not to interfere, Lahana!" he yelled.

A chuckle came from deep within the Goddess, her voice a mix of both grief and pride. "Oh—that's not me, Father."

As if responding to a cue, Orah's power ignited and the wind picked up, creating a wall of wind and dirt that circled around Orah, Jes, Lahana, and Roan.

Nothing could break it.

Nothing could stop *her*.

Jes's eyes widened at the display of Orah's powers. Her rage felt all consuming as she stared at him.

How could he so easily hand Roan over?

Hand them over?

The wall of wind grew as though Orah had created her own cyclone of rage. Jes pulled himself from the ground but flew back again when a large rock pulled from deep within the earth and slammed into his side.

Orah stepped toward him. The hairs on her arms stood as if electrified. Taking a deep breath, she thought of all the weeks she'd spent training with him.

Watching him.

Learning about him.

In an instant she was on him. Her hands out like claws as she wrapped her arms around his neck and swung herself over him. Gasping at the hold she had on him, he pulled his arm back and slammed his elbow into her stomach. Startled by the blow, she released him and stepped back.

He whirled around, pure amusement and fascination now danced wildly in his eyes. "You want to spar, Orah?"

That deep, monstrous voice replaced her own. "I want to *fight*, Jesiel."

With a smile he ran for her, swiping his leg out as if to kick hers out from under her but she was too fast for him. The wind swirling around them picked up, right on time, propelling her higher as she jumped, avoiding his kick. His eyes widened while she landed a few feet from him.

Standing in the fighting stance he'd spent weeks teaching her, she smiled at him.

Accepting the challenge, his wings flared out at his side and he launched upwards, planning to attack her from above.

But she expected that.

Her wind grabbed hold of one of his wings and he screamed while she pulled him back to the ground. Landing with a crash in front of her he smiled again. "Nice trick."

Letting her ego get the best of her, she smirked right as he moved and grabbed hold of her arm. Twisting it backwards he pulled her against his chest. "Calm down, Orah," he whispered into her ear, as if he had any right to be so close to her.

Screaming she threw her head back, slamming it against his chest. The shock of the blow pulled a grunt from him. Orah smiled, taking advantage of his shock and flicked her finger. He let out a shout at the rock that pulled from the ground and collided with the back of his head.

Throwing his hands up to rub his head, he released his hold on her and she whirled around, swiping her foot out she kicked his legs out and he crashed to the ground. Her rage was hot and untamable as she made starlight shackles appear, tethering him to the earth. Sweat ran down her back while she stared down at him.

Cocking his head to the side he smirked.

He actually smirked at her and her rage unleashed. She ran to hit him when an enraged scream off to the side stopped her in her tracks. Looking over, her eyes widened in shock as Marek burst through her wall of wind and his shadows wrapped around her ankle, pulling her to the ground.

The shock was enough to calm the cyclone around them and her head slammed against the ground. With a laugh, Marek approached, and his shadows pulled her closer to him, and farther from Jes.

Vines from the earth appeared all around Orah and she desperately tried to grab hold of something as Marek pulled her closer to him. But despite her attempts, each vine broke with the force of his shadows tugging at her.

Kicking against them, she screamed, and more lightning cracked in the sky. Eyes widening, Marek pulled her upwards with his shadows. "If you hit me with one of those again, I will kill you."

Unphased by the threat, her power surged through her and the hairs on her arm prickled once again. She grinned wide and tilted her head to the side in a clear show of disregard for his threat. Marek's shadows released their hold on her, and she fell to the ground abruptly.

Laughing, she stood, confident she had struck him again.

Her eyes widened though as his hand shot up and he caught her lightning in one swift movement. Grinning, he looked back at her while the light appeared to seep into his skin and his arm glowed briefly.

Stepping back, she considered his threat and readied herself for his wrath. He stalked closer to her and flicked his hand up. She watched with near feral anticipation as a ball of light appeared in his palm then quickly tendrils of shadows extinguished the light while he drew closer.

Her heart beat against her chest in a panic while the ground shook beneath her and she stared at him. An icy cold hit her back and she looked behind her at Roan. Lahana's sob pierced Orah's chest and she turned to face Marek again. "You did this." The words came out deep and low, but choked and pained.

Cocking his head to the side, he smiled. "And? He could have fought back."

Lahana's responding sob fueled Orah's rage and she ran for Marek.

He smiled arrogantly as if he knew what she would do next, but he didn't expect the ball of flames she shot from her hands right into the center of his chest.

He stumbled back, grabbing his chest from the shock of the blast.

Thinking she'd made her point she turned to run back to Roan when something tugged at her feet and she looked down to see his shadows wrapped around her ankles again, slamming her back into the earth.

The shadows climbed up the length of her body, flipping her onto her back and splaying her arms out. Her eyes widened as he finally finished his approach. His casual saunter enraged her, and she screamed, fighting against his shadows. Their hold on her tightened and she cried out as the same hand of light from the night before flew toward her.

With a smile, he stood over her, grinning while the hand of light hovered right above her throat—taunting her to fight further.

Her scream echoed in the air as the hand wrapped around her neck for the second time. The pain from the pressure on her bruised skin pulled tears from her eyes. Staring down at her, his eyes narrowed. "I didn't want to ruin that pretty neck any further, but you've left me with no choice."

As if it took no effort, he flicked his hand, softly commanding his shadows to climb farther up her body until they reached his hand of light. She couldn't breathe and his hold on her tightened. She was sure she was going to die. He wouldn't let her live after that.

"*Life.*"

Jumping at the sudden voice, Orah's eyes wandered to where Lahana sat on the ground looking up in shock.

Roan was no longer in her lap.

Orah's eyes snapped back to Marek and she smiled.

His eyes flared and he grinned down at her, tightening his grip. "I knew there was something dark inside of you. You like that. Don't—" His inaccurate observation was interrupted when he was suddenly thrown backwards.

The ground shook around her while she tilted her head up, watching Roan drag his brother across the ground. Marek let out a terrified scream and the sky went black.

"I told you I would kill you." Roan's threat echoed in the air.

Roan's starlight replaced the sun and Orah stared in awe, not caring she was still shackled by Marek's shadows.

Flames appeared in Roan's hands and he gripped his brother's neck, pulling him upwards. Orah watched, sure Roan was going to kill Marek when footsteps pulled her attention.

Snapping her head up, she found the King now standing above her, staring at her with evil intent.

"Roan," the King said calmly.

Roan's eyes snapped to his Father and he dropped Marek with a loud crash. "Don't touch her."

The King bent down to where Orah was still tied to the ground. He smiled at her then glanced back at His son.

"*Death.*"

Orah let out a scream before Roan registered what was happening. Lahana ran across the lawn but was unable to stop the knife of shadows Marek stabbed through Roan's back.

"NO!" Orah screamed and thrashed, helplessly watching Roan stagger in shock. Everything moved in slow motion while blood trickled down his torso, pooling at his feet and seeping through his hands clutching his stomach. She fought, trying to break the shackles, but the strength she'd felt when she'd first hit the lawn was sucked away by the dimming light in Roan's eyes. The beautiful blue eyes that were now barreling into her soul. From the distance she couldn't hear what he said but she could clearly see what he mouthed before he collapsed.

I love you.

In an instant Marek was above her again, his eyes burning with uncontrollable rage. "Now that he's out of the way." His hand slammed down as though he intended to choke the life out of Orah. The King's clearing throat distracted him though, giving Orah the perfect opportunity to catch them both off guard.

Struggling to breathe past her shock of watching Roan fall, she willed her power to obey. Tears ran down her face while she thought of Roan. Of his laugh, his smile, his touch. She thought of the look on his face when she'd descended those stairs the night before. She breathed out shaky, grief-ladened breaths, feeling the hum of her powering responding to her love for Roan. She looked down right as her body ignited and the light of the sun returned, filling her with its direct light. Marek's shadows hissed and slithered back into the ground in response.

Pulling herself to her feet, she looked up and grinned.

Marek and the King stared at her, both of their mouths hung open and she pointed at them. "You're going to have to do more than that to kill me."

Screaming, she threw her hands out, hitting Marek with another bolt of lightning. His own scream of rage echoed around them and he ran at her. Her body froze where she stood, and he smiled wide.

She couldn't move and she stared, frozen in fear as he approached her. The same feeling she had on the roof when he ripped her dress rushed through her. Smiling wide, as if knowing she had sensed what was on his mind, he approached slowly. She tried to move against his hold but no longer had any control of her body.

Standing in front of her, he brushed her cheek softly. "It's not as much fun when you can't fight me."

She couldn't move when he grabbed the back of her head and kissed her. Her stomach flipped with disgust while he claimed her mouth, then she bit down on his lip as hard as she could. Letting out a yell, he stepped back, holding his bleeding lip, glaring at her. She prepared herself for another blow but instead Marek didn't move while the King held up his hand.

Stepping backwards, Marek held his bleeding lip, his anger collided with Orah and she smiled back, tasting the iron of his blood in her mouth.

The King glanced at where Lahana once again cradled Roan on the ground then looked at Orah. A groan behind her turned her head and she twisted back to find Jes standing. The fight with Marek and shock of his attack on Roan distracted her enough for the shackles she had on Jes to disappear.

Looking back at the King, she jumped to find him staring at her with something like intrigue in his eyes.

Leaning forward he brushed a piece of her hair from her face. "I'm going to need all this back, you know."

Not sure what he meant, she spit Marek's blood that coated her mouth in the King's face in response. A look of disgust and anger flashed across his eyes and he stepped back.

Looking at Marek he snapped his fingers. "Take care of this mortal."

Orah knew she should have felt fear in his tone but instead her rage built, she would not allow herself to be helpless. Staring at Marek she let out a scream and her body jerked forward, finally freeing herself from Marek's hold. His eyes widened and his fear hit her like a solid wall. Grinning, she threw her hands out again and watched in delight while he flew backwards, slamming so hard into the ground that a crater formed around him.

A prickling sensation behind her told her that Jes was approaching and she threw out her other hand. She didn't see him but the sound of him slamming into a tree behind him echoed across the lawn.

Narrowing her eyes, she walked closer to the King. He smiled softly as if baiting her, hoping to see what she would do next.

Her entire body ignited into white hot flames while she smiled back. Stepping back, He shook his head in disbelief. Orah smiled. He thought she wasn't a threat.

He was *wrong*.

Her power sang triumphantly, begging her to unleash and she listened.

With another scream she threw out her hand, ready to blast her rage right through the King when the coin in her pocket suddenly heated, burning into her skin. She let out a surprised scream and her power flew out from her hands but split into two. She watched in horror as one white hot blast raced toward the King then bounced off him. The other went right toward Jes, whom she hadn't seen approaching again.

The blast that bounced off the King diverted straight into Jes's back while the other barreled right into his chest.

Orah let out a choked scream while she watched Jes crumble to the ground.

In the group of guards someone screamed Jes's name. She watched the guards all part as Moros rushed past them to Jes's side. Cold grief lingered in the air and she held back her own sobs as Moros's tears his Jes's cheeks.

Whispering softly, Moros brushed his hand across Jes's face. "Jes. My love."

Lahana's gasp was the only sound beside Moros's sobs. Blinking back her own shock, Orah looked back at the King.

His eyes were on fire and a very bright crown of light now sat on his head. Shaking his head, he motioned behind him. Orah had forgotten that Arno was there and paused as the giant of a Beskermer approached her.

The King let out a sigh, staring at her. "Arno, the mortal."

Turning to look at Roan and the now large pool of blood circling his body and Lahana, the King shook his head. "What a shame about my son." His eyes fell back to Orah and he grinned wickedly. "I guess the Fates will have to wait for their challenge until I make another."

Fear hit Orah and she turned to run back to Roan when large hands grabbed hold of her shoulders. Thrashing against Arno's hold she screamed Roan's name.

"Let me go! Let me go to him!"

Tears ran down her cheeks. She had to say goodbye. She had to say goodbye.

Cold shadows wrapped around her and she was suddenly pulled from Arno's grip, crashing back to the ground. Looking over she watched Marek slowly stand from the crater, his eyes full of pure rage. Fear settled lower in her stomach and she thrashed against his shadows.

Another choked scream came from her as Marek's shadows crept up her body, into her body, and grabbed hold of her lungs.

Holding up his hands, the King sighed. "Marek, enough. Arno bring the mortal with us."

Grinning, Marek flicked his hand and Orah's head slammed into the ground. A loud crack echoed in the air and somehow, she was aware enough to realize that sound had come from her head hitting the earth. Her vision blurred as Arno picked her up like a doll, slinging her over his shoulder. Bouncing against his back she watched the King approach Roan, stepping into his son's own blood and lifting his chin softly.

He appeared to be whispering something before He stood and stared at Orah. Tears fell down her cheeks, soaking Arnos back and she watched while Lahana sobbed and screamed, holding her hands to Roan's still bleeding wound.

"Death."

"FUCK!" Orah screamed out, cursing Death's call. Cursing herself for allowing this to happen.

She watched through her blurred vision thinking she thought perhaps she could see Etta running across the lawn to Lahana's side.

Moros suddenly blocked Orah's view of Roan. He didn't look at her though, he kept his eyes solely on Jes's lifeless body in his arms. Orah's head swam while she watched the God softly kiss his partner's forehead.

She considered briefly whether or not she should have felt guilt for what she'd done to Jes when Arno abruptly threw her down onto the wooden floor. Her head crashed against the hard surface and she tried to look around through the daze.

Chariot seats surrounded her, and Marek sat directly to her right. With a smile he waved his hand, and the chariot lurched upwards to the sky.

Arno stood above her now, placing his hand in the crook of her neck. Looking up at the sky, Orah thought she saw a winged shadow high above them as Arno squeezed his hand and the darkness took over.

Lahana's tears hit Roan's face and he slowly forced his eyes open. His chest was barely moving but he could feel the blood pooling around him. Like a warm blanket trying to heat his now cooling body.

He didn't expect Marek to stab him—if anything he was slightly impressed Marek was able to trick him.

He couldn't move or react as he watched Marek's shadows wrap around Orah. Her screams of fear reached him, and he begged his power to respond, but his body couldn't move, he could do nothing to protect her.

Roan watched anxiously while his Father commanded Marek to stop, and his brother flicked his wrist, causing Orah's head to slam into the ground followed by a loud crack. Roan couldn't let out his cry as Arno threw her over his shoulders, carrying her toward the golden chariots on the street.

Moros followed close behind, holding a limp Jes. Roan watched, unsure of what he was watching while a tear ran down the side of his face.

He blinked trying to comprehend all that was happening around him when a figure approached. Lahana's grip on him tightened protectively. His Father leaned down with a grin, briefly looking back to Arno and Orah. Softly caressing Roan's cheek, He laughed. Suddenly, Roan could no longer hear Lahana's cries while their Father leaned down.

With a whisper, He grabbed Roan's chin. "You took my fate bound from me. It's only fitting that I take yours."

Roan's eyes flew open in response and he stared up in shock. His Father smiled down an evil, vile smile, before dropping Roan's chin and casually walking away toward the chariots. Helplessly, Roan watched as they took flight, taking Orah—his fate bound—with them.

Words were unreachable while he closed his eyes. He had meant to protect her from his Father, he had intended for his Father to take him, not her. Now, there was nothing he could do to keep her safe.

His chest rattled with each breath he took, and his wound continued to bleed. His body ached and his arm throbbed, but he felt no pain. No—he felt no pain—only a growing numb cold. Struggling to take his last few breaths, Roan let out a choked laugh. He had always thought he would become the God of Death, but it appeared the Fates had different plans for him.

Feeling warmth on his face, he forced his eyes open once more. A bright light blinded his vision, and from the brilliance the Pegasus of Death descended and landed before him. Accepting his fate, he took one last ragged breath, allowing the cold hands of Death to embrace him.

Acknowledgements

First, I want to say I'm sorry for the ending. Please forgive me.

Now that we've gotten that out of the way, I'd like to thank you, the reader, for your support. Hopefully you're not too enraged with me over the ending, and you can appreciate these acknowledgements.

To my husband, the love of my life, my own fate bound, and my soulmate literally written in the stars. I would have never been able to accomplish this without your support and love. Thank you for all of the hours of storyline development. For handling life and the kids when I was immersed in getting this novel written and refined. Thank you for your jokes about my characters and for your help in creating a world readers will love. Thank you for never doubting my ability to complete this novel and for hyping me up to anyone you could. Thank you for holding me up along this journey, especially when I felt like I was going to crumple. Thank you for finding me all those years ago and continuing to tell me you loved me even when I was too scared to say it back. Thank you for seeing who I am in a way no one else ever has. I love you forever.

To my children, thank you for your patience and love. Thank you for telling me how proud you are of me. Thank you for loving Mommy's story even though you have no idea what it's about. Thank you for inspiring me to go after my dreams. And especially, thank you for always reminding Mommy that she's not too old to try new things.

To my sister, my rock, my village, and my kids' second mom. Thank you for reading my book and never telling me I shouldn't put this story out into the world. Thank you for being the person I can cry with. For allowing me the space to mess up as a mother and never judging me. For holding my hand for the last 28 years and being my safety net in the middle of all the chaos. My world would have been so dark without you in it.

To my Nama, thank you for being an inspiration. For the weekly phone calls, laughter, and tears. For being a woman I have always admired and who has always shown me, my siblings, and my children the most unconditional love. Thank you for years of love and comfort. Thank you for always being a steady hand in my life.

To my mother-in-law, Rebecca, I wish you could have read this. I wish I could have handed you this book and gotten one of your strong, comforting hugs. I'm not sure if you would have read it, especially chapter 37, but I still wish you could have seen it. Thank you for seeing who I strived to be and for providing comfort and encouragement. Thank you for your son, and the wonderful man he turned out to be.

To Michelle, my best friend, who grounded me through some of the darkest years of my life. Thank you for adopting me into your life despite my 'Don't burst my bubble' hoodie. Thank you for always supporting me and loving my family like your own. And thank you for not running away from me after being asked to make bread at two in the morning.

To Anna, my first reader and dear friend, thank you for all the funny book reels and laughs. Most especially, thank you for the constant support and for immediately diving into my world and story. I'm sorry you have to wait so long to find out what happens in book two.

To Sydney and Stephanie, thank you for your years of friendship. For helping be part of me becoming who I am today and for jumping at the chance to read my book. Thank you for all of the memories and love.

To my beta readers, Mel, Nikki, and Katie, thank you for your insight and guidance in helping make this story what it is now. Thank you for helping me catch funny errors, for helping me cut a staggering 11k+ words, and thank you for still talking to me after the ending.

To LJ Andrews and your incredible indie author scholarship. You quite literally changed my life and opened the door to opportunities I wouldn't have had otherwise. Thank you for acknowledging the work that goes into self-publishing and making sure the world is aware of it too.

To my editor Sophie, thank you for hopping in at the last minute when I was in a panic. Thank you for loving Roan as much as I do and for your amazing comments during your edits.

To my proofreader, and beta reader, Brittany, thank you for helping me comb through this story to perfect it in the best way we could. Thank